On Wings
of Magic

On Wings of Magic

Witch World: The Turning
Book 3

Andre Norton
with
Patricia Mathews
and
Sasha Miller

TOR

A Tom Doherty Associates Book
New York

ON WINGS OF MAGIC

A Tor Book
Published by Tom Doherty Associates, Inc.
175 Fifth Avenue
New York, N.Y. 10010

Tor® is a registered trademark of Tom Doherty Associates, Inc.

Edited by James Frenkel

Library of Congress Cataloging-in-Publication Data

Norton, Andre.
    On wings of magic / Andre Norton : with Sasha Miller and Patricia Mathews.
        p.   cm. — (Witch world : the turning ; bk. 3)
    ISBN 0-312-85026-3
    1. Witch World (Imaginary place)—Fiction.   I. Miller, Sasha.
II. Mathews, Patricia.   III. Title.   IV. Series: Norton, Andre.
Witch world ; bk. 3.
PS3527.O632O5   1994
813′.52—dc20
                                                              93-33504
                                                                  CIP

First edition: January 1994

Printed in the United States of America

0 9 8 7 6 5 4 3 2 1

acknowledgments

A very big acknowledgment is due to a very great lady, Andre Norton. Not only did she create this world and allow me to live in it for a while, but she also handed me Alizon as my own little piece of it to develop. Therefore, thank you, Andre. Thank you for everything.

—Sasha Miller

My thanks to Dr. Suzette Haden Elgin, inventor of Laadan, a language created by and for women, for her permission to use this language in "We, the Women."

Thanks also to Linda Piper for the tale told by Arona to the travelers in Chapter 13, *Toads*.

—Patricia Mathews

The Chronicler

THERE are places in this ancient land of ours which are pleasant to the eye and yet are meant for traps for the unwary. Though Lormt (which I have come to see as my Great Hall, I, Duratan, who am kinless) is filled with knowledge gathered from years untold, still we who delve there also realize that there are secrets so well lost in the ages that they may never be made plain. Even if reference to them is found, it will not be well enough understood that its message can be clear to those for whom it might have the strongest meaning.

We live now in a time of ceaseless change, never knowing what the next day will bring. Once I was a fighting man who needed to come instantly alert to the blast of the war horn. Now I am again engaged in battles, but mostly far more subtle ones. Some are fought in a lamp-lighted room, upon a time-ridged table, my weapons not word nor dart-gun, but crumbling rolls of parchment and books so pressed by years their thick wooden or metal covers have glued their fragile pages together and it takes the lightest and most careful of handling to free them. Then, far too often, the near invisible lines on those pages are in some tongue foreign to that we know in this day, and so provide puzzles for even the scholars among us who have been the longest in the pursuit of such.

After the Turning of the southern mountains brought down two towers and some walls, opening thereby numerous secret rooms and crypts which held even more records, we were like to be swallowed by a sea of lore which we could not even list nor find places to store. What surprises might hide therein we could not even guess.

There were those who had their special subjects for which to search, but many among the oldest of the scholars simply became bewildered by this new wealth and could be found at times picking up a roll, a few minutes later abandoning it for a book or a scroll, and then sinking into a kind of daze as might a child who was faced by too great a supply of sweets on a feasting table.

However, there was danger and some of us knew that well. Nolar, who was witch talented but not trained, had testified to that when she had written her own account of the Stone of Konnard. That there were, in addition, other unchancy discoveries to be made was brought home to us in later times.

Yet the start of it all began with no stench of evil but rather a thing which had long provided a thorn to prick Nolar.

Spring came later for several years after the Turning, and our winters were longer. Lormt had changed in more than the sudden loss of towers and walls. The Witches had never had any interest in what was stored there, and, while they ruled Estcarp, few found their way down the single road which linked our storehouse with the outer world.

We had a spread of small farmsteads without the walls but within a ring of forest which held us as a center. There were a few traders who sought us out to bring what we could not raise or make by our own hands. Otherwise what lay beyond our narrow boundaries took on shapes of legend and to most did not matter.

However, when the forest was storm-flattened at the Turning, the river Es thrown from its bed, our world whirled about us and changed. First came refugees—though none of those lingered. Then followed seekers of special knowledge. The long rule of the Witches broken, other changes arose. Escore had been opened—that age-old land from which we of the Old Race had come very long ago. There war raged between newly-awakened evil and those who stood for the Light. We heard reports no one would have given credence to in other years.

Yes, evil came, and twice near to Lormt. There was fighting of another sort and in that I had a part.

Kemoc Tregarth, who had proven the worth of what Lormt held, made calls upon our records. So did others who faced clearly the fact that the old way of life had vanished and new must be hammered out with all the skill a swordmaker expends upon a trusted blade. There was a coming and going, and more and more of those who saw that the sharing of knowledge was of great value at such a time were called upon for help and advice.

So it fell on Ouen, Nolar, and I, and sometimes Morfew, who was the most approachable of the older scholars, to handle the requests from abroad, to answer many concerning what might lie in the past.

At the same time we heard reports and rumors enough that for the first time Lormt was forced to look to defenders. Chaos brings to the fore masterless men who quickly may become outlaws. Also what had been loosed in Escore did not always stay within the boundaries of that land. I found myself again a leader of fighting men, with Derren of Karsten as my second, and a force of landbred boys and a few stragglers from the old Border companies to command. We sent out scouts and had sentry posts in the hills, though the severity of the winter season kept us mainly free from raids while it lasted in these new years.

I was returning from my first round of sentry posts for the spring when I came upon a cup of green in a bit of the forest which was of the old growth. There was such a fragrance on the air that I reined in my mountain pony and looked groundward. There grew a small clump of those flowers called Noon and Midnight by the shepherds and found only near Lormt, their shaded, nine-petaled heads nodding in the breeze. I slid from the saddle and limped to gather four of them, and those I guarded very carefully while I rode to Lormt, eager to give Nolar this token of spring.

She was with Morfew and her face was very pale except for that stain on her cheek which was her birthmark and for which she had been shunned by those too dense to see aught but that which did not truly cloak a very brave and gallant spirit.

"Of a certainty her way has been hard, and when she came here she was hardly more than a child. Also she has listened too much to the Lady Nareth and that one—" I heard the sting in Nolar's voice as I entered Morfew's study "—has ever kept herself apart. There is good in Arona and a quick cleverness, also a love for what she does. I have long hoped that those prejudices born and fostered in her, the bitterness which has ridden her these past years, could be assuaged. Me, I think, she might trust if she would let herself. Mainly, I suppose, because I am a woman. There are few enough of us here. That is why she has listened to Nareth. I cannot think why a girl of Arona's intelligence would put up with the arrogance of that one. And now that Nareth is so old— Well, I shall make one more attempt, but if she takes on Nareth's airs and graces—"

"I believe, my daughter, that Arona is one who has not been able to fit herself to change. She sees that as an enemy. There are many others within these walls not unlike her in that. Still, she likes you. I have seen her watch you at one of our common meetings and there is plainly a struggle within her," Morfew said slowly.

"Does anyone else keep back knowledge, closed against the use of others?" Nolar retorted. "I am about to speak to her again—if she says once more that she will not share what she knows with me—because I am one with Duratan—!" Nolar's fist struck hard upon the table so that the inkwell before Morfew gave a little jump.

"What is this of Duratan?" I laid hand upon her shoulder and reached around to hold the flowers before her.

For a moment she stared at those, and then she laughed, but also shook her head.

"Do not try, Duratan, to make me see this other than what it is, a waste. Arona has so much to offer, not only of herself, for she was born to the task of recording, saving the past, but she has also the records of one Falconer village and legends which may open many closed doors. You know what might well have aided the Mountain Hawk!" She gave a little sigh. "I have that which I should be doing myself but I shall try again, put to the test that she does have some trust in me. Now that the Lady Nareth cannot make trouble, there may be a chance."

Two days later she came to me and her eyes were bright with triumph.

"It is done! Arona will allow me to view her treasures if I promise to do so only with her. So I must vanish for a space into that women's world, and during my absence you will have a chance to learn my value by missing me."

She smiled and put two fingers to her lips, then those to mine, and left, leaving the scent of Noon and Midnight behind her.

WE, THE WOMEN

by
Patricia Mathews

One

A Lady Scholar at Lormt

$\mathcal{A}$ solitary mounted figure plodded down the mountain trail, brown cloak and hood blending with the brownish-grey mule, one more shadow on a tan hillside. The mule's worn leather saddlebags were just large enough to hold a few necessities and a change of clothing; four long leather cylinders strapped alongside the saddle gave the impression that the rider might also be an archer—or a messenger.

The scholar's apprentice guarding the entrance to Lormt knew the cylinders for scroll cases. The mule's saddleblanket, though worn and faded, was a work of art—an original Jommy Einason, or Nolar missed her guess. The lean trousered figure who dismounted at the gates and looked around directly was no peasant boy, but a young woman with the sharp features and hot coloring of the Falconer breed.

Nolar's whole body trembled within her skin from fear and from anger, for her Falconer stepmother had loathed her birthmarked face. But this woman of the same race merely looked at Nolar with relief and said, "Good afternoon, sister. Arona Bethiahsdaughter of Riveredge Village. May I see a scholar? Not a he-scholar, if you please—if that's possible."

"Nolar of Meroney," the young student answered, taken aback. Her mind raced over the female scholars at Lormt. Dame Rhianne had always welcomed a new girl, but she was old, and dreamed in the sun. Nolar knew a few student-assistants, and there were some older women who were little more. Only one name remained; with a sigh, Nolar called out and a young boy appeared. "Visitor to see the Scholar Lady Nareth, if she will," Nolar said briefly.

The boy stared frankly at Arona and asked, "Falconer lady?"

"Was," Arona said curtly. "The old ways are gone forever. I could not endure that." She was speaking to Nolar directly now, the boy dismissed and forgotten. "Nor would I have our story lost and hidden through *rarilh.*"

Nolar turned, puzzled; Arona smiled briefly. "Deliberately failing to record and tell the tale, from malice. He-scribes have strange notions on what is important and what is not." Her eyes searched Nolar's face and she said bluntly, "Do you fear me, that you look so grimly at me?"

Nolar blushed. "I beg your pardon, Lady. I . . . my father's wife was of your people. She. . . ."

Arona's eyebrows raised. "Do I know her name and clan?" she asked, and then put a few brief questions to the girl; then the Falconer woman whistled. "An aunt of Lennis the Miller! An angry and stiffnecked clan, those of the mill. Mine, now, is said to be bitterly proud and disastrously impulsive; the Mari Anghard are known even to outsiders, at least by reputation."

Now Nolar whistled a bit. *"The* Anghard? She who was nursemaid to the three Witch children?"

Arona smiled in truth now, and her whole face lightened. "The very one." She took cloths and a currycomb from her pack, and began to groom her mule as she spoke, looking around for water. The creature was already nibbling at what grass there was by the gate. Then she laughed. "I had a mule named for me once by Cousin Jommy, though he thinks I don't know it, for I can be stubborn."

They talked earnestly and happily together, until at long last the boy returned.

"You're to follow me, Mistress Arona," he announced. She did so, leading the mule until they came to the stables and left the beast to Lormt's care.

*   *   *

The Scholar Lady Nareth was past her middle years, with dusty brown hair and piercing grey eyes. "Sit down, my girl," she ordered, indicating wine on a side table. Arona sipped it gratefully. "I understand you have some scrolls for me. Do you know what they contain?"

Stung, Arona answered coolly, "I wrote or copied most of them. I was the scribe in our village until the elders decided to preserve the peace by giving the post to a refugee boy. We are of the Falconer Women's village by the river, under the crag; this is the account of our lives."

Nareth studied her, then held out one well-groomed hand for a scroll. She unrolled it, frowned, and said, "You say nothing of life in the Eyries here, nor anything else concerning Falconers; yet you are of their blood. Of course, they keep their women apart."

Truly annoyed now, Arona said, "We saw very little of them, thank the Goddess. This is the account of *our* lives, not theirs. We do have lives, and kindred, and songs, stories, and a long history. Very little concerns those things men think important, such as wars and battles; this is why I would rather not see a he-scholar."

Nareth's eyes flashed grey in her cool, pale face. "Calm yourself! And tell me what wisdom is in these scrolls that merits your long journey to Lormt. You do realize we do not trouble ourselves with such records as what Falconer's woman gave him a son when, or how many measures of grain were issued to each woman at harvest time, or that one pulled the other's hair over her man's favors or her allowance or her ribbons."

Arona's lips were white now, and her hot Falconer eyes blazed. In a thin voice she said, "We bore no sons to any man. We bore our children to our own names, and saw the boys stolen from us as soon as they could walk or before. We were given nothing. All we had or did, we devised with our own hands and minds. We saw much of it destroyed time after time as the Falconers in their madness raged among us."

She lifted her chin. Proudly she said, "Our tales go back over twenty generations of women, to the Far Shore, when we were queens in our own lands, and prospered. Only an invasion of armed men in overwhelming numbers put an end to that. Uprooted in a strange land, alone, with nothing, with our own men turned against us and blaming us for their military failures, we built and survived and endured, and still prospered. But I see not even Lormt cares to hear that! Your pardon, scholar's handmaiden. I should have known." And to her complete horror, the Falconer girl broke down in tears.

Lady Nareth, on the verge of having the girl expelled for her extraordinary rudeness, did not. Behind the veil of her grey eyes was a scholar's mind, logical, unemotional, detached. "You are overwrought and overworn," she said with the same detachment. "I will forgive that outburst. You may guest in the wing used by our maidens and she-scholars; there is food in the refectory. I will read these scrolls and assess their worth myself; then I will speak to you again. I warn you, there are to be no more hysterics in my presence; we are scholars first, here, not women."

Arona looked up; Lady Nareth nodded sharply. "Thank you, my girl. You are dismissed."

As Arona went in search of her quarters, and food, Lady Nareth thought with regret of her own mentress, Scholar Rhianne. Rhianne had taken every stray female chick under her wing, not as a mother, but as if they were younger versions of herself. She protected them fiercely, and grieved when they—like Nareth—left her to deal with the more important scrolls and scholars.

Nareth's disciples were all boys. She had little but contempt for the average girl. Most of them were weak, fuzzy-minded if not mindless, subservient, and sly. Or they were strident and rude, forever in hysterics about some imagined slight. Every year there were some—the little sluts—who dared accuse this master or that of scandalous conduct towards them, and had to be turned out of the community.

It was plain that she and Arona would be crossing swords every day the Falconeress was at Lormt. Yet, Nareth's duty to the community forced her to read the scrolls, and therefore Arona must stay until she did. With a dire vision of a firebrand being touched to a keg of old oil, Nareth opened the first scroll. On top of it was a letter, to her (though not by name), from Arona, in a fine square hand. Intrigued, Nareth began to read.

TO WHOM IT MAY CONCERN

All accounts of Falconer life deal with the men and birds in their high mountain eyries. For the rest, it is said, "They keep their women in villages apart. They also keep their dogs in kennels, their horses in stables, and their sons in nurseries." Does nobody find anything lacking in this statement?

I, Arona Bethiahsdaughter of the Foxlady Clan, a woman of the Falconers, have come to complete that record. From time immemorial, since the days the Sulcar mercenaries set us down on your shores and before, we have had a life, a tradition, a culture of our own. We had our songs, our stories, our teachers, and our scribes, of which I was one.

We fell, not from force nor under oppression, but from peace and under freedom. Perhaps, if this is so, it is time we did, but I cannot help but mourn the life I was reared to. In many ways it was a good life: proud, self-sufficient, and but for the Falconer visits and their grim aftermath, free. Here, then, before our tale is lost and our lives go down to dust, is our story.

Arona, Chronicler

Two

The Falcon Cries at Night

Falcon Moon, a little past full, rose huge and red above the treetops to the east. To the west, Falcon Crag glowered in the blood-splashed grey of sunset. The women of Riveredge Village whispered together in tense little groups from which the children were excluded, glancing up at the crag as if afraid of being seen, then down again.

Where were the Falconers? The first full moon of fall always brought the strange, masked madmen to take the boy babies away, and to start daughters growing in the villagers. Elders and children peered restlessly out of their hiding places in the caves, ready to bolt and run again. Those volunteers of child-bearing age whose names had been drawn in the summer lottery drew their Visit veils about them and dug in the trailhead gardens in swift, jerky motions, saying almost nothing.

A thin, nervous girl with hot bronze hair and yellow eyes threw back her unaccustomed veil and whispered, "Tell me again about last time, Aunt Natha."

The woman beside her glanced up at the Crag again and whispered softly, "They fixed the Visit huts, and cut us several cords of wood. They redug the outhouse trenches, and after generations of ignoring this place, made everything as snug as if we truly lived here. Why, they did not say. Does anything in the records speak of this?"

The girl Arona shook her head and looked up at the sky. Thunderheads were forming in the east as they did most evenings in the early fall. The sky was darkening. Natha Lorinsdaughter, coguardian to the young Keeper of the Records, took her hoe and Arona's and turned back towards the cluster of cabins around the trailhead. They were small and barren, of log chinked with clay, with crudely thatched roofs and tiny stone hearths by the door. The Falconers had built them long ago when, strangers to these lands, they deserted the village to seek their fortunes alone. Some said they had been expelled for extreme ill-behavior. Arona wondered.

She lit the fire as Aunt Natha filled an old ceramic pot, chipped around the edges, with water. They unrolled the sort of bedding usually given to animals on the rough dirt floors. A shepherd on duty would find this adequate, but for the closeness and the fear; many a young girl sleeping out in the woods for this reason or that had less comfort. To go without weapons or jewelry or any other adornment, and to drink neither ale nor beer, made this a religious vigil of sorts. It was only the apprehension that made her uncomfortable, she told herself. For a moment she even believed it.

She and Aunt Natha had eaten a rough meal of field rations, washed down with water, cleansed themselves clumsily from their only pot, and given thanks to She Who Guards Women, when an odd sound made her stand up suddenly. Arona raced for the hut's open door frame and put her head out. Far above her, a lookout's throat twisted itself into the harsh sounds of a falcon's cry. "They're coming," the girl blurted out, turning back to the door. "Now!"

She was almost too late. Racing hoof beats drowned out the sounds of the lookout's warning. Arona covered herself hastily, begging the Goddess for protection as her heart pounded. Above her, shadowy mounted figures raced down the well-worn trail between this meeting place and Falcon Crag.

Mounted Falconers in bird masks, with metal pots over their heads and metal plates binding their jackets, thundered into the village on the backs of horses, like horses fleeing before wolves. Long, curved butcher knives hung from their belts, and wolf-spears were bound to their saddles. They swung themselves out of their saddles and moved with grim purpose towards the huts. Without a word, one took the girl by the shoulder and shoved her into the hut. Well warned at her Initiation, she made no outcry, though she was bitterly angry that she must endure this three times in succession. Was this how daughters were started in a woman's womb? This was the central mystery of their lives, that she had been so eager to experience?

But birth was also painful and bloody, and lasted longer; nor did the Falconers enjoy the deed that makes a child, either. They seemed driven and desperate.

Before the last Falconer was finished with his duty, a low-voiced, harsh mockery of her own lookout's call sounded, very close. The Falconers in the hut swore, rapidly made themselves fit to ride again, and raced for the door, herding the two women after them. A golden-helmeted Falconer stood in the center of the cluster of huts. "Females," he barked, harshly. "We go now. Keep your sons. We cannot see them now. We will see them later. Now go." He prodded one with a short, nasty-looking eating-knife. Awkwardly she moved at a rapid walk, not daring to run, until she reached the shelter of the forest. The others followed, each going their separate ways. The central figure said, even more harshly and loudly, in that unnatural deep voice, "We must do this. Enemies must not find you. Forgive."

He barked an order and, efficiently, the mounted Falconers rode into the huts and gardens, trampling everything that could be trampled, knocking the straw from the roofs, tearing down the log huts, as the women watched in stunned silence. Then they rode away to the south, without venturing deep into the forest where the real village was.

As soon as the last Falconer was gone, Arona and the younger women picked up their skirts and ran along the hidden forest trails to their comfortable, safe homes under the trees. Then Natha Lorinsdaughter opened her throat to sound the all-clear, followed swiftly by the call for possible trouble ahead. Arona wondered dry-eyed *what trouble?* And what worse enemies they could have than these bird-faced creatures? Then she ran into the House of Records, flung herself across her bed, and wept as if her favorite dog had savaged her.

In the village of Cedar Crest, Morgath the Blacksmith's house and forge were burning like the bonfires of an angry god. With one last, hastily stifled sob, Morgath's wife Huana—no, his widow, now—looked down from the hillside to which she'd fled, and laid a hand over her young daughter's mouth. The trees, thick as winter fur, hid the sight from the women and the women from the Hounds of Alizon. But the village square was empty.

As Huana watched, people began dashing out of houses and barns to the forge where lay several bodies, as still as death. All but a few of the gathering crowd wore skirts, and those few were very young, or very old. The blacksmith's widow laid her finger across her lips and whispered, "Stay here, Leatrice, and don't make a sound unless one of our neighbors comes." She thought a bit and said, "If it's a pack of lads alone, don't answer even if it's our neighbors."

"I'll climb a tree," Leatrice promised, hushed by her mother's manner. But excited as well.

Huana groaned. "It's unseemly and unwomanly, but—better that than spoiled for marriage, I suppose." She said so as if grudgingly. "I'll be back." Purpose came back into her voice then. "If I'm not back by next sunset, wait till dawn and try to reach your Aunt Markalla in Twin Valleys. And, Leatrice—keep to the back roads if you do!" And as silently as possible, the woman slipped down the hillside.

Every woman, child, and old man in the village of Cedar Crest seemed to be in the square, and all the women were wailing fit to wake the dead. Huana shoved her way through the crowd to the smithy, where her dear husband Morgath lay dead at his own forge. And for what? Huana strangled another sob. The soldiers had demanded that he shoe their horses and repair their swords and spears. The first he had done willingly; the second he claimed to be beyond his power and, for that, they slew him and ransacked the house, burning it.

She knelt beside the body, weeping for the blood flowing from his many wounds, and laid her ear to his mouth, then his chest, to listen for his breath. There was none. She laid her hand to his mouth then. It came away bloody. Under the heavy, coarse shirt with its stiff collar, his throat had been cut.

Now she keened like any of the others, howling, "Oh, Morgath, why did you ever defy them? I told you and told you, do as they ask and send them on their way. I told you!"

Tears running down her face so she must blow her nose on her apron, she shoved her way through another crowd to the village well, and dipped that same apron in the bucket without a by-your-leave as a neighbor woman hauled it up. Then back to where her husband lay, and with the wet apron, washed him as best she could. But how could she bury him decently, with no men around to dig the grave? She looked around, desperate to see any man of her kindred at all, but saw only her son Oseberg, who would be fourteen in the spring.

"Oseberg!" she called above the noise. "Oseberg, come here, immediately!" Accustomed to obedience, the hulking young boy pushed through the crowd as she did, to stand by her side. Softly she said, "We must bury your father." White-faced, he nodded. "Do you run to the house and see if a shovel remains, and if not, find one. No, help me move him to our yard first."

The boy gulped and looked around to see if anyone could help. He caught the eye of Lisha the baker's wife; she moved more gracefully to his side and asked gently, "Can I help?"

Huana sighed deeply in her relief and threw her arms around the other woman. "Oh, I am so grateful for your help, cousin. Has a shovel or spade survived in your house, and does your husband still live? Oh, yes, and—Leatrice!" She lowered her voice. "Leatrice is in hiding from the soldiers."

Lisha patted her cousin on the shoulder. "I'll send my sons to get her." Noting her cousin's look of *oh-gods*, the baker's wife nodded understandingly. "I'll send Hanna and her sister," she corrected. "We'll need our big boys to dig graves and help rebuild."

Gratefully, Huana patted Lisha's shoulder in return, and the three of them—two women and a boy—helped carry the boy's father back to Huana's scorched houseplot.

Then, wiping the sweat from her forehead, Huana said, "I can't stay here, with Oseberg too young to take over the forge and not done with his apprenticeship yet. Who would take care of us? We have no close kin here."

"What will you do?" Lisha asked practically.

"Try to make our way to my married sister in Twin Valleys," Huana said grimly. The thought of living on her sister's husband's charity was not at all appealing. She could only pray his charity extended to finding his wife's nephew a new master in the only trade the boy knew. She who had been mistress would become a drudge in another woman's house. But she and her children would not starve, nor be reduced to begging or harlotry, and surely nothing else awaited her here. Why, after three invasions in as many months, scarcely a man was left to support any woman, let alone one in her late twenties with two children. She sighed heavily.

Lisha nodded in sympathy and said, "Let us rest a while, and see if we can ask others to help in this. Then, after we've buried Harald and Morgath together, we can help them, too."

Huana, who had not looked beyond her own needs, said in hasty horror, "Oh, Lisha, I'm so sorry! I had no idea they killed Harald too."

"Trying to defend us," Lisha said, her eyes dark with anger and grief. Only then did Huana notice Lisha's torn gown and headdress, hastily set to rights. Instinctively, the blacksmith's wife pulled away. If Lisha had been dishonored, Huana could not associate with her without sharing the stain, and then not even her good name would remain to her. She would be destitute indeed.

Lisha's mouth twisted cynically, but she said nothing but, "Shall we see to the burial, then?" And because the needs of the moment came first, the women and boys began to dig their loved ones' graves.

Little enough was left to the village after this last raid. Hands wrapped in rags, the women and children dug through the ruins for anything they could salvage: iron pots, a few plates and utensils, a bit of farm gear. Huana and Lisha managed to capture a few fowl that had run, squawking, when the raiders rode through. Leatrice had managed to rope an aged donkey belonging to the village priest, whom for some reason the wicked child heartily disliked. "Well, the priest won't miss it where he is," Huana dismissed the matter in her mind. It would not do to tell Leatrice this, of course.

Then the sky darkened suddenly as the earth shook under their feet and the very land rumbled and belched like a giant with indigestion. "Run!" cried Huana, abandoning her quest for goods. She shouldered her heavy bag of salvaged goods and slapped her young son across the backside. Oseberg Smithson gave his mother a resentful look, picked up an equally huge bundle, and served his sister as his mother had him. Lisha and her five children followed. Other bewildered and leaderless women and children from the ruins of Cedar Crest plodded along into the forest at the greatest speed their burdens would allow. It was not a quiet exodus. Cattle lowed, children sobbed, fowls in their cages cackled, and an occasional mule or donkey brayed.

Luckily, there were no pursuers to hear and follow them. These were not the doings of men, but of the gods.

The small party of bedraggled refugees picked their way through trees and over rocks, through sticky mud and slippery moss, scratchy briars, and up a steep hillside, speeding away from the source of the turmoil with all deliberate haste. Children fell down and had to be picked up; harried mothers often slapped them to send them on their way again. The youngest babies whimpered their hunger and fright. There were sharp sounds of anger and quarreling as they forced their way uphill, skirts heavy with mud and torn with briars. The sickly-sweet voice of Yelen the carpenter's wife chirped desperately, "Now, now! Little birdies in their nests always agree!"

"Oh, shut up!" Gondrin the alewife snapped in fury.

"We've been through too much," Lisha said sagely to Huana beside her, as their children struggled in game silence up the hill. "We're all worn to the bone by now."

Wondering who had appointed her possibly-defiled cousin the village priest, Huana glared and said nothing.

They scarcely noticed in their fear and exhaustion when the steep hill rounded off and began to slope downward. When they found a way relatively free of briars and brambles, it took them a while to realize what was happening. Leatrice Smithsdaughter spoke first. "A path, Mama! A path! I wonder where it goes?"

"A path, a path," cried the weariest and the least thoughtful.

"A path to where?" Huana asked sharply. "Do we know the ones who made it? What if they turn us from their doors as beggars?"

"As you always did," the alewife whispered in a voice that carried all too well.

"A path to an enemy stronghold, perhaps," Yelen the carpenter's wife said fearfully.

"Or maybe to refuge?" Leatrice answered stoutly. Then they all began to talk at once, occasional voices rising briefly above the babble until Huana groaned. "Oh, if only we had a man here to lead us!" That got instant, vocal agreement.

"Well, we have not," Lisha snapped, "so let's try to settle this like grown women. Those who would go on, gather over here where I am. Those who would not, make up your minds what to do. For me, I am going on. Whatever awaits us, it could never be as bad as being alone in the woods at night, unless, as you said, it's an encampment of soldiers. If it is, why, we can send somebody ahead to find out. Egil?" She called her oldest boy.

"Sure, Mama," the youth answered in a reassuring tone. He

was almost seventeen and already trying to cultivate a mustache.

"That's settled," Lisha said cheerfully. "It's getting dark. Shall we try to camp here, or push on?"

"If we camp here," a young girl's voice quavered, "won't wild animals get us?"

"Not if we light a fire," Egil Bakerson said with amiable scorn.

"If we light a fire," an older woman asked more rationally, "won't wild men see it and find us?"

Lisha thought about that as voices babbled around her again. "Some of us must stand guard," she finally said, "and take turns. Who has anything long and heavy or sharp? A pitchfork? A kitchen knife?"

"Do we have enough big boys to keep watch?" Yelen asked, trying to count them by eye.

Gondrin had taken a stout stick in her hand. "If Lisha will take the first watch, so will I," she declared. "If anything comes, you all be ready." She saw Yelen look fearfully towards boys of ten, eleven, and twelve, and said in scorn, "Oh, grow up, Yelen, and don't lay your burdens on their shoulders yet. Anybody else?"

Leatrice looked around and found the shovel they had used to bury her father. "I'm with you," she answered bravely.

"No, you're not," Oseberg shoved her aside. "That's my business; I'm the man of the family now."

"Oseberg," Huana decided. "Go with them."

The women and children slept uneasily that night on the wet ground. The forest was filled with strange noises and stranger, deeper silences. The women and boys on watch shivered in fear and exhaustion and longed for even the small comfort of their cloaks on the cold ground. It was hard to keep from dozing off. When they were relieved, Oseberg, Gondrin, and Lisha were replaced by Egil, Leatrice, and, hastily, Huana—who did not want her maiden daughter up alone after sunset with a grown lad like Egil. The boy glared at her discreetly, disappointed. Huana intercepted the glance and smiled grimly, watching the children more than the oncoming night.

They woke to a forest cold and damp, with the fire nearly out. The women dug in their bundles for what food they had, and managed to find a few eggs from the fowl they had brought. Their one goat was dry. In a tone that brooked no argument, Egil Bakerson announced that he and the boys would snare small game for their hungry families. "You just wait here," he ordered them. Yelen quavered acceptance; Lisha gave them till midmorning. The women used the time to check and rearrange their bundles; several bitter fights broke out over what food was left.

The first and second watches rested. Leatrice and her mother were relieved by Lisha's daughter Lowri and a tough old beldam, the widow Melbrigda, from a farm on the edge of the village. The boys came back empty-handed, but for Oseberg, who had found some sour crabapples on a tree. Even those were welcome. Wearily they picked up their bundles and moved on.

One day followed another, cold, wet, and hungry. A light rain began to fall, but it was no common rain. It felt nasty, as if fireplace ashes had been mixed with it. The earth had ceased to rumble, but the clouds overhead were a baleful orange-grey, as if the very heavens were on fire. Huana and Lisha could go no farther, but sat down on the ground and wept helplessly.

Then a dove called out of nowhere. The fog parted enough to show a tall, tumbled crag in the distance. Closer yet and to the north were the vague outlines of a mountain range, shrouded in mist. Below them was a wooded valley. The dove called again, and her cry became a falcon's screech. Huana looked up, terrified, to see a great woman-headed bird part the clouds.

She circled high in the sky, closer and closer to the wet, bedraggled group of refugees, then glided in on silent wings. Old Melbrigda, whose husband had once been in service to a lord, said, "Why, it's a ladyhawk. Come on, pretty, come to

Mother." She wrapped her shawl around her arm to make a thick padding, and held her arm out. The ladyhawk settled down on the padding gently and dug her claws in.

"There is refuge by the river," the bird said in a barely understandable accent, "and sanctuary in the valley. If all women are your sisters, you may enter there as sisters and mothers and daughters. I have said it."

"Who are you," Huana whispered in terror, making a sign against evil.

"I am a goddess," the bird whispered back, "once a maiden, then the living spirit of vengeance, which was my only justice. Now I am a guardian spirit. Take an oath of kindness, woman, for those I guard set much store by it."

"This I swear, gladly," Lisha said promptly. "Is there any here who would not? Assuming that you trust the bird and those who sent her, which I do."

Gondrin stepped forward. "In my trade you learn to read people, and I say, follow the bird."

Lisha looked over the small crowd, none of whom had gone another way nor turned back at the path. "Lead, Mistress Hawk," she decided. "I, for one, will follow. Come on, children." She picked up her pack again, sighed, settled it on her shoulders, and went forward.

The bird who came to them in early morning left them in late afternoon. Twilight thickened in the forest. Slowly, fearfully, the little party made their way down the path. Leatrice, near the front, kept looking around curiously, then nudged her mother. "Look, Mama, in the trees. Isn't that a house?"

Huana peered through the forest gloom, but saw only a dim shadow that might have been anything. She shuddered. "Leave it be, Leatrice," she whispered. "The gods only know what lives out here all alone like a wild beast."

For a moment, Leatrice's heart ached with longing for her father, who feared as little as her mother feared much. Then, resolutely, she again shifted the weight of her heavy pack and kept looking for houses. She saw dim shadows here, traces of paths there, and many things that might or might not mean human life, but at last it could not be mistaken. She saw the gleam of firelight through cracks in a shutter. She nudged her mother again. Grudgingly, Huana said, "It may be a house." Then she and the other women started talking.

Egil looked disgusted. "These women are going to chatter all night. Shall we wake the householders up?"

"Are you prepared to fight them if they're bandits or shape changers?" Leatrice asked.

Egil's lips twisted in scorn. "I shouldn't have asked a girl," he conceded, the last word accented like a deadly insult.

Leatrice shoved ahead of him and found the door. "Help," she called out. "Help us. We're lost and starving and there's no men with us and we won't hurt you. Please?" Egil swore a mild oath at this disgusting, unmanly conduct.

The door opened. A thin, bronze-haired girl of about fourteen answered and rubbed her eyes. "I'll call the elders, sister. What's your name? And—what's a 'men'?"

Arona, roused from a painful and uneasy sleep, stared at the strangers in shock. So many, many people she had neither grown up with nor seen born! They spoke the tongue used by the only other outsiders she had ever seen: Gunnora's Daughters—the wise women who came to trade each year; and the strange woman of power who called herself The Dissident. Wind rattled her open door, blowing in the first drops of rain of tonight's storm, recalling her manners to her. "Come in and share my fire," she said laboriously in the same tongue they used. "I am Arona Bethiahsdaughter of the Foxlady Clan, apprentice Keeper of the Records. My mistress is out, but do come in."

They crowded in, some dozen and a half of people. The young apprentice bit her lip. She would not leave these people alone; yet, someone must be told. On a sudden thought, she put her head out the door and raised her voice in the call meaning

"Unidentified strangers, trouble but not much." Satisfied, she put more wood on the fire and set the cooking pots over the coals.

The cat called Little Red Pest walked over to the strangers and the girl who had first knocked on Arona's door put down her hand to pet her. A tall girl in sheepherder's trousers made rude noises, and her mother swatted her across the rear as she would a mule. Then the mother said to Arona, "Is your (something?) or your (he-mother?) home, maiden?"

Drat this wretched language, Arona cursed silently as she found words to frame an answer to a question she did not understand. "I no longer live in my mother's house. My mistress is the record keeper here. I have the right to offer you this kindness," she reassured them. In the distance she could hear the sounds of rainclad women sloshing through the leaves. Let an elder who spoke this tongue have this burden! Then, because Huana had used a title to her, she corrected her. "I may soon be not maiden, but mother, for the Falconers came last night."

"Falconers!" the woman demanded, her voice rising to a strangled squawk, and she stared at Arona as if the girl were being Shunned and had not warned her. As if a fox had raided the henhouse, the women all started shouting at once. The rude big girl, whom Arona could see had faint hairs on her face like a crone, said, "Don't worry, mother, I'll defend you."

"You're a good boy, Oseberg," the woman said gratefully as the village elders trooped in, one by one, crowding the small room beyond its comfort.

Eldest Mother Mechtild swung her head around with a suddenness that made Arona's teeth ache. "Boy?" she said ominously.

A babble of voices rose all around Arona, who by now was starting to get a headache. "Boys are the young of the Falconer breed," Lennis the Miller shouted hysterically. "We've seen what this one's cousin Jommy did, left unchecked, for all her Aunt Eina's careful rearing. It killed a Falconer! That's why they tore down the huts! The Jommy has done violence to me, too!"

"Falconer?" Huana was screaming. "You belong to the Falconers?"

Another Jommy, Arona thought, looking at Oseberg curiously. The rain was beating down harder and the wind was whipping it in through the door. Arona's headache was slowly growing worse. She had liked the gentle, lame Jommy who was so conscious of his anomalous position in the village, boy or no boy; she had taken a dislike to Oseberg even thinking it was a girl. From her pain she said sharply, "We cannot keep them all here all night while we debate, sisters, for they are on the verge of collapse, and so am I."

"Mother," Egil spoke then as if handing down a decision, "the young mistress is quite right. There are too many of us, and we cannot all impose on her people like that. Suppose you ladies let us shelter in some outbuilding tonight, and Oseberg and I will be quite willing to do chores for you in payment."

A baby cried thinly from hunger and cold. Noriel the Blacksmith pushed forward. "Noriel Auricasdaughter of Wolfhame Clan," she said. "There is plenty of room at the forge, if any of you would shelter with me."

Huana's head jerked up sharply. "Forge? Uh, Mistress Forgewife, does your (something) need another apprentice?"

Noriel's plain, heavy face was transformed by radiance. "Do you offer me an apprentice?" She looked hopefully at Oseberg, who grinned, then looked dubiously at his mother, who nodded agreement. "It is settled."

Asta Lennisdaughter was staring at Egil, and now tugged at the hem of the miller's heavy rain cloak. "Mother, these people seem so hungry," she said sadly. "And their oldest girl is so well-spoken." She lowered her voice. "And looks s-t-r-o-n-g," she whispered so only her mother should hear. "Of course," she added slyly, "it will put Aunt Marra's nose out of joint." That last comment brightened Lennis's eyes vindictively.

Arona's head was aching violently now. Viciously she recalled that every child in the village referred to Lennis's two daughters as Roldeen the Bully and Asta the Sneak. Plainly the Sneak wanted the well-spoken Egil for a sisterfriend—as did Arona. Mostly the young record keeper wanted to be back in bed. She found a wooden mallet and brought it down, hard, on the table. Everyone looked up. And Arona spoke as if she were an elder or a householder.

"Everyone willing to take in these people for even the rest of the night, speak in turn," she said, taking her spindle from its place beside the fire. "Not you, Dame Noriel; why don't you and your strangers seek a nice, warm bed? And you, Dame Lennis, will surely want to tell your strangers where to stay and what to do in more comfort than this."

Lennis looked at her through narrowed eyes that looked small, piggy, and shrewd. Then the miller laughed, sharply. "A clever little girl for one who was a child yesterday. All right, Little Missy Recorder, we will obey your orders indeed."

Arona held onto her temper as tightly as she did the spindle. The miller's rudeness, like every other detail of this night, would go into the records exactly as spoken, of course. But then, Arona reassured herself, Dame Lennis had never been too bright. She pounded for silence again and held out the spindle to the next person to speak. As the woman speaking began a long argument both for and against taking in strangers, Arona said, "Yes? Or no? These poor people are exhausted." The baby cried again.

Another called out, "I cannot bear to hear that poor thing whimper! We have only the front room floor, but if you are agreeable, Mistress, you can stay with us."

And wasn't it true that the poor were more willing to share than many of the prosperous? That deserved an aphorism, when Arona could think of one.

Gondrin raised her hand for the spindle and Arona passed it over. "For what it's worth, I am an alewife and a brewmistress, and can earn my keep at the local tavern."

Arona translated that, and said, "What is a tavern?"

"A place where men come and drink, and discuss things, and meet their friends," Gondrin said, then looked around. "Oh. I see no men here," she said suddenly. "This is a village of Falconer women, you said, didn't you? I'll bet they don't drink . . . here . . . and it's certain they wouldn't allow you to!"

That started a noisy, angry cascade of voices. Her head pounding as if it would not cease for days, Arona shouted, "Order! Mistress Gondrin, nobody will stop you from having your house of ale. The Falconers do not tell us what to do except at the trailhead, once a year, to the volunteers. They do not concern themselves with our daily lives, which in any case we do not let them see. Please, my sisters, if any of you will help those left, this ancient mother is asleep," she indicated Melbrigda, "and needs a bed." By keeping everybody here strictly to the point, she could at least hope to regain her bed before daylight made sleep impossible.

One of the he-hens started its morning salute to the dawn, and Arona groaned. Now they would all be here all day. Why had none of the elders taken this from her hands? It was their place. No, they were too busy debating the long-range consequences of taking in the strangers. Suddenly she said, "Your pardon, Elders; I *am* sick."

Old Floree Anasdaughter suddenly recalled that she was a healer as well as an elder, and strode over to where Arona sat, nearly fainting. "Great Goddess, child, you're as pale as snow. You! Clear out and move this meeting to the village hall, you fools; this should never have been laid on that child's shoulders." She held up the fainting recorder and said, "Can you walk, child?"

"I'll help," Oseberg said eagerly; for he and his new comother had hung around out of curiosity. The blacksmith was shy, but for all that had to know everything, Arona remembered. The hulking youth put one hand under her arm, but then moved it stealthily to one of Arona's breasts. She took it off.

"Can't blame a boy for trying," he said cheerfully under his breath. "You're no maiden, you said. How about you and me . . . ?"

Arona tried to shake off his grip. "I can walk," she said. Then she turned on him. "Why are you fondling me like a pet cat?" she snapped, loud enough for all to hear. "Stop it. Or does this village have a second bully?"

Huana, who heard this, sniffed. If the wench was shameless enough to announce what was being done to her, she was not worth a moment's consideration. But Oseberg should be warned not to fall into her doubtless-many traps. She took the lad by the ear. "Come along," she said firmly.

Floree put Arona to bed in the back room of Healing House, where the girl slept for two days with the worst headache in her family's history. The first strangers ever admitted into village life settled with their adopted families. Riveredge Village would never be the same. *And I'm only fourteen,* Arona thought as she lay down with a wet cloth over her eyes and gave in to the pain.

Three

New Wine in Old Bottles

A rona woke in Healing House, the senior recorder by her bedside. The girl sat up, rubbed her eyes, and washed her face in icy water from the bedside basin. "I was dreaming of First Times." As she found and donned her robe, she accused, "Where were you during that dreadful racket last night?"

Maris, who woke whenever a cat twitched its tail, smiled a little and handed Arona her sandals. "Two nights ago. But you were doing quite well, dear."

The village women were already up and about their business, but more of them than usual were clustered together talking in low tones. Arona stopped while a group of them wearing tool aprons hauled logs to a rundown abandoned cabin now being rebuilt.

Gondrin the alemaker saw her and waved cheerfully. "Thank you for helping us!" she called out, pounding a peg into the cabin side. Feeling better, Arona strolled down the path to Records House, looking around curiously as the strangers passed by.

She stopped to watch two of their children playing a game with sticks. They were clashing their sticks against each other, and as Arona watched, the big blonde's stick touched the little brunette. Ah! A fault against the big blonde! No, the big blonde was crowing, "Gotcha!" to her friend. Arona watched a bit longer, then realized the object of the game was to keep the other child's stick from touching you.

It was a game of self-defense. A shudder ran down Arona's body. What sort of world was out there, that little children played games of self-defense?

The one called Huana and her daughter Leatrice passed. Arona spoke; Huana jerked Leatrice aside and glared at the young recorder as if Arona had done her some harm. As Arona stared after them, Egil Lishasdaughter came up beside her and said graciously, "Don't mind her. She's terrified for her daughter's virtue. For myself, I'm grateful you took us in. Now, let me see, you're the village scribe's daughter, aren't you?"

Arona slowly puzzled out as much of this as she could. "I'm Maris's apprentice, not her daughter," she said carefully. "Thank you for your thanks; you're welcome. Please tell Huana not to fear; her daughter is safe now." Then, "You do not speak our language at all, do you? Any of you? You'll have to see the priestess and learn what we all learn as children."

Egil looked at her thoughtfully. "At home, I was told schooling is for priests and my betters. Not for the likes of us. My mother may not be able to spare me, but I can talk her around. If your schoolmaster's around, I'll be glad to talk to him.''

Arona frowned again, working out the meaning. "The he-priestess did not want to teach you? You seem bright. Let me take you to Sacred House to see Dame Birka. Our priestess.''

Egil's eyebrows went up. "Gladly! You know, Arona—that's your name, Arona?—you seem to have quite a sharp mind, for a girl. You're not exactly in the common mold, but many a girl who counts herself a beauty would die for those cheekbones and that hair. Interesting, that's the word I want to use, interesting.''

The stranger had an unusually deep voice, Arona thought, and a pleasant one, but what a chatterbox. It, she, whatever was the proper term, seemed to want to be friends, but sounded like a big girl talking to a tagalong. How old was she? At least eighteen, from her size. But as breastless as a little girl, and with hair cut so short Arona wondered if she had been ill. Surely so, for a maiden so sensitive to beauty in others would surely treasure her own beauty. But that crack about having such a fine mind for one so young did not sit at all well with the proud Recorder, who was used to being the eldest and the brightest in her family. *I have a rival here,* she thought. *But, possibly, a friend.*

They came to the Sacred House farmyard, and Arona stopped. "Do you like books?" she ventured suddenly.

"Yes. Yes, I do . . . when I can find one.''

"And beauty. I can tell that about you.''

"Yes, indeed!'' Egil's grin grew wider. Suddenly his face was over her and Egil was kissing her, not as children who are friends nor as kindred do, but a strange sort of kiss that fascinated and frightened her. She yanked her face back and stared. "What—why—Egil, that was—even best friends do not do such things by surprise.''

Egil bowed solemnly, a gesture Arona had never seen. "My humble apologies, Mistress Arona, and I hope indeed we will be friends.'' The door opened; he bowed again.

Arona disappeared in the direction of Records House as the priestess nodded a clear dismissal. *Not only a chatterbox,* the girl thought of Egil, *but smooth, slick as a snake. I wonder what she wants of me?*

Arona and Egil understood each other less than either of them thought; Noriel and Huana's family understood each other not at all. Noriel knew it and was not bothered by it. She guided the little party to the forge house and waved her hand expansively at the loft, the kitchen, the main room, and her bedroom off the kitchen.

When she gestured that the children would sleep upstairs, Huana threw a wet-hen fit. Noriel shrugged; maybe Leatrice and Oseberg made too much noise together. Huana talked on until Leatrice went to the loft, and Oseberg to the main room floor, then glanced into Noriel's room, stared long and hard at its one bed, and with much complaint, climbed the ladder to the loft.

In the morning, Noriel greeted them cheerfully. Of course, her strangers could neither speak nor understand any more than small babies could, but women still talked to small babies and in time they learned to understand. She splashed water on her face and showed them where all things were, dressed, and went out back to the woodpile. Huana stood in the kitchen doorway, hesitant; Noriel beckoned her out to join her and picked up several chunks of wood. Huana hesitated, then shoved Oseberg out to join Noriel.

Noriel then made hand-over-hand signs of drawing water from the well and beckoned Leatrice to join her; saw Oseberg, and handed him a pile of plates. Huana's heart sank. Bad enough she should be a drudge in a stranger's house, but for her son to be put to women's work? They had fallen very low indeed! She started to weep silently.

Noriel poured water into a huge ceramic pot that stood in the hearth, added some dried cracked grains, and motioned Huana over to stir it. Oseberg handed the plates to Leatrice, then sat

down, waiting to be served. Noriel took two long steps to his
side and motioned *Up!* She handed him a knife and some tree
fruits and made peeling motions. Huana opened her mouth in
outrage, then remembered she was a beggar, living on charity,
moaned, and hung her head.

Noriel's heart filled with pity for these strangers, alone and
far from their home. To distract them and to open communica-
tions, she pointed to herself. "Noriel," she said. She pointed to
Huana.

Leatrice said, "Mother."

"Mother," Noriel called. Huana looked up and stared, wiping her eyes with her sleeve.

"Huana," Leatrice corrected. She pointed to herself. "Leatrice." And to her brother. "Oseberg."

"Leatrice. Leatrice Huanasdaughter, Oseberg Huanasdaughter," Noriel said, pleased.

Huana gaped and stood up straight, confronting this huge,
foul-mouthed forgewife. "He is not Oseberg Huanas-whatever-
you-said!" she exploded. "I'm a respectable widow, I'll have
you know, and these are the true children of their father in
honest marriage. How dare you! Beggars or no beggars. . . ."

Noriel looked at Leatrice, who pointed to herself and said
"Leatrice Morgathschild." She tried to pronounce it as Noriel
had, then pointed to her brother and said "Oseberg Morgathson" in her own language. By way of further explanation, she
held her hand up high beside her and pointed to the imaginary
person she measured. "Morgath. My father," she explained.
She drew an imaginary knife across her throat, hung her head
limply, looked up with her eyes full of sudden tears. "Morgath," she said, and snuffled.

Noriel took the girl in her arms. Ah! Their birthmother was
dead, murdered by Falconers or something like, it seemed, and
Huana their co-mother wanted it made clear that her sisterfriend was to be remembered. More charitably, she wrapped an
arm around Huana, too, and said, "I'm sorry." She wished she
had three arms, one more for Oseberg, or that the child would

come over for comfort instead of standing with its back to everybody, shoulders hunched over as if refusing comfort. Oh, well, they were among strangers themselves.

"Oseberg Morgathsdaughter," she said, and beckoned him over. The boy obeyed, his face streaked with tears too. Huana said sharply, "Big boys don't cry, Oseberg, and you have to be the man of the family now."

"Oh, mother, leave him alone," Leatrice protested.

Noriel, understanding none of this, sighed. *Wet hen,* she dubbed Huana. Oseberg was just a child. Leatrice seemed to have some sense. She dished out four bowls of porridge and gestured to the nearest of her guests to pass them around. Oseberg took the first one to reach him, dug in, and started eating; sharply Noriel said, "Oseberg Morgathsdaughter! Show some manners!" Startled, the child looked up. *Pampered,* Noriel decided, showing him by gestures to pass things around.

Somehow or other, the morning meal was served and eaten. But when they rose from the table and Oseberg headed out the door without a word, Noriel cornered him. Indicating the bowl, she gestured *Up! Up!* Reluctantly he cleared his place; Leatrice and Huana did the same, and Huana set about washing the dishes, ordering Leatrice most sharply to help her. Oseberg followed Noriel to the forge.

Huana sighed. She and her daughter were drudges in this forgewife's house. The only one who spoke a human tongue besides the old crones was that insolent whore with red hair, Arona, and even her son must play the servant. These would be hard times indeed.

Down by the mill, the irresistible force had met the immovable object. "Well-spoken!" Lennis snorted, hands on hips. "I don't care if this Egil Lishasdaughter is the Bard Ofelis herself. It's still a Jommy, and I'd sooner have a rattlesnake in the house than a Jommy. Do you hear me?"

Asta Lennisdaughter's lip quivered, something she'd had much practice at. "Mother," she said reproachfully. "Just look at these poor little children and their hard-working mother. See how cute little Soren is? We'd have a baby in the house again," she coaxed, "without all the mess and bother of getting one yourself." The girl held up the golden-haired refugee infant and cooed at it.

Lennis pounced and in one swift motion, stripped away little Soren's blanket. "Another Jommy," she pronounced, and turned on her youngest viciously. "What's wrong with you, you wretched girl?" she demanded in a fury. "Do you have a perverse taste for the very beasts that killed your grandmother and violently attacked your mother?"

Her eyes narrowed as she looked at her daughter. It came to her, not for the first time, that too many things came out as Asta wanted, even when Lennis started by firmly opposing whatever it was Asta was after. "And none of your tricks, young woman," she growled.

"Mother!" A loud outraged scream from the other room distracted the miller, who promptly abandoned Asta to see what ailed Roldeen. Bursting into the kitchen, the harassed miller gasped in outrage at the sight of the soft-spoken Egil with its filthy madman's hands on the arms of her eldest! In the corner, the Jommy called Egil, sounding thoroughly annoyed, was spouting off in its outlandish gabble at Roldeen.

Quickly, before it could progress from bad words to worse actions, Lennis clouted it along the ear and raised her hand again threateningly.

Instead of retreating as the original Jommy Einas he-daughter always had, or having weeping hysterics as the Jommy had always done in childhood—the little baby—this one stood tall and stared her in the eye. Without first being spoken to—the rudeness of it!—it began babbling at her. Then, seeing she did not understand, it pointed to its sister. Then it pointed to Roldeen and made pinching motions, hard and vicious, over its own arm. It had been about to pinch Roldeen!

"Out!" Lennis shouted, her opened hand sweeping a huge arc

that encompassed Egil and the crying child in the corner. Lisha and her remaining children poured into the room.

Lennis pointed to Egil, then to the door. "Get that thing out of here," she said darkly. Then, with greater generosity, to little Hanna, "you can stay."

Egil turned to his mother. They talked back and forth in their unknown tongue, the weeping girl Hanna adding her bit. Egil put one arm around his mother and spoke tersely. The sense was clear to all: "We're leaving."

"Leave, you ungrateful wretch," Lennis called after them. "After I was kind enough to take you in and give you a place and feed you, and this is how you repay me?"

Egil turned and spoke briefly. Lennis caught Lisha's eye in outrage. "You just stand there," she howled, "and let that thing speak for you as if you were witless? Let me tell you, I'd put my daughters in their place instantly if they ever tried to speak for me, their mother." Her eyes narrowed again and a triumphant smile spread over her face. "Witless. Of course! Well, if you'd sooner starve than live on my kindness, of course, you're all free to go." She turned back to Asta. "As for you, young woman. . . ."

Arona spent all day in the records room hunched over the scrolls, getting every detail of the hectic late-night invasion right. She had to guess at the spelling of the strangers' names, and put them in phonetically. Who had come and when, and who they went with. As her penpoint dulled, she cut it fresh with her tiny penknife; as it wore down, she went to the goose pen to find another quill. Her ink block was growing sticky and her shoulders hurt.

As she finished the first list, she stood up and squinted into the golden western sunlight of midafternoon. And the chores undone! With a sigh, she went to the woodpile and fetched in enough to keep the fireplace going. She went to the well and hauled water enough for Maris to cook their meal and herself to refill their basins and pitchers. The cow would need to be milked later on, but somebody had fed the geese and collected the eggs. The garden could stand weeding, but that could wait until tomorrow. However, she would have to water it.

She drew bucket after bucket of water from the well and sprinkled the plants thoroughly with her hands before laying down water along the roots. She swept the floor of the house and picked several ears of ripe sweetgrains and her choice of vegetables, placing them on the kitchen table for Maris. Then she set off for the village to see what was happening.

Walking down the familiar path between Records House and her mother's carpenter shop, she ignored vague cramps in her lower abdomen. Bethiah Anghardsdaughter, her mother, was sitting on the front porch chatting with her longtime crony, Noriel the Blacksmith. Arona smiled to see the blacksmith and called out "Hello, Aunt Noriel." She had been fond of the smith since her fifth year.

For when Arona had just begun to use a precious metal needle instead of a baby's bone needle to mend her clothes, she had to her great shame lost it. Little Arona searched for the needle in all the ways taught her, but before admitting the accident to anyone, had tried one last thing. She had seen how certain things, rubbed against a cat's fur, called hairs and threads to them. Racing into the kitchen, she took one of her mother's precious glass drinking glasses and rubbed it against the fur of Smokey Patchesdaughter, the most docile of the cats. Then she took the glass into the front room to see if it would pick up the needle.

Her mother scolded her then for playing when she should be sewing. Her explanation made no sense to any of the adults, and she was scolded again for playing when her needle was missing. They called in the blacksmith, who had metal magic, to find it.

To Arona's delight, the blacksmith's ritual for finding needles was as unusual as the glass-and-fur one she herself had invented. She took from her apron pocket a tiny metal horseshoe, stroked it with a bar of metal kept wrapped up in her apron pocket, and ran it over the wooden floor. Noriel's little horseshoe found the needle in a crack in the floor.

When Aunt Natha and Mother were in the kitchen fixing cider and cookies for the blacksmith as courtesy required, Arona crept up to the formidable woman and told her about the cat's fur. The blacksmith not only had heard her out, but seemed impressed.

"She's very B-R-I-G-H-T," the woman spelled out to Arona's elders. "I'd certainly like her as my apprentice, if she had the strength for it." Then, sadly, "but it's too much to ask of any woman, to give up having children for The Art."

"Why must your apprentice give up having children?" Arona asked, patting Noriel's hand in sympathy.

Noriel touched her finger to her eye as an unexpected tear formed. "I am very strong, and Falconers do not like that. They kill very strong women," she said frankly. "So I must stay away from them. But only they can give us daughters. The village asked me to do this anyway, and since I love metal, I did. But it is hard."

Arona hugged the woman then. "I'll be your daughter as well as Mother's and Aunt Natha's if they'll let me," she promised. And so it had been through the years.

But today, Noriel looked like a woman who'd had a hard two days, and Aunt Natha was nowhere to be seen. The stranger woman Yelen was sitting by Arona's mother and seemed to hang upon her every word. How she could do that without a common language, Arona didn't know.

"How are your strangers, Aunt Noriel?" Arona called out, joining them on the porch like an adult.

Noriel chuckled. "That Huana! As fussy as a wet hen, always flying up into the treetops over something. She hovers over Leatrice like a broody hen and orders her around like a busybody."

"And your new apprentice?" Arona was suddenly very curious about the strange children of the strangers, for one day she would have to understand them in full. "How glad I am that you've found one! Do you think it will work out?"

Noriel shook her scarf-tied head and laughed. "Oseberg's a good worker in the forge," she said, "but an incredible know-it-all. You can't tell that girl anything that her old mistress Morgath didn't do better. In some cases, it's even true, but getting Oseberg to listen to anybody else is like getting the attention of a mule. Sometimes I think she has been pampered like a princess," she went on. "Her mother takes advantage of her strength, though, quite as much as she takes advantage of Leatrice's willingness to help. But—Arona! Even when they knew you were bookish and going to be a priestess or a recorder or something like that, did your family set you apart? Let you get out of your chores? As if what you were doing was so much more important that you shouldn't have to be asked to do them?"

Arona whistled. "That spoiled?"

"That spoiled," Noriel said. "Though a good worker, still and all." Then her huge shoulders shook with laughter. "Oh, well, I'm teaching her manners. We may even make a fair cook and housekeeper out of her, though I despair of her ever learning to sew decently. So did her mother! For Huana threw another of her fits when she saw me trying to teach the child. How dare I try where her own mother has failed?" She threw back her head and roared.

Arona started to chuckle, then giggles poured out of her as she remembered her encounter with Egil. Natha Lorinsdaughter walked up the dooryard path, her nose looking thoroughly out of joint. "That Lennis!" she exploded.

"What's she done now?" Arona's mother asked without real concern.

"Driven her stranger-guests out into the night with a wild tale of them bullying her daughters," Natha said sourly. "The stranger's oldest daughter tells another tale, of Roldeen pinching her sister and Lennis beating them both. I must say, of the two, I tend to believe the outsiders." Having delivered this shocking statement, she hung up her shawls. "I promised to ask about finding them another place before my mother and the other elders got dragged into it. What's for supper?"

Chicken, in honor of their stranger-guests, fixed in a strange style. Yelen smiled very smugly as they ate their fill. She was indeed an excellent cook, Arona thought as she took second helpings, then thirds. The parts had been dipped in a heavy batter and cooked in hot grease like frybread. It was served with whipped tubers with a chicken-flavored sauce. That was a new idea, and very, very good.

Her cramps slowly started coming back. Arona, who was fourteen years old, had a suspicion what they were. So that dreadful day and night at the trailhead had borne no fruit? Not that she wanted a baby now anyway. She was only the Recorder's apprentice, not the Recorder. Her mother and aunt and cousins and sisters always had room for one more, but it wasn't the same as having her own household.

She had nobody to share a baby with. That was the problem. In a village where all the girls had their best friends from childhood—and changed often, but still had best friends—she was too bright, too intense, too quick with her tongue, too interested in things they were not. There were several girls she liked, who liked her, but they were never very close.

Egil was bright, and interested in the same things she was. Egil was strangely-behaved, though, and that worried her. But maybe she and Egil would end up as sisterfriends one day. That would be nice.

She had left the records unfinished! Excusing herself from the table, she said, "Thank you, Mama, all, but I did leave something undone at Records House. We still have a little light left. Will you excuse me?"

"Certainly, dear," Bethiah said placidly. Yelen murmured agreement.

Arona raced down the path back to Records House and all but ran into Egil. He caught her by the arm. "Where are you going in such a hurry?" he asked.

"Records House, and if I'm in a hurry, you should know better than to grab me," she snapped, annoyed. He looked as if he were starting to argue; she grabbed his fingers. "Don't tease, Egil! The light's almost gone, and I have my work to do." He made no move to let her go. "Oh, Egil, Aunt Natha's even now looking into finding your family a new home," she remembered to tell him, then wondered if she would need to pry his hands off her. To her relief, he removed them himself and bowed, saying, "Thank you," then dashed off.

She went to the familiar records room and lit a candle to enter one last line.

"Ay-gill Lishasdaughter accused Roldeen Lennisdaughter of violence against her sisters. She made this accusation to Natha Lorinsdaughter, who said Lisha and Lennis quarreled over this and Lisha left Lennis's house with all her children. They want a new home. Natha Lorinsdaughter is asking about this. Ay-gill wants to go to school." Arona sat and thought about the next item and decided, reluctantly, it must be recorded in case matters between the strangers and the village ever came to judgment.

"Ay-gill also kissed this recorder Arona Bethiahsdaughter for no reason and apologized later but gave no reason for the kiss, except that she wants to be friends. She also laid hands on me even though I was in a hurry and serious, which was rude. Their manners are different. Nobody knows how different."

She blotted the ink and weighed down the scroll's corners to let it dry overnight, then made ready for bed. Her supposition was correct: there would be no child. There would be other years, other Falconer visits. Maybe if she wanted a child, Egil would do this for her. That would be a lot better than another Falconer visit. Egil would make a marvelous best friend once she learned manners. It would be nice to have a friend she could talk to. Maybe. One day.

Egil Bakerson stared after Arona thoughtfully. No, not at all in the common style. Even that young lout Oseberg Smithson couldn't keep his eyes off her. Or his hands, from what Egil had heard. Pity he hadn't thought of it before trying that kiss! Well, nothing ventured, nothing gained.

Oseberg had been sure, with so many girls in the village and so few boys, they'd both have all the girls they wanted. Oseberg hadn't stopped to think that these girls were used to grown men, not boys, and Falconers at that. It would take a most uncommon boy to compete with Falconers. Of course, it might be to their advantage that the Falconers were seldom around and the boys were. On the other hand, that might just make the boys seem commonplace compared to the girls' remote, glamorous Falconer lovers.

Arona wasn't giving Egil a second glance. That wasn't surprising. A homeless, landless, penniless nobody and stranger to the village, he'd have to be somebody first. Luckily, their interests coincided. He liked what little taste he'd had of reading, writing, and keeping records, and she obviously took the recorder's office seriously, almost too seriously. Arona would consider the village recorder to be somebody. If he were the villager recorder, she'd have to consider him.

He walked away whistling, planning how to do this, then dreaming of Arona's love, in detail that would make his elders blush if their memories were short. First, to take care of his mother and the little ones. Then, to win Arona's seat. After that, he could win Arona.

Four

Elders' Business

*H*eavy dark clouds hung in the sky, and the ground trembled under everyone's feet. Maris Guidasdaughter, the recorder, was often away from Records House, and spoke very little when she was there. She stared at the walls facing Falcon Crag, ate what was set before her without comment, cleared her place, then closed herself in the scroll room without a word. She came out hours later with dust on her hands.

Arona was left to record the names and placements of the strangers, and feared she was doing it wrong. "Mistress Maris," she said. Then, louder, "Mistress Maris!"

The recorder looked up. "Yes?" she said, sharply.

Arona shoved the newest record scroll into Maris's hands and waited, trembling.

"I'll look at it later," Maris promised, laying it down and looking west again.

Was her mistress sick? Arona considered calling the healer, then instead set water on the hearth to boil for an herb brew and the morning dishes. From there she went to sweep out the henhouse and lay the sweepings on the compost pile, and from there to the garden that had gone neglected that past week. She was weeding the vegetables when Dame Maris appeared at the back door. "You speak the strangers' tongue as well as I do," she said. "Will you help Egil Lishasdaughter find her family a new home?"

Arona straightened up and dumped the last weed on the pile of dead ones. Maris went on, "And, dear, you should use the masculine suffix for those strangers you know to be he-girls. You can correct it after you wash up; Egil's in no hurry."

"Mistress, is it wise to set the he-girls apart?" Arona argued. "Dame Noriel is civilizing her new apprentice very well by refusing to set it apart."

Dame Maris blinked her weak blue eyes. "But, dear, they are different," she answered. "Go wash up."

She was back being the recorder again! "Wretched he-girls," Arona complained cheerfully in her own tongue, as she drew a bucket of water from the well.

"Oh, we aren't all that bad," Egil said cheerfully, in his own language, from somewhere behind her. He snatched the well rope from her hands, saying, "Here. Let me."

The bucket jerked, splashing water on the wellhead. Egil laid a hand on her shoulder, a delicate touch, just as gently withdrawn, and walked back to the house with her, carrying the bucket. "You shouldn't have to strain your eyes over those 'wretched records,' " he said, using the negative ending of the village tongue on the end of the word in his own. "I liked seeing you gardening."

The two statements meant nothing together, but Arona felt the small hairs on her arms stand up. She shivered. He looked curiously at her; she shrugged. "A ghost walked over my grave," she said, then dismissed him to the parlor. She dared not say the ghost wore Egil's shape.

Maris had always insisted that Arona leave plenty of room between words for corrections. Carefully the girl squeezed '-id' onto the end of every noun and pronoun she knew to refer to a stranger boy. A few times she scraped off the ink to rewrite, much smaller. At last, proud of her work, she straightened up and brought the scroll to Maris.

The Recorder wasn't there.

A crow fluttered in Arona's bowels; she ignored it and went upstairs to dress for visiting. She tied a yarn braid of many colors into her own hair braid on impulse; Egil gave her an admiring look as she came back down.

"We're still looking for a place," he said immediately. "Gondrin the Alewife let us spend the night with her in return for some heavy builder's work, but I would really not like to see my sisters reared in an alehouse, with all due respect."

Arona glanced at Egil's mother, who sat silent in the other chair, her lips pursed. "What trade were you reared to?" the girl asked, wondering why the elders had left it to an apprentice to bargain between grown women. Well! Arona would show them what she could do!

"I was a baker's (something), a miller's daughter, and somewhat renowned for my embroidery," the stranger Lisha answered, a little doubtfully.

All women baked and did embroidery. They had already tried the miller. Noriel the Blacksmith already had a stranger family; so did Arona's mother, who was a carpenter. Who did not? Floree the Healer had a houseful of them, sick, weak, and wounded. Arona looked up. "How are you with the sick, Mistress?"

"Squeamish," Lisha admitted. "Hanna, here, is an excellent nurse, though. She brings home all sorts of wounded animals and birds. Harald used to laugh about it and complain we had a howling menagerie at the bakery!"

That was a start. She and Egil were the only ones old enough for apprenticeship. Embroidery. Great-aunt Lorin, who owned several pair of scissors, did most of the sewing for the village. Would she be interested? They called on her. Egil did most of the talking. Aunt Lorin heard them out with a scowl.

"I have enough on my hands these days with poor, dear Eina," she said bluntly, "without taking on another such." Great Aunt Eina was slipping rapidly into senility.

Elthea the Weaver was even more blunt. "I need no witlings," the old weaver said. "And when daughter speaks for mother and manages her affairs, what else have we but a witling and a busybody?"

Arona stood helplessly, looking from Elthea to Egil to Lisha. The woman seemed sensible enough, but then, why indeed did she let Egil speak for her? The girl settled her shoulders and translated directly. Egil bridled. "What you call witless," he said directly, "I call a decent modesty. I promised my father I'd look after her. . . ."

Weak of wit, Arona translated in her thoughts, sadly, as Lisha nodded agreement. Though the older woman was frowning at her oldest child! Well. Loyse Annetsdaughter was rich, and noted for her kindness. She lived between the forest and the caves, a choice location, well-watered and well-hidden. The sky was clouding over again. "We'll try Dame Loyse," she said.

It was a bright, crisp morning at the forge. Several strong young maids in trousers and sheepskin jerkins, carrying spears and ropes and backpacks, came past the dooryard fence. "Roundup!" one of them called. "We're going out after the sheep. Everyone's welcome."

Noriel nudged Leatrice. "Go ahead," she urged. "Your sister works for two, and you've never been on a roundup."

Huana straightened up, mouth open, and blazed forth, "A decent, gentle maid like Leatrice, go with those trousered ruffians? Alone? Out on the open range with nobody to safeguard them and take care of them? What if they should meet strange men? It is not seemly. What can their mothers be thinking of?"

Leatrice looked from her mother to her mother's employer to the girls. From the middle of the group, Nelga Olwithsdaughter called, "I'll lend you a spear! I have two! Bring your harp and sing for us!"

"Just a bit," Leatrice called back. "Mother, you know Nelga. All the other girls are going!"

"All the girls take their turn," Noriel agreed, wiping her hands on her apron, "And you can't tie her to your apron strings forever. Did you know Ofelis the Bard wants to apprentice your daughter? You have a girl to be proud of, Huana."

Leatrice, taking that for permission, handed her apron to her mother and dashed upstairs, shouting "Thanks!" And to Huana, "Daddy would have let me!"

Huana couldn't deny that. It was one of the things that wrung her soul when Morgath lived. Huana moaned. Why did they have to find refuge in a village where all thoughts of propriety and decency were lost? Though, she had to admit, she was neither starving, begging, nor reduced to harlotry!

Huge black thunderhead clouds had formed as Arona walked back from Dame Loyse's farm. From Lookout Mountain came the sound of a dove call. Arona left the path leading back to Records House and detoured towards the trail leading East through the forest, away from Falcon Crag. The spectacular sunset started to fade. Gunnora's Daughters, if that's who was coming, would have to spend the night. Maybe one or two of them would guest with Maris and Arona! Quickly she slipped down the trail, waiting to greet them.

Her heart sank as she saw, not the usual russet trade cloaks of those who followed the teachings of the good goddess, but three women in plain silver-gray hooded robes. Still, one saw so very few strangers! Though now there were more than one could get to know in a lifetime. How had they come here, and why?

As Arona watched, one of them took a thong which hung around her neck, and pulled forth a blue jewel. The gem shone with an inner light of its own even in the rapidly-darkening forest. The woman turned and looked directly at the girl hidden in the trees. Gently, in the tongue of the outsiders, but with a slight accent, the stranger said, "This is no place for curious children. Go home to bed, now, and forget you saw us."

Arona suddenly felt defiantly adult, and would have insisted on her right to stay, but her mouth and her feet took on lives of their own. "Yes, ma'am," her tongue said meekly as her heart raged with no meekness there. Slowly her feet began carrying her to Records House despite her will. She struggled to free herself from whatever bound her, but as she struggled, her purpose faded with the memory of the encounter, growing dimmer and dimmer. At last, she looked up to the treetops and saw it was quite dark. *I must have stayed later than I thought at Dame Loyse's,* she thought, and went quickly and quietly to Records House and her own bed.

On the plains to the west of the village, the girls ran and chased each other, shouted across the fields, and played tag with each other and the dogs. Leatrice Huanasdaughter, feeling her legs naked in the baggy, floppy trousers of the shepherdesses, followed. The wind blew her hair, and no skirts entangled her legs. "Come *on,* slowpoke!" Nelga called back. "You'll never catch any sheep that way!"

Leatrice had to stop and catch her breath. "Mother always made me slow down and walk," she said, panting a little. "Like a ly-dee!" she mocked the last word. "Sorry!"

The sun was hot on her unbonneted head and sweat ran down her unprotected face. It tickled and itched. She wiped it off with her bandanna and raced after the other girls again. They called back and forth and she tried raising her voice experimentally. It carried over the hills until she thought they could hear it clear to Falcon Crag! She imagined her mother hearing it and winced a little inwardly. A lady does not raise her voice. A proper maiden speaks softly and sweetly at all times. "Damn!" she said, resoundingly, to the empty, Huana-less air.

Nelga fell back. "Are you all right?" she asked.

Leatrice nodded, her breath coming short. "Just thought of something," she explained. "Back home, I mean."

Nelga held out a leather canteen full of water. "Here." Then they were off again, Nelga twirling a rope with a loop in the end to throw over strayed sheep—and bushes and anything else she could rope. She showed Leatrice how, but the outsider girl's hands had yet to learn the way of it. Both girls laughed at last. "Come on, let's chase some sheep," Nelga offered, and showed her how to whistle for the herd dogs. Leatrice was delighted and shocked. "Whistling girls and crowing hens," she quoted her mother under her breath, and finished defiantly, "have more fun than henhouse hens and henhouse maids!"

By the end of the day they were all tired, and when they had built a fire and started toasting their waybread and dried meat on green sticks, Nelga said, "Too out of breath for a song?"

Leatrice bit her lip. "I don't know any of your songs," she said. "I can sing some from home. You won't know the words."

An older girl said, "Sing. I'll interpret. My mother's a trader." Leatrice placed her as Elthea the Weaver's granddaughter; she couldn't remember her name offhand. Leatrice found a pitch and started singing, a little selfconsciously, an ancient ballad of star-crossed love. Elthea's granddaughter was making a hash of the translation, turning it into old friends parted by a family quarrel; Leatrice, unsure in the new tongue herself, let it go.

Nelga giggled. "How about 'Four Falconers Down From the Crag?'" The other girls seconded this with enthusiasm, and Nelga began to sing.

Leatrice listened, at first puzzled, then totally sure she was not hearing what she thought she was hearing, and then shocked and embarrassed beyond words. She had seen male farm animals; she had seen them mating. She had heard boys bragging of the strangest things and competing in truly loathsome ways. But unspeakable matters like this? Mother would have a fit if she knew!

Mother was never going to hear one word of this, and neither was Aunt Noriel, nor any other adult.

Elthea's granddaughter nudged Nelga. "I don't think she's Initiate yet," she whispered when the song was over.

"She's got to be," Nelga protested. "She's older than her sister, and Oseberg's been Initiated—I think. She knows some of the things, anyway. Leatrice! Have you been Initiated?"

"Initiated?" Leatrice looked from one to the other, suddenly afraid. "I'm a maiden," she said in a voice now shaking. She quietly put her hand to the knife Noriel had given her.

"Oh, we know that," the oldest girl, Nidoris—her name came back to Leatrice suddenly—said. "But are you still a child?"

"Have you had your moon-blood?" Nelga clarified.

"Oh, yes! For over a year now! Mother was after Father to find me a husband before I dwindled into an old maid," Leatrice answered, blushing.

The logs on the fire crackled and one broke. Nidoris poked the coals with a large stick and added another log. "But you haven't been to the priestess to learn those things a maiden should know," she stated. "Have you?"

Nidoris drew in her breath in a soft whistle. "You poor thing! Well! Just as soon as we get back, you go see Dame Birka. She'll teach you all the right things, so that even a Falconer visit won't be so horribly dreadful as it could be."

Now Leatrice's whole body shook with a chill that would not let her go. "Falconer visit," she croaked.

"How we get daughters. You don't have to if you don't want to," Nidoris said in a soothing tone, "but most of us want babies, sooner or later, so we put up with it. You'll see."

"Oseberg's not like a Falconer," Brithis's voice came from the other side of the fire. She pulled her stick back and tasted her meat tentatively. "Ow! Hot! He's nice, like a sisterfriend, only I don't think anybody ever told him what to do, either."

Leatrice stared in shock at the friend she had thought so nice. She and Oseberg—she had—she had done—they had done— Leatrice felt her face burn as she tried to imagine it. She tried to picture soft, puppydog-like Brithis as disgraced, a hard-faced outcast who brazenly made up to men for her living. She shut her mouth and then said, "Are you and Oseberg betrothed?"

"You mean are we promised friends?" Brithis asked with a cheerful laugh. "Sort of. We're promised best friends, but he doesn't want me over to spend the night because of, sorry, Leatrice! Your mother, well, she's. . . ." Her voice trailed off.

Leatrice tried to imagine Huana permitting Oseberg and his betrothed to bundle under her roof and failed miserably. She tried to picture Oseberg introducing Brithis to Huana as his intended bride and realized, with a shock, that her mother would make difficulties there, too. "If you have a great dowry," Huana's daughter suggested, "Mother might not mind as much. Uh, would your family accept the match?"

Brithis was silent for a while and ate her meat, while the wind started blowing chill around their backs. "No offense, Leatrice. My mother likes Oseberg, and Aunt Noriel's one of her best friends. But she's having trouble with another stranger-woman in the family right now, and, well, everybody thinks, I mean, nobody wants to quarrel with your mother, too."

Leatrice, dismally aware of her mother's reputation as a champion fussbudget, nodded. It was like the ballad she had just sung, she thought miserably, with her own mother as Lady Capela. Well! Then, she could be, could be—Priestess Laura! She leaned over, her face closer to the fire. "Listen, Brithis," she said confidentially. "We'll think of something. All right?"

"Right—sister," Brithis agreed.

They clasped hands over the top of the fire, sang one more song, rowdy without being offensive, and curled up in their bedrolls as close to each other and the fire as they could get, against the autumn chill.

The morning was cold. Arona had stopped weeding the garden, and started laying the vegetables and fruits out to dry for the winter. The tree leaves were starting to turn golden yellow and a spectacular scarlet. And Mistress Maris, closeted all day with the elders on elders' business, had almost ceased to live at Records House. Arona was the one left to record the death of the old stranger Melbrigda and the coming-of-age of Nelga Olwithsdaughter, one of her own agemates.

She had nobody to talk to. Her mother and Aunt Lorin, like her mistress, were away most of the time. Aunt Natha could only complain about that mealy-mouthed bird-chirping Yelen who sucked up to Bethiah and agreed with everything. Her agemates all had their own concerns. Egil, now stable helper for Darann Mulemistress and errand-girl for the elders, could only try to wheedle Arona into sewing torn buttons on her blouse.

"I can't believe you can't do this for yourself," she exclaimed, and offered to show the stranger how. Egil stood by, quite pleased, until she put the needle in his hand. Then he backed away as if it would bite him, and looked at her as if she had already bitten him.

Nelga's coming-of-age lifted her spirits somewhat. "I've really come to invite you, your mother, and your sisters to a maidenhood party," she said as he stared at the button sourly. "One of my friends has left her childhood behind. I'll bring enough food for all of us; that's courtesy to strangers. And, don't get your back up, I know you haven't had time to make yourself any pretty clothes or trade for them. We lend clothes back and forth here, and I have a cousin about your size. What do you say?"

Egil frowned. "You understand Mother is no longer her own mistress."

Arona stared at him. "Egil! Nobody would stop her from coming to something like this! Come on! Let's go find out."

Egil set his face stubbornly. "No." Arona shrugged and left, puzzled.

Elthea the lame weaver came to borrow a mule. "I'm heading for Dame Loyse's farm. Isn't that where your mother lives? Is there anything you want me to say to her?" Egil scowled and looked at the ground. "Tell her I'll get her free one day."

"What?" Elthea exclaimed, and rode out, thinking. In Dame Loyse's yard, she was shocked to see a huge iron cooking pot, filled with dirt and planted with flowers, sitting by the door. This was *raduth,* conspicuously using a useful thing only for show. There were tales that Dame Loyse's daughters did no work because they were too rich to need to. Elthea snorted in disgust. *Raduth.*

The old weaver dismounted and sat in Loyse's polished wooden rocker, drinking cider and eating little cakes while she dickered over a beautiful length of embroidery. At a break in the talk, she said, "Egil has a message for her mother."

Loyse's eyes widened. "The witling? Oh, dear, is it wise to ask after her? The poor thing gets *so* hysterical so easily. But," she shrugged gracefully.

Elthea scowled at her new embroidery as Loyse left the room. No witling had made the cloth she was looking at.

As soon as Loyse left, Lisha sidled into the room, dressed in an ill-fitting hand-me-down of Dame Loyse's, a child of about eight in her arms. "Help Lowri," she begged in badly accented speech. "Please help." She glanced around as if afraid, though Loyse had a name for kindness. A witling? Hysterical?

Elthea unwrapped the rag that bound the child's arm. It was swollen and red, and hot to the touch. Lisha set her face. "Pardon. I no speak so good your—language. A—geeth?" She formed her hand into a head and snaked it back and forth, hissing.

"Goose. One goose, two geese."

"Bite Lowri." She feigned biting with her hands. "I ask Mistress please help." She bit her lip, distressed. "Mistress say," she shook her head with a sweet smile and caroled, as if to a child, "No get in temper, Lishakins." She looked up again. "Need," she searched for a word.

"Healer." Elthea rose, took the child's arm, and hobbled to the door. "I will. You stay here. I'll be back. With elders."

"Mistress not let me go. Nowhere." Lisha said, very softly, glancing around again as she followed the weaver to where her mule was hitched.

Loyse came bursting into the yard, wide-eyed. "Oh, there you are, Lishakins! You naughty thing! Did she bother you? I have to watch her constantly," the farmer confided, "or she wanders off everywhere. Now, Lishakins," she caroled.

Elthea set the child behind her on the mule and snorted. "Nonsense! She's no more witless than you, young woman. They speak a different tongue, that's all." She clucked to the mule. "I'll be back."

Lowri dug bare feet into the mule's side. *"Mistress,"* she said with a curl of her lip, "keeps her locked up and talks to her like a baby."

"I heard," Elthea said curtly. Loyse was shouting at her to come back. The rode into the village center and dismounted at Dame Floree's. Healing House was empty but for a young stranger-woman with a broken arm and bandaged ribs, who sat on the front porch stringing pungent vegetables with one hand. "Where's Floree?" the weaver asked.

The stranger pointed. Elthea shook her head. "Tell me." A flood of the strangers' tongue followed. Elthea shook her head again and rode over to Records House. Arona understood this gabble. The old woman sat in the dooryard and called, "Arona Bethiahsdaughter!"

Arona put her head out the door. "What's wrong?" she demanded, alarmed.

Elthea snorted "The stranger ain't witless. Shy, maybe. Daughter's hurt. That wretched fool Loyse don't listen, keeps her mewed up. You speak that gabble. Well?" she challenged.

Arona looked down, her face scarlet. "I thought Dame Loyse would be kind. Everybody says she is."

"Where's the healer?" the weaver demanded.

"I . . . I don't know, Mistress Elthea," Arona admitted, tears starting to come from her eyes. She blushed more furiously, wiped her eyes on her sleeve, and glared.

"Come on," Elthea ordered. Arona grabbed her sandals from the porch and followed, running. There was nobody at the healer's, nobody at Sacred House, nobody at the meeting hall. Grimly the old, lame weaver, Lowri in her arms, searched the village on muleback. None of the elders were anywhere to be seen. Lowri was starting to look pale, though she doggedly sat upright on the mule and clutched her wounded arm to her fiercely. The clouds were covering the sun again, and the mule laid its ears back. A dog ran around in circles, then dashed under a porch.

Elthea stopped and pulled a handful of divining sticks from her pocket. She shook them and cast them, studied them, and shook her head. "The witch's place," she said.

The log cabin they came to had been long abandoned, for its

owner died without daughters. The Jommy, who'd had to leave the village in haste, came back a year later with one of Gunnora's Daughters, and a strange woman in a dun robe, who carried a shining blue stone. It hurt to look at the stone. The strange woman gave no name, saying it was against the custom of her kind, but with a wise, sad smile, said, "You may call me The Dissident." As nobody had heard that word before, she explained, "The Witches of Estcarp loathe the Falconers, for Falconers set themselves apart from women."

"Or we from them," Natha Lorinsdaughter muttered that day.

"So, for that reason, they will give no help to you Falconer women."

"That doesn't make any sense!" Arona had blurted out that day. She was very young, with a front tooth missing, and her mothers hastened to hush her, with apologies to their visitor. But the strange woman shook her head sadly and laughed. "Out of the mouths of babes," she said, and said no more.

What she did in the village or why she was there, nobody knew, except perhaps the elders. She had lived there for years now, helping Floree the Healer and Birka the Priestess at times, and working her garden like any other woman the rest of the time. A few families had offered her a strong girl to cut her wood and haul her water; The Dissident politely thanked them and refused.

Of course the divining sticks would point to a woman who helped the Healer, Arona thought, politely not speaking her thought, as they dismounted. Smoke was rising from the chimney; somebody was home. Elthea sat on the mule in the dooryard and called, "Hello the house!" There was no answer.

Arona added her louder, higher voice. "Dissident? Dame Witch? We have a hurt child here. Can you help us?" Again no answer, but now Arona felt very sure indeed someone was home and choosing not to answer. Anger boiled up within her: at a woman who healed not answering a cry for help; at elders vanishing when people needed them; at Dame Loyse for dismissing Lisha as a witling; at herself for believing in Dame Loyse's kindness and arranging for Lisha and Lowri to live with Dame Loyse; even at Egil, for being so pushy that people got the wrong impression. Boldly, rudely, she picked up Lowri and went to the door and knocked.

". . . think we should postpone the maidenhood party?" she heard the priestess ask anxiously, in a lowered voice.

"No," the Witch answered, "or you'll tip people," her voice trailed away, "off," and she rose. "Arona," she said in a cool, remote voice.

They were all there, gathered around The Dissident's hearth, cakes and cider and needlework at hand as at any gathering. Dame Floree, Dame Maris, Dame Birka, Great-Aunt Lorin, about five others, and a velvet-haired gray cat with blue eyes. They were all looking at the angry girl who had, with unthinkable rudeness, burst in without a sign of welcome. Lowri Lishasdaughter rested in her arms. "She's hurt!" Arona protested, her voice cracking on the last word. "We couldn't find anyone to help! I. . . ." Then, her face scarlet, she thrust Lowri into Dame Floree's arms, stared at the women, and fled.

She would have run right past Elthea's mule, but the weaver turned the animal around and called, "Well."

"They're all in there," Arona said, choked. "Talking."

Dame Birka had come out on to the cabin porch, and beckoned Elthea over. "You could have been among the elders," she said in a severe voice. "You chose not to. Accept this as our business for the while. Arona, you will say nothing to anybody, not even to hint. On your mother's name?"

Arona had shrunk away from them and now looked up sideways. "On my mother's name," she vowed, chilled to the bone by what she had imperfectly sensed in that cabin. Then, hiding her face behind Elthea, she walked back to Records House.

Five

Bad Vibrations

$\mathcal{L}$eatrice learned to race out with her new friends after sheep, practiced roping, stood watch in the night against wolves, and speared rabbits for supper. Day followed day, and her face grew brown with the sun. Her hair grew tangled, and she tucked it up under a cap like the others.

Then, very near the end of roundup, a foxwolf called from the hills, very close. She was on watch. She shivered. Her roping and spear-throwing skills were still raw. What could she do if the flock were attacked now? Cry for help? Restlessly the sheep baaed behind her, and the dogs stirred in their sleep. One lifted his head and woofed softly.

A lamb began to bleat, high, shrill, and terrified. Leatrice raced around to the source of the sound to see the foolish little beast several hundred people-lengths away from the flock. Where was the other watchgirl? Who was she? Why hadn't the dogs given notice? She roused the nearest dog with the butt of her spear, then raced after the lamb. A slinky grey shadow hovered over the lamb, its teeth at her throat. "Wolf!" Leatrice cried, a ringing cry her mother would surely have slapped her for. "Wolf!"

The beast looked up at her, unafraid, bared its bloody teeth, and then went back to eating. Hoping she was holding her spear correctly, she drew her knife with the other hand and drove the spear into the predator's throat.

It wasn't there! The wild beast slipped past her and ran into the night. She knelt beside the lamb to see if she could help it.

Too late she saw the grey beast leap for her own throat. In haste she threw her arm up to protect her face. Its teeth closed on her forearm. In searing pain she raised her knife with her free hand and stabbed again and again, only hoping she was doing some damage. Then she felt hands on her shoulders.

Nidoris whistled as she pried the dead beast's jaws from the new girl. Her sleeve was in shreds, and blood runneled forth from the bite marks. Brithis and Nelga held Leatrice down while Nidoris painfully picked every scrap of anything she could see from the wound by the light of a burning stick Saris, the missing watchgirl, held. Then Nidoris uncorked a skin nobody had been allowed to touch, and bathed the wound in it over and over. Leatrice tried not to scream in pain, for these girls were so much like boys, they'd surely despise her tears and hysterics. The cries came out anyway.

Nidoris patted her shoulder. "Where's your clean bloodrag?" she asked.

Shamefaced, for such things were not talked about in her home, Leatrice whispered, "I'm using it."

"That's why it attacked," Brithis whispered. "Oh, Leatrice, why didn't you tell us?"

"She didn't know!" Nidoris snapped. "That does it. That wretched village of hers neglected—does *anybody* have a clean bloodrag?" Brithis handed her a rag and she bound Leatrice's arm. "Saris! Where in Jonkara's name were you?"

"Same thing as Leatrice," Saris said simply. "It came on suddenly. You know how these things are."

Nidoris made a nasty noise. "Next time, wake someone first. There!" She put her arm around the trembling, whimpering girl whose head was now buried in her other arm. "That was brave of you! And you get the skin. Did you know that? Be proud." She led Leatrice back to the fire, where half the girls were now awake and watching. "Here! Our Leatrice killed one of Jonkara's Dogs all by herself!"

The girls set up three cheers. Leatrice, her head full of pain and reaction to fear, realized fuzzily she was being made a hero.

She, the girl who could never please her mother! But somehow she doubted Huana would take her feat this well. And they were going back tomorrow. She started trembling.

Nidoris offered the special skin to her and Leatrice obediently gulped it. It was harsh, raw ale, the very soul of ale. "Lifewater," Nidoris said as Leatrice sputtered and choked. "Dame Gondrin makes it well. It's for healers." She and two others helped settle Leatrice in her bedroll.

I'm a hero, Leatrice thought in wonder. Then she slept.

Oseberg Morgathson squirmed as Noriel the Blacksmith touched a hot curling iron to his hair. It was shaggy by his old standards; she clucked over how cropped it was. His sister Leatrice, curled and robed, her wounded arm proudly displayed in an embroidered sling, refrained from laughing until Aunt Noriel brought out a gown she had worn as a girl. "I can't wear that!" Oseberg protested as Leatrice put her hand over her mouth. Giggles poured from her in a broken stream, punctuated by hiccups. Their mother, Huana, squirmed worse than Oseberg, though she looked lovely in a dress borrowed from the birdlike Eina Nathasdaughter, the Jommy's own cousin and named for his mother. Pride, Noriel decided. Huana was poor and Oseberg was far too big for beauty; Huana would accept neither.

"There," Noriel said, satisfied. She looked at Oseberg's face, critically. Coming closer to him, she whispered "You'll want a sharp blade to take the hair from your face." He balked; she said softly "I know how cruel these girls can be; they'll tease you about being an ancient, and laugh. Only crones have hair on their faces, and even they take it off."

Oseberg twitched. "The girls will laugh at me?" he asked in a low voice. She nodded; he accepted the blade and went to the other room.

"Good children," Noriel said, patting Huana on the shoulder. "Oseberg's coming along very nicely; you should be proud.

And when they taste your cooking, Huana, your name will be made. Imagine, Bethiah making so much of Yelen's chicken! Oseberg, are you sure you don't want a hair ribbon?"

"Quite sure!" he howled, and nearly tripped over his unfamiliar skirts as they came down the steps. If Egil saw him all dolled up like this, he'd never live it down, but Aunt Noriel assured him this was the way people dressed around here, and the girls would think him a bumpkin if he wore his old clothes to this party. What was it about? Nelga somebody was newly marriageable. Not that apprentices married. Was she as pretty as Brithis?

The party from the forge met another group on the path, a family with a girl in her early teens. "Hello, Dame Noriel," Brithis called out. Oseberg tensed, terrified of her laughter. "Oseberg! Your hair looks cute. It's different. Is that the style where you come from?" She raised a hand to his carefully made curls. "Good evening," she said politely to the others. Huana set her lips tightly; Leatrice stepped back a bit so Brithis could walk beside Oseberg. Oseberg suddenly walked more lightly, and smiled. "Hello, Brithis," he said.

Egil had an equally pretty robe one of the elders had given him, but he belted it and tucked it up to the approximate length of a man's holiday tunic. He carefully combed his budding mustache, polished his boots, and offered one arm to his sister Hanna when he called for her at Healing House. There was no way to detour by Records House in hopes of seeing Arona; he had delayed as long as possible, but she had not appeared.

"You look very pretty this afternoon," he told Hanna as he escorted her to Nelga's mother's house. "Four more years, and you'll be the queen of your own coming-out party. Are you happy working for Dame Floree?"

"Oh, yes! I got to watch her sew up Lowri's arm and cut away the proud flesh. Lowri cried and cried and Dame Floree had me cuddle her and give her a sweet to help her."

Reflecting on the kind of child who would enjoy seeing such

surgery, Egil nearly missed the women on the path intersecting his. When he saw them, he swept off his cap in what he imagined to be a grand sweeping bow. "Mistress Arona," he said.

"Hello, Egil. How's Lowri?" the girl answered, distracted. The hens had been upset that morning, cackling and fluttering as if a fox had been at them; Dame Butthead the goat had nearly refused to be milked; and the cat, Little Red Pest, was under the bed and would not come out. Did that presage a whirlwind, or an earthquake, or simply trouble in the house?

Egil ground his teeth. One day he'd be worth her notice! Suddenly, the earth started to rumble and the path shook like a giant stirring. From Lookout Mountain came the cry of extreme danger, and it rang throughout the village as if every throat had taken it up. Egil felt an urgent, "Run for the caves!" command and his voice echoed his thought. "Run for the caves!"

"Run for the caves," Arona repeated, as the danger cry came again and again. Then, "The hens! Dame Butthead! And the cat!"

"For the love of . . . are you worrying about a stupid cat *now?"* Egil shouted.

"The goat and the hens!" she cried out, racing back to Records House to the back fence.

Dame Butthead was tossing her head restlessly and trying to find a place to hide. Expertly, Arona looped a rope noose and called the goat, then tossed the rope around her horns. "Egil! Catch!" she called out, heading for the henhouse. The ground was shaking under their feet so she could hardly stand. She found the hen cage and shoved three of the squawking, terrified biddies into it. Then the chicken house started to shake. "Run, Arona!" Egil screamed, shoving her with one hand. The hen cage banging against her knees, she ran. The barnyard tilted upwards, then back. She threw herself down, flat on her face; Egil threw himself on top of her.

With a shivering roar, the chicken house collapsed. Arona looked around cautiously, got up, and began to run north.

"This way!" she called to Egil. Then she lifted her skirts and raced through the woods so fast he could not catch her.

He lost her in the woods and called "Arona? Arona!" with his heart beating ever faster. He pictured her lying helpless with a broken leg, or lost, or pinned under a tree, or with a wild animal holding her at bay.

Another group came running down the path. A huge, muscular woman in an embroidered pink holiday gown grabbed him by the arm. "This way!" she shouted, dragging him along the path. "Hurry!"

His lungs gasping for air and his throat raw, he wrenched himself free after a while and simply followed her. They came to a tall cliff he would never have approached during an earthquake, for fear of rockslides. The woman went straight to what he now saw was a cave mouth. Egil followed her deep inside.

Then the trembling began in earnest, as if the whole mountain were shaking itself apart overhead. No, Egil decided, the entire mountain range. Blue light danced around the cave mouth, and the beasts outside howled as if in mortal terror. Strange lightning danced around Falcon Crag and laced through the peaks. A cold wind blew. At last, exhausted, Egil sat against the cave wall, his head between his knees, and let the storm rage while he slept.

Arona sat on the battered hen cage, her back against the cold, rough stone of the cave wall. The hens, finding it dark, had mercifully fallen quiet. The cave wall shook under her back, but held. Near the cave mouth, a high-voiced stranger woman cried "It's stupid to hide in caves during an earthquake! We'll all be buried alive here!" Huana of the forge, who had thrown an epic fit when her daughter came back from roundup injured. How did Aunt Noriel endure it? She seemed proud of her tiny housemate's fierce temper! But with a chill of fear, Arona realized the woman was right. Good thing few others could understand her; the last thing they needed now was a panic in the caves.

In her mind, as if someone nearby had spoken over the noise, came the words *We will prevent that.* The voice was utterly cool, utterly calm. *Be still, now.* She recognized the Witch called The Dissident.

As her eyes adjusted to the darkness, she looked toward the cave door. The faint blue lights she had thought came from Falcon Crag came from several hooded figures by the door. They danced in light, and light danced around them. Between Arona and the lights, Nelga Olwithsdaughter said in a shaky voice "What a—an adventurous coming-of-age. Nobody will ever forget this."

"Well!" Asta Lennisdaughter whined. "I don't think it's fair!" Asta was not invited to many parties, Arona reflected. She'd cherish the few she could attend.

The noise started up again, louder than a thunderstorm, as if the entire mountain range were falling about them. The blue lights intensified, and a low humming filled the air. The sharp smell of a nearby lightning stroke hit Arona's nostrils. A dog barked in protest. She felt a large shoulder next to hers, and put out her hand for comfort. The hand that took hers was big, with stubby strong fingers, heavy calluses, and more hair than most women, but smooth-skinned.

Then she felt its mate feeling for her breast. All comfort fled. She grabbed the hand and bent it back sharply as the storm raged outside them. "Ow!" a familiar voice yelped.

She sighed and dropped the hand. "Oseberg Huanasdaughter," she said in disgust. "Why are you always doing this?"

"Some girls like it," Oseberg said, hurt feelings in the strange-accented voice.

"Cousin Brithis," Arona agreed, startled. Brithis Nathasdaughter had to pat every animal, cuddle every child, and touch every object. She felt suddenly hungry, and traced the hunger to the smell of food arising faintly from somewhere. She refolded her shawl, setting it behind her back, and tried to lean against the wall again. Outside, she heard a sharp crack, as if lightning had struck within the village. There was a sound as if the greatest houses in the village were shaking themselves apart, and the whole mountain shivered. A goat baaed and a baby cried thinly. Arona breathed in deeply, and caught the smell of terrified people and animals packed close, with odd smells of food.

"How long will we be in here, does anybody know?" she called out suddenly.

Oseberg nudged her. "I have a dish of stew here," he whispered. "It was for the party. Have some."

Arona dipped in a tentative finger. "Your mother's? Delicious! She and Mistress Yelen should sell it as Mistress Gondrin does her ale, for many of us are too tired to cook at day's end. I know Aunt Noriel was."

Oseberg lowered his voice. "Arona. Mother says Aunt Noriel is probably a lover of women. Is that true?"

Surprised, Arona said, "I think you're right. Despite her shyness, she truly likes people. Don't you think?"

Oseberg fell silent. A cold blast of wind poured in the door, chilling everybody, followed by a searing blast of hot air. "I'm sorry about you missing the maidenhood party," Arona whispered as they dipped further into the party food. "Did you have a good one in your time? Or are you of age yet?"

"If I was of age, I'd have been made to fight in the army," Oseberg whispered back. "That's where all the others are. We have nameday parties, though, and we come out dressed like adults when we're old enough. Leatrice put her hair up for her fifteenth. That means she's old enough to marry. Father was in no hurry to marry her off, though."

Arona had to ask what an army was, and marry, and marry off. Oseberg did his best to explain, but kept returning to, "You people don't marry?" while Arona tried to intuit the concept of self-defense in large groups. She dipped her fingers into the stew bowl and felt hot ceramics beneath them. The whole mountain shivered and a thin handful of women screamed. That caused several children to set up a howl. The Dissident's voice, as stern as Dame Birka's when she taught naughty girls, came to all their ears: *Be still, for your very lives.*

The shaking seemed to go on forever. The cave was filled with an intense, glowing blue light that seemed to come from the rear. The sharp smell of ozone filled all their lungs. A hideous roar deafened them all, and went on for hours and hours. Then there was utter stillness. Children started to cry again.

This quiet will not last, The Dissident's mindvoice told them all, sounding like their mother. *Mistress Maris, you have time to call the village rolls.*

Arona could hear the relief in the recorder's voice as she called out, "Arona Bethiahsdaughter!"

"Here," Arona said, her voice shaking in the powerful stillness.

One by one they answered, by family, the mothers first and children second, apprentices third, and strangers fourth, until all were accounted for. "Eina Parrasdaughter!"

"I answer for her." The calm, deep voice of Great-aunt Lorin.

At last the roll was over. The recorder said then, "I think we should apologize to Nelga Olwithsdaughter, whose maidenhood party was ruined by this disaster. Sisters, let us share the food properly."

"Uh-oh." Arona and Oseberg said to themselves, very quietly.

"If the growing girls have left us any," Dame Birka put in, and Arona felt like curling up into a tiny ball.

Egil Bakerson was jammed against the wall between the oversized blacksmith, Mistress Noriel, and his friend Oseberg's mother Huana. He still held Dame Butthead's rope, and groaned when the frightened goat decorated his boots in barnyard style. When roll call came and he heard Arona's name, he let out a breath he didn't know he was holding.

Brave girl! She didn't sound a bit hysterical. He thought to call out to her, to reassure her he was still here, but dared not interrupt the roll call. Organized, these women were, almost like an army. Well, they were Falconers' women. When they came to his name, he called it out loud and clear, so Arona might hear him. And his mother and sisters and baby brother, too, of course.

"Lisha Sigersdaughter!"

"Elyshabet," his mother corrected. Egil's eyes widened. She had always hated the long form of her name and never, in his memory, used it. His grandmother had, when she was angry with her daughter-in-law. Loud, clear "Elyshabet Sigersdaughter, of Elthea's Weavery."

"Hanna Lishasdaughter . . ."—a giggle—". . . Hanna Elyshabetsdaughter of the Infirmary."

"Oseberg Huanasdaughter, apprentice blacksmith."

"Oseberg Morgathson!" Huana howled like a wounded dog.

Arona sighed and thought of all the corrections she would have to make. Why couldn't these strangers know their names and stick to them like grown women?"

"Soren Elyshabetsdaughter," Mistress Maris called out, making her correction with no difficulty.

"I answer for him," Mistress Lisha said with sharp precision and dignity. No, not the witling Lennis and Loyse had called her. *Shy,* Arona decided, her face flooding hot at her part in that mistake.

Slowly, into the silence, a low humming started again. The mountain started to vibrate again, and blue lights laced themselves across the cave door. In a flash of common yellow lightning from outside, Arona saw the face of the nearest Witch. She looked drained and aged. Sweat stained her plain robe, though it was a cold fall night.

The noise intensified, and Oseberg nudged Arona again. "Arona," he said in a low voice, sounding desperately serious. "Mother says Aunt Noriel has nothing to teach me about metal and I'm only with her to keep my hand in until I can find a real blacksmith for a master."

"Have you learned anything new from her?" Arona asked, growing mighty tired of Huana's opinions.

"Well, sort of," Oseberg confessed.

"You do things one way in your village and we do things another way here," Arona dismissed that. "Your mother has no use for our ways, but if you find them useful, keep them to you until you have your own forge. She's not a blacksmith, after all."

"She says neither is Aunt Noriel, but that isn't true," Oseberg confessed. Perhaps he, too, was tired of his mother's opinions.

"When you are Initiated," Arona informed him, "you will not have to answer to her, only to your mistress or employer. You still owe her respect, but not obedience. Feel better?"

Oseberg beamed and planted a big, wet kiss on her cheek. Then, "Oh. I'm sorry, Arona."

She patted Oseberg's hand. "Forgiven. This once."

The storm started again. People raced for the dungheap, the food, or to find their kindred. A babble of voices started to rise against the gathering hum. Huana started to complain again about the names given her children, and Yelen started chirping again about everything being for the best. Loyse heard Mistress Elyshabet and sniffed, "Well! She certainly deceived me!"

Huana found Oseberg and took him by the ear, yammering at him. The cave began to sound like a family quarrel much multiplied. The blue lights flashed again, and one of the Witches sagged against her sisters, who held her up. One forced water down the fallen one's throat. The Dissident said something urgently to Dame Birka, who sighed and answered back. "Sisters and daughters!" Dame Birka called, in the loud voice she used to address village meetings. "Sisters and daughters!" Her announcement was echoed by a firm but weary-seeming mind-voice of The Dissident. Silence fell over the exhausted people. "How about a tale of brave women in ancient days, to keep up our spirits? Maris? Arona? Ofelis?"

Ofelis Kemisdaughter, the ancient bard, shook her head unseen in the darkness. "My voice cracks with a long tale," she said hoarsely. She had been among those elders dealing with the

Witches beforehand. Maris also passed. After thinking a bit, Arona began an old tale of ancient days, then another, then another.

Six

Lormt Again

*S*cholar Lady Nareth laid down the Falconer scroll and frowned, looking off into the distance. The tales seemed to be, not sober history, but fantastic legends of a land across the sea, where women ruled, and each clan had an animal protector. Yet, there were oddly compelling bits—Theora's tale for instance—that matched known facts. The script was ancient, and the parchment and ink seemed to be of great antiquity.

The writer, if she translated correctly, was one Warina Falconlady, "written on the shores of exile, after all our men went mad." A drop of water splotched the parchment. A tear? Or simply sea spray? The austere scholar read the tale again, across the gap of centuries, and trembled.

Queen Theora and her once-loyal man, Langward, stood on the cliffs above the shore and from her last, besieged keep at Salzarat, watched with hot, angry tears as the last of the old Houses took sail with the Sulcar pirates. Behind her stood the man whom she had raised from nothing to the second highest office in the land.

"Madam, be sensible," Langward now said without inflection. "You will find nobody to join you in a mad last stand to preserve the rule of your whims."

"Whims!" she choked, remembering the hard thought and agonized balancing that had gone into each decision.

"But if you choose the plainslord, you will still be Queen. I know you cherish the title and honor."

She stared at him, but he would not meet her eye. Did he count her as foolish as the ladies of the conqueror's court? Forever they squabbled over the fine points of precedence that depended on their husbands' ranks. Nobody knew nor cared for their own worth, but only for their chastity or lack of it, their obedience, and their silence. Become as they? Indeed!

"As Queen, I rule, a mother to my people, not their conqueror's pet slave," she said firmly. "No."

"You would not like the other, Madam," Langward said stolidly. "He offered you to me. As a favor." As her hand flew to her long dagger, Guardian of the Queen's Honor, he reminded her, "You made me the same offer once."

"You refused, saying you would not be my lapdog. Well, I will not be yours. Are you oathbound to this man, then?"

"No." It was a flat statement.

Theora looked at him a long second. "If you join me in my last stand, it will neither be death nor the impossibility you imagine. We have one recourse left—the old magic. The Goddess still stands by Her children. I know She is proscribed in this land and Her worship outlawed. This is the greatest outrage of all. Will you suffer it, Langward?"

Langward looked up then, and raised one hand. An armed plainsman came in from behind the door, his face grimly triumphant. "You were right, Langward. I have heard enough."

Shock and rage took the Queen's reason and speech for a fleeting moment. Then, crying, "Langward, this is treason!" she plunged the Queen's Guardian blade into the man's traitorous heart. The plainsman drew his sword and advanced on her, more pleasure on his face than had a right to be there in the face of his accomplice's sudden execution—for murder it was none.

"And you, woman," he gloated, "by raising weapon to a man in the King's service, are guilty of treason both high and low, and will hang."

The window was too far to reach, or she would have jumped and cheated them of seeing a queen in chains on the gallows. She thought to rush his sword; something in his stance told her he was well prepared for this. Desperate and cornered, she cried, "Jonkara! Avenger of Women! Stay his hand and grant me vengeance on them and theirs, until one of their race learns again we are their mothers, not their cattle."

The plainsman's lunge slowed and halted. Langward's body, slowly toppling, ceased to fall. Theora could neither move nor speak. At last her thoughts froze as her motions did, and her last thought was a burst of bitter laughter as she recalled the old fairy tale about the sleeper awakened by the kiss of a princess. "I'll settle for a fishermaid, or even a Sulcar pirate lass," she thought. Then her thoughts stopped altogether.

It was several days before Scholar Lady Nareth summoned Arona. She said little but, "Whence comes this tale?"

"It is one most ancient," Arona said promptly, "attributed to Warina Falconlady, friend of the mother of my clan. Whether this is true, nobody can know for sure, but we have no reason to doubt it."

A true scholar's answer. Unaccountably dissatisfied, Lady Nareth dismissed the girl, and did not summon Arona into her presence for quite some time after that, while she continued reading.

In those several days, the Falconer girl wandered around

freely. She checked on her mule and watched the stablehands at work. She explored the ancient, ruined complex, both the towers that stood and the towers that had fallen. She looked up at their lofty heights, and down at the tumbled stones, and wondered how they had been built. She learned the ways and hours of Lormt.

Nobody bothered her in her austere stone cell, and nobody served her. Her first night there, she carried a full chamberpot through miles and miles of corridors before finding someone to tell her where the midden was. She did not starve only because, upon leaving Nareth's office, her guide-boy, as hungry as she, showed her the refectory.

There was food of a sort at all hours, and Arona wondered what Lormt gave the cooks in exchange for their food. Or were they students and apprentices doing a tour of kitchen duty, as it would have been at home? But when she asked one, the cook only laughed and said, "Me, Mistress, one o' them learnt women? Not for me."

Arona continued to prowl, ready to leave if anyone bid her go. None did; many an elderly scholar simply looked up, distracted, and grunted, or said with varying degrees of politeness, "What can I do for you?"

She saw rack after rack of scrolls, many shelved carelessly or left out to gather dust. She saw a cat asleep on a pile of manuscripts, in a large scroll case. (But it was quite a small cat, neat and black and white, and Arona grew fond of her in due time.) The Falconer girl's hands itched to set each scroll back in its own place; slowly her mind began devising a system of places for them. She read a few, but found she was more curious about Lormt itself. Who founded it and for what reason? How was it fed and supplied and, once again, in exchange for what? How was the community governed, and what was its relationship to the scattered holdings roundabout? How were disputes settled, and what was counted mannerly or unmannerly among them? This she had to learn above all, for she had seen in her own village what strife had been caused simply by differing ideas of manners and decency.

"Long, long ago, when he-women lived among us in peace and harmony across the sea," Arona took up a long tale for the terrified villagers of Riveredge, hiding in a huge underground cave from the dire deeds above, "there lived a maiden of thirteen summers called Myrrha Foxlady, who was head of her family, because her mother was dead. She had two loyal he-sisters, older than she was, but she was family-head because she was the only daughter.

"It was her custom, as with all family-heads, to ride a tame horse around to all her kindred to see how they did. But this time, ill luck befell her."

Arona lowered her voice ominously. "Wild males from across the plains had come raiding, like wolves, knowing neither decency nor kindness. These found Myrrha Foxlady and killed her guards with great violence in their madness. They did to her and the bodies of the guards as Falconers do. Then their he-mistress, one named Tsengan, nobody knows whose child, took the body of Myrrha Foxlady upon his great tame horse and rode to the gates of her great fortified house, shouting for her he-sisters to come out. To them he promised to spare her life if they promised to treat him as mother and mistress in all things, and to save her life, they agreed."

Egil, listening in the darkness, frowned and shook his head. No romance, for so this seemed to be, could rally terrified women and children; though it might distract them. He had thought better of Arona, too. Oh, well, she was only a girl after all.

Arona's voice grew rich with anger. "This Tsengan locked Myrrha in her room and would not let her speak, nor do her duties as head of the family, but beat her into obedience like a cruel mistress, and every night he did with her as Falconers do until he started a daughter within her. Then he spoke of giving the unborn daughter to another wild man to be bondservant to him as Myrrha was to Tsengan, and this she could not endure.

"He also oppressed her household miserably, making each of his wild men mistress over some woman's house, and giving them leave to beat their bondmaids and their bondmaids' children, these who had been free people and proud! He killed the Healers and the Wise Women. Every maiden was made bondmaid to some wild man, while for those who were women, it was like a Falconer visit that lasted forever." Arona's voice grew deep with horror. Leatrice shivered. She had little idea what a Falconer visit entailed, but plainly, things unspeakable were happening at Castle Foxlady.

Arona's voice grew softer. "Then, as Myrrha sat in her room, seeking a way to escape and free herself from this madman, a falcon flew in the window. Some say it was Jonkara Herself. The falcon lighted on Myrrha's shoulder and said 'Over the mountains, over the sea, Falconer ladies intend to flee.' Then Myrrha knew her release was at hand. She sent her tame fox with a collar and a note tucked under the collar to follow the falcon back to the Falconlady House. She waited. No rescue came."

A sigh ran around the cave. Arona's voice grew clear and strong. "She must save herself. Then one day her mad he-mistress accused a village woman of witchcraft and made Myrrha, dressed as family-head, watch the woman burn alive, in silence. This was so all would think she had ordered it, for she had argued day and night with him to do justice and cease to do wrong, and no beatings would stop her from pleading for her kin. Then she knew what she must do."

Egil frowned. No, this was no romance. It seemed, rather, a ruined woman avenging the loss of her honor.

Arona dropped her voice significantly. "Myrrha spoke quietly among the women in her house, those who knew she defended them and tried to care for them and protect them from the madmen. She spoke to the cooks and those who served the tables. Her he-sisters she did not speak to, for they had promised to obey Tsengan and not harm him, to save her life, and they never went back on a promise. She begged her women to make some excuse to bring those two into a room apart, with a lock on the door. She put something in their wine to make them sleep. She locked them in, so they could truly say they broke no promise, being helpless."

She paused. "Then she put even stronger doses of the medicine in the wine of the madmen, and killed them all. Some she had to kill with her knife, and some died of the drug, but all died. Then she found her tame horse and fled as fast as she could to Falcon House, where the madmen had been raiding and plundering for years but had not taken the house, to tell her cousin the Falconlady she was free and the wild males were dead."

There was a dead silence in the caves as Egil pondered on the extraordinary ruthlessness of this long-ago maiden. Arona's voice took on a mourning tone.

"It was the custom in those days," she said simply, "for every woman to take to herself a he-male who was as a sisterfriend to her and more, and she would let him start her daughters within her. Such a one was called her—" She used a word Egil did not recognize; plainly it meant *husband*. He would be glad to take her aside later and set her straight on this and related matters. Arona was speaking again.

"Myrrha's kinswoman, the Falconlady, had such a he-sister-friend, who had done as the wild men did," she said in a lowered voice, "and made himself mistress over Falcon House and Falconlady, and had made bargains with Tsengan, to stand together against Tsengan's fellow bandits. When Myrrha Foxlady came to him, torn and bleeding and weary, this false kinsman scolded her, calling her betrayer of her *husband* and their people. He scolded her for a wicked child who did her own will without thinking who it hurt!"

Arona's voice took on a sharp, rapping anger. "Myrrha was very angry, for she had saved them all from a wicked bandit at great cost to herself and great suffering. But Falconlady's daughter came to her and swore to be sisters with her forever and ever for her courage, and so it was. Later, such as Falconlady's *husband* became Falconers, and killed Myrrha Foxlady as they killed all who crossed their will, and we women went on alone to live alone, for there were no he-women left who knew decency and kindness any more. None of us has ever known why they stopped behaving well and started behaving like madmen, but we could not endure it. Thus, we only let them among us every year, and then only at the place they built for us, apart from where we live, and then for one purpose only, to give us our daughters. In exchange for which, they take our sons to live among them as Falconers."

Arona took a deep breath. "May we all be as brave as Myrrha Foxlady, but may we never need to kill or be killed."

Egil scowled. A feeble disclaimer for such a vicious tale! If Myrrha were not a woman ruined, but Tsengan's lawful wife— the stupid wench should have made that clear from the beginning!—then her actions were foul and treacherous beyond belief. Was Arona making a heroine of one who poisoned her husband? He could not believe it. She must be reciting an old folktale by rote, ignorant of its implications or how it should be framed for a proper moral lesson.

When they got out of this cavern, if they ever did, he would properly recast it. It was only his duty as future village recorder; and certainly doing so was a major step in attaining the office. That is, unless the crones had the usual old-woman attachment to what they knew, whether or not it made sense. Well, he'd fix that, too.

The lights by the door flamed higher and thunder rolled across the mountains like a frenzied giant's drum roll. The wind, rising throughout, now whipped icy rain into the cave mouth. The huddled villagers moved farther and farther back into the cavern's recesses. Nelga Olwithsdaughter, her voice shaking, whispered, "I will *never* forget my coming of age!"

Leatrice Huanasdaughter laughed through her terror. "You

mean you'd rather stand by the wall waiting for Oseberg or Egil to ask you to dance? When we have parties, Mother always makes me sing and play the lap harp for the guests."

"But you're a bard!" Nelga whispered. "Oh, Ofelis will be so pleased to have a girl in the village who can sing! She lost her last journeywoman to childbirth. It was two-headed twins and so horrible; she cried for weeks, then made a Teaching song for the Healers, and has never spoken of it again. Oh," she remembered Leatrice's question. "In our village it's courtesy for the host to invite the guests into the dance; I'm glad you told me your ways. I wouldn't want Egil to think us rude. Leatrice, could you try to sing the storm away?"

The thunder rolled again, as close as if lightning were striking this very mountain, and rain lashed the doorway. Leatrice gaped at Nelga and began, unsteadily, the ballad she had sung for the herd camp. Oseberg took up the tune, adding a few bass notes; Egil, on the other wall, sang counterpoint. From that song they went to the tragic "Witch Vow," the jolly "Swamp Maid," and a merry tale of a farmer and his wife who tried to do each other's work one day. Then she began an even merrier tale of how a rabbit outsmarted a fox.

The mountain shuddered as if it were giving birth. Leatrice clapped her hands, singing, "Don't throw me in that bush, don't throw me in that bush. And the rabbit cried merrily to the fox, oh, don't throw me in that bush."

The nearest village maids giggled and clapped, repeating the chorus, "Don't throw me in that bush, don't throw me in that bush. . . ."

The mountain began shivering and a noise like thunder began to roll, but did not end. It slowly grew louder and deeper, deeper and louder, as the mountain shivered, then shook. The cavern floor tilted to the right, then to the left, throwing the crowded villagers and refugees across the rough stone. Children screamed and the animals packed in with them howled or cackled according to their breed. The mountain shook itself as if to rid itself of vermin.

A sheet of blinding white light flashed across the door. Arona held up her hand to shield her eyes, and stared in horror at the plain outline of her bones seen clearly through the flesh. Behind this shield, she could see the familiar outline of Falcon Crag crumble and disintegrate like a child's snow house in the thaw. The light vanished, and the newly-blind cave dwellers cried out. Somewhere a woman started sobbing. Outside the cave mouth, the rain fell, a bit more gently than the usual late-summer afternoon thunderstorm.

A faint whimpering came from the heap of robed bodies lying by the cave door. Arona slowly made her way to them. The Witches who had stood guard at the door lay there, unmoving, but for one whose foot twitched slowly. "Dame Floree!" she screamed then. "Dame Healer, come quickly!"

It was the stranger-child Hanna who came, her mistress close behind her. Between them, the three women turned over the first body. Dame Floree leaned down, ear to the Witch's chest. She felt the woman's face, and breathed her breath into her mouth. This she did with all four of them.

Two were dead. One lived, sick and weak. The Dissident lay as if dead, her pulse a thin thread, her face a grayish-white.

Dame Floree called for help. Slowly, under a night-black sky, the women of Riveredge Village came to the cavern mouth to see. They made up pallets from their shawls and cloaks, blankets, and extra skirts, for the two sick Witches to lie on. Then, weary unto death themselves, they tried to sleep.

When dawn came, cold and grey with glowering red clouds overhead, they came out to see what had become of their village.

There was very little left. They would have to build it all again, from the root cellars up.

And the entire year's crops were now destroyed.

Seven

After the Storm

Che records! Arona raced from the cave mouth to Records House, and cried out in dismay at the wreckage. Little Red Pest dashed up out of the storm cellar stairs, winding herself around Arona's legs. "You fool cat!" Arona exclaimed with joy, wrestling the great door open. "Whatever made you hide yourself down there?" It must be that the Goddess whispered to cats in times of need.

The records, stored carefully on their own shelves in a room beside the root crops and the oil jars, had all withstood the storm. The recorder's apprentice ran from one to the other, checking each one with mounting cries of joy, then let out a ringing whoop of delight. The records had survived the storm! She ran back into the village to see what else still stood.

Noriel's anvil and Lennis's millstones were intact. Many heavy tools had not been blown far. Most peoples' root cellars remained. But the fields, the houses, the pots and weavings which were their only trade goods, and anything else above-ground smaller than a huge boulder, were debris-strewn wrecks.

A huge fallen tree had crushed the roof of the village hall. Oseberg and Egil, each taking one end, were struggling to move it alone. Noriel laid down her hoe and strode forward, lifting the middle. It barely budged. "Darann!" she called. Egil gave her a foully insulted look.

"Egil, Oseberg," the crisp voice of Darann Mulemistress snapped across the ruined fields. "Try not to wear yourselves out; we have a long stretch of work ahead of us."

Arona lifted her head and shielded her sensitive eyes against the bright fall sun. "With all due respect, Mistress," Egil Elyshabetsdaughter answered back crisply, "see that your ladies do not overwork themselves. Oseberg and I will handle the heavy work."

"Egil Insolence," a woman whispered, and snickered at the newcomer's widespread nickname. *Egil Arrogance,* Arona thought, as she started digging out whatever could be salvaged from the Records House ruins.

Grimly the women and girls put their backs into the salvage work as if they faced a house-raising after a fire, but so much multiplied, no end seemed in sight. The village hall and Healing House first, with the young and sick and elderly crying in the cold. Any root crops that could be salvaged were shared equally, despite the outcries of those who had planted them, for people were starving. Dame Butthead's milk, like that of her sisters, was doled out by the half-cup, and any hens' eggs were served by the slice. Cats, dogs, and chickens were turned loose to forage for themselves, and the big girls took the sheep back to the open range to graze in what scrub grass remained.

Egil and Oseberg worked like mules, and all the village watched, amazed. They started earliest and ended latest, and hauled the heaviest loads. Quietly some of the weaker workers began taking on the camp chores for the two of them, saying, "It isn't fair they should work so much harder than the rest of us."

Suddenly, on the tenth day, the lookouts on the mountainside sounded a strange call: not the falcon's cry for Falconers; nor the dove call for the Daughters of Gunnora come to trade; nor the vulture's cry for bandits; but a quail's call. "Strangers. Misdirect them!"

"I went last time," a woman shrilled.

"Well, it's not my turn," another argued sourly.

"Where in Jonkara's name are the veils and robes?" a third demanded.

"Arona, you speak the strangers' tongue," the new Eldest Mother, Raula Mylenesdaughter, ordered. "You, you, and you," she pointed to several experienced traders, all of child-bearing age and perfect in form, none of whom had gone on the last visit, except for the girl. With a curse of, "Wretched strangers," Arona fetched her veils from the storm cellar, behind the onions.

Egil, who was hitching a downed tree to Darann's mule team, stopped. "If it's strangers, you'll need protection and someone to speak for you," he said, in a firm, reasonable tone that brooked no argument. Strapping his knife to his belt, he started to follow the women.

Noriel and Darann each took one of his arms. "You will not. To let them know you strangers live here could bring death on all of us. Let those with experience handle this, lass."

Egil stared at them. He started to tell them, bitterly and in detail, how far too far they had gone. Arona, a young maid, was being sent out—against all prudence and propriety!—to meet strangers, while he stayed home like a field hand in her father's service. He spat on the ground. Then he stopped. Darann was his employer. Field hand in her father's service was exactly what he was, until he established himself. Tasting gall in his mouth, he went back to hitching up the mule. This would have to change.

Eager with curiosity, Arona followed the women to the trail-head, where a band of strangers astride tame horses waited. She caught her breath in fear. They wore no bird-masks nor helmets, but they were Falconers in form. But *this is what Egil will look like when grown,* she thought suddenly.

The leader was almost as young as Egil, though he had hair on his face like a goat. He addressed the women with Egil's gravity, using the tongue Arona had been hearing from the strangers all season. "Do not be afraid," he said very slowly and carefully. "Your men have sent us to help you."

Another Falconer visit to endure, so soon after the last?

The young male must have noticed their dismay, for he repeated, "Do not be afraid. The Falconers are our allies. We will give all the courtesy due our sisters, mothers, or daughters."

One of his troop stared around at the huts, all torn down, and exclaimed in a rough voice that was almost a shout, "What in the name of the Gods has happened here?" Then he checked himself. "Oh. The Turning."

"We will help you rebuild your homes," the young leader said, and shouted an order. The men of the pack train dismounted and sprang into action, working like daughters of one mother. When the women rose to share the work, the men waved them aside. "You just keep a fire burning and cook what we provide," the leader said in a kindly tone. "I'm sure you must all be pretty hungry by now."

An even younger man was looking at the youngest girls as if to see what lay beneath the crude and ugly veils. Asta Lennisdaughter looked up and marveled, "You're so strong! I couldn't do all that."

The young man smiled. "You don't have to. That's what we're here for."

The leader looked up sharply, frowning in puzzlement. "I was told you ladies did not speak?" The oldest woman among them stood up and gestured drawing her veil across her mouth, sharply. Asta fell silent. The leader watched this byplay, frowning more deeply. "I was sent here to find out what you needed," he addressed the eldest of the group. "Food? Medicines? Seed grain?"

The eldest bowed her head and mimed the acts of hoeing, shoveling, sawing, and chopping. The young male leader scowled. "I understand your need for labor, my lady, but we cannot stay long. I wish we could, but needs must. . . ." His voice trailed off and he scowled again.

The eldest shook her head and fingered the iron fittings on the pack horses, then, very gingerly, the long knife that hung at the leader's belt. She was not understood. The women looked at each other silently. Then Marra Annetsdaughter, normally a trembling rabbit, spoke up with more courage than any woman there knew she possessed. "Tools," she said in a quavering voice. "Hoes. Knives. Axes. Shovels. Metal. And salt. We have no salt where we live. We will trade pots, weavings, jewelry."

Asta was leaning over, whispering to one of the offloaders, "Do your kind do all the heavy work where you come from?"

"Well, of course there are menservants and laborers to do most of it in many places, and I'm sure farmwives do their fair share of hard work, but yes, Mistress, heavy work is for men to do, not women."

"What do women do?" she asked, like a hound on the scent of a fat hare.

The man looked at her, puzzled. "Why, stay home, tend the house, mind the children, look pretty, I suppose." He was very young.

"But then," Asta persisted, "how do they get their living?"

The man laughed indulgently. "If your face is as fair as your voice, Mistress, you won't have to worry about that." Seeing she did not understand, he added, "We men make the living for our women. Isn't that so even among Falconers?"

"Oh, yes, indeed," Asta said hastily. "I just wondered about—about strangers. We see so few."

The eldest of the women had come over to Asta and was glaring at her, repeating her gesture with the veils; the leader of the men stepped over, too. "Lorryl," he snapped. Then, more softly, "these ladies are of the Falconers." It was a warning.

They set their bags of grain and dried foods, together with whatever metal tools they could spare from their own packs, in one of the ruined houseplaces. They rebuilt the huts, outhouses and garden plots and all, exactly as the Falconers had the previous year. They carried stones to build hearths, and even staked out garden fences behind the huts. They were twelve in number, but they worked like twenty women, and all the volunteers had to do was cook.

At night, they set up their bedrolls well away from the huts where the women sheltered, but one of them came to Arona's hut in the twilight, glancing around like a thief. She understood almost none of his words, or why his voice sounded so sly. Then he tried to handle her as Oseberg had done, but roughly, like a Falconer. To resist a Falconer, to cry out against one, meant death! But these were not Falconers, and she had not come to get a child. Twisting to release his hold, she cried out, then dug her bare foot into the dirt and tried to pull free.

Three leaders among the strangers burst into the hut, running, and without more than a glance, one swung his arm upwards under the intruder's chin, then rammed the other hand into the rough one's belly. He fell to the ground, moaning, and his leader said coldly, "I warned you, Haroc, these ladies belong to the Falconers! Five lashes." The other two dragged Haroc out; the leader bowed as Arona had seen Egil do. "My most humble apologies, my lady; this man will be disciplined severely."

Arona heard him mutter as he left the tent, "If the Falconers ever hear of this, Haroc will be dead—or I will."

If they ever came to hear of it, Arona and all the women there would be dead. Somehow the girl did not feel like saying this.

"I like these strangers," Asta Lennisdaughter said thoughtfully.

"Their customs are very different," Marra Annetsdaughter whispered. "One asked to start a daughter in me, and her eldest spoke very sharply to her."

"Not at all like Falconers," a third woman agreed, "nor women, either. Who can fathom such strange beings?"

Asta looked up, then, quickly, looked down.

Egil straightened up and mopped his brow. The last of the fallen trees was out of the fields and stacked neatly to the side, where several strong young women were chopping it into firewood. What was that noise? Cheering, and applause! The women gathered round were giving their two young men three cheers and hearty praise. At least Arona, back from the trailhead, had heard! So had Asta Lennisdaughter, who was staring at him with frank admiration. His heart glowed warmly.

He never thought he'd be glad that manual labor had saved him further schooling, but he was learning nothing from Dame Birka. A headful of weather-lore, crop-lore, beast-lore, and similar old wives' tales, worthwhile if he'd ever intended to set up as an herbwife. Some talk of male and female that he blushed to hear from a decent granddam, and was entirely women's business besides—or else frivolous beyond belief. What he wanted to learn was his letters and his numbers. If women knew these things, surely *he* was not beneath such teaching!

Oseberg's new employer came up and slapped her foster son on the back heartily. "Good work, lass," she boomed, and beamed at them both impartially. Then she sat down on the nearest log and sighed. "I hope the trailhead party brings back some metal to forge into tools."

"Will an iron pot help?" Loyse Annetsdaughter asked innocently. The huge cauldron had once held flowers by her doorstep. Now, hastily cleaned of dirt, it held whatever possessions she and her daughters had salvaged from the ruins.

Egil's mouth dropped. "My mother's kettle!" he exclaimed.

Loyse looked at him and sniffed. Her face was dirty; her robe was torn and muddy; she wore breeches, soaked and filthy from her knees to their front hem. Yet, she carried herself as if she were the wife of the mayor of Cedar Crest. "Mine by fair trade," she said with gentle reproach. "I was kind enough to offer your mother and sisters a fine home when they had nowhere to go; they offered me this in return."

Noriel glanced at Egil sharply. "Tell me, quick. Is it true your mother is halfwitted, as Loyse puts about?"

Egil picked up an axe and put it back down, standing straight and tall. "My mother," he said soberly, "is in full possession of all her wits and faculties. She came here ignorant of your—customs and your language; but then, under normal circum-

stances, she would have no occasion to need such knowledge."
He spoke in a mixture of the village tongue, to the extent he
spoke it well, and his own, for concepts and words he still
lacked in theirs. Loyse scowled; so did Noriel.

"She is no halfwit," Egil clarified, flatly, in their speech. "She
does not know your ways or tongue." He started to say "Why
should she?" but knew it was his outraged, angered pride speaking and would hurt his mother's cause beyond all healing. He
started to argue, then said, "I would take this before a . . ." he
searched his mind for the word, "one who . . ." he tried again.

"Judge," Noriel supplied the word. Then she defined it: "one
who decides who is right and who is wrong." Egil nodded his
thanks. Noriel scowled. "The Eldest Mechtild died in the Night
of the Storm. But I think you're right. This should be heard by
a council of elders, at the very least." She looked around for the
nearest child and called, "Leatrice! Run find the stranger Elyshabet for us; we have matters to discuss here." Then she turned
and said, with unmistakable dismissal, "Thank you, lass."

The new eldest, Raula Mylenesdaughter, brushed the field
dirt from her skirts, took a worn spindle from her pocket, and
held it up for silence. Elyshabet Sigersdaughter and Loyse Annetsdaughter each came from where she sat and stood before
the hastily convened elders, not looking at each other. The
elders spoke to both women at great length, then summoned
everyone except the man it most concerned, Elyshabet's son.
Egil found a seat next to Arona on a rock, watching her mark
a wood-bound clay tablet, salvaged from the ruins and crudely
mended.

"In the matter of the pot," said the eldest after interminable
wrangling, "We find it did belong to Elyshabet Sigersdaughter,
who traded it to Loyse Annetsdaughter for food and shelter.
Three people have told us the trade was Loyse Annetsdaughter's idea, and that Elyshabet Sigersdaughter consented because
she felt she had no choice. Seven people told us Elyshabet
Sigersdaughter had no idea of the pot's value."

"She's a witling, poor thing," Loyse Annetsdaughter put in, stubbornly.

The eldest pounced on her like a cat upon a rabbit. "If Elyshabet Sigersdaughter is lacking in her wits, no trade with her can be fair, and therefore is not valid. How say you, Elyshabet Sigersdaughter?"

The stranger woman flushed. "Is true, I much slow at your tongue. Mistress Loyse no speak mine none. I say," she burst into her own speech, "if this makes one halfwitted, then Loyse Annetsdaughter has no wits at all, for I understand her somewhat, but she does not understand me. That's not the issue. The issue is the value of the pot, which is greater among you than in my home village because we trade with mining districts and you do not. I did not know that yet; you can't learn everything there is to know about a strange place in a few days!"

"Speak so we can understand you!" came the cry from several corners of the crowd. "Speak our speech!"

The Witch quietly joined them and now was quietly translating for those elders who did not trade with the outside. When she stopped, she raised her own hand, and, recognized, said, "I suspect we have a language barrier in many of these quarrels, good women, for it is harder than you know to learn a new tongue in later life."

"She made a fair exchange, her pot, which meant little to her, for her life and her children's lives, which meant much," said Loyse Annetsdaughter gently. "Who can call that unfair?"

Egil nudged Arona. "The priests say a bargain made under duress is no bargain at all. Pity nobody here has any education."

"Perhaps you will enlighten them?" Arona snapped, moistening her stick to work it deeper into the clay. Egil looked over her shoulder. The system of signs she was using was not the usual alphabet, but some sort of abbreviation which he did not understand. He scowled and went back to his own thoughts.

Dame Floree put up her hand. The eldest pointed the spindle at her and said, "Yes, Healer?"

"The trade was a bad one, for Lowri Elyshabetsdaughter hurt her arm, and Loyse Annetsdaughter neither brought her to me, nor allowed her mother to."

Elthea the Weaver then put up her hand and was recognized. "Loyse sold me some embroideries Lisha made," she said gruffly. "Well worth the few days' food and shelter she had of the woman."

Egil started to comment again. Arona nudged him. When he did not speak, she put up her own hand. The elders looked startled. "Recorder?" The Eldest asked in a voice cold with disapproval, for recorders did not take part in such debates.

"Egil Elyshabetsdaughter told me they teach in her home village that a bargain made under duress is not valid," she blurted out rapidly, her own face scarlet. How often as a little girl had she been reprimanded for speaking out in meeting? But this was not a formal meeting, and the matter was important.

The eldest turned to Egil's mother. "Is this your custom?"

"I no take part in matters village," the woman said in her halting village speech. "But I think yes. Harald say so once."

The Elders conferred, and examined the embroideries Elthea produced, and Egil nudged Arona again. "Do you people really bother to write down every petty squabble between old women? Your industry is admirable, but. . . ." He fell silent as the eldest raised her spindle again.

"In the matter of the pot," she said sternly, "we find several matters. First, that by the customs of Elyshabet Sigersdaughter, there was no bargain, so that she went into the agreement falsely. Second, that Loyse Annetsdaughter did not keep her agreement, for Lowri Elyshabetsdaughter's arm festered unhealed while in her keeping. Third, that the embroidery we saw is a fair trade for the food and shelter the Mari Elyshabet family had. Finally, that Elyshabet Sigersdaughter did not fully understand the bargain, for it was not put to her in a tongue she understood."

The Eldest paused. "Henceforth, all bargains between strangers and ourselves shall be made with an interpreter helping, and all strangers closely questioned on their customs concerning this bargain. But in this case, we order the pot returned to Elyshabet Sigersdaughter. We also offer her the Virdis Nilyrasdaughter farm, now empty, in exchange, if she will consent to have the pot reworked into plowshares and tools."

Egil stood up. "Done," he said, as if the pot were his. The eldest ignored him. "Is this acceptable to you, Elyshabet Sigersdaughter?" she asked. The Witch translated in full detail. Lisha frowned and scratched her head. "I'll have to think about it," she managed, and fled into the fields, where she took up her labors again. Egil rose and joined her. *Pushy,* Arona thought, not for the first time, as she hastened to record the verdict.

As the gathered women dispersed, Arona craned her head to overhear Egil and his mother. "We will be landed," he coaxed her. "You need not be a maidservant to that old woman any more."

"I'm not exactly a servant," Lisha said, scowling.

Elthea turned their way and said, "Your mother's happy with me and she don't like farming."

"I realize you'd be losing an excellent sewing-woman," Egil agreed, with almost poisonous reasonableness. "Mother," he turned and put both hands on her shoulders. "You wouldn't have to work the land as women do here. You have me for that! You'd be mistress in your own home again, and my little sisters and brothers would all be taken care of, and of course, I know you, Mother, you'd never put your whims above the needs of the family and the village. Would you?"

"I have to think, Egil," she said calmly, and nodded in dismissal.

Egil slammed his axe into the last fallen tree with all the strength of his fury. One day, one day, he would be somebody in this village, and not dismissed as a beggar lad. Then the recorder Maris—the one literate woman in this village—walked by with her own clay tablets. "Mistress Maris?" he called politely, "May I ask you a question?"

Eight

On Trial

*I*t had been a long and hungry winter, with much to write about, for tempers were short. Huana Guntirsdaughter in particular quarreled with everybody in the village at one time or another, and dragged everyone else into her quarrels. She brought her daughter Leatrice and the sheepherder Nidoris before the elders, howling about Leatrice's wound, the negligence of those who were supposed to watch her, Leatrice's sheltered rearing, and the horror of sending one's daughters to herd at all.

Leatrice bit her lip and, eyes averted, edged as far away from her mother as possible. When the elders asked to hear Nidoris, the young herder put an arm around Leatrice's shoulder. "She did well. She was brave, and got the wolf who was stealing our lambs. If there was any negligence, it's her mother and her home village, letting her get to maidenhood without Initiation. She didn't even know enough to cry off night watch during her moon time."

The eldest beckoned Leatrice closer. "Is this true, what Nidoris says?"

Leatrice snuffled in the cold. "It's true I didn't know about—about wolves and blood," she quavered. "I never herded at home and neither did any of my friends. Nidoris didn't know I didn't know, and she looked after me like a big sister. I don't know what your initiation is, so I can't tell you, but I don't think I've had one."

The verdict was foregone. After talking at length to all the girls who had been on roundup and their mothers, Nidoris was absolved of negligence. Huana was ordered to consent to her daughter's Initiation immediately. A few weeks later the little woman had slammed Dame Birka's barn door in her rage, but nobody knew why. Then Huana made a dreadful row when Leatrice left to live with the bard, Dame Ofelis, as an apprentice.

Another set of traders had come through before the snows, and Asta Lennisdaughter's bruised face spoke of her mother's violently expressed displeasure at the way Asta made up to them. The women of the village sold almost everything they owned for food, tools, and salt; many had been forced to crowd into the Visit huts the first strangers had rebuilt, and work the gardens there. And then the matter of Elyshabet Sigersdaughter's iron pot had come up. Arona still squirmed at the memory of her part in urging Egil's mother to work for Dame Loyse!

Egil, now, was like a cat who had found the creamery. He had started learning to read and write in mid-fall, and worked on his lessons every minute he could be spared from the rebuilding, his work with the mules, and putting his mother's new lands in order. He not only came to lessons faithfully, but he asked many, many questions. "Why do you have so many words for such a simple thing as this?" he'd ask, about love, about pregnancy, about kinship, about moon-blood time.

"Why do you have so many words for tools of self-defense?" she'd ask, and he would run on for hours as if such technical distinctions really mattered! His legendary arrogance proved partly to be his foreign accent; he had—just once—commanded Arona to fetch him a tablet, in the presence of Mistress Maris, and the recorder had boxed his ears thoroughly. Then, as if he were a backward child, she had carefully pronounced the same word in command mode and request mode. One could see a great light dawn across his face.

Even more of his arrogance was simple ignorance of grammar. "What are these little words at the end of each sentence?" he asked on his seventh lesson.

"They tell how you know what you know," Arona began, then stopped. He had ended every statement of his with the word meaning, "It's self-evident." She spent the rest of the day teaching him the differences, and while he was still overly fond of the "opinionated mode," as Arona and her friends promptly dubbed it, he learned others. One mode even made him laugh. "Arona! Does this ending really mean the speaker is a wretched liar?" He went around using it for days, chortling to himself.

He had all the faults of an overindulged maiden. He was as lazy as a cat about the common chores of Records House, and managed to bungle every one beyond recognition until Mistress Maris threatened to stop the lessons. Then he learned, very quickly, and was as neat-handed as Arona herself. And he was as full of ideas as a hen was of eggs. "When I'm recorder," he would say, "I'll see to it these old tales are properly explained, and the moral made plain. When I'm recorder, I'll separate out old crones' nonsense from solid fact. When I'm recorder. . . ."

When the Falcon Goddess laid an egg in the center of the village square!

They had wrangled happily for hours and hours over many of the myths and legends of the village. It was a good thing Egil was never going to be the recorder! He was shocked, for instance, that Myrrha Foxlady, whose tale Arona had told in the caves, was a hero of her people. All he could see was treacherous death-dealing and some sort of oath-breaking Arona never had understood, since nowhere in the tale did it say the Foxlady had ever sworn an oath to her conquerors. Egil—when and if he took the office from Mistress Maris and her apprentice— planned to alter the tale beyond recognition, and keep the old version away from any but the elders. Did he count himself among those elders? Even so, Arona shuddered at the implications of a would-be recorder altering the records. *If only Mistress Maris could have heard all his boasts,* Arona thought. But Mistress Maris was forever away, closeted with the elders on the goddess only knew what business, and Arona felt very much alone.

* * *

Now hunger, cold, and cabin fever had brought village matters to a head once again, one cold day in Snow Melt Moon. The early spring sky was cloudy and the air was wet and cold, even at midmorning. It was foul weather for a village meeting. Arona, her shawl damp and her boots muddy, trudged through slowly melting slush to the new Mulehouse. There were too many people here for even the village hall, and this dispute bid fair to last all day. Unheard of this early in the year!

She carried a couple of apples in her skirt pocket and a large pack of clay tablets on which to record the latest confrontation between villagers and strangers.

Mistress Maris, walking beside her, nodded her head in the direction of the heavily-laden Egil following them. "He's coming along very well," Maris commended him.

Now Egil caught up with Arona, saying, "Let me relieve you of that load, beautiful one."

The small hairs on Arona's arms stood on end again, for no reason she could understand. Yet, it would be shockingly rude not to accept such a kind offer! "Thank you, Egil," she said reluctantly.

As she gave him part of the load, she saw he also carried tablets. For her? Or for himself to practice on?

The wind from the mountains drove into Arona's face as she followed the people through the gate to the Mulehouse, the only place in the village large enough for such an assembly indoors. Several young girls were on the roof, laying down heavy rocks to fasten blankets across the top of the stable courtyard as shelter from the coming rain. Firepots stood around and outside the Mulehouse, carefully guarded against an accidental spill. They gave more smoke than heat.

Five elders, with the Witch called The Dissident as the now-compulsory translator, sat wrapped in blankets on a bench under the stable roof overhang at the back of the building. The Witch looked haggard and old. So did Mistress Maris. Arona dragged a bale of hay from the pile and spread out her blanket to sit on. Maris would be on the other side of the assembly, so that nothing would be missed. Egil sat beside Arona and set down the tablets to his left; handy for him but not for her. *Inconsiderate,* she thought, angry beyond reason.

Huana Guntirsdaughter and her family filed in, without Noriel. Huana looked triumphantly angry; Oseberg looked miserable. He followed his mother, but looked into the throng. He caught Brithis's eye and looked away. Brithis, starting to show the child she carried, gave him a cold stare and deliberately put her arm around Nidoris Esthensdaughter. Huana looked at Brithis and curled her lip as if she'd seen a bug in her stew.

The eldest, Raula Mylenesdaughter, waited until all were inside the shelter or as close to it as they could reach. Then she held up a bare spindle, age-old symbol of speaker's authority, and called the village rolls. Almost everyone was present; every woman absent had a kinswoman to answer for her. Then the eldest began to speak.

"I worried about taking in the strangers," she began, "because of the he-children. I was wrong. What have we seen? Childish fighting; our daughters complaining of stranger rudeness and strangers complaining of ours; maidens choosing sisterfriends and quarrelling and breaking up, and such matters." Her tone dismissed this as unimportant.

Arona glanced at Brithis and Oseberg. No matter? Maybe an elder could take that view. What had parted such fast friends? She glanced at Mistress Huana and scowled.

"But!" the eldest said severely. "In the past season, seven cases concerning the stranger women have been brought before us. Now we must look at whether the strangers should stay with us, and if so, who?"

Arona's mouth dropped. Exile these women, with winter still upon them? And what of the children? Oh, some had, at first, been louder and noisier and rougher than most, like Oseberg. Then, some were very shy and timid, terrified of disarranging their clothes or coming home covered with sweat, or swimming in the river, and had been natural prey for bullies like Roldeen Lennisdaughter, who now stood before the elders with Yelen Andersdaughter and three of her children.

Roldeen was now complaining that Mistress Yelen's daughter Karmont had offered her violence. Karmont Yelensdaughter faced the accusation boldly. "This *girl*," she said in scorn, "is as big and mean as any he-woman, and she's been picking on our little sister Betza. Just ask her!"

Betza Yelensdaughter was one of the timid ones, and would take no part in village fun. The first time Roldeen had bullied her, Mistress Yelen had said, "We'll see about that," and stalked off to the mill to have it out with Lennis. She had come back in tears, crying, "Who do you go to in this Godforsaken place to see that justice is done and the decencies observed?"

Lennis and her nasty daughters had a complaint or two coming. "The elders!" their neighbors cried enthusiastically. "Take it to the elders!" And so it seemed she had.

The elders conferred briefly. "Roldeen Lennisdaughter to stay away from the daughters of Yelen Andersdaughter, and they from her, until they all can get along. Nidoris Esthensdaughter, would you be willing to teach Betza Yelensdaughter something of self-defense? Since she has not learned it of her sisters."

The chief herder rose. "I will, since it seems to me the two eldest daughters of Yelen Andersdaughter have been playing the bully themselves. I have a question for the elders concerning Rannulf Yelensdaughter."

The tale she told was utterly unheard of. One of her herders, a child not yet Initiate, had confided to her that she did not like the secret game Rannulf Yelensdaughter was playing with her. "They were playing at Falconer visit," she said shortly. "Now, where did that child learn this? Must we treat it as a young Falconer?"

The elders were talking to each other, the Witch, and the sheepherder. An errand-girl ran to summon Rannulf; Arona caught the age-old little-girl's excuse, "She started it!" The recorder's apprentice laid her used tablet down and reached for another. Her pile was empty. "Egil?" she asked. He gave her a black look. "Could you hand me one of my tablets?" she asked politely.

"You don't need one for this," he answered curtly.

"Yes, I do," she argued, and when he refused to budge, she reached across him to get one. Losing her balance, she fell over into his lap. He grabbed her and held her, nuzzling her ear. "Egil!" she said sharply. "Let me go and give me a tablet!"

"Recorder!" The voice of the eldest cut through the crowd like an icy wind from Falcon Crag. "Do you have something to say at *this* meeting?"

Humiliated beyond words, Arona answered, "Egil Ely-shabetsdaughter is keeping my recording tablets from me and is playing games with me. Tell it this is no time for childish pranks!"

Egil loosened his grip and politely handed her three tablets, saying in a soft but carrying voice, "You had only to ask, my dear."

"And I am *not* your dear," she whispered viciously as she regained her seat, close to tears from rage and shame. She barely managed to catch the verdict of the elders, that Rannulf Yelensdaughter should cease these games on pain of Shunning—as a young Falconer—and Dame Birka should talk to Mistress Yelen about teaching him what he was still too young to know.

The next question was, "Should the strangers be allowed to meet the traders from the outside?" That caused a storm of commentary loud enough that the eldest had to leave her seat to silence them. "No, never! We have enough to deal with!"

"What if the Falconers learn of this?"

"What if we're invaded by more strangers?"

Asta Lennisdaughter raised her hand at a village meeting for the first time anyone could remember. "I think," her voice quavered, "we have a lot to gain from welcoming traders and strangers. Look how kind they were after the Turning! They know things we don't."

"That's not the point," Natha Lorinschild argued.

"When I get you home, young lady," Lennis growled, for she had always led the isolationist faction.

Egil Elyshabetsdaughter then raised his hand. "Suppose some of us have families who miss us," he suggested. "Wouldn't it be a kindness to let them know we live and are safe here?"

"Good point!" someone shouted, and the debate was on. It raged for over an hour, while Arona ate an apple and noted the high points from time to time. Egil leaned over to whisper, "Sounds like a flock of hens with a fox in the coop."

"Do you have anything more to say at *this* meeting, Master Recorder?" Arona asked frigidly.

"You sound like one of these small-minded, vindictive girls forever pulling each others' hair," he said, sounding disappointed. "I thought you were better than the rest of them." He fell silent as Huana Guntirsdaughter now came before them. Noriel Auricasdaughter stood across from her, head down, her huge red hands twisting her head scarf. The eldest raised her spindle.

Dame Noriel was alone, her head held stiffly high. She looked as if she'd been crying. Had Mistress Huana quarreled with her, too? Now what?

The elders took their seats, and little girls fed the firepots, stirring the coals.

Huana glared at Noriel. "I charge the women of this village with foul, unnatural practices. You don't marry like decent women; you have no idea who fathers your children; you rut like wild beasts in season. Well, now I know what else you do!" she cried vindictively. Since most of the insults were in her own tongue, only a few raised their eyebrows. "And now this *she-male,* who looks like a man and acts like a man, has made an unspeakable suggestion to me!"

The big blacksmith wiped her eyes and stammered, "I

thought you liked me. We seemed to get on well together." She turned to the elders. "I asked if she wanted to be sisterfriends. I never dreamed she disliked me so as to take offense."

Gently The Dissident asked in Huana's own tongue, "And what did you understand this to mean?"

Huana bridled. "To be her wife! Why, even that recorder's wench told my son she was known to be a lover of women!"

Noriel's face brightened as if this were high praise, and several voices immediately cried out agreement. "She fed me and my daughters the time I was so sick," one woman shouted, "and only asked that we do the same for the next woman in need."

"She defended my little Jommy against that big bully Lennis," Dame Lorin added, "and has never failed in kindness to anyone."

"She was the first to offer food and shelter to the strangers when they came to us homeless," a third put in. *And look how they repaid her,* hung in the air.

A youthful, but large and hairy, hand went up from where Lisha's family sat, and a smooth, too-familiar voice stated with almost insulting kindness, "Apparently we have another mistranslation here, my good ladies, for it seems the word she used would mean, in our own tongue, *philanthropist.*"

The eldest nodded in gratitude. "Thank you, Mistress Egil. I may call on you to translate again this day." Now it was Arona who ground her teeth in anger. The eldest pointed her spindle at Huana and then asked "If you were so offended, why did you remain with Noriel Auricasdaughter?"

Huana ducked her head and admitted, "She made Oseberg her apprentice. I would give anything but my honor for that."

Noriel shook her head. "I needed an apprentice. You had no need to feign friendship for this." She blew her nose vigorously. "And I'm no Loyse Annetsdaughter, to bind anyone to live with me against her will." Her eyes started running again, and she turned away.

The eldest said, "This matter seems plain. Huana Guntirsdaughter may leave the home of Noriel Auricasdaughter and go where she will; you did not need to bring such a simple thing before us. Is there more?"

"Yes!" the stranger cried passionately. "You ordered my daughter to be taught things no decent maiden should ever know!"

The eldest frowned. "I think we have another difference in customs here. I must hear what is taught in your village about maidenhood and womanhood." Huana's mouth fell open. She blushed scarlet and pulled her shawl up to shield her face from view. Gently the eldest offered, "Those not Initiate need not hear this. Maidens, will you take the children out?"

"And the boys," Huana said in a strangled tone. Arona was vindictively gratified to see Egil led out with a pack of small girls. Once that was done, the eldest prompted, "What were you told about your moon-blood time?"

Huana blinked back tears of shame. "My mother slapped my face, to bring the blood back to my cheeks. She warned me that now I could bring shame to our name, so I must always conduct myself modestly from now on. So I have taught Leatrice, though Morgath allowed her to be far too hoydenish for a virtuous maid."

"But how daughters are made, what did you learn of that?"

"That children are gifts from the gods to married women," Huana said promptly, "But to unmarried women, they are the fruit of wickedness. This is why a maid must guard herself so carefully."

The priestess said then, "But Leatrice knew nothing of how this was caused. It was the first thing she asked me."

Huana beamed. "I have kept her as innocent as a babe, for when maidens know such things, they may be tempted to try them; at any rate, these things are not to be spoken of before decent people."

The eldest frowned. "It is cruel to send a maid to get a child without knowing what will happen to her. And if she does not want one? She may still find one forced upon her."

Huana sniffed. "If this is done to her by force, she is disgraced, and that is why her best defense is to stay home and mind her mother! My mother reared me most straitly to never incur even the slightest shadow of disgrace, as her mother reared her. Her mother was a lady's maid in a lord's castle, and knew the ways of the better sort of people. She was widowed before she came to Cedar Crest, but Oseberg is named for her dear late husband."

The witch drew in her breath and looked at Huana compassionately, but said nothing.

The eldest said then, "Explain this matter of 'wedding' to us, Huana Guntirsdaughter."

Huana looked at her, puzzled. "It means that a maid is given to a man to keep his house and to bear and rear his children, to," she blushed, "submit to his will. He keeps her and makes her mistress of the house, and she obeys him all her days, or his."

The eldest raised her eyebrows and then asked, "And are you happy with such a life?"

Huana purpled. "No decent married woman ever answers that question, nor asks it! A decent woman does her duty, which is to be a modest maid, and obedient wife, and a watchful mother, all of which I have done no matter what! Men, even your own husband, will try to shake your virtue; children will defy you and run around like hoydens, or fall into the clutches of a slut who got herself with child by your son and then have the gall to claim him the father; others will laugh and sneer, but I have never failed in my duty!"

Mistress Yelen leaned over and whispered to Brithis's mother apologetically, "She's always been a rigid stickler for propriety."

Natha Lorinsdaughter answered sourly, "Does that mean 'as full of spite as a hen of eggs'? She hates everything and everybody; haven't we all seen it? But now she's cut off her skirts to spite her petticoat, you wait and see." She nodded in the direction of a mask-faced Noriel Auricasdaughter.

The eldest held up her spindle again. "Huana Guntirsdaughter," she said gently, "our customs have served us well for generations, and it seems, better than yours have you. Just as Leatrice Huanasdaughter—"

"Morgathschild!" Huana howled.

"—has been Initiated, so shall all the stranger maidens be taught the same lessons as our own. Those who are male will be taught the same lessons given our Jommy years ago." She nodded at Huana. "You may go back to your place now."

The eldest looked up at the sky and decreed a halt, so people could eat a hot meal. Huana looked around in the watery noonish light. A gust of wind tugged at her shawl. She thought of the warm, cozy forge house and its friendly hearth, with everything arranged exactly as she liked it. Noriel had given her a free hand, almost as if she were mistress and not maid. She could make them a nice cup of herb tea, and a bowl of hot soup for their midday meal. She could—then, like a blow to the belly, it struck her. She was not going back to the forge house. She was going—where could she go? She had no kin to take her in. The faces of the other strangers were closed against her. Some of the villagers were positively gloating. She seized on Oseberg, who looked at her helplessly. Brithis grinned nastily at her, the little slut.

She found a bale of hay in a sheltered spot, and began to cry.

Arona gathered up her tablets and edged her way towards the exit. Maris joined her on the path to Records House. The old recorder's face was as icy as the wind, as icy as the Eldest Mother's voice. "That was a sorry spectacle you made of yourself this morning," she told the girl.

"Me?" Arona blurted out, angered beyond endurance. "Egil was the one who. . . ."

"Childish scuffles at a village meeting are unworthy of a girl your age, Arona, especially of my apprentice."

"But, Mistress," Arona pleaded.

"Say no more about it, Arona Bethiahsdaughter," the recorder ordered, then stopped. "And I have wanted to discuss with you for some time the errors you have been making in records dealing with the strangers.''

Arona could no longer control her tears. The injustice of it all overwhelmed her, and her eyes and nose ran until she must use up her pocket rag and part of her shawl as well. ''These strangers keep changing their names and their stories, and there has been more to write since they came than there has ever been before! I've had to give lessons, and my he-student loves to plague a teacher younger than he is. I tried, Mistress, I did try, but there were times I was all alone without help last fall, and, you were away on elders' business so much!''

The recorder steered her into Records House and dipped out a cup of hot water from the kettle which always hung on the hearth. Arona blew her nose and let her mistress sprinkle some herbs in her cup to steep.

''I can see it's been too much for you,'' the old recorder said, her voice remote and thoughtful. ''Perhaps I should take on another apprentice. The matter's been put to me.''

Arona's tongue froze. Another apprentice, instead of her? After all her efforts? It wasn't fair! One look at Maris's closed face warned her it would be useless to say so. *The matter's been put to me.* By whom? Had the elders complained? She had taken risks and now she was being punished. She had spoken up in meeting and had burst into The Dissident's house with Lowri. She should have—no, for a hurt child she'd do the same thing again no matter what they did to her.

But she should have kept silent in meeting. That she could do. Her head started to pound again. Slowly she sipped her herb tea and ate a bowl of soup. She looked at her mistress for reassurance and found none. Sick to her stomach, she wondered who the new girl would be. Would she do any better? She finished the soup and excused herself. Outside, the wind was growing colder and the clouds deeper. That was a relief. The wet light after a storm always hurt her eyes and gave her headaches.

She stored the tablets in the writing room—for the new girl?—and supplied herself with fresh ones wrapped in damp towels. She stopped to get a fresh handkerchief, and on second thought, made it two. Her nose always ran in nasty weather.

She hurried back to her old place, and shoved the hay bale aside, so that she would be alone. As the elders and the villagers started trickling back in to the Mulehouse, she stopped Brithis, and out of her own misery, asked, "Cousin, what happened between you and Oseberg?"

Brithis tossed her head. "Well, anyone who's so jealous she can't love any baby but her own, doesn't deserve to have friends." Her face was red and her eyes were puffy. "That horrible mother of hers got to her," she then admitted miserably. "Well! I'm glad Dame Noriel kicked her out! I hope she freezes, starves to death, and all the wolves eat her, and the Falconers find her, and, take her to Falcon Crag to feed their birds!"

Arona had to laugh, and she gave Brithis a huge hug. Egil's prissy contempt for vengeance like this was even funnier, and after a while, Brithis began to laugh too. The eldest raised her spindle again. Maris Guidasdaughter came forward with Egil. "In the matter of the petition of Egil Elyshabetsdaughter, maiden, to be apprenticed to the recorder," the Eldest began.

The clay tablet dropped from Arona's numb fingers and fell face-down into the stableyard mud, obliterating some of the characters. Arona scarcely noticed. She stared at Egil, her mouth hanging open, her belly frozen, and at Maris, for whom she had worked so hard and so well. She gasped as tears began to flow down her cheeks. Her head suddenly seemed to explode.

"Petition granted," the eldest said. There was more, but Arona could only hear it as a babble of noise. She could not pick up the tablet; she could record nothing. She sat, as in a bad dream, while Egil came to join her.

"It seems we'll be working together from now on," he said cheerfully. "Hey! Arona! What's there to cry about?" He handed her a handkerchief, looking puzzled and annoyed. "Aren't you happy for me?"

Nine

Falcon Winter, Falcon Spring

$\mathcal{T}$he sunlight was as icy and wet as the snow that still clung to the houses and barns. Arona wiped her eyes again and trudged down to the well-worn path to Records House. She was drawn and gaunt, and a stubborn weariness clouded her face as did the long bangs which obscured her eyes. It had been a hungry winter.

Now Egil Elyshabet's he-daughter, may Jonkara's talons tear its lying soul from its beautiful flesh, was going to live at Records House, as of tomorrow morning. "Mistress, how could you?" she burst out, hastening to catch up to the old woman.

Maris sighed and took Arona's hand. "It's as you said, dear, there's too much work for one person, and Egil loves the work as much as you do. It will all work out; you'll see."

Sourly Arona persisted, "Have you heard his wild ideas about what he'll do *when he becomes recorder?*"

Maris coughed, then chuckled softly. "As I recall, all bright young girls have their own ideas. Weren't you going to turn Records House into Magic House, and learn every ritual you could find for doing things?"

Arona didn't answer. Since the strangers came, she had no more time for hobbies. Even in the depths of winter, there had been Egil's lessons to work at, and knitting until her fingers were sore, to replace garments lost in the Great Storm of the Turning. Her own scrolls, tucked away behind her bed, had gathered dust.

She could only lie sleeplessly in bed that night and hope Egil would be less a rival and more a friend.

He came very shortly after dawnlight, authority in his very walk. Arona bristled, for all she had promised her mistress she wouldn't. Maris wasn't well and couldn't deal with nonsense.

"I know you have quarreled in the past," Mistress Maris said gently, laying one arm around each youngster's shoulder, "but now my apprentices must lay their quarrels aside and be as one. Arona, please show Egil your room, and then show her her chores, that's a good girl." She sounded tired and looked frail.

Egil unaccountably whistled when he saw the low-ceilinged loft room, with Arona's robes hanging from pegs in the wall, and he looked at her speculatively. But downstairs, when she said, "We'll take turns doing the housework," and handed him the dishpan, he cocked his head to one side. "You're enjoying this, aren't you?"

How could she? "I'm only trying to be fair," she said stiffly, still not looking at him.

Egil shook his head. "If one person is better at outdoor chores and one person at indoor chores, doesn't it make a lot of sense that each one do what she's best at?" he argued.

This was one of their standing arguments. "If Mistress Maris wants to change the custom, she may; I won't," she said, wrapping her hands and shoulders to draw water. He followed her outside, carried the buckets back in, and winked at Arona when Maris, seeing this, handed the dishtowel to Arona. She glared at his unrepentant grin of triumph.

From morning dishes to record room, to mending and sweeping, to the records again they went, arguing as they went. "The first thing I'll do," Egil said thoughtfully, "is take that horrid tale of treachery and add the proper interpretation to it."

"You do just that," Arona challenged. "What Mistress wants is a complete account of yesterday's meeting, as well you know."

"Oh, come on," he scoffed. "One granddam crying that another's child blacked her son's eye? Be serious." But he was too canny to let their mistress know how lazy he was, and applied himself to the task as diligently as if he wanted to. When they finished, he rolled up the scrolls and capped the inkstones carefully. But he raised the expected fuss over peeling dried vegetables for the supper stewpot. *Lazy,* Arona thought in contempt. One day Maris would see it.

That night, in what was now their room, she started to undress, then turned around and saw Egil frankly staring, as if he would devour her. "Egil," she said firmly, "that's rude."

He laughed softly. "I never expected such false modesty of you, Arona, since you know what we're here for." He moved closer to her, and then held her in a bear hug while he kissed her, as hard as he had that first time. Taken unawares, she twisted back, pushing with the heels of her hands against his chin. She tried to gasp out, "Stop it!" but he laughed a little and said, "If that's the way you want to play it," and she saw he was like a Falconer about to do his duty.

She had not come here to get a child! What made Egil think she had? She struggled with hands, feet, and teeth, until she managed to free herself. Then, totally undressed, she scrambled down the ladder. "Mistress," she gasped, and started to sob. The old recorder, dozing in a rocker by the hearth, snapped her head up and focussed sleep-blurred eyes on her. Arona knelt by the rocker and laid her head in her mistress's lap. Through choking sobs she said, "He tried to do as Falconers do." She used the ending reserved for Falconers and rutbeasts, spitting it out with a sharp-sounding negative. "He said I knew it would be so. Mistress," she begged, "did you tell him he could do this?"

Maris blinked. "Were you having a bad dream, dear?" she asked, seeming confused. Her face was hot from the fire.

Arona gasped and extended her arms, scratched and bruised, into the dying firelight. "Is this a dream?" she cried.

"You were fighting," Maris said severely. "That is unworthy, Arona."

"He tried to—Mistress! Didn't you hear me?"

"Go back upstairs, dear, and you two make peace."

Arona bit her lower lip, tears rolling down her face. "It is not right to send me to get a child without telling me. You even heard the elders say so. If you keep Egil upstairs, I will sleep down here."

Maris sighed and looked closely at Arona. She was badly upset about something, to be sure, but then, she had been badly upset about a good many things ever since Egil Elyshabetsdaughter had come to the village. What was this about a child? Nobody had said any such thing; she told the girl so most firmly. Then would she go back upstairs? Arona wiped her nose on the back of her hand. "Only if you tell Egil he is not to do this!" she insisted.

Maris peered at her more closely. She did seem frightened. It was hard to imagine the softspoken, deferential Egil as a bully, but the old recorder remembered a few old humiliations at the hand of the equally soft-spoken Peliel Laelsdaughter long ago. "Egil?" she called. "Egil Elyshabetsdaughter? Please come down."

Egil threw on his shirt and trousers, thinking furiously. This Maris Guidasdaughter had made him recorder's apprentice in Arona's stead, had put them in the same room, and had told them they must now be as one. What other meaning could this have, but that she had given him Arona as his handfast wife? And Arona was no blushing innocent; he had heard from many sources how explicit was the instruction of these Falconers' women. Was there some necessary preliminary she expected? Kisses, flowers, eternal vows? Well, she would have them! But he would not be treated as an outlaw for simply claiming his rights.

As Egil came down, Arona raced for the ladder, scrambling into her heaviest and most concealing robes. She braided her hair tightly and put on soft house boots. Egil and Maris were talking softly together. The old recorder broke off in the middle of a sentence, and said, "No, Egil Elyshabetsdaughter, I do not understand. Now, what I want you two girls to do is go upstairs and promise to live like sisters as long as you both are here."

Arona's eyes searched Egil's face in the dim firelight. She made up her mind. "I can stay here by the fire," she answered. Both Maris and Egil shook their heads. She examined Egil's overmuscled arms, remembering their strength as he held her against her will. "Egil," she said desperately, "you go on upstairs. I won't be able to sleep; I'll stay down here and keep our mistress company."

His hand closed around her upper arm. "Don't be foolish, Arona," he said in the grim voice of a bully about to have his way.

Arona dug her short, strong fingernails into his hand, to no avail. "Mistress!" she cried desperately, once more.

Maris jerked her head back, now totally alert. "I do not wish to think I have made a bully my apprentice," she said firmly. "Arona, you must not be afraid of her. You must learn to stand up for yourself."

Trapped, Arona said softly, "You go first, Egil. I'll come along later." Then, to the recorder, "Dame Lennis is right, Mistress. They are different." She blew her nose on a fresh rag the old woman handed her. "They act like Falconers. We don't understand them. Do you? Maybe the Witch does." She glanced towards the door.

Maris stroked her hair. "The hour is very late for one the age of the Witch, but if you really fear Egil's bullying, you can sleep with me tonight—just this one night. You really will have to learn to live together, you know."

She knew. That's what frightened her most. The next morning, Egil, dressed and washed, put his head next to hers. "What do you require, my little sisterfriend?" he asked softly. "An oath of lifetime fealty? Do you wish me to beg you on bended knee? Pay a (something) price to your family? All you need to do is tell me; just remember, I'm a stranger here, and do not know your customs."

"Egil," she said, distressed, "what you must do is ask."

"Well, then! I'm asking now."

"No. Not yet. Not while I'm afraid of you."

"You told me," he spat out in a nearly inaudible fury, "that all I needed to do was ask. So I did. And now you refuse me? I don't know what game you're playing, but you'd better be a bit more honest with me from now on."

She twisted loose again. "You think you own me!" she exclaimed in shock. "Well! Go ask Loyse Annetsdaughter how that works! And leave me alone!" She went about her chores and continued writing up the village meeting, shoving the relevant sections under Egil's nose.

He stared at her, brooding, all day: at work and at chores, at meals and after, when they sat knitting by the fireplace, and shortly before bedtime. She excused herself early, and heard him on the ladder. Scrambling back down, she dragged her quilt behind her with, "It wants mending." Then she sat stitching at it until she could keep her eyes open no longer. Egil was still watching her like a cat at a mousehole. She yawned, stretched, and excused herself with a remark about the outhouse. Then she wrapped her quilt around her and quietly slipped out of the gate and onto the darkened path.

It was too dark to run. As quickly as she could, she picked her way along the path, eyes alert for obstacles. Which way was the House of the Witch? From the plains to the west, one of Jonkara's Dogs cried mournfully. The end of the quilt dragged on the sodden, half-frozen ground. Lips tight, she fumbled for it and wrapped the heavy cover tighter around her. The path was rough under her soft house boots. She stopped, breathing very softly. Was there a sound behind her? If Egil came after her, she would sound a warning call as loudly as possible, and see this taken before the elders.

Why was he behaving so? Like Roldeen and Asta Lennisdaughters and the Falconers all rolled into one! She caught her breath and set off again. The familiar village pathways looked entirely different after dark, and she had not dared take torch or candle. She heard a very soft, faint footstep again, close behind her, and stopped. Something soft and furry wound itself around her leg. She stooped down to touch it. A familiar voice demanded, "Yow?"

"Little Red Pest!" she breathed, picking up the cat. Then she set it down again with, "Show me the way to the Witch's House, kitty. Please?" The cat darted off. She followed. The path did not seem familiar, and the night was chill. *Oh, Dame Witch, help me,* Arona's mind begged as the wind knifed through her hair. Her ears felt made of ice, and hurt painfully; her nose was full of ice. She set down one foot after another, and, stepping on the side of a rock at an angle, fell heavily on one leg. *Dame Witch!* her mind screamed. In the distance, Egil was calling, "Arona? Arona!" She struggled to her feet.

Then she felt her mind held fast by the mind of the Witch. Her feet, with no volition of her own, now held her up and began walking her down the path she had thought went the wrong way. With no light from sun, moon, stars, or torch, she could see every detail of the ground underfoot. Her legs moved faster and faster, until she was running like a message-girl. Egil's voice sounded louder and louder behind her. With one last effort, she burst through the Witch's open door and flung herself, gasping for breath, against the haggard old woman's plain, heavy robe.

"Just sit," the old Witch said dispassionately. A kettle hung over the fire, and from it, rich soup smells rose. Arona recognized root vegetables and what had to be the eldest of the he-hens, boiled for days. She fell, nearly fainting, onto the Witch's plank-wood settee. "Arona!" Egil was calling. The Witch dipped out soup into a red pottery bowl, handed her a spoon of the same material, then stared into the distance. The calls ceased, and the girl sensed Egil turning back to Records House. Satisfied, the Witch watched her eat until the bowl was empty.

"I knew this was bound to happen," the Witch's voice came from a distance as Little Red Pest jumped on top of the girl and settled between her legs, purring. Then the old woman set herself to contact the recorder, whose ultrasenses were sharper than either her sight or her hearing.

Egil was at the Witch's house at dawnlight, followed by a distraught Maris. The Witch sat them both down with herself and Arona. "We can take this before the elders if you wish," she said judiciously, "or we can settle it here." The frail old recorder's face, clouded at the thought of another meeting, brightened. It was a horrible stain, not to be able to keep order in her own home.

"Maris, under no circumstances do a girl and a he-girl share a room, but one: that 'wedding' you heard Huana Guntirs-daughter speak of the day before yesterday," the Witch said with mild distaste, for her order rejected all that. "Egil acted according to his own customs. Every dog gets one bite, not two. We must now warn people to keep the he-girls and the girls apart. Shall I call the meeting, or will you?"

Egil brooded at Arona over his bowl of the witch's porridge. "I cannot believe you people had no concept," he began, stopped, and the Witch nodded. "Arona, I would never hurt you. I will be honest. I want you for my—'sisterfriend' is the closest I can come in our common tongue, but there's another, used only in the ancient records. Do you understand me?"

Arona called the most ancient scrolls to mind, and all the lines concerning this. At last she said, "I understand. But I will have to think long about this. Will it be as Huana Guntirs-daughter said, all submission and duty and obedience like a bondsmaid?"

"Great Gods, no! That woman hates men, marriage, and everything about it except the respectability of a married name, and that's because I sincerely doubt her la-di-dah grandsire ever existed except in her granddam's imagination. Did you notice, 'Oseberg' is a town's name and not a man's? I'd love you, cherish you, protect you. You'd be somebody of importance, for I'm already well on that road. Our sons could be big men in this town."

He spoke largely in his own tongue, which had too many strange concepts for Arona to understand fluently. She sat watching him, her yellow eyes unreadable. "Would it be as the old scrolls said, how these he-sisterfriends became masters over their ladies?" she demanded.

He scoffed. "Fairy tales and legends. I should hope I'd be better to you than they! Though I should also hope you would never poison my soup for a moment's harshness. Truce?" His eyes solemn, he reached for her hand. "I can see I outraged your modesty, and to tell you the truth, it's all to your credit." He took her hand, not as a bully, but as a friend. He cocked his head and said gently, "It's a foul rumor among us . . . strangers . . . that you girls have no modesty to outrage. I know that to be false. But it's plainly not like ours. Accept my apology?"

"Done," she agreed reluctantly. When, on the way back, Egil insisted on moving his things to the records cellar or the barn, her suspicious heart melted a little. But she slept lightly that first night, dressing and undressing in haste and—Maris would have a fit if she knew—taking one of the kitchen knives to bed with her.

Ten

A Quest for Wisdom

I am the recorder's apprentice; one day I shall be the recorder. Arona stared out the loft window and tried to convince herself. Up till now, she had never questioned it.

Egil was determined to succeed to Mistress Maris's post. Did the recorder know that? The hungry winter had been hard on the frail old woman. Now that a few green shoots showed through the melting snow, Dame Butthead foraged more freely and gave a bit more milk. Arona could find fresh greens along the stream and in the woods. The nights, still bitterly cold, gave way to middays that were pleasant if she wrapped up well. Yet, the old recorder was still sick. Slow to wake in the morning, confused when she did wake, she could deal with nothing until she had eaten, and her appetite was poor. It had come about that Arona tended her mistress while Egil took over many of the other chores of Records House.

Yet, he was as docile and kind as a beloved big sister these days, unfailingly polite, deferential to Mistress Maris, and considerate of Arona's wishes. With a smile, he relieved her of the heaviest and most unpleasant chores. Joyfully he talked history and legends with her, sitting on the front porch in the rocker with his feet propped up on the rail. Acknowledging his junior status in the house, he slept in the front room and left Arona the bedroom-loft.

He courted her friendship. With gentle tenderness he would offer hugs, kisses, and small gestures that made her wonder if every day were to be her nameday. He began sentences with, "When we are together." He talked of the babies she would bear, and of his own desire to start them. Maris began beaming like a doting mother whenever she saw them together.

He dreamed of working with Arona as partners, like sisters. *With him as the eldest,* she thought viciously. For he was still a sneak and a bully. Four times he had handled her against her will, once in connection with that nasty prank which caused such trouble with the Mistress. Several times she had seen him watching her exactly as the cat would watch a mousehole. Had Mistress Maris seen it, too?

But one day, when the old recorder had fallen into a deep sleep, Arona thought of her old scrolls and went down to the records room to look for a parchment scrap. The door was bolted and fastened with a heavy knot.

"Did you tie up the records room door, Egil?" she asked,

tracking him down in the writing shed. She looked over his shoulder to see what he was writing; he moved to block her view.

"We can't let stray animals and curious children make free with the records," he said, his voice making plain his surprise and disappointment that Arona hadn't realized this immediately.

"Yes, but I need to get in," she retorted.

"If you need to get in," he answered patiently, "all you have to do is ask me."

She seized his shoulders in both hands then and tried to turn him around. "I will ask my mistress for access to the records," she exploded. "I will not ask another apprentice! We have never locked those records up, and never have children or animals disturbed them until you came." She turned around, found her utility knife, and began sawing at the rope. Egil left his writing to stand behind her. "That rope was not easy to come by," he said darkly.

"Pity," she said angrily, and rummaged through the scrap pile. He had rearranged things down there, she saw immediately. Several of the scrolls had been set apart. After much searching, she found a scrap barely large enough to write her name on. "Is this all we have left?" she demanded. "What happened to the rest?"

"I'll see to it we get more," he answered, still patiently. "Why don't you see if the recorder is all right? Or if you really need something to do, I'm sure the garden needs attention."

"I have plenty to do," she retorted. "It's just that somebody has hogged all the materials to do it with. Let's have the rest, Egil; I need them. Now!"

He smiled indulgently. "A little more honey in the asking might get you further than temper tantrums, sweetheart." He put his arm up to block the door. Arona shrugged, turned around, and began examining the scrolls he had set aside. "I can let you have three sheets," he said then. "That's all I can spare."

Leaving with her precious gains, she looked inside the writing room. He had used twice that amount recording the ballads he had sung to her. Annoyance mingled with understanding: of course he would not want his peoples' stories lost; and he had never learned to share things fairly. But why would he lock up the records room?

What kind of people had lived in Cedar Crest?

She called at Elthea the Weaver's just to talk to Egil's little sister about him. Lowri adored him. She told no tales of mean pranks or petty cruelty, but boasted, "Nobody pesters us when he's around."

His nearest age-mate among the strangers, Leatrice Huanas-daughter, doled out her words like precious spices. "He's handsome," she said. "He's ambitious. Everybody says he'll be a man of importance some day." In other words, Leatrice loathed him.

Mulemistress Darann said, "Good worker. Smooth talker. Bossy. Had a way with the mules."

"Egil?" Oseberg said enthusiastically. "He's great, the best ever."

Arona perched herself on the edge of a worktable at the forge. "He's not jealous that you found a sisterfriend in Brithis?"

Oseberg hooted. "Jealous? He's glad. He told me so. Anyway, she's not his type." His face fell. "But it's awful, only seeing Brithis because Mother's out there all alone." Oseberg loved Egil. Whatever his manners had been, Oseberg's heart was kind.

Brithis was pleased to tell Arona what it was like to live with a he-stranger. "Nice. Like a sisterfriend, only better. Oh, Oseberg has a few funny ways," she conceded. "She was terribly upset about me going to the Falconers and asked me not to any more—not that I need to, now!" She giggled and ducked her head, then peered up shyly. "Starting babies their way is nice. You should try it." She thought a few minutes. "She likes me to do the inside chores while she does the outside, but she's so strong and does so much, that's fair enough." She pursed her lips. "She wouldn't see me, though, until she found out her horrible old mother wasn't going to starve or freeze after all. I guess that's only fair; she's her mother."

Was there something in Egil Arona was too blind to see? She made one last call, to the new farm Egil's mother had traded her pot for. Dame Elyshabet, her skirts tucked up and her hair bound in a scarf, was out in the fields with a hoe. Egil had promised her, *You won't have to work the land, Mother; I'll do all that.* Then he had run off to Records House, leaving her with a farm she had never wanted, and all the work to do. He was a liar and a bully and hopelessly spoiled. Arona stood in the path, irresolute, then hailed the house.

"You know he was the eldest," Dame Elyshabet said as they sat on the porch drinking hot herb tea. "For so long I could not rear a living child; perhaps we made too much of him. He had neither uncles nor cousins nor older brothers to cut him down to size. And of course, he stood to inherit Harald's bakery." Her eyes asked Arona just what the girl was interested in knowing.

Arona, herself the eldest in a large family and the one earmarked for distinction, nodded. Dame Elyshabet, so inarticulate in the village tongue, was as wise as an elder in her own. "Why do you let him speak for you?" she blurted out. "And tell you what to do and force you to do things you don't choose? You're his mother, and he's still a maid! Why does he play the bully sometimes and then be so sweet and kind? Why does he think Aunt Noriel would act like a Falconer and why is he always so sure he alone is right?"

Elyshabet shook her head and laughed softly. "You never met his father's mother. Norine was as rigid as Huana in many ways, but clever and smooth-spoken . . . when she needed to be. Egil takes after her, and while she lived, he was always her favorite. That's the trouble."

Huana Guntirsdaughter appeared in the kitchen door then and sniffed contemptuously. Dame Elyshabet shook her head. "I couldn't let her starve," she apologized.

The last Arona had heard, Huana Guntirsdaughter had taken refuge in one of the Visit huts, working the garden there and living on whatever meager food supplies and tools she could borrow from hard-pressed villagers and blood-bound kindred. *Serves her right,* the girl thought intolerantly, remembering Aunt Noriel's face that day. But Oseberg Morgathschild didn't deserve to be torn between his mother and her enemies.

Egil openly admired Huana's folly, and sang Arona several ballads of women who chose death before "dishonor"—having a child started in them by force. Demanding to know what that had to do with Aunt Noriel's offer of partnership, she heard him out with growing amazement. "Egil! That's a contradiction in terms! Besides, even if Aunt Noriel *could* do that, she never would."

Dame Elyshabet was too kind, and it made her easy prey, Arona realized with a sinking heart.

The Witch refused to speak of Egil, saying the privacy of a mind was inviolate unless a life was at stake. Arona bit her lip at the thought of the Witch. How much help could Dame Witch be these days? People in the village were starting to look oddly at the Witch, muttering as she passed and making Falcon-away signs behind her back, to ward off bad luck. "They blame me for the disasters of the Turning," the Witch told Arona when she asked, tablets in hand.

"You saved us from the worst," Arona argued, remembering the night in the caves.

"They remember it was my kind who started these events," the Witch said gently. "And if I had the power to save them from the worst, why did I not save them from everything that befell them this winter? It's an old, old tale, child. But I'd take your doubts about Egil to the Elders."

Arona shook her head. "It's too soon after the last meeting. All I've heard from anyone is that they want no more quarrels. And Egil's manners are beautiful when older women are about," she said bitterly. "Mistress Maris will hear no evil of him."

It seemed to Arona that the word *senile* hung in the air between them, but neither dared say it out loud. She left Witch House and went back to look in on Mistress Maris.

The recorder lay in bed, feebly coughing, wheezing as if the effort to breathe had worn her out. "Egil!" Arona shouted. There was no answer. Arona ran for the healer.

Dame Floree and her apprentice Hanna Elyshabetsdaughter came into the sickroom. As the healer placed an ear against the old recorder's chest and bade her cough, her apprentice cried out, "Egil!" The girl's face lit up as he entered the sick room.

Egil scooped up his little sister and hugged her tightly. "Hello, apple blossom," he said lightly, then set her down. "What ails the recorder?" he asked Dame Floree directly, as if neither Arona nor Hanna were there.

Dame Floree shook her head. "It's a lung fever. I'll make up a potion for her cough; keep her warm and make her drink plenty of liquids."

"Did you hear that, Arona?" Egil asked. "I'll be in the records room." He left; Dame Floree raised her eyebrows, but said nothing.

They had no honey in the house. Frowning, Arona scraped up whatever she could spare of her ornaments to trade with Olwith the Beekeeper. Egil put his head out of the writing room to offer a bracelet Darann Mulemistress had given him, which was gracious of him. But whatever was he writing in there that he could so neglect his sick mistress? Friend, bully, bully, friend, what was Egil Elyshabetsdaughter?

The beekeeper could only spare a little honey; Brithis, her apprentice, was pregnant and needed it more. The lookouts on the mountain gave a quail call, and Arona suddenly decided on one last desperate course. She would beg Cousin Jommy to advise her and the Elders about Egil.

The first boy ever reared in the village of women, Jimmy had a twisted foot. Most sickly or deformed daughters were given the Mercy of Jonkara by the midwife, at their mother's word. Jommy was male, and males belonged to the Falconers, who gave Her Mercy to all such. His mother, almost past the age of bearing, had no living daughters, and vowed to keep him and rear him as a girl.

To the fear that a male in the village was as a wolf in the flock, his mother Eina had said, "Dogs are the daughters of wolves, but we took the pups in at birth and brought them up to be members of our families, and we are all glad now."

Mistress Maris, then young, had spoken for Jommy. "The first woman to adopt a wolf pup was attacked as a danger to the village and to us all," she said. "The first women to fashion ourselves spears and knives against wild beasts were told they would bring all the Falconers down upon us to kill us all. The first to ride forth in search of metal was nearly Shunned for her daring, and the first to build herself a house nearly had it burned down by her sisters for fear of the Falconers. Would any of us do without the gains they made?"

He had dealt with grave matters while still a boy. He had lived outside and seen their ways for a year and returned under a great cloud of scandal, for he had killed a Falconer. Now he lived self-exiled, seeking wisdom. Every full moon the elders sent up provisions for him, and whenever he finished weaving a rug, he sent it back down again in payment. It was time to trade with him again. Generally a woman rode with the pack mule. The next moon it would be Arona.

But before she could do so, she was summoned once again to deal with the traders from outside.

The lookouts gave the quail cry again. The trail was clear and traders were riding again. Arona grabbed her Visit veils and ran. She had loaded a borrowed mule with every pot the kitchen could spare, every piece of jewelry she owned, every weaving not needed to keep them warm. From the other direction came Asta Lennisdaughter, dressed in her best clothes, with a finer mule equally laden. Several other women, some with donkeys and some with mules and one—Nidoris—with a baby tame horse!—joined her at the trailhead huts.

"Arona!" one of them called. "You speak the traders' tongue. Could you teach me when you get a chance? I have some onion and egg salad for your mistress."

"Nidoris, what a cute little horse!" someone called. "Did you catch her when you took the sheep out?" Half a dozen girls crowded around to pet the filly and admire her. The first women in the village, seeing there were wild horses on the plain, had tried to catch and tame them. But where could they ride one that a mule or donkey, cheaper to feed, couldn't go more easily? Only on the plain, and Falconers left their long arrows in any riders they found on that particular plain. Horses were pets, mothers of mules, or wild herd animals running free.

"Traders ride tame horses," Nidoris said with a bold grin. "Maybe they'd like a baby one to bring up."

She tethered the filly to a tree by the huts and looked around. "These aren't bad!" she exclaimed. "Sheepherders would love them!"

The trade caravan, a pack of perhaps twenty horses and donkeys and mules, rode into sight. It was led by bearded he-people with hard leather jackets and as many knives as a butcher's kitchen, but there were hooded and cloaked women in divided skirts riding with them, and one robed Daughter of Gunnora. Arona ran forward to greet the cowled woman and asked, "Where are the rest of you?"

The Daughter of Gunnora laughed. "We have always been very, very few on this side of the ocean, child, and it comes to me you no longer need us. But we are here if you do!"

Asta Lennisdaughter was searching the caravaners' faces for the youngster who had talked to her that fall. Failing to find him, she cornered a bearded one who seemed receptive. "Is it true that in your homeland," she began. Arona didn't listen to the rest, for one of the traders' packs held just what she needed.

"Parchment," she was saying a few minutes later. "We make our own, but someone used it up without taking that into account." The trader woman smiled indulgently. "And honey for my mistress's cough. The bees were all shaken up last fall and their Eldest Mother never got over it."

The trader woman conferred with one of the bearded ones briefly. Arona caught the word, or name, Lormt. Another recorder? Or another village whose recorder she was. She asked; the woman tilted her head and raised an eyebrow.

The bearded one said gravely, "Lormt is a place where old scrolls are kept, and scholars go to learn of them. It is," he peered at the mountains and idly sketched in the sand with his knife-tip, "roughly north and east of here. You leave these mountains and cross the valley of the river Es, of which your river is a tributary, and you'll see a small mountain range joining a great one. There where they join is Lormt, and there we go to sell the parchment you ask for. Why? Are you a scholar, too?"

"An apprentice," she confirmed, and began haggling with him over whatever parchment he could spare. Then she asked the trader woman, "Mistress, tell me of the customs of your land." And soon, because her heart was sore and she was desperate for advice, she was asking the stranger woman how to deal with Egil. The other traders gathered round, full of advice.

"Just don't let him bully you," the trader advised, but didn't say how.

"Have your kindred knock the fertilizing horse-dung out of him," the bearded he-person suggested. Good idea. Pity she wasn't kin to the pugnacious Lennis!

Come to think of it, Asta Lennisdaughter knew all about dealing with bullies. Arona looked around and didn't see her. Where was Asta? Not that the miller's daughter was any friend of hers. Oh, well, she was probably farther back in the pack train, talking to one of the trader friends she loved so.

Arona led the mule back along the path, deep in thought. It was becoming clearer and clearer that Egil was making himself he-mistress over Records House with every deed he did. He was not above bullying if that would get him what he wanted. The trader and her he-people said this was very common outside, but not necessarily the rule. She returned the mule to Mistress Darann with suitable thanks and a small gift, and, still deep in thought, let herself in by way of the kitchen. Mistress Maris apparently still slept in the main room, and Egil was sitting by her. Relieved, she hung up her wraps and started to take her parchment to the loft. Before she was out of the kitchen, she heard Egil growl softly, "Die! Die, you useless old woman, and get out of my way!"

With the greatest effort of her life, Arona stifled her cry of outrage and slipped out the back door again. Grabbing her cloak, she ran to Healing House. She stopped, took a deep breath, and composed herself. "My mistress is much worse," she told Dame Floree with only a trace of agitation. "I begin to wonder if someone, god or woman, has ill-wished her." As Dame Floree found her cloak and summoned her helper, the girl added, "I have parchment enough to copy your remedies for you, for your apprentice."

"Feeding my apprentice will be payment enough," the healer said dryly, for Hanna Elyshabetsdaughter was at the hungry age.

Arona shook her head. "She'll have to fight Egil for it." For she had his measure completely now. *I'll have to fight Egil for Records House,* she thought, *and he fights most foul. Jonkara, help me; I don't know how to fight one who fights so foul.*

Mistress Maris died as the first of the spring birds were starting to discuss nesting sites, when women were talking about plowing the fields, a month after Asta Lennisdaughter disappeared with all her mother's trade goods, to the great scandal of the village.

"It was lung-sickness," Dame Floree said, as she had on the first visit. "The winter gave it to her, and no goddess." She glanced at Witch House sideways and made a falcon-away sign, as if Dame Witch might have ill-wished Mistress Maris.

"I'm sure you did all you could and more," Egil reassured her. Arona wiped her streaming eyes and glared at him. How dare he pretend to mourn Maris when he had ill-wished her? All the village had come with food and gifts to mourn her passing. The hospitality had fallen entirely to Arona. She did not try to force Egil to take part; the less he had to do with the business of Records House, the better.

"Arona!" Now he spoke sharply to her, as a mother to a daydreaming daughter. "We need more ale here."

"Then go get some," she snapped back.

He shook his head and murmured to their guest; she caught the word "distraught." At last, with a martyred sigh, he fetched the pot; the guest turned to Arona. "Who's to be in charge of Records House now?" she asked.

Arona's head jerked up. Giving it to Egil was intolerable; he conceding it to her, improbable; fighting him for it, unbearable. "We'll have to take it to the elders, Aunt Olwith," she said.

The beekeeper shook her head. "More division in the village," she said sadly.

Eleven

Judgment Day

$\mathcal{T}$he elders of Riveredge Village convened in the village hall, with The Dissident among them, since the case concerned a stranger. Among them, but not with them; the elders sat slightly apart from the Witch, and gave her the uneasy looks they had given the strangers when they first came. Egil and Arona sat before them, well apart. The glance Egil gave Arona as they entered promised her he'd be well revenged for this when he had the chance.

Arona spoke first. "I come as apprentice to Maris Guidas-daughter, now dead, to take her place. I have served her faithfully since childhood. She brought Egil, Elyshabet's he-daughter, to help me when the strangers came, for she was busy on Elders' business, and there was more work than one woman can do. Then she was sick, and needed both of us to tend her. That time is now past, though," she said graciously, "I thank you for your help, Egil."

Egil smiled indulgently. "The records do show you were overworked," he conceded, "with the large number of errors and corrections in your hand." He nodded to the Elders. "Don't worry. I corrected all that, and will keep it from happening again. But why," he turned back to Arona, "could we not live together as one, as our mistress expected?"

Arona trembled and took a deep breath. "If you had helped me with our mistress and with the other chores at Records House, I would have been glad to have you as my apprentice and assistant once," she said. "Elder Mothers, he did only the work that he liked, and tried to keep me from my own work. He admits to me that in any partnership between us, he expects to be the elder. He enforces this with pranks and bullying where need be. He often did this behind our Mistress's back when she lived."

She glanced at The Dissident. "On one occasion he acted as a rutbeast, and Dame Witch said he had misunderstood us and thought that by his customs this was right. Dame Witch, you understand their customs. If he was made my helper, would he expect to play the rutbeast again?"

Egil's hand flew up. "That's not fair!" The women turned around, and The Dissident nodded. "I made a vow from the beginning to love Arona, and cherish her, and treat her kindly. It is true, I want her as a man does a woman, but unless she is one of those," his voice took on a note of distaste, "who think that all men are beasts, and the act of generation a thing to be endured—for which I do not blame her," he said gently, with kindness spread like butter in his purring voice, "since the Falconers have made it so. I would not be as a beast to her."

"Then why," Arona rebutted, "have you bullied me? Ordered me about as a mother to a small child? Dame Floree has heard this and so has Mistress Olwith and many others. Why have you laid hands on me to keep me from my business? Kept my tablets from me in public and locked up the records?" Briefly she summarized every incident. "Dame Witch," she appealed, "you understand their customs. Is this conduct accepted among them?"

The Dissident raised her hands for silence. "To your first question. If you were partners, he would expect to, as you say, play the rutbeast, at his will and not yours. This is their custom, and he is one to stand on what he accounts his rights. He would also expect, as you said, to be the senior partner in all things. He would consider himself to be the recorder and you his assistant, and would take any steps he counted necessary to make this happen. Those pranks you both speak of had one end: that you must come to him in order to ply your trade."

Arona sat down, stunned. So it was. She had not thought of that. The Witch continued "Would you accept that?"

"Certainly not!"

Egil was recognized. "You could give it to me freely," he suggested. "Do you doubt that I love you and would cherish and protect you?"

"Only when it was your will to do so. Not if my will crossed yours. Elders," Arona said flatly, "we cannot be co-recorders. He has admitted this with his own lips. Unless," she said as a sudden idea came to her, "he recorded the tales and doings of his own people, and I of ours, and both of us, those that are in common."

The Elders conferred together. Eldest Mother Raula Mylenesdaughter said then, "If you cannot live together, why should we choose you above Egil Elyshabetsdaughter? By all accounts, Egil is the better recorder, more diligent, with a neater hand, making fewer errors, and as you said, elder than you are."

"More diligent!" Arona exploded. "Honored elders, while he locked himself in the records room writing Jonkara knows what, my mistress lay ailing, and I must tend her. He never offered! I could have fought him for use of the records room and bid him tend her, but—" she looked around at them. Then she said, tears welling from her eyes, "He wished her ill and not well. I heard this with my own ears. I had been out, and came back quietly, and he was saying 'Die! Die, you useless old woman, and get out of my way.' "

The elders gasped and conferred again. Dame Floree gave Egil a severe look. Only Arona and the Witch noticed that Egil looked not at all surprised.

The stranger sighed. "I should have prayed for a miraculous recovery rather than a merciful death," he admitted, hanging his head. "My grandmother," his voice trembled, "died after a long illness, wasted and in pain, until I could no longer bear her suffering, and prayed the Gods to save her. My old hound Beller," and now a true tear came to his eyes, "was savaged by a wild boar when I was a boy. I could not help him, but had to put him out of his misery, and remember thinking later that men are more merciful towards their dogs than the Gods are towards men. That's all."

What an actress! Arona thought indignantly. The Witch glanced back at her in full agreement. Several of the elders had tears in their own eyes, and were nodding agreement. One of them looked reproachfully at Arona.

The Dissident raised her hand. "It seems to me," she said calmly, "that the question is, who would be the better recorder?"

Arona raised hers. "Egil Elyshabet's he-daughter is a stranger, not reared to our tales and customs. He has often told me he wants to rewrite the scrolls to accord with his notions and customs, which his own mother tells me are like those of Huana

Guntirsdaughter. I say we examine the writings each of us has made, even the ones we have made privately, and you can also see how he stores and cares for them. I will give you all mine for inspection, even those I did as a child."

"Agreed," Dame Floree said at once. "Those among us who are lettered, come down to Records House with me." Then, to the visible dismay of many of the others, she added, "Dame Witch, will you join us? You have your letters, and you know the minds of women."

"Gladly," said The Dissident, wrapping her cloak about her.

The inspection was a long and tiring business. Several of Egil's scrolls were the records of his own people, and Arona wondered again, why not make him recorder for his own kind and leave the village records to her? She spoke her thought again.

Then the Eldest Mother Raula demanded, "Where is the record that Asta Lennisdaughter vanished with the traders and all her mother's goods?"

Arona gulped and had to admit, to her own horror, that with their mistress sick and Egil doing all the scribes labor, she had not thought to record this major scandal herself. She hadn't even remembered it! Her stomach turned over and her head slowly started to ache again.

Dame Floree unrolled one of Egil's private writings. "This seems to be a retelling of the tale you told in the cave, but from the viewpoint of Tsengan the Madman," she remarked.

Arona wiped her eyes and nodded. "He has often said the tale should read that way." She let that sink in with the elders, then led them upstairs.

Arona's scrolls were the accounts of her experiments and others, most of them made as a child. As she unrolled one, her eye fell on the last line. "This has been altered!" she cried in outrage.

The elders hurried over. She pointed an indignant finger at the last word. "These I did myself, and on each one wrote, 'I know this because I have done it with my own hands and seen it with my own eyes.' But look! This now reads, 'This is a farrago of utter nonsense.' " A choked sound came from Egil, who covered his mouth hastily, but the hairs on his upper lip still quivered. "Egil, this goes beyond a prank!" she raged. "You altered a scroll!"

"How do you know it was not your mistress, expressing her just opinion of what was within?" he asked innocently.

"What other scrolls have you altered?" Arona demanded. "Oh, Respected Elders, now we will have to look at them all!"

The Eldest Mother sighed and found a place to sit down, for her back and her feet ailed her, and her legs grew numb and ached after too much standing. Egil, solicitously, fetched her a cup of hot herb tea. Arona glanced at the Witch, who shook her head gently. Dame Floree sent Hanna to Mistress Gondrin's for food and ale. Another thought occurred to Arona and she glanced at the Witch in terror. The Dissident nodded.

"Elders," she remarked in her cool, pleasant voice, "this will last more than one day. Since there is a question of the scrolls being altered, I think Egil and Arona should each return to her mother's house to live until we have finished, and a guard be set on the records room."

"Agreed," said the Eldest Mother, with a sour look at Arona.

Back at Bethiah's carpentry, Arona could not sleep. Her bed was narrow and unfamiliar, and now belonged to one of Aunt Natha's little girls. There was no small red cat to curl up at her feet, and walk back and forth on her chest in the morning, nudging her to get up. The sisters and cousins had noisily begged to hear every detail about the case and life with Egil. Karmont Yelensdaughter, who showed signs of growing into a he-maiden, asked why she didn't just find out what Egil wanted and give it to him, in exchange for what she wanted?

"Because we want the same things," she said crisply, "Or in some cases, we want opposite things."

She pushed her chair back and excused herself from the

supper table. "Mother, Aunt Natha, Aunt Yelen, I'm really not hungry." She fled to the porch and began to cry, for Maris, for herself, for the records, and for all that had happened since Egil Elyshabetsdaughter had come to the village.

If Egil won this case, what could she do then?

She could live here and go to Records House each day to keep an eye on the records. Egil would not allow that, but could he stop her?

Suppose he did. Then she could steal the records and put them away somewhere for safekeeping. But where? And if the elders made him recorder to begin with, they might—they would—make her give them back.

Suppose she hid them some place they'd never find them, and refused to give them back? The worst they could do was exile her. Mad Bethiah the Murderer had been exiled. Grandmother Anghard had exiled herself, and Peliel Laelsdaughter, and Cousin Jommy. Asta Lennisdaughter had run away with the traders. That was one way to get away from a bully.

If only she'd had the chance to talk to Jommy! The records said he'd found exile lonely and scary, but not terrible. He was a weaver and had made his living without any trouble. Where could an exiled scribe make a living?

Suddenly she sat up in bed. The he-trader had told her where a scribe could live, and where the records would be safe from all meddling. Lormt. He had even shown her the way. Had the trader sensed she was up for exile? That was even more scary.

It wouldn't happen. The elders would never give the records to a stranger, to someone who changed them, to a liar and a bully who had wished the old recorder dead. Or they'd give him his and her theirs. That made so much sense, why didn't everybody agree to it at once? Why didn't they see it?

She turned over in her bed again. The blankets felt twisted and the pillow lumpy. Her hair itched; she got up and brushed it, slowly. They had to see it her way. If they didn't, the consequences were just too terrible to think about.

*   *   *

The days wore on, and the elders began to grumble. Reading the scrolls was a laborious job, and they began blaming Arona for the inconvenience. Full moon went by, and someone else took provisions to Jommy the Wise. Egil brought in one of the dogs Eina Parrasdaughter, and Parra Lorinsdaughter after her, was so famous for raising, and played with her by the hour, happily. He called her Fang. Arona's nerves were ragged.

Then Dame Birka called, "Arona! Come here and tell me if this has been altered?"

The girl ran to the priestess's side. One long, gnarled finger pointed to the last word on the last scroll of the Tale of Myrrha Foxlady, as written by her sisterfriend Warina Falconlady. One small accent mark had been changed. It was enough to change the meaning from, "I count this true because I had it from somebody trustworthy," to, "I count this false because I had it from somebody untrustworthy."

"Oh, yes," she said, her eyes filling with tears at the thought of this sacrilege. "It's been altered, and by one who would invalidate the tale. See?"

Egil, confronted, smiled confidently. "Are you sure? When did you last read this scroll?" he asked Arona.

"Over a year ago. What of it? I have memorized them all," she said indignantly. "Alter my writings for a jest, yes. Rewrite an old tale for your own amusement, yes. But alter what was written long ago? Oh, Egil, how could you?" she raged. "And what else have you done?"

"Found our mistress's private writings," he said, producing a parchment scrap with a flourish.

On it was written, "I am gravely disappointed in the flighty conduct of Arona Bethiahsdaughter, and henceforth name Egil Elyshabetsdaughter my true successor in Records House." It was formally signed "Maris Guidasdaughter, Recorder," and ended with the scrawled initial that was her mark. The hand was shaky, as befitted an invalid. Arona studied the writing closely, stunned.

"It's a forgery!" she shouted. "This is none of her writing, but his, no matter how much like hers it looks."

Raula Mylenesdaughter took Arona by the arms. "We have had just about enough of your spite, young lady. Whatever you have against the new recorder, pursue your feud elsewhere."

"Eldest," the Witch said softly, "he who altered one record, and wants his way at all costs, may alter another. You asked me here as Truthsayer; I say now, Arona is to be trusted; Egil is not."

The eldest released the girl and glared at the Witch with a hard, suspicious look. "Who can be trusted and who can not? You said you know the language and customs of these strangers, but do you know as much as you claim? Are you above the loves and hates of common women? I think not!"

The eldest turned and scowled at Arona. "Since the strangers came here, Arona has changed out of measure. Three times she has interrupted meetings. She has made one scroll with nothing but corrections upon it. She dabbles in magic instead of doing her work, and cannot see clearly where Egil's kind are concerned any more than you, Dame Witch, see clearly where Arona is concerned. Did you not come between those at Records House against the will of their mistress? Arona's hatred of Egil has caused strife among us which cannot be endured, and I fear, will continue to cause strife unless they are reconciled. As for the sort of recorder she'd be, we have the dying words of Mistress Maris herself on the matter! Can anyone here dispute a deathbed wish?"

The Witch started to speak, looked at the set faces around her, and fell silent.

Eldest Raula held out her spindle. "Egil Elyshabetsdaughter!" The boy stood suddenly tall and straight; she looked him in the eye. "Do you swear by your mother and your foremothers, by the Good Goddess, and in fear of the wrath of Jonkara, if you are made recorder, to copy the scrolls faithfully as written? To never alter any of them in the least, but to correct your own errors? To faithfully record all that happens in this village as it happens, omitting nothing and changing nothing?"

"I do."

The eldest stepped back. "Egil Elyshabetsdaughter has sworn an oath of great power to do these deeds no more. Arona, will you join him in this work as two sisters of one mother?"

The sky seemed like a crystal wherever Arona looked, and all sounds were sharp and clear. No remnant of feeling, whether fear or outrage, was left to her, only her mind, which saw all things plain. "Only as I said before, if he confines himself to his records and I to ours," she answered, drawing her shawl around her.

The eldest sighed again as Egil shook his head slightly. "Is there no hope of reconciling you two?" she asked then.

"Yes." Arona had thought of this, one last-ditch measure, two nights before. She had hoped never to have to use it. "I will cook you one last meal before," her voice shook, "before I move back to my mother's house. In exchange, I want my private writings, pen and ink, half the parchment I bought from the traders, and the little red cat you pay no heed to."

Egil smiled and shook his head. "No, indeed, my little Myrrha Foxlady. Those vicious old tales have put too many wild ideas in your charming little head. The cat and the writings are yours for the asking; the writing materials are not mine to give away."

"Accept the meal and end the feud," The Dissident said suddenly, "and I will eat it with you, to prove there is nothing lethal in it. Elders, for the sake of peace in the village, can we not spare Arona pen, ink, and a few scraps of parchment? It is hard, not to practice the only trade you know."

The eldest looked at Arona's stricken face, and wondered if she had been too unkind to the girl. "Done," she said promptly. Egil nodded acceptance.

Twelve

Long Gone

The fireplace at Records House burned high and bright, with colors of the sunset in its flames, and the faint aroma of incense coming from the evergreen logs. Egil leaned back in the room's best chair and sipped his ale slowly, half an eye on Arona. The girl smiled nervously back at him, and sipped her own ale even more slowly. A lifetime of training kept The Dissident from peals of unbecoming laughter.

By Egil's feet, Fang gnawed a good half of the meat Arona had nearly beggared herself to provide. The dog was having more pleasure in the steak than was the boy, growling and tugging and wagging her rear end until Egil had to laugh and scratch her ears. "But don't call him a her, Arona," he said with a grin. "There's but one she-pup in this room, and that's by your own choice. Where was the poison, in the sweet cakes? Or in the bread?"

"In the greens," she retorted, knowing how he hated them. Covering her mouth inadequately with one small hand, she stretched and yawned mightily. The dog's growls grew softer as she settled down to chew her meat in earnest. Little Red Pest jumped into Arona's lap and began purring softly. Arona tickled the cat's ears; the cat twitched the end of her tail. Arona took the rest of Egil's plate without a by-your-leave and set it on the floor; Little Red Pest jumped down and began licking it happily.

Egil raised his eyebrows and took a long draught of his ale. "You would gladly poison any man who got in your way," he conceded, "but not that stupid cat." He poured out a little into a small bowl and set it on the floor. The cat sniffed at it and lapped it experimentally. Arona seemed utterly unconcerned. The Witch grinned openly, and yawned and stretched herself.

"I could use some fresh air," she remarked. "Arona, could you show me the way to the, uh, the little house?"

"I guess," Arona mumbled ungraciously, rising and fetching her shawl. Egil watched both women intently as they left. As soon as the door closed behind them, he was down on the floor examining the dog and the cat. The puppy, her legs stretched out in front of her, growled softly in a digestive stupor. Her tiny tail moved back and forth. The cat passed under his chin, turned around, and backed up so that her tail was in his face. He stood up suddenly and sneezed, his nose full of cat hairs. He took his seat again and sipped his ale, musing.

Arona was up to something. He could tell that by watching her. The Witch knew it, too, and was forestalling whatever crazy scheme that silly girl had dreamed up. From the front of the house came a soft, low humming, as gentle as a lullaby. Somewhere in the distance, someone was singing a gentle old ballad of peace and love. Egil breathed deeply of the sweet-smelling, fire-warmed air. The cat jumped onto his lap; idly he petted her, then, one hand still on her fur, closed his eyes. Slowly his head fell to one side. Then he began to snore.

The huge, heavy knife Arona had borrowed from the butcher moved back and forth through the rope binding the records room door. Silently the Witch moved through the tall weeds surrounding the cellar, and laid an axe in her hand. Arona nodded thanks, looked around, and drove the axe into the rope—once, twice, three times. The rope parted under each blow, until only a few strands remained. The Witch held forth her jewel, which shone with a dim blue light invisible a finger's length away, brought out a pair of Great-aunt Lorin's scissors and snipped the last of the rope.

The huge wooden cellar door creaked loudly enough to wake the dead as Arona and the Witch pulled on it. Arona stopped short. The Witch kept pulling. "He'll sleep deeply at least till morning. More, if the fire keeps burning," she said softly. Hearing no sound from above, Arona put her back into the job. Egil had hung this door after the storm; did he know it would take two women to move it? He had been very proud of its sturdiness.

The door gave way, and the two women tiptoed down into the darkened cellar, their way lighted only by The Dissident's jewel. Arona went unerringly to the scroll shelves, chose a double handful of the records, unrolled them to remove the roller sticks, and rolled them back up inside each other. When three or four were rolled together as tightly as possible, she eased them into tight leather cylinders. "He won't bother with the 'who bore whom' scrolls or the quarrels and lawsuits," Arona whispered grimly. "Only the hero tales and the First Times tales."

One of their running arguments was Egil's insistence that someone must have taught the women to build houses, tame sheep and horses, and spear wolves. "Could you have done this?" he prodded her. "Could anyone you know? Well! There you have it! So, who taught them? I mean to discover this."

There was a quick dove call from the woods. Arona answered briefly and returned to her scrolls, until four cases were loaded. She popped out of the cellar, the Witch close behind. Leatrice Huanasdaughter waited with two saddled mules and another laden with bundles. The moon began rising in the west over the ruins of Falcon Crag. One of the mules hee-hawed. The Witch laid a hand on her head and the noise ceased.

Darann Mulemistress, leading a string of mules laden with all the contents of Witch House—the price of three mules—stopped beside them. "Something havey-cavey going on here," she let them know. "If it were anybody but Dame Witch, I'd call the elders."

"She wants a B-R-I-B-E," Leatrice translated cynically in her own tongue.

The Witch laughed softly. "Go home, good woman; you saw

nothing. I told you and many others it was time for me to go back to Witch Place."

Darann Mulemistress's eyes turned inward and her face grew abstracted. Then she clucked to her mules and slashed the lead animal with a tree branch. The mule train moved on.

Arona moved softly and carefully to the door of Records House. "Kitty? Little Red Pest? Kitty, kitty, kitty." The cat did not move. She started to slip through the door; her foot did not move. *The cat will not go,* the Witch's mindvoice told her firmly.

No! Arona cried silently, and mentally called the cat again. It stretched thoroughly and moved on into the back room.

Let her go, the Witch ordered. *She's her own mistress.* Arona had to accept that, and with one backward glance and *Farewell, kitty,* she slipped back out and found her mule. A bundle of sheepherders' trousers, jerkin, and poncho was tied to the saddle with a pair of boots on top. Quickly she slipped them on under and over her gown and cloak. She slid the butcher's biggest knife, now somewhat rope-scored, into her sash, and a smaller eating knife into her boot. She clucked to her mule and both women were off.

It was eerie, riding at night through the eastward trail. Her only light was the full moon, which gave no depth to the eternal shadows, and the stars. Dame Witch had extinguished the blue light from her jewel, saying it tired her as much as a long ride. "Why are you doing this?" Arona asked when they were well into the woods.

"You were telling the truth," The Dissident said simply. "I am sworn not to interfere, but, *in for a lamb, in for a ewe.*" She fell silent.

The sounds of the forest at night fell soft and strange on the girl's ears. She listened for the howl of Jonkara's Dogs, but they were silent that night. The mules plodded softly over the spring-damp ground. Arona, busy with her own thoughts, said little; neither did the Witch. It was hard to stay awake, even in the saddle, and soon she yawned and dozed off. Her mule put its head down to graze; only when it was full did they start again.

Near dawnlight they passed a tiny, rustic shrine with a painted wooden image of the good goddess. Under the rooftree was carved a ripened stalk of wheat and the richly laden branch of a fruit tree, interlaced. There the Witch called a halt, and tied their mules on the far side. The weary Arona unloaded her saddlebags and fetched water for the mules from the tiny stream behind the shrine. The two women wiped down the mules and entered the shrine with a prayer, the Witch with a spell also. The air inside smelled of fresh herbs and flowers; an enormous welcome awaited them.

Arona lifted her head. "Did you know? This was built by two of our own, Freyis Ingneldasdaughter and Ylsa Dorinesdaughter, and a Daughter of Gunnora, Ragny Grethirsdaughter, and thus was trade opened between our village and the outside world, only with the Daughters of Gunnora, until you came."

The Dissident laughed. "Arona, Arona, sleep first and history second." She yawned and stretched. "Good night, child."

Arona wrapped herself in her saddle blanket and lay down with her head on her saddle. "Good night," she said sleepily.

The path wound slowly upward, between two gently sloping mountainsides covered with forest, towards the rising sun. Arona, hopeless with spear or arrow because of her short sight, laid snares for small game when they camped the next night, catching an unwary coney. A day and a night they had slept in Gunnora's shrine, rising refreshed and strong. There was no pursuit.

"I thought so," said the Witch. "It takes much to move your people from their village."

"The stolen records are not 'much'?" Arona asked, aghast. The Witch shook her head compassionately.

They came to a fork in the road; the Witch unhesitatingly chose the northward road, deeper into the mountains. That evening, just before sunset, they passed a ruined village. Charred stones and an occasional doorframe, a fireplace and chimney standing alone in a field of rubble, spoke eloquently of fire and destruction. "The Turning?" Arona asked, awed.

"War, more likely," the Witch answered somberly. "This must be the village your new neighbors fled."

Arona's eyes searched the ruins and grew wide as she contemplated such anger. "Who could hate them so, Dame Witch?"

The Dissident found she had to explain nations and armies to the girl, scribe and chronicler though she was. The people across the sea, from whom she was descended, had been no nation, but a loose alliance of Great Houses on the edge of the Waste, linked by blood and common language and customs. They had not been peaceful: every spring after planting time, their men banded together for forays deep into other lands, returning just before harvest with treasures for their ladies, their mothers, and their sisters.

For each man rode under the banner of his mother's house, and bore her name. "As mothers are to daughters," Arona told The Dissident around the campfire that night, "so each he-defender was to his sister's he-child, and each he-child to his mother's he-sister. We, the women, owned and worked the land, and carried on all necessary trades and crafts, saving only weaponscraft."

And these raiding bands and loosely-linked houses had proven sadly easy, if brave and gallant, prey for the first invading nation with an army. The remnants of this once-noble people had fled the Waste, across the mountains and over the sea, under the leadership of the Falconlord, their customs altered out of recognition by long warfare and defeat. Arona closed her eyes in silent tribute to their fall, then said, "It comes to me, Dame Witch, that their many-times great-grandchildren still roam the wastes, riding to foray on the backs of their great tame horses, with the guardian spirit of their houses—whether lion or mountain cat, bear or boar or badger, wolf or fox or eagle or falcon, still painted on their shields, still defending them at need."

The Witch had a sudden vision of a young-old man riding

across the plains, a mountain lion painted on his shield, his man's form shadowed by the form of a great cat. Beside him rode a woman of her own pallid, dark-haired race, wearing an embroidered tabard of her own design, his companion and his wife. "I think they do," she said. "But their sisters are no more."

"I know," Arona answered, abstracted. "We are here."

For six days and more they rode, higher and higher along the winding path that broadened into a track holding two mules abreast. Among the sweet-smelling evergreens that lined the road appeared tall, slender white-skinned trees whose tiny new leaves quivered in every wind. Deep snow still lingered in the shaded places, and where the sun shone daily, they rode hoof-deep in mud. There began to be houses along the roadside, and there they would stop and ask the farmers' hospitality. Arona saw how the Witch was treated with deference, like an Elder; but she watched the men and women of the farmsteads together more.

She wore the clothing of a sheepherder, for they were on muleback, and tucked her hair up under a cap as they did. The farmers, men and women, would call her "lad" and speak to her one way; when she removed the cap, they called her "lass" and spoke to her another. As a "lad," she saw the daughters of the farms stare upwards at her through half-closed eyes, and speak in the tones of a dove to her; as a "lass," she heard their sons speak in the persuasive voices of Egil at his most charming. The Dissident did her best to explain love, marriage, and courtship to her, but hers was a virginal calling, and Arona's soul had been too early hardened by Falconer rape and Egil's charming, foul deceit. The girl's only concession to these things was, "I'll leave them to those that like them."

The road started to descend through the hills again, and The Dissident stared off into the distance, to the west. "I will have to leave you soon," she said. "Arona, you have not yet learned how to read people, and there are all sorts on the roads. Yet,

most are kind and decent. Go armed, and if you sense wrongness, do not stay to find out." She seemed to confer with folk
at a great distance, as in a trance. Then she pulled an amulet
from her neck.

"Take this to Lormt. It is of great antiquity, but of no use to
me. The runes upon it speak of caverns of the Old Ones. I found
it years ago in the hills east of Es, but am neither scholar. Nor
do I want any dealings with the elder races." She grinned,
crookedly. "Our own is trouble enough! But it might be they
will protect you from human evil. They, and your own wits and
strength." She hugged the girl, and was suddenly gone.

Arona stared at where she had been. Or had she been illusion? She felt more alone than she had ever felt before, and it
came to her then that she was hopelessly exiled from her family,
her village, Records House, and all the dear, familiar things she
had always known. A great bitterness then rose up in her
against Egil and all his kind, and the elders who heeded him
above her, and the outsiders who had taught him from the
cradle that he was as a princess, to have his way over all other
women.

"May he starve and freeze and be eaten by wolves," she
repeated Brithis's curse against Huana, "and Falconers find
him and take him to Falcon Crag to feed their birds. May
everyone else he meets deal with him as he dealt with me and
my mistress, and may he weep in the night for what he has lost."
Then she gave way to weeping.

Egil, now recorder of Riveredge Village, awoke with the thick
headache and sticky eyes of one who had been drugged. The
sun was low in the western sky, and the fire had long since
burned out. Fang was whining to go out, and had made a mess
by the door. The remains of last night's supper stood sticky on
floor and tabletop, flies swarming around it. They seemed to
take no harm from it. Had he drunk that much?

Arona was angry at him. She'd come around. She could no
more stay away from Records House—or from him—than a

horse could cease to run. He was the only one in the village she could talk to about things they both cared about; in time she'd come around. He had pushed her too far, too fast; he had known that while he was doing it. His accursed impatience! But a season or two of patient courtship should undo the harm. For he truly loved her, and if she had the sense the gods gave a goose, she knew it.

He yawned, stretched, and rubbed his sleepy eyes. Splashing cold water on his face, he went to inspect his new domain.

The rope on the records room door had been cut—again— and he knew whose work that was. No, she could never stay away from Records House. Several scrolls were missing. Not his private writings, and not the tiresome daily business of these farmwives and their crones, but the fascinating, obviously false, tales of heroism and invention, great deeds and desperate times, that she so loved. "Arona!" he called. "Arona?" He shook his head, combed his hair, ate a few bites, and set out for her mother's house.

Bethiah hadn't seen her. "Isn't she with you?" she asked, and plainly, believed. He strode down the path to the forge house, then broke into a run. None of her friends had the slightest idea where she was, but all thought she was with him. He broke into a cold sweat. "Arona!" he bellowed, running towards the caves. Several villagers followed him, with torches. There was no sign she was there, or had ever been there.

It was useless to ask the Witch; several villagers informed him that she had left the day before, as planned. "Didn't you know?" the eldest, Raula Mylenesdaughter, accused him.

Arona was gone, and half the village history with her. *Oh, well,* he thought, *the tales were patently untrue anyway. Women ruling a town. Were-raiders defeated by an army of common men. Falcon Goddesses taking vengeance on mortals.* The town was better off without such fantasies. *Arona!* he cried miserably. *Why did you have to do this? If I'd had any notion how much these silly tales meant to you, I'd have given them to you as a gift. Come back to me, and let me make it up to you.*

Thirteen

Toads

Share my fire?" The lone traveller who offered wistfully was roughly dressed, but as clean as a traveller could be on the road, and well-spoken. Gratefully Arona dismounted from the mule she had named Lennis, and approached the fire. She felt no sense of wrongness then, nor later as they talked. She spoke of her mission to Lormt, her and Egil's struggles for the recorder's office, and the decision of the elders. He spoke of his wife at home, his children, the daughters who were the light of his existence. She told tales, and they shared food and wine.

Then she took off her cap. His eyes widened. "A lass? Well! The gods have smiled on me beyond measure! I could use my bedroll warmed this night." She shook her head and retreated; he brought forth a length of fine lace from his pack. "You won't find me ungenerous," he coaxed.

"Thank you, but no," she said firmly, retreating further, loosening the knife. He sprang at her, one hand on her throat, the other holding a dagger he had drawn faster than her eye could follow. "What are you if not a whore?" he snarled. "A robber's wench, lying in wait with your band to prey on such as I?"

"A traveller! I told you!" she cried, struggling to free her knife with one hand, driving her nails into his hand with the other. "You bid me share your fire, and now play the rutbeast and the bully with me? Oh, Lennis was right about your kind. Our miller," she explained, "and never right about anything before. But, oh. . . ."

"If you didn't want this," he asked, honestly bewildered, "why did you show me you were a lass? I thought it meant— what any man would have thought it meant. How old are you? And what's your real story?"

"Fourteen," Arona choked out, "nearly fifteen, and this Egil I spoke of, he wanted—he tried—I ran away—"

The man retreated. "For that, I am sorry. But if you mean to keep on with this mad course, keep to your boy's disguise until you reach your aunt or whoever you are fleeing to." He sheathed his knife and sat back down. "You need not fear me any more. I believe you, and, great gods, I have daughters." He shook his head in pity. "Forced to choose between a lustful master and going unprotected on the road. So might it be for them if my ventures ever failed. What's your name?"

"Arona Bethiahsdaughter." She sat down well away from him, but accepted the drink he offered as apology. Why did he look at her with such compassion? "Dame Witch, who rode with me a way, told me much, but," her voice shook, "not the whole. But this is a land where little children play at self-defense."

"The wars," he agreed. "No, your Witch companion—it was prudent of you to take service with her. Brave lass!—is protected from what you have had to endure. Sleep now," he said gently. "With your knife in your hand if need be. I will not harm you. But most other men—you do well to go armed."

She slept, but warily, and woke still tired. From now on, she would ride only with women, or alone.

The rough, bearded men around the campfire chuckled as the youthful storyteller lowered a clear, unbroken voice dramatically. ". . . And the foxwolf cried out in amazement, 'Sister? Why are you calling me Sister, you foolish little hen?' And as she spoke," the storyteller paused, "the hen ran out of the foxwolf's mouth, and got away. And never did the foxwolf get one bite of the little brown hen!"

The men chortled, and their children clapped and cheered.

"More! More!" shouted a young maid from the family group that clustered to one side of the campground.

The storyteller called Aaron Bethiahson rose, bowed to the women and children, and emptied the last of the pack mule's burden into the saddlebags of the riding mule called Lennis. Ride with women or alone. What a fool's vow, in a land where men abounded on the roads, and no woman rode alone except as bait in a trap as the man had said! And those who rode with men had no say in anything and could not be dealt with, for which bile rose in Arona's throat every time.

The moon had waned and waxed again since she had left Riveredge Village. The broad valley of the river Es lay behind her, and the mountains wherein Lormt lay, ahead. Wearily, eagerly she looked back one last time at her first taste of the lands of the outsiders. Some had been kind, and some, cruel. Some drove her from their doors as a vagrant; others shared their last crust. All had been scarred by the bitter marks of war, their homes in ruins, their fields fallow, the very stones themselves tumbled and scorched by the enormous energies let loose the night of the Turning.

The bargain sealed with the caravan master, she fingered the copper and silver coins in wonder the next morning. Such small, plain things to be worth so much in trade! And such an elegant concept, in a land too big for simple barter. Coinage; moldboard plows; tame horses with metal rings upon their feet; people who lived by their trades alone and not as farmers; and the women Cousin Jommy's tales mentioned, who lived by letting men play the rutbeast with them. Men who practiced with her at the art of self-defense, thinking her a boy, who would never have taught the girls who needed it more.

Arona shivered, and fingered her butcher knife again. The mountains ahead, with their predators in fur, would be safer than the cultivated lands, with their predators in men's clothing. She scratched the old pack mule behind the ears one last time and patted her muzzle. "Goodbye, Raula," she said. The mule's new owner smiled at her indulgently; Raula brayed loudly. The children laughed again, and the caravan moved west. Arona turned Lennis's nose to the northward path, into the mountains.

Several days she rode, eating lightly of her provisions, living off the forest as the sheepherders were taught to do. She sheltered from the rain in huts of green branches, covered with a tightly-woven blanket, and listened to the familiar sounds of the night woods alertly, but without fear. Then, in the bright blaze of midday, she heard muffled hoofbeats in the hills to her right.

This one place, the steep dropoff to her right and the sheer cliffs to her left had broadened out into a meadow, where cattle grazed and wildflowers bloomed knee-deep. At the back of the meadow, against the face of the cliff, a tumbledown log cabin stood. The porch rail alone was new, and long enough to tie several horses to.

She rode a slow mule and not a fast horse. Looking to the left and the right, she urged Lennis along the path with all speed. Ahead on the path the hills rose steep around her on both sides as the trail wound into a pass between two peaks. Turning around, she saw a dust cloud and picked out the vague shapes within. One, two, three mounted riders, far down the trail, and moving fast. She drew her knife.

She knew now she could give a good account of herself with the weapon, but the odds were great now. If only she'd brought a bow and some arrows! But, no, what use had a shortsighted maid for distance weapons? Better rely on her snares.

Dismounting quickly, she rummaged in the saddlebag for her rabbit snares, all the while casting terrified glances down the road to where the riders were gaining on her. She tied a snare between two white-barked willow trees, then jammed the others in her pocket and struck Lennis on the rump viciously. The mule brayed and headed down the path at a mule's fastest pace.

Arona's amulet began to hum. She took it in her hand as she ran down the path, desperately seeking a hiding place. If she could see one, any other person could, for her sight was short and most hunters' sight was long. *Dame Witch,* she mentally prayed as she ducked off the path and into the trees. *Power behind this amulet. Save me, and save the scrolls, or all this has been for nothing. Jonkara, Falcon Goddess, Avenger of Women, save me.*

As she ran and searched, she attuned her mind to the amulet. It hummed louder, and began glowing softly, the scarlet of the mountain leaves in Falcon Moon. A deeper humming came from the sheer rock face ahead and to her left. The sound intensified, and became a rumbling like thunder. A huge slab of mountain granite slid back like a curtain, and a cave mouth gaped behind it. Lennis the mule plodded up beside her and brayed her rebellion at the musty, tangy air that came from within.

Arona edged closer and closer to the cave mouth. An eerie blue light that seemed partly too bright to be seen by human eyes shone deep inside. Outside, the bandits' hoofbeats raced closer and closer. Only a moment she weighed her terror of the unknown against her certain fate if she lingered. She took a deep breath, and shoved her mule through the curtain of light, following swiftly before she changed her mind. Unless they were most unusual bandits, they would not follow her here.

She was in a huge vault, deep underground, lit by the same blue light that protected the cave. A faint, crisp smell touched her nostrils, as if the place were preternaturally clean. There was no visible source of either smell or light. The mule laid back her ears and would go no farther; with a sigh, Arona looked around for a place to tether her and found none.

Oh, Jonkara's droppings, I'll stay, a voice grumbled in her mind as plainly as her own breathing. It was a rough, steady, stubborn, ill-tempered voice, and long-familiar to her. In gratitude she thought back, *Good mule!* and walked down through the vault, staring about her in wonder.

Row upon row of pallets lined the vault. On each pallet was a living being, shielded by a cylindrical covering of the same light that protected the cave. Many of them were human; some were not. Most of the humans were men; some were women. She lingered long over one, a redheaded young woman in a sleek cloth-of-silver suit that fitted her like a second skin. The woman wore boots and a plain silver helmet and carried a long silver lance of odd shape that Arona knew, without being told, was a weapon of great power. The recorder frowned. Was it right to rouse such a powerful warrior and use such a great weapon against a pack of common thieves? As well kill a mouse with a meat cleaver!

She looked up and down the rows, noticing that some of the men looked like those very bandits she had left outside. When had it come to her that she must wake somebody here? And for what purpose?

It came to her then. *Wake the one you need the most.*

She stood among them, eyes closed, concentrating, and finally admitted, *I don't know which one I need the most, but trust You to do so.* For now she realized the cavern itself was sentient in some way she did not understand. Moreover, she could trust it. That caused her a moment's panic so intense she nearly lost control, for what better bait for a trap than that feeling of absolute trust?

The cavern seemed to laugh at her, a dry chuckle, and it directed her to a small side room where she could take care of her needs, wash her face, and drink from an artificial spring of cold, delicious water. *Unfortunately, my supply of human food is quite limited,* it advised her. *The War That Sealed The East put a great burden on my facilities. This one seems a little less destructive.* It sighed. *Low-tech wars always are, but for disease, famine, and such things.*

"Who, what are you?" she said out loud.

"A refuge." The cavern seemed to be thinking. Then, by subtle shifts of the light around her, it led her to a pallet from which a frightening, repulsive creature was rising. The creature was short and squat, with grey lumpy skin. It was clad in some sort of harness and very little else. Arona's guts churned within her.

The creature rose and looked at her steadily through huge yellow eyes set far to either side of its head. Its wide lipless mouth moved, though the cavern gave her the sense of its words.

"Hello. I'm Krakoth, once recorder of Grimmerdale."

Grimmerdale! The Daughters of Gunnora had tales about the Toad People, and Arona was now looking at one. Nay, conversing with one. Trying to keep the bile from her throat, she extended her hand. "Honored Dame Toad, I'm Arona, once Recorder of Riveredge Village."

Krakoth blinked, upper and lower eyelids meeting. "Well met, Ape Woman."

"Ape Woman!" Arona's fear gave way entirely to anger.

"You call me Dame Toad," Krakoth pointed out. Arona realized then that they were speaking her own native language, and in that tongue, she had accepted the hideous being as people. Well? Was she not? The Toad Woman spoke, and practiced Arona's own trade.

"My apologies," she managed to stammer. "It is the only name I know your people by." But of course, if they had such a homely thing as a Recorder, they must have many of the other homely and familiar things of her own kind. *Ape People,* she thought, and suddenly laughed out loud at the picture of her relatives and neighbors in fur, with protruding muzzles and little stub tails. With it came a parallel picture of toad people herding sheep—what *were* a Toad Village's sheep?—and tending gardens, toad mothers and toad children. . . .

Krakoth chuckled. "That's the mammal way," she pointed out. "Our tadlings fend for themselves until they are of an age to learn speech and civilized customs. Then we adults choose among them and take them into our houses as servants until they are old enough, or settled enough, to strike out on their own."

Remembering certain women in her village, she ventured, "And I'll wager some of them are kept obedient, tending their foster parents long past adulthood and into old age."

Ruefully, Krakoth answered "Quite right! All adults try it. But we have a tradition, that younglings as they come of age must rebel, often violently, against adults and all they stand for, for about a year. Then they are drafted into our army and lead a totally regimented life for two years. Upon discharge, they take their places among the adults and begin the cycle anew. But enough of that. How may we do business?"

Arona, finding the Toad Peoples' rites of passage bizarre beyond human understanding, wrenched her thoughts away from contemplating them. "I have lost the road to Lormt and was beset by bandits. That's the need that drove me in here. If I have a deeper need, and the cavern seems to think so, it tells me you are the person to meet that. How you can get me past the bandits and back on the road, I don't know."

"And what do you offer me in exchange for my help?" Krakoth asked with muted eagerness.

"What do you want?" Arona answered with the practicality of a trader.

Krakoth mused a while, then seemed to throw bargaining and haggling to the winds. "Are the people outside still as suspicious of non-ape life forms as they were the last time we met?"

Arona considered this. "The common person, yes. I don't know about the scholars. All the tales they tell of your people are tales of fear."

"We took one of your young adults for experimental purposes," Krakoth admitted dryly. "It was bulging with young in the manner of mammals; the Gormvin decided to see if a few adaptations could be performed and a mindlink established between our races. None of us expected the—person—to react with such violence, nor to cling to the tadling despite all. What bargain did it make with its partner in this adventure, that the partner joined it in such a desperate deed? It did not seem wealthy."

Arona nearly burst with disbelieving laughter and horror. Whoever or whatever the Gormvin were, they had so little

understanding of human beings one could almost call them
innocent, not evil. Were such deeds commonly performed
among their own kind? Almost certainly they were.

It came to her then, with wry amusement, that as the ways of
men were to her, so were the ways of toads to men. Was this the
lesson Dame Cavern had to teach her? The cavern seemed to
chuckle in agreement.

"So you want to understand human beings."

"If you will. In return, I will give you a hand weapon and a
mask of illusion. The weapon does not kill unless you deliberately set it so. It stuns the victim, who wakes up with a horrible
sensation of pins and needles all over its body until full sensation returns. It is quite a deterrent to possible attack. Your
people are not scientifically advanced enough to take it apart
and discover its secret, or I would not trade it for so little; but
I have others."

"The mask of illusion?"

"Creates the image of a horrible monster." Krakoth thought
a minute. "It now projects a human bandit. I will reset it to
project my own face, but made frightening and horrible." She
deliberately made a face, in the manner of a child trying to scare
another child. Arona realized suddenly she was seeing the toad
being as a mild-mannered woman of books and scrolls, much
like herself—and she imagined that human beings, Ape Folk,
who did not know her, would also see her that way. She laughed
suddenly. "Your own face is strange enough to them they will
not look twice," she assured her. "Fear of the alien is still quite
common around here."

Krakoth laughed, the gurgling croak her throat was designed
for, and nodded. She made some adjustments to the device and
gave it to Arona. In form, it was a huge pendant or locket-
necklace. "Don't use it forever," she warned. "The power
source will run down in a few cycles of the moon. Same with the
weapon, but sunlight will recharge it if you give it enough time.
All day, perhaps, at most."

Dame Toad settled comfortably on a bench designed for her

kind. One designed for Arona extended itself from the wall across from Krakoth's. "Let me read these records," she said, "and that will be payment enough."

The hour was late and Arona was hungry. Excusing herself, she went back to the place her mule was tethered, pitying the poor thing being kept that long. Had it fouled the cavern's clean floor as the hoofed kind do? She found it in a blue-lit metallic stable, constructed from the cavern walls exactly as her seat and Krakoth's had been built, munching on a load of dry grass and sipping from a standing pool of water in a niche in the wall. If this were illusion, it was remarkably complete. The floor was clean.

She found her saddlebags and pulled forth a cloth-wrapped bundle. "Cavern. Can Krakoth eat any of this?" she asked.

"Try it," the cavern advised. She took the bundle and the scrolls back to the benches, where Krakoth had been provided with a fishy-smelling stew. They agreed the others' food would take more getting used to than such a trade was worth, fell to, and a pallet extended itself from the wall for Arona.

Panic struck. Was this how the others had been entrapped here? Lay down on a pallet, sleep, and wake up when a stranger wakes you, perhaps hundreds of years into the future? "Cavern," she called. "I do not wish to sleep more than one night! When the sun rises outside, I wish to waken."

"Understood," the cavern answered dryly, a little disappointed, it seemed to her.

Three, four, five days and nights went by. Krakoth not only read her scrolls, but scanned them with a large jewel held to her right hand by a leather band. Lights within the jewel danced with a life of their own. She in turn read the records of the Toad People, shown in moving pictures and a strange script projected onto the cavern wall. She could not read Toad; the cavern had to interpret.

It was an odd, alien way of life, and strangely barren, it seemed to her, but in truth they were clever artificers. Grimmerdale was one of the smallest of their villages, but almost entirely centered around the Gormvin, where strange things were done with their own folk, human beings, other life forms, and even the rocks themselves. Yet, Toad Folk lived there, and took their food from huge halls where nothing else was shown, and watched pictures move upon their walls of an evening, or played games of sorts that seemed entirely concerned with mutual rankings and scorekeeping. Some of the toads raced noisy machines at very high speeds over rough country roads, often crashing them into each other or against rocks or trees, or fought each other for pleasure.

"Grimmerdale, on our side of the barrier, is a very small town," Krakoth apologized. "There is little for the tadlings to do except such things as you see here. If you work for the Gormvin, you live a comfortable life, with all your needs taken care of; if not, well, it's a small town. Many go elsewhere. But it's the only facility doing research on Ape Folk, uh, human beings, in the area, and I'm a bit of a humanologist myself." At last she yawned and stretched. "A pity you can't take our records to Lormt, but they have no way to read them."

"I will take copies anyway, and maybe one day they will."

"To transcribe them would take longer than you have, Arona," Krakoth said, a little disappointed. "However, I'll give you a film canister against that very day. Guard it well."

Arona put forth her hand, then decided Krakoth deserved more. Catching the Toad Woman in a surprise hug, she bade her farewell as a woman of Riveredge would to a close friend.

Krakoth grunted and wiped her face. "Whew! Human customs are strange indeed! No offense, Arona, I can see you meant well, but do not ever do that again."

Egil, she thought suddenly. *I said those very words to Egil. Under the same circumstances. No wonder he was angered.* But it was too late; she had made him an enemy and he had made her one.

Krakoth looked up suddenly. "You have been calling me by the names used for egg-layers. I am not. Let us be precise. I am one of those sperm-sprayers you have come to hate and fear."

Then it chuckled. "I have adopted the pedantry of the Labs," it confessed. "Sound body, prosperity, and many clever tadlings to serve you, Arona."

"The same to you, Dame—he-Dame—Krakoth," Arona called back. She retrieved her mule, thumbed off the safety catch on her stunner, and went forth to face the bandits.

They had not waited for her. The sun was high in the sky as she rode back down the trail to Lormt. She mulled over the lesson of the cavern. It was not at all obvious. It plainly concerned the toad in some way. How?

Krakoth had been, at the end, a friend, for all its strange customs and beliefs and looks. For all that, she would not let a daughter of hers fall into the hands of the Gormvin. Did she hate the Gormvin? No, they had done nothing to her. Would she if they did? Or were they acting according to their own needs and nature? Could they be taught better? Would they accept such teaching? But she was not likely to meet any more Toad People; the lesson the cavern set for her must be far greater than that.

Strange beings, strange looks, strange customs. All of these, she had dealt with this spring, and would deal with again. In what way? With hate and fear, as if all men were wolves?

Great-aunt Eina's words came back to her. *Dogs are the daughters of wolves, but we took them in and reared them properly, and now they are part of our families.* A wolf stole sheep to feed her young, and not from any evil will. Who could hate the wolf? It was only acting according to its nature. For all that, though, a woman had to guard her sheep and her daughters from the wolf's hunger.

Arona's mind ranged over the men and women she had met on the outside. The witch had said, "Where you sense wrongness, flee." She had not spoken of vengeance. "Give every dog one bite," she said of those who did not seem predatory. "Not two."

Not all men are wolves, Arona realized, *and not all women are people.* Was that the lesson of the cavern and the toad? That all beings must be dealt with for what they were, according to their own needs and nature? That this meant guarding against danger, without hate or needless fear? Somehow that seemed such a simple lesson even a small girl could understand it. Such a lesson would stand her in good stead among strangers. She would need that at Lormt.

Wondering what lay ahead, she rode around a steep switchback. Surely she had not been this high in the mountains before? There, below her, the entire mountain range lay at her feet, shrouded in a blue-grey haze. She lifted her eyes. Ahead of her, the great stone complex that was Lormt sprawled. Heart rising in her throat, she urged her mule onward, and through the gate.

Interlude

That is what she brought us." There was disappointment in Nolar's voice. "Oh, I have copied all the earliest legends. But the daily records of that prison-town, what are they to us, save a curious bit of sidelight in history?"

She shifted in her chair, and impatiently brushed back a wandering wisp of hair which fluttered against her cheek in the warmth of a new spring breeze. "Though it is true that now I can even better understand her—" she added. "Once I thought my lot, until I met Ostbor, was a hard one, but I think I was blessed not to have been born in a Falconer village."

"Not all villages are alike," I said. "Surely Mountain Hawk and his men could not have been so feared and hated. I know little of their ways, and that hued by rumor and gossip. But of men I know more and he was not so cruel, nor could any under his ordering be."

Nolar hesitated and then nodded. "That may indeed be true. There are all manner of men—my father and Ostbor—yes, as winter and spring those two differed. But also there may be more of worth in her accounts than I first thought. Those who may have to deal with her kind in the future will have a guide. So—" she looked a little happier, "at least all this may serve some good purpose in days ahead."

"Change works. Two days ago when I rode with Derren, to see the newly planted forestland he is so justly proud of, I met a Falconer—"

"A messenger from the Lady Una, from Mountain Hawk?"

"On the contrary, a young man who has chosen his own change and made it well, though it was not easy. He has a wedded wife and a daughter, and finds life, if strange, very pleasant. They have settled in a village not too far away and he is a hunter for the people there. I would call him a happy man and we should arrange a meeting between Eirran, his very capable—and beloved—wife and Arona so she can see that change need not come harshly. His name is Yareth, and he spoke of visiting us with his family later in the season. His wife is a student of herb lore and would like advice for that."

Only that visit was not to be, because the Dark reached out to blot out the brightness for that eager young hunter, and from his own despair, rage, fear and triumph came . . . but that was the end of his story before it struck at us.

FALCON MAGIC

by
Sasha Miller

One

I

$\mathcal{E}$irran tied a clean cloth around the compress on Belda's forehead. Unconsciously, she tightened her lips into a straight, disapproving line. Rofan had really gone beyond any limit of decency this time. One of Belda's eyes was swollen shut—the result of a blow from Rofan's fist—and Eirran shuddered to think what had caused the lump on Belda's forehead. This was the third time in the two weeks Yareth had been gone that she had been called to Belda's cottage to repair the damages after Rofan had beaten her. Now, at the end of winter, when food was running low and tempers running high, everyone was a little on edge from hunger. Everyone, that is, who hadn't had the foresight to put away stores of grain, dried or salted meat, and dried fruits and vegetables. Or who, like Rofan, ate like the glutton he was when it was available and had to go without when it was not. And who then angrily turned to beating his wife when she could no longer set food in front of him.

Didn't the fool realize that Belda and the children were even hungrier than he was, that they stinted themselves trying to keep the man fed and satisfied, so his temper would not overflow and drown them in the flood? Eirran shook her head and clicked her tongue against her teeth. No, obviously he did not. This time Rofan had been very late coming home from the distillery he and his cronies kept outside the village. As far as Eirran could determine, he'd beaten Belda not only for offering him thin soup to eat, but also for failing to have it hot and waiting for him. It was a good thing he had left the cottage then, presumably to return to his still and drink himself unconscious, or she would have been sorely tempted to tell him what she thought of him and risk a beating herself.

Far better I should have called three or four of the village men instead, she thought. But it wouldn't do any good now. It never does when he's so drunk he can't even remember.

"He doesn't mean it," Belda said defensively. "He is always sorry after."

"That doesn't change anything." Right, she thought. When he sobers up, he'll be sorry. And then there's no use in beating a sorry dog. He gets out of it at every turn, except when Yareth is in the village. Eirran selected some dried herbs from the sacks in her carry-bag and began measuring out individual doses and wrapping them in bits of cloth. "You still wind up with injuries. It's a wonder he didn't kill you this time. One of your teeth is loose. Here, make tea of this leaf each morning for five days, and drink it as warm as you can stand it." She took a small bowl and pestle out of her carry-bag, and a jar of solidified sheep's grease carefully refined and strained until it was nearly white in color. Eirran used it in all sorts of preparations for the skin. Her concoctions for relieving chilblains were so popular she was running low on the oily base. But clearly, Belda needed the salve far more than another woman needed a cream to improve her complexion. She measured out other herbs and began pulverizing the leaves and dried flowers. The scent rose, pleasant and comforting. "Do you have anything to put this in, after I've mixed it?"

"Yes." Belda motioned to Erman, her oldest. The boy came forward awkwardly, half afraid, half curious. "Go get that jar from the time before, when the Wise Woman was here. You know where it is."

The boy bobbed his head and vanished through the tattered curtain that served both as door and wall, separating his parents' sleeping area from the rest of the tiny, rundown cottage.

"I'm no Wise Woman," Eirran said, sighing. She began blending the dust-fine herb fragments into the sheep fat. "Back in Karsten, old Juvva didn't teach me half what I need to know, just in order to look after the few people here in Blagden."

"You're the only one we have, and you're learning more every day. I don't know what we—what I would have done without you."

Eirran could feel herself blushing under Belda's praise. And yet, she knew better than anyone that the woman was right. If she hadn't always been available, Belda might well have been dead by now, from one of Rofan's beatings.

It was a too-familiar story. Blagden was a small village, its inhabitants mostly decent people able to survive from one winter to the next if they were careful and frugal with their resources. Their sorest lack was missing the luxury of having their own fully qualified healer, and having to rely on someone only half-trained like Eirran. And there were always men like Rofan, to make good times bad, to make bad times worse. Eirran wondered how they had managed before she and Yareth had come.

"Here's the jar, lady," Erman said. Shyly, like a wild thing, he slipped it onto the table beside her. He had a sharp, wild smell, like a ferret, and he skittered away again as if wary of coming too close.

Perhaps he had learned better, through contact with his miserable excuse for a father. Eirran sighed. There were other children in the room, all sizes, from Erman on the verge of manhood to a baby crawling about and playing in the mess on the floor, all as dirty and most as smelly as Erman. They lined the room, staring at her out of wide and wary eyes. They reminded her of half-tamed little animals, their hair long and tangled, their faces grimed, their expressions suspicious. A girl, not quite a year younger than Erman, watched her from behind a pile of unwashed and malodorous clothing. Eirran thought of her own immaculate home. At the best of times, Belda was scarcely a tidy housekeeper, what with all the children she had to look after. When she was ill or recovering from injuries, things grew much worse. The older children could lend a hand, if they just would. But then, Eirran thought, I shouldn't be so quick to judge. Perhaps Rofan had beaten all the spirit out of everyone in the cottage.

"Come here," she said to the girl. The child just stared, as if she were lacking in wit, or perhaps Rofan had hit her too hard once too often and scrambled her brains. Eirran wondered if she should command, or coax. "Come here," she said again, making her voice soft. Very cautiously, the child moved a step closer. Eirran held out her hand and the child flinched. But gradually, she moved nearer until she stood next to Eirran's chair. Eirran put the jar of herb cream in her hand and the girl had to grasp it lest it fall.

"What is your name?" Eirran said.

"Rawfa," the child whispered.

"Well, Rawfa, do you think you can help your mother with her bandages when it's time to change them and put on more medicine?"

The girl brightened. She clutched the jar of salve. "Oh, yes, lady, I can do that. I've watched you each time you come to tend to Mama, and I think I know just how it's done."

"Very good. There's something else you can do to help her, you know."

"What?" The girl looked up at her, a spark of interest in her dull eyes.

Eirran gestured around the dirty room. The air was stale, heavy with the presence of too many unwashed and malodorous people crowded into too small a space. "You could pick up things and put them away. You and the little ones could even help with the washing. You could give the young ones a bath, and have one yourself. You could sweep the floor."

The spark went out and Rawfa's shoulders slumped. "No use. Pa just comes home and messes it up again. And sometimes he's sick. It's the drink, Mama says."

Eirran had smelled it when she first entered, overriding all the other foul odors—the splatters of vomit on the floor, scarcely wiped away.

"You have to try," she said firmly. "What other people do is their business. But what you do is altogether different. You cannot allow yourself to let go, to slide down into dirt and despair. Your father is not himself sometimes. Then he is ill and his sickness makes him do things he wouldn't do if he were well." Eirran pushed down the feeling she was telling the child a lie. Even if Rofan had never touched a drop of the harsh liquid he and a couple of men very like him made from grain that would be better used to feed their families, he might have behaved much the same. Eirran was no stranger to spirits; she had grown up serving tables in her uncle's public house in Karsten on the main road between Kars and Verlaine. She knew good brew from bad, and knew what sort of men used it to excess, what sort used it merely to ease the harsh outlines of their daily lives. Rofan was a brutal man, and the drink only gave him the excuse he sought in order to exercise all the cruelty in his nature.

She sighed. At least Rofan and his cronies didn't make bad liquor, the sort that could blind a person, or even kill. She wasn't at all above keeping a jug of Rofan's brew herself, on a high shelf in the cabinet behind her work-table. As a stimulant it was excellent, when used in small quantities. And a little poured into a cut or wound virtually eliminated the danger of infection. It never ceased to amaze her that something with such beneficial applications could be so misused—the way Rofan did.

"Come," she said briskly. "And you other children as well. We can make a game of it. Each one of you pick up something that is out of place, and put it where it belongs. We'll have this cottage tidy in no time!"

Under her insistent urging, most of the children began moving reluctantly or resentfully, according to their natures, but doing as she ordered. Some, however, just stood, staring vacantly.

"You're so good with children," Belda said. "I'm not.

Strange that I have to go and have a new one every year, while you've got just the one."

Eirran peered at Belda closely. "You don't mean—"

"Yes. I'm carrying again. I think it was the prospect of having still another mouth to feed that set Rofan off this time."

"As if he feeds the ones who are already here." Eirran bit her tongue but not in time to call back the words. She had to leave, now, before she found herself saying even worse. "Here, Rawfa, you're in charge until your mother gets better," she said briskly. "You see to it that things are kept tidy. And you help your mother with the little ones. You all have to work together."

"Yes, lady," the girl said.

But Eirran knew in her heart that the words were just that— words. Those who lived in this tiny cottage on the far side of the village came into this world beaten down, already defeated by what life had to offer. She felt sorry for the new one, so tiny he or she didn't even show as a bulge in Belda's weary body.

Eirran wished with all her heart that Yareth were back from his spring hunting trip. The stern Falconer who was now her husband brooked no nonsense from anyone, man or woman. The first time she had gone to treat Belda after Rofan had beaten her, Yareth had sought him out and had given the man a sound thrashing from which he did not recover for a week. Now Rofan dared beat Belda only when Yareth was absent from the village, and he seemed determined to make up for missed opportunities at such times.

She gathered her things into her carry-sack and left, declining the offered guest-cup of watery broth. "Save it for the children," she advised Belda. "Or for Rofan, when he returns. I'll be back to see you tomorrow, and bring another mixture that's good for women who are carrying. And maybe a little flour, if I can spare it. Use it to make something for the children."

"Thank you, lady," Belda said humbly. "Thank you, Wise Woman."

II

The day was already fading as Eirran trudged along the path leading back to the warmth and cleanliness of their cottage. She missed Yareth with a pang that cut through her like the early spring wind. She slipped and caught herself before she fell. The footing was uncertain; with the coming of dusk the mud was beginning to freeze and a skin of ice to form on the puddles. She looked forward to the dish of hot stew Jenys was certain to have waiting for her. Only six years old, Jenys was one of those rare children who seemed to have been born grown up. From the time she could toddle, she had enjoyed "helping Mama." Eirran loved her as much as she loved Yareth; the two of them were her entire life.

In spite of Rofan and the occasional unpleasantness like the medical emergency that had drawn Eirran from her snug, warm home, Blagden was a pleasant little village and Eirran was happy enough to be living here. Most of the year she and Yareth made do quite well. Only the winter's end was hard to bear, when food stores dwindled and bitter nights gave way to chill, dank days belying the start of spring.

The two of them had traveled a long way since their excursion into the Barrier Mountains seeking the ruins of the Eyrie. When they had first met, Yareth had had some idea of rebuilding the Falconers' ancient stronghold and, driven by his dream, had stolen Eirran to become the mother of a new generation of Falconers.

She had hated him at first, and felt contempt for someone who would steal her away in her sleep, but she had never feared him. The man who had sat the previous evening in the shadows of her uncle's public house on the road between Kars and Verlaine, watching her as she worked, had attracted her interest, as she had his. But Eirran was never one to accept her fate tamely; when she discovered she had been bound, gagged, blindfolded and abducted, she all but screamed the broken mountains down around his ears the moment he removed the gag. Even his falcon, Newbold, fled from the noise. She stopped screaming only when she got the hiccups, as she always did when upset or angry. They had had their first quarrel then. He had expected her to tend the camp; she angrily retorted that as she was his captive, it was his responsibility to look after her instead. Eventually, after a day of stony silence, they reached an uneasy peace. Afterwards, as they traveled they made the best of a poor situation between them until they actually got into the mountains and found themselves under attack by a creature so horrible Eirran was glad she had been thrown to the ground and stunned before she could get a look at it.

They took refuge in a narrow cave, the four of them—Eirran, Yareth, Newbold and the Torgian horse, Rangin. And there in that shelter—despite the chill of the evening breeze Eirran grew warm at the memory—Yareth had stripped her half-naked to examine her bruised shoulder. They touched, moved closer, and then without either of them willing it, they made love. Later, the monster found their trail, tearing at the cliff face trying to get at them; they huddled together in darkness, waiting, and both had been certain they would die that night. He gave her his hunting knife. Without speaking, they knew how they would make a clean death. Eirran would kill the Torgian, Yareth the falcon. Then, as he held her, she would die by his hand and he would kill himself with the same weapon before the terrible beast could touch any of them. Mercifully, morning had come and driven away the beast before they must put their plan into action.

Knowing what sort of monster now inhabited the mountains where the Eyrie had been, they had to depart. They could not fight it alone, and the rest of the Falconers were now scattered to the winds, their society as fragmented as the riven mountains where they had once lived.

An experience like this forges strong bonds between a man and a woman. Even the falcon accepted her, coming at last to ride on the special Y-shaped fork on the saddle horn close to where she rode in the circle of Yareth's arms, and the horse, Rangin, allowed her to feed and brush him. There was no question that Yareth and she would stay together even though Yareth's dream of rebuilding the Eyrie was now for naught. Eirran refused to return to the public house where her uncle had begun to urge her to bring in a little extra coin by being "nice" to the men. Her dream had always been of a cottage, clean and tidy, with a baby in a cradle and a cat purring on the hearth; only her fantasy now seemed to have any chance of coming true.

They made their way to Estcarp, rejecting holding after holding as they passed through. Either it was a forsaken nook in the mountains, where Eirran could not be comfortable, or it was a town on the plains where Yareth felt like an interloper. Finally they had chanced upon the tiny village of Blagden, a few miles south of Lormt. Blagden lay in a notch of the Barrier Mountains where they branched out from the Great Mountains to the east, which pleased him. And the village occupied a low valley, flat enough to make her happy. Here, at last, Eirran opened the store of coins she had acquired so painfully over so many years and that Yareth had brought when he had abducted her, and they bought a cottage with enough land to sustain them. With a few more of her dwindling supply of coins Eirran bought another horse, a gentle old gelding to pull the plow, for the Torgian was no farm horse.

And so they settled down at last. Eirran had almost begun to despair of finding a suitable place for them in time; she knew that the child growing in her belly was ripe to be born.

That first winter was a lean one, for they had not had time to put food by. But Yareth went out and hunted rabbits, squirrels and birds, and these he traded for other foods, and for seed to plant the following spring. Eirran spent the last of her coins for furnishings for their cottage—a bed, a table and benches, a kettle. Yareth displayed an unexpected talent when he turned to whittling wooden spoons and bowls for them to use. Later he built a cradle for their daughter with his own hands. Nor was

Eirran idle. She plowed, she planted, she scrubbed, she cooked. And everywhere she went, she carried the infant Jenys on her back. The little cottage fairly glistened under her hands; likewise, the vegetable garden flourished, and the herb garden threatened to overrun its boundaries. Then, as if to complete her dream, a young tiger cat showed up one morning on their doorstep, strolled in, and made himself at home. At first, Newbold eyed the interloper warily and Pounce, the cat, walked very softly indeed when Newbold was indoors on his perch. But somehow the two worked things out between them, even as Eirran and Yareth had. Newbold's territory was with Yareth, in the wilds, and Pounce's with Eirran, in the cottage and the area immediately surrounding.

Falcon and cat competed for chasing the vermin with the result that nowhere in all of Blagden was there a cottage and garden so free of mice and rats as the Falconer's. So thorough were the animals that they had to expand their hunting grounds to the cottages on either side, much to those occupants' gratitude and sometime amusement.

"It's as if those two were having a contest, seeing which could bag the most mice," Aidine, Eirran's next-door neighbor, was wont to remark laughingly. "Who would have thought of such a thing?"

If there was a flaw in Eirran's and Yareth's lives now, it was that Yareth was no farmer nor would he ever be one. But he continued to go up into the mountains and bring home fresh meat for the villagers. In time he became the chief huntsman for Blagden. He had no sword, only the long dagger, and his dart gun was no hunting weapon even if he had been able to find fresh ammunition for it. But he could rig nets and deadfalls, and he could use a sling with great efficiency. One of the men in the village, no archer himself, gave him a bow he had unearthed from some hiding-place, and Yareth used it until he could make a better one for himself. Evenings, he fashioned and fletched arrows when he was not making other things for them both to use.

And they loved each other. Stern though he was, his Falconer upbringing strong in him, he loved her. They had occasional differences of opinions—sometimes quite loud and vigorous, as she had never been one to hide her feelings under a veneer of submission—and though they might shout at each other now and then, or he might stamp outside until both their tempers cooled, he had never, ever raised a hand against her.

He's ten times—a hundred times—the man that miserable Rofan is, Eirran thought grimly to herself as she turned down the lane where the dwelling that had come to be known as the Falconer's cottage stood. I cannot believe how lucky I am to have him.

Eirran was so deep in her thoughts it took her a moment to realize that something was wrong. The little house near the end of the pleasant lane had an oddly deserted look to it. There was no welcoming glow of lamp at window, no curl of smoke from chimney. Pounce didn't wait on the stoop for her return. Aidine opened the door of the cottage next door and came running toward her.

"Oh, Eirran, she's gone, she's gone!" Aidine cried. She burst into sobs.

With an effort, Eirran kept herself steady. "Be calm, Aidine," she said. "I can't help you unless you can tell me what's wrong. Who's gone? What's happened?"

"It's Jenys." Aidine swallowed hard, visibly trying for control of herself. "She's gone."

It was Eirran's turn to panic. "Jenys! Gone? Where? What happened? Is she hurt—?"

"No, no, nothing like that. Please. Come inside. Warm yourself. You must be half-frozen—"

"I don't have time for that! I must go look for her—"

"No, Eirran. *They* took her."

"They who?"

"Armed men, on horseback. And a lady, dressed all in gray. She had five other children with her, riding on ponies. There was a sixth pony."

"And Jenys rode off with them? Is that what you're trying to tell me? My Jenys would never do such a thing!" Eirran brushed past Aidine, opened her door and rushed inside her empty home. Pounce came out of his hiding place and began winding himself around her legs, miaowing plaintively.

She searched through the cottage, hoping that Jenys, like Pounce, had merely been hiding, making a joke. But the fire had burned down to ashes on the hearth, and a forgotten pot of stewed vegetables gave off a stale, burnt smell. There was no sign of Jenys anywhere.

Automatically, Eirran picked up Pounce, cuddling him in her arms. He nudged her chin with his cold nose, the way he did when he wanted food or attention. She stroked his ears. "She really is gone," she told him numbly. "My Jenys really is gone. Oh, whatever shall I do?"

III

For a day and a half Eirran fretted and waited, worrying herself almost into illness. She took the promised herbs and a small sack of flour to Belda, being careful both to pick a time when Rofan wasn't at home and to school her face, voice and manner in calmness. There was nothing to be gained by alarming Belda. That task done, she alternately lavished attention on Pounce and threw herself into heavy springtime chores. That evening, she attempted to mend one of Jenys's dresses and found herself weeping over the stitches. She ate only because Pounce reminded her of mealtimes. On the afternoon of the second day, Yareth returned.

To keep herself from thinking, she had begun digging out the tree-root that interfered with planting this year's vegetable garden, enlarged from the year before. Intent on a stubborn coil of root deep in the earth, she didn't hear the commotion when Yareth and the other hunters returned to the village and only looked up when Rangin snorted, greeting the gelding. Yareth slapped him on the flank, sending him into his stall. Unsaddling and grooming could come later. Now the Falconer smiled, hurrying toward her with open arms.

"I told you to wait until I came home so we could tackle that chore together!" he said in a half-scolding tone of voice. "Here I find you covered with dirt, not exactly what I pictured when I thought about holding you again—"

She jumped up and flung herself sobbing into his arms, nearly knocking him off-balance.

"Eirran, Eirran, a little restraint!" He laughed, holding her so he could look at her. Then he grew serious. Hers weren't tears of joy. "What is it? What's wrong?"

"Jenys. . . ."

It wasn't at all the way she had practiced telling him, calmly, showing none of the fear and panic she had known when Aidine had met her at the door. As the story emerged he began to shake; somehow they found themselves on their knees in the dirt, clinging to each other as Eirran told him all that she knew, all that she had learned since that night.

Then he stood up, drawing her to her feet, and they walked back to the cottage. He sat down at the table and by habit, Eirran set about brewing some tea. Newbold was already on his perch and he bated and screeched at her in greeting.

"How many armed men?" Yareth said coldly.

"Five, Aidine said. Five men, one woman, six children."

"And the woman wore gray? Are you sure?"

"Aidine said so. I didn't see them. I—I was away."

He frowned. "You left Jenys alone?"

"It was no different from any other time I've done the same. There was need elsewhere in the village. Jenys was minding the cottage until I returned."

"Where were you?"

"Belda was hurt."

Yareth slammed his fist down on the table. "That worthless man! You were out tending the damage he did to his stupid wife while the Hags of Estcarp were stealing my daughter. . . ." He started to get to his feet. "I'll kill him—"

"No!" Eirran pushed him back into the chair. "That won't solve anything! What did you mean, the Hags of Estcarp?"

He scowled. A muscle twitched in his jaw. "It could be no other. The woman in gray, the armed men, the children—they were all girls?"

"That's what Aidine said."

"Then it's certain. The Hags nearly eliminated themselves and their entire malignant strain when they worked the Turning and destroyed the Eyrie. More than a few in Estcarp hoped they had. Now they're trying to build up their ranks again, coming by stealth and taking the daughters of unsuspecting—"

"Surely they didn't steal all six of the children, didn't wait until all their parents were away—"

Yareth got up. Decisiveness radiated from him. "After this much time the trail has gone stone-cold. But it doesn't matter. I know where they've taken her. I'm going to Es City and get my daughter back."

"You won't go alone."

"And why not?"

"Because she's my daughter as much as she is yours!" Eirran glared at him fiercely, unaware that she had put her hands across her abdomen. "Even more so. I carried her in my belly all those months. I'm the one who bore her. It was my pain that pushed her out into the world. Don't you think I would have followed that very night, except that I felt I must wait for you? And now you think you'll leave me behind? Never! I am going, and that's final."

Yareth glared at her out of yellowish-brown eyes as fierce as those of the falcon, Newbold. Another person, even a warrior, might have quailed before that gaze; Eirran could imagine that kind of look being used many times in the past, when a Falconer confronted one of those who dwelt apart in the Falconers' Village. A mere woman. But she was much more than that; she was Yareth's wife and Jenys's mother, and she was going with him to demand the child be returned from those who had taken her.

"I won't make Rangin carry double the whole way to Es City," Yareth said.

Eirran's knees trembled a little and she realized that somewhere within her, she had feared he might find a way to force her to stay behind after all. "You forget we have Dorny. Give me a few minutes to get ready."

He looked away. "I am wasting time, waiting on you."

"An hour either way won't matter. You've just come back from a week up in the mountains. Surely there are a few things you must do before starting out again."

"Very well," he said reluctantly. "An hour, then."

Eirran had long since packed her bedroll and what food remained to them, had laid out the shirt and trousers for the road, and the cloak to wear over them. She hastily washed the dirt off herself and changed clothes. Then she picked up Pounce and hurried next door.

"Will you look after him?" she asked Aidine. "We're going after Jenys and I don't know how long we'll be gone—"

"Of course," Aidine said. She took the cat and he snuggled into her arms. "I'll get Hefin to finish planting your garden and I'll look after it until you get back. Don't worry about anything. Be careful. The roads aren't very safe these days."

"I know, I know. But we'll be back."

"Luck, then."

"Thanks. I have a feeling we'll need it."

She ran back to the little stable. Yareth had already fed Rangin and given him a hasty grooming. Newbold waited, perched on a rafter, and Yareth whistled. At the signal the falcon flew to the saddle fork just as Yareth mounted.

"Wait—" Eirran said.

"You'll have to hurry if you want to go with me." He nudged Rangin and the Torgian trotted out of the stable. Once he would have danced out, tossing his head and nickering, as if to show that the prospect of a hard journey on the heels of a long hunting trip was nothing to him. But the years were beginning to show on the horse, as they were on Newbold. The falcon kept to his perch more these days rather than winging skyward at every opportunity.

Hurriedly, Eirran secured her carry-sack over her shoulder. She slipped a bridle on Dorny and scrambled onto his back, wishing they owned a second saddle. By the time she maneuvered the gentle, splay-footed old gelding out into the lane, Yareth was well ahead of her and she knew she would be looking at his back most of the way to Es City.

Two

I

*J*enys had had a busy day. She had gotten up at dawn when Mama did, and the two of them had worked in the garden most of the morning, getting the ground ready for spring planting.

"Every year there are more weeds," Mama said. "And nastier ones." She tugged at a big, ugly growth that Jenys had tried to pull but couldn't so much as budge. Finally, with the two of them working at it, it came loose. Jenys was almost certain she heard it growl and snarl as they pulled it from the ground. Mama threw it onto the pile to be burned later. "We're going to expand the garden this year, and take in that section over there." She pointed toward a spot where a dead tree-stump stuck jagged edges above the ground.

"But Mama," Jenys said, "Papa said not to touch that until he came home to help."

"Oh, you were listening to us, were you? Well, I'm not going to wait for Papa, what do you think of that? I think I know how to do it myself. We've got to harness Dorny anyway for the plowing. I'll dig around the stump and get it loosened. Then we can hitch him to the ugly thing and let him pull it out. Papa can chop it up later for firewood."

"That sounds like a very good plan," Jenys said seriously.

Mama laughed. "You are my little old woman," she said, as she frequently did. "You're six going on forty if you're a day."

Jenys had never quite understood why Mama said that or why she thought she was a little old woman. She knew how old she was. Six, going on seven. And she only said what was sensible, after all.

They pulled weeds until the sun reached its zenith. Then they went inside to rest a while and eat a little cheese and bread. Mama made very good cheese; she traded her Wise Woman services for extra milk now and then, and Jenys enjoyed helping her with the straining-cloths and the press. And she loved taking the leftover whey out to Dorny and Rangin. They made such funny, snuffling noises as they drank it. Mama said it was good for them. And they did seem to like it very much, almost as much as the lumps of barley-sugar Mama sometimes took them, as a treat.

After lunch, Mama harnessed Dorny and started to plow. The soil was still muddy and wet from winter and Dorny's hooves made heavy, sucking noises as he plodded along the furrow. But the freshly-turned earth looked very black and rich and Jenys liked the smell of it.

"Do the herb garden next, Mama," she said, "and I'll plant it for you."

Mama smiled at her. "All right. Dorny needs a rest," she said. "Get the shovel for me." At the end of the furrow, she looped the reins over the plow handle. The gelding dropped his head with a grateful sigh and began to nibble at some early grass.

Jenys ran into the stable and returned at once with the shovel. She and Mama had three gardens, one for flowers at the front of their cottage and the ones for food and for herbs at the back. The herb garden was the smallest. But Mama didn't need a large one, not when she had Jenys to plant it for her. Ever since Jenys had been a little girl, she had been able to make Mama's herbs grow large and strong and healthy. She had no idea how she did it; she simply sang to the seeds as she put them in the soil, the way that seemed perfectly natural to her, and the herbs did the rest. Without anything being said between them, she and Mama kept this part of the gardening their own secret. Somehow, they both sensed that Papa wouldn't have approved.

Papa wouldn't have approved when Erman, from the other side of the village, came asking for Mama early that afternoon, either. Jenys didn't need any special knowledge to realize that. She didn't like Erman. He always smelled funny.

"Please," the boy said, "it's Mama. She's bad."

But Mama didn't even hesitate, regardless of what Papa would have said, and regardless of how bad Erman smelled. She just brushed herself off and unharnessed Dorny. She went inside the cottage and washed her face and hands. "I'll be back as soon as I can," she told Jenys.

"I know," Jenys said. "I'll have supper waiting for you when you come home."

Mama smiled. "Yes, definitely six going on forty," she said, and pinched Jenys's cheek affectionately. Then she picked up her carry-sack of medicines and left with Erman.

Without needing to be told, Jenys knew that Rofan had been beating Belda again. He always waited until Papa was gone and this was the third time Erman had come for Mama since Papa had left for the first big springtime hunt. Maybe Papa would beat Rofan again, the way he had done once before. It had been all the village talked about, behind closed doors, for weeks and Jenys had found it very exciting. Papa didn't approve of Rofan, and Jenys knew he would be very cross when he found out that he had been mistreating Belda again in his absence. The only thing she didn't like was the way Mama and Papa would be cross with each other for a while.

Still, she didn't mind being left in charge of the cottage and the garden. She felt very grown-up indeed as she finished singing Mama's herbs into the ground. Then she turned to the rest of the garden. Though it was only partly plowed, she could do the bean and turnip seeds, and maybe the carrots. She had never sung over vegetables before; it would be fun to see if they needed a different song from the herbs.

Interestingly, Jenys discovered that they did, a little, and each vegetable had slightly different requirements from the others. She grew absorbed in her task; before she realized it, she had finished one entire row and was ready to start on another. She wished she had been planting honeyberries instead of dull old vegetables. But Mama always said vegetables were better for her. They could always dry the surplus and put it away for later. Honeyberries were good only during their short season. What was worse, they didn't even make good jam. Mama had tried making jam often enough, but the results were always disappointing. Papa always laughed and said she just didn't have the knack for jam-making but Jenys refused to believe it. Her Mama could do anything.

She finished the carrots. Then she found the flat stakes Mama used as markers and, as she hadn't yet learned to write anything but her name, she drew a picture of a bean, a turnip, and a carrot on three of the stakes and pushed them into the ground at the end of the furrows.

"There, now, that's that," she said aloud. Imitating her mother's actions, the child brushed the dirt off her hands and clothing. Then she went inside and washed herself clean.

She looked in the larder and took down the sacks of dried vegetables. They would make a good stew if she seasoned it with enough wild garlic, and there was a patch of it growing out near the old tree-stump. She took three handfuls of different vegetables—Mama measured one handful for each of them but Jenys had to use three because her hands were so small—and set them soaking in fresh water while she went out to gather the garlic. She also picked an early crocus from the front garden. By the time she returned the vegetables were softened enough that she could chop them into smaller pieces. But first she found a cup to fill with water and put the crocus in. That done, she started on the dinner, humming to herself while she worked. A little meat would make the stew taste very good, but she knew better than to use the last of their dried venison. Not until Papa came home, even though Jenys knew the hunt would be a success. Her Papa was simply the most wonderful man in the world, and by far the greatest hunter who ever lived.

She put the vegetables into the pot, added more water, and set it over the fire, moving a sleepy Pounce so his fur and whiskers wouldn't get singed. He scarcely blinked when she moved him, the lazy old thing. Later, she knew, he would wake up and go sit on the stoop waiting for Mama, the way he always did when she was gone during the day. Then Jenys set out the wooden bowls and the spoons Papa had carved, and put the crocus on the table. She always liked to make the table look as pretty as possible.

Outside, Jenys heard the sound of horses' hooves and men's voices. She flew to the door and flung it open, heart thumping, sure that Papa had come home early. But a lady dressed all in gray stood at the threshold, her hand upraised, as if about to knock. Jenys and the lady just stood there staring at each other, and it was hard to tell which one of them was more surprised.

"You!" Jenys said.

"Yes," the gray-clad lady said. "You've been expecting me."

"I have?" Jenys said, blinking in surprise. She thought about it. There was something so very familiar about the lady, though she was certain she had never seen her or anyone like her before. But there had been that time a few weeks ago when she had wakened from a sound sleep, thinking her Mama had been speaking her name, only Mama had been asleep also. "I thought I heard something, once—"

"It was the Call. And now I've come. These other children with me, they heard the Call as well."

Now Jenys looked past her and saw the other people with the lady. There were five little girls, about her own age. Some stood and stared at her boldly. Others hid behind the lady's skirts and peeped out at her, giggling. One of them had her thumb in her mouth and Jenys couldn't help thinking that she had given *that* up long ago. All of the little girls looked very much like the lady. Startled, Jenys realized they also looked like herself—sharp-featured, with great gray eyes dominating triangular little cat-faces. There was a kind of *rightness* about them, an air of self-possession, that was somehow not quite right at all, considering what very little girls they were, and suddenly Jenys understood what Mama said about her being six going on forty.

Waiting out in the lane, keeping themselves a little apart, were five men on horseback. They wore chain mail and tall helmets with chain scarfs at the throat. One of the men had a falcon, just like Papa's. Though there were only five little girls, there were six ponies idly nuzzling at the new grass.

Jenys looked back at the lady. She stroked a milky gray oval gem that hung from a silver chain around her neck. With a pang that brought a sharp taste into her mouth Jenys realized that she wanted one just like it, more than anything else in the entire world.

"We're ready to go now," the lady said, as if it were the most natural thing in the world. "Come along."

"Yes, lady," Jenys said. She thought it would be unmannerly to close the door in the lady's face, so she left it open while she took her small russet cloak from the peg and put it on. She wanted to say goodbye to Pounce, but he had disappeared. She tied the strings at the throat just as Mama had taught her, and went outside. Then, carefully, she closed the door behind her.

The lady laughed. "How neat and tidy you are!" she exclaimed. "Like a little mouse."

Jenys couldn't keep from giggling. The very thought of a mouse with Pounce and Newbold ready to grab it if it stuck its head out of the corner made her forget all her manners.

"What is it?" the lady asked. "What's funny?" When Jenys told her, she laughed as well. "Nevertheless, that's what we'll call you from now on," she said. "Mouse. Do you like that?"

"Oh, yes, lady, I do, very much!" Jenys—Mouse—stared at

the lady in open admiration. "Where are we going, if you please?"

"We are going where you and others like you can go to a special kind of school."

Mouse's brow wrinkled. "School?" she said doubtfully.

The lady laughed again. "Oh, it's that and more than that. It's where you are meant to be." She turned to the other little girls. "Come, children. Bring Mouse's pony. She doesn't know which one is hers. Can you climb on it by yourself?"

"Yes, thank you, lady," Mouse said. She had watched Papa mount Rangin many, many times, so she knew exactly how it was done. She was far too small to reach Rangin's stirrups and Papa had to lift her up when she rode in front of him. But the pony was just the right size for her and she scrambled into her saddle unaided.

Then without another thought, she and the lady, the other little girls and the five armed men rode out of Blagden, leaving everything and everyone behind.

II

The lady's name, Mouse quickly learned, was Bee. They took the road north, riding behind Bee two by two, trotting along at her horse's heels as if they had been doing so all their lives. The Guardsmen rode before and behind; Rhinfar, their leader, accompanied the lady, and the other four brought up the rear. Rhinfar carried a furled banner at his side.

The road they traveled was the one, Mouse learned, that would bring them to Lormt if they stayed on it and didn't turn west at the Great Fork. She had heard about Lormt before. Sometimes Mama talked about going there to study but she never had found the time. Lormt sounded like a very interesting place, with its scholars and scrolls and learning. Even the stones in the walls must be simply full of knowledge. And especially now, since two of the four towers had fallen, uncovering much new material the scholars could spend lifetimes cataloguing.

Mouse and the other girls looked forward to seeing it. But Bee seemed completely indifferent to Lormt; she ignored any and all mention of the place. She chose to avoid it and the Great Fork as well by cutting across country to pick up the main road, and the men followed without comment.

The main road was a very good highway, excellently maintained. It was hard-packed and bordered on both sides with a wall, low enough for Mouse to step over, of gray-green stone the color of the river they traveled along. Mouse had never seen stones this wonderful color in all her life. Around Blagden the stones were red-brown and the ground itself had a reddish cast to it except when it was freshly-plowed or wet. Then it was a dark brown, almost black.

Mouse thought surely everyone would laugh at her, the way she couldn't stop looking this way and that as they rode. She had never been this far beyond the edges of Blagden in all her life, and the world outside was at once strange, exciting, and a little scary. But she soon discovered that the other girls were staring just the same way she was, except for Star who was the most self-possessed of them all. As they rode, the girls talked and Star seemed to have been everywhere and seen everything. It was Star who told them most often where they were and what they could expect around the next turn in the highway, or over the next rise.

Mouse's first impression had been correct. They all looked very much alike indeed. Every one of them, even Bee, was slight of build. Besides the triangular little cat-faces, they all had dark hair and eyes, and pale skin. They might have been six cousins out traveling with their aunt. They all had new names now. Mouse never knew what they had been called before, and she found she did not particularly care. Nor did it seem possible to her that she had ever been anybody but Mouse. For the first time in her life she had friends, real friends, who were enough like her to understand the vague sense of *otherness* that had been with Mouse all her life. All of them had, she discovered, felt the same way while they were growing up. They were very much at home in each other's company and they realized that, before they had met, they had all been very lonely in a way only they could comprehend. Now, it was as if each had suddenly discovered five new sisters. Mouse's companions were Bird, and Flame, and Star, and Cricket, and Lisper who couldn't pronounce the letter "s" very well. She was the one who sucked her thumb when she felt unsure of herself. She called Mouse "Mouth," which made everyone break into uncontrollable fits of the giggles. Before long, Mouse began to discover why the lady had decided to call them as she had.

Bird was bright and inquisitive, cocking her head to listen and then flying off in a different direction altogether the moment another thought struck her. Flame fairly glowed with the fires within, and whenever she spoke, she spoke with great conviction and earnestness. Cricket was unquenchably cheerful, while Star was probably the most knowledgeable person— besides her Mama and Papa, of course—that Mouse had ever met. And as for Lisper, well, her nickname was obvious.

Bee, Mouse learned, had started out from Es Castle and made an enormous circle through Estcarp, heading south and working her way eastward and then north again until she finished her questing at Blagden, and all six little girls were safely in her care.

Like Mouse, Bird, Flame and Cricket had come from ordinary families living in small villages; Lisper was the child of an important family whose stronghold lay near the ruined Barrier Mountains. Star had come from the poorest background of all—itinerant peddlers, dealers in trinkets, without a permanent home of any kind beyond the wagons her family traveled in. Her mother and the man whose bed she currently shared, awed by the gray-clad woman accompanied by soldiers who had found them unerringly in their wanderings, had let Star go without a murmur. And after all, it made one less mouth for them to feed. Star told this story so matter-of-factly that Mouse knew that either she wasn't at all hurt or upset by her parents' attitude or she was very wounded indeed and determined not to show it. Mouse resolved that she would be a very good friend to Star, in any way she could. Her own Mama and Papa—

Mouse blinked in surprise. This was the first time since she had left home that she had even thought about Mama and Papa! She had all but forgotten them, and hadn't even missed them, not once. Would they be grieving? Worrying about what had become of her?

That night, instead of going directly to sleep, Mouse wept softly into the blanket covering her. The sound of snuffles and sniffles nearby told her that she was not alone. She sat up and discovered that most of the other girls were weeping as well.

"I want my Mama," Cricket said miserably.

"Me, too," Flame said. Bird and Lisper nodded agreement. Lisper sucked on her thumb as if she would never leave off. Mouse wanted more than anything to reach out, to try to make Mama *hear,* the way she had used to sometimes back home. But somehow, around Bee, she didn't dare.

"Better be quiet," Star said. She alone was dry-eyed. "Bee will hear you."

"I already did," Bee said. She moved into the middle of the group and sat down, taking Lisper onto her lap. Cricket cuddled up in the crook of her other arm and the rest of the children crept as close as they could get, even the independent Star.

"Please, lady," Mouse said. "We forgot to tell my Mama and Papa where we were going. They don't even know where I am!"

"And that troubles you, does it?" Bee said. "Well, you don't need to worry. By now they know what's happened."

Lisper took her thumb out of her mouth long enough to say, "I mith my Mama and Papa." Back went the thumb; Lisper snuffled mournfully.

"That will pass. You are in safe hands, and you are where you need to be. Remember that. Now, go to sleep, all of you." Bee shooed them all back to their places and tucked them in. She kissed each one, lingering a little over Lisper.

Like Mouse, the other girls seemed to find more comfort in what Bee actually meant than what she had said. "Thank you, lady," Mouse said. "We'll be all right now." Then she fell asleep.

III

It was wonderful, being in Bee's company. She really was like an aunt, a young aunt they could tease and laugh with, and who was as much fun as anybody they had ever known. At the same time she was someone they knew they must obey without question. They sang songs and Bee told them stories. "It makes the miles go faster," she said. And it did seem they must have a magical wind at their backs, helping them along.

At first Mouse eyed the men warily. She had seen chain mail before, of course. Papa had a chain shirt, though he almost never wore it. And his helmet, though not new, was just as intimidating as the ones these Guardsmen wore. But these men had long swords at their sides, and it was plain that they had plenty of ammunition for their dart guns. Papa had run out of darts a long time ago, and now he kept the gun on the wall by the door, just for looks. The men guarding Bee and the girls didn't talk much except among themselves, and then in low tones. Mouse was surprised to discover that the men took all their orders from Bee. Then she began to wonder all over again. Papa would never do this, take orders from a woman, and yet there was that Guardsman who looked like he might be one of Papa's distant relatives. Somehow, though, she was not tempted to speak to him with any degree of familiarity. Like Newbold, his black and white falcon rode on his Y-shaped saddle-horn. But this bird was as different from Newbold as the man was different from Papa. This bird screeched and screamed every time she tried to come near, so she left him alone. Still, she knew the man must be one of the wonderful Falconers who were Papa's people before he married Mama, and she wished he would talk to her sometimes.

Each night, before they went to sleep, the little girls had a lesson from Bee. Mostly it was on the nature of magic, but one night it was about how to act when they got to Es City.

"We'll be there very soon. You must be on your best behavior," Bee told them. "The Guardian rules us all—yes, even though you have never even met her. She is now your mother. Indeed, she is now your only parent, as she is mine. You must not shout or skip or run, but must walk quietly in her presence and speak when you are spoken to."

"Will she beat us if we're bad?" Cricket said, giggling. "Will she send us to bed without our suppers?"

"Of course not!" Bee tried to be firm, but the corners of her mouth twitched. "Oh, you scamp. You're going to lead them a merry chase at the Place of Wisdom."

"And what is that, please, Bee?" Mouse asked.

"It is a place leagues and leagues beyond Es Castle. In fact, it is a day's ride from the sea."

"Hooray!" cried Lisper. "My Mama and Papa and I uthed to live bethide a lake, and they would take me thwimming thometimeth. Ith the thea like a lake, pleath, Bee?"

"Yes, you might say so, only bigger. I remember outings to the seashore now and then while I was at the Place of Wisdom, when we had all been very, very good. Now, speaking of being good, you must all go to sleep now. Another day and we'll see the towers of Es City on the horizon."

Mouse was so excited she thought she would never be able to sleep again. And the other girls were, too. They huddled together, whispering and giggling, until Bee hushed them and sent them to sleep. She held her mysterious jewel and spoke a few words Mouse thought strangely familiar though she had never heard any sounds like them before in her life. All at once her eyelids grew so heavy she couldn't keep them up, and the next thing she knew it was morning.

The last few miles to Es City were a sheer torment for the overexcited children. Instead of rushing them through their mid-morning meal, Bee allowed them to play Catch Me.

"Run and shout all you like," she told them. "I hope they'll tire themselves out," she added to Rhinfar. "I do believe this is the healthiest, most energetic group of children we've had in years."

"I wouldn't know, lady," Rhinfar said. "But they do seem strong, and vigorous."

"New blood," Bee said somberly. "We've nearly exhausted ourselves, we Witches. And nearly extinguished our line, during the Turning."

"Were you there?" the Guardsman asked.

"Yes, I was in the second circle. I had been chosen to be one of those who stood by to give of our strength when it was needed while the strongest worked the spell. The Power came—" Bee broke off, shuddering. "It was terrible. If I hadn't closed my eyes and covered my ears, I might have died with so many of my sisters. Their Jewels shattered, disintegrating into dust and the Witches died—" Again she broke off, shuddering, and clutched at the stone hanging from the chain around her neck. "A few others in the first circle were less fortunate. Their Jewels went black, and they were left alive—if you can call it living, the state they were in. Many have never recovered to this day."

Mouse, who was hiding nearby, kept very still, listening. She had heard about the Turning, of course. Everyone knew how the mountains had fallen between Estcarp and Karsten, and Papa's home, the Eyrie, had been destroyed. But she hadn't had any idea how it had happened until now. The thought of such power as the Witches had wielded made her dizzy. . . .

Bee took a deep breath. "But those terrible days are over," she said. "We have a new Guardian now, a younger one, one with new ideas. She is willing to accept that the world has changed, that different ways aren't always inferior, that the time has come to try new things. Expansion, Rhinfar. Perhaps an entire change of direction. And the children are the key— Mouse! What are you doing here!"

Mouse jumped, full of guilt and ashamed of having been

caught eavesdropping. "I was hiding, Bee," she said. "It was part of the game. I didn't mean to listen, really."

"Well, no harm, I suppose. You go with Rhinfar and find the others. If we want to get there before nightfall we must start now."

Obediently, Mouse went with the Guardsman while he broke up the game, much to Star's disappointment. "I was winning!" she said.

"No, you weren't," Flame retorted, and Lisper agreed.

"You couldn't catch me no matter how fatht you ran," she said. "You couldn't even thee me if I wanted to hide, and I can run much fathter than either one of you. Tho there."

"Then we'll let you three run all the way to Es Castle," Bee said with mock exasperation. "Unless, of course, you'd rather ride with the rest of us."

That ended all complaints and arguments. Obediently, the little girls rushed to climb up onto their ponies at once and fell into line in the familiar twin column.

Estcarp had become a silvery, gray-green land, far different from what Mouse had been used to, close to the mountains. Back at her old home, the trees were tall and fragrant, with spiky needles instead of leaves, and prickly, sweet-scented cones grew at the tip of each branch. Mouse had loved to gather the cones and always kept the basket by the fireplace full, for they made the fire smell very nice. But the cone trees were far behind. Here the woodland smells were far different—earthier, more like the memory of the tame crops they bordered, and less like the wild sweetness of the mountain forests. Mouse wondered what the people used to perfume their fires.

In this part of Estcarp, where there were no early crops planted as yet, the native rocks shone greyish green in the sun and what vegetation had begun to come in leaf displayed much the same muted hue. The trees were modest in size. And they didn't grow just anywhere, as they did outside Blagden. Here there were tidy, well-defined forests and occasional copses and trees lining either side of streams, the trees' domain drastically reduced by the farmlands. But many fields lay fallow, un-plowed, and Mouse wondered if the war she had heard about had left Estcarp needing to produce less food than it once had.

Es City seemed at first to be just another grey-green smudge on the horizon. But then as they grew closer, Mouse could see that the city walls and the castle they enclosed were built of the silvery grey-green stone that was so plentiful throughout this part of Estcarp. Now she understood why this highway they traveled was bordered and, in many places, paved with the same kind of stone that made up the great central city-castle. Running as it did all the way from the Great Mountains to the sea—so Bee told them—the road served as a proud reminder to all who traveled on it that they were in Estcarp, the land ruled by Witches. Pride surged through Mouse as well. Soon—very soon—she would be riding through the gate of Es City. Then, with her new-found sisters, she would go into the presence of the Guardian and, if she were found worthy, would begin the training that would some day make her a Witch as well.

She sat up very straight in her saddle. Glancing around, she discovered that the other five children seemed affected in the same way as she. Spontaneously, the little girls struck up one of the trail-songs that had made the miles go by so pleasantly on their journey to this wonderful, magical place. Their voices rose high and sweet and tremulous, and men atop the wall paused to look down at them.

As if that were a signal, the Guardsmen pulled themselves up smartly, and Rhinfar unfurled the silver banner to let it float freely in the freshening breeze. Some of the men added their deep voices to the treble of the children's, and Bee joined with her rich alto.

And so, singing, the Witch children passed through the gate of Es City and into their new life.

Three

I

*I*n spite of her best efforts, Eirran couldn't keep up with Yareth. Old Dorny simply couldn't match Rangin's pace. Grimly, she grew accustomed to the sight of Yareth's back. He maintained a distance well ahead of her on the stone-lined main road leading to Es City. Each evening, though, she would catch up with him as he was beginning to make camp, and the two of them would feed and tend the horses before preparing their own meal. And they slept close together, even though they didn't make love. Eirran remembered their last night together before Yareth had left on his hunting trip. That night they had well and truly loved each other. She warmed at the thought. How close they had been, how they had clung to each other. How long ago? She counted on her fingers. Three weeks, perhaps. And how much had happened in the meantime!

As they journeyed, Yareth found and searched the places where Jenys and her abductors had camped. "It's clear. There were five men," he said, examining the boot-prints in the dust of the campsites. "One woman and six little girls. Just as Aidine told you. They don't seem to have been in a great hurry."

Hope made a lump in Eirran's throat. "Do you think we can catch up with them before they reach Es City?"

He shook his head. "No. These tracks are nearly a week old. They've arrived already. But I'll get there in time to stop them before they can do anything to my daughter."

"Our daughter," Eirran said automatically. "We'll get there." But Yareth didn't acknowledge her words. She sighed.

Though Yareth's trail-knowledge told them the ones they were following had taken at least five days on their journey, he and Eirran, traveling with far more urgency, arrived in only three. Eirran gaped openly at the round grey-green stone towers, looking as if they had erupted from the grey-green soil in which they were rooted. As one approached the city, the surface of the road improved, going from packed earth to stone paving. Evening shadows lengthened and the hooves of Rangin and Dorny rang loudly on the paving stones as they rode through the dauntingly strong gate of Es City. The main street led directly to the castle. They pulled up before the immense gatehouse.

It was as if they had been expected. A Guardsman came and took the animals away to be housed, fed and watered. Another, a Falconer by his looks, slipped Newbold's hood on him. "I'll take him to the mews, brother," he said. "Our birds aren't allowed inside. Witch law."

"Thank you, brother," Yareth said. "His name is Newbold. Guard him well."

"My life on it."

Another Guard guided them through the intricate castle entrance, into an area outside the vast main building, then left them to find their way as best they could. There didn't appear to be any way inside; no windows, no apparent doors pierced the towering walls. Es Castle turned a stony face to those who would enter without knowing its secret. Nevertheless, Yareth strode forward boldly, but Eirran stopped a grey-clad woman as she went about some unknown errand.

"Please, Lady, will you help us?" she said.

"What is your business?" She spoke to Eirran cordially enough, but cast a suspicious glance in Yareth's direction.

"I've come to reclaim my daughter from your Guardian's grasp," Yareth said.

The woman eyed Yareth coldly. "Ah. I see," she said at last. "Come this way."

At a gesture from her, an entrance appeared where there had been none before. Eirran realized that she had been taken in by an illusion of solid, unbroken walls. Perhaps windows hid behind illusion as well.

They went inside. The grey-clad woman led them through a maze of corridors until they reached a closed door. "Wait here," she told them. "I'll find out if the Guardian will receive you."

Yareth made a move forward and Eirran laid her hand on his arm. "No," she said. "This is the Guardian's place, and she is within her rights. But," she added in a voice pitched so that their guide could hear, "if she will not see us today, then we shall return tomorrow and the next day and the next, until she does."

Eirran could tell by the way the woman's head went up a notch that her message had been clearly understood. She entered the chamber and it seemed to Eirran that she and Yareth waited an hour or more before the Witch returned.

"The Guardian has consented to see you now," she said. "It is a great honor she does you, you must understand that."

Yareth brushed past and went inside the room at once, but Eirran paused in the corridor a moment. "Thank you," she said. "Thank you for your help."

The Witch merely shrugged and walked away, presumably to return to the errand that Eirran's and Yareth's arrival had interrupted. Eirran took a deep breath and hurried to catch up with her husband who was already inside.

II

The room was a small one, perhaps one of the Guardian's private offices. Eirran couldn't imagine such an important person using such a tiny room for official matters. It was brightly lit by globes set in holders on the walls. The leader of the Council of Witches in Estcarp was standing in front of a tall-backed chair. A cluttered table beside her indicated that she had been seated there, working, when the Witch had interrupted her with the news that Yareth and Eirran waited without.

"I was told there were two of you," the Guardian said. There was a hint of mild reproof in her tone and Eirran regretted having lingered in the hallway. No breach of etiquette, however small, would help them in this interview. Eirran knew instinctively that Yareth would be well advised to speak softly to this formidable lady.

But he was in no mood to be conciliatory. "You have stolen my daughter," he said bluntly. "I have come to take her back home with me."

"Your daughter?" The Guardian raised her eyebrows slightly. "You had a daughter?"

"I *have* a daughter," Yareth retorted. "And you have stolen her. Give her back."

"I have no idea who you might be referring to," the Guardian said.

"She is here somewhere. If I have to take this place apart stone by stone—"

"You?" The Guardian was amused, and allowed herself to show it. "By yourself? Your ardor becomes you, Falconer. I had no idea your kind even cherished your male children, let alone your daughters."

"There is much you don't know, but more that you do and won't speak about. Again. I demand that my daughter be returned to me."

"I could call a dozen Guardsmen and have you thrown into the street," the Witch said. "Or I could do other things. . . ." Her hand stole to the blue-gray jewel that glowed on the silver chain around her neck.

"Threaten me if you will, but I will have my daughter back."

"Enough. You tire me. There is nothing more to be said." The Guardian turned away and sat down again. Stone-faced, she picked up a packet of papers. With deliberate, unhurried movements she began untying the silver ribbon that bound them.

Eirran knew that she had finished with the interview. But a faint hope remained to her. Witch though she might be, the Guardian was still a woman, wasn't she? Perhaps the pleadings of another woman might touch a responsive spot in the Guardian's heart. Eirran took a step forward but Yareth stopped her, putting his hand heavily on her shoulder.

"No," he said, his tone harsh. "We'll receive no help here, no consideration. No—no mercy." He spoke this last word with heavy irony. "We'll have to look elsewhere."

"I have to try." Eirran shook off his grasp and moved closer. Despite herself, she had begun to weep. To her mortification she recognized a certain uneasy feeling in her midsection and knew also that she was going to begin hiccuping the way she always did when she got upset. "Oh, Lady," she said. "Please—*hic!*— please don't turn us away. Jenys is our only child. I don't think we will ever have another. We have to—*hic!*—have to know what has become of her!"

She went to her knees, and then, beyond shame, prostrated herself at the Guardian's feet. For a moment there were no sounds in the room except for Eirran's sobs and hiccups. There was a faint rustle of clothing as the Guardian leaned forward in her chair and touched Eirran.

"Get up," she said. "Stop weeping. Your Falconer is ashamed for you. I can read it in his face."

"I don't care, I don't care," Eirran said miserably. "*Hic!* All I care about is having Jenys back." She pulled herself up to her knees again, and clasped her hands. "Can't you understand that? My child. That is all either of us wants."

The Guardian glanced from Eirran's tear-stained face to Yareth's stern one. "I see that you both love your daughter deeply, in your different ways. I am sorry."

"What does that mean, Lady?" Yareth's tone, it seemed to Eirran, was just a bit less truculent than before.

The Guardian looked up at him. "It is too late," she said.

She got up and moved away from the table to a nearby window where she moved the curtain aside and stood staring outward. Yareth helped Eirran to her feet and put his arm around her as she clung to him for support.

"Do you mean—" His voice broke a little and he cleared his throat. "Do you mean that she is dead?"

"In a way," the Guardian said. She turned to face the distraught parents. "It might be easier for you if you thought of it in that way, for in fact, she is dead to you. We all die, as far as the outside world is concerned, when we come here. All ties with family, with friends, with anything but each other, are severed when we become Witches. Yes, Falconer, and you also, Falconer's lady. Your daughter is dead."

"But you have seen her," Yareth said stubbornly.

A flash of emotion swept over the Guardian's features, as quickly stifled. "There were some girls here. Your former daughter may have been among them."

"Six little girls? Accompanied by a woman, and five men?"

"When there is an Ingathering, we always send one of our own under guard."

"Then you have seen Jenys," Eirran said. "*Hic!* Oh, please, you must have." She moved in Yareth's embrace as if prepared to cast herself at the Guardian's feet again.

The Witch closed her eyes and compressed her lips. Then she looked at them, and the first sign of compassion softened her features. "Yes. She must have been one of the ones I interviewed. She has been here, but is now gone to the Place of Wisdom. I'm afraid it really is too late, Falconer."

"Place of Wisdom?" he said. "What is that? Where is it? I'll go there at once—"

"And you would perish before you even reached the walls," the Guardian said. "Believe me. The Place of Wisdom is the academy where Witches are trained. It lies many leagues west, and it is guarded by magic. If, by some miracle, you could win past the outer defenses, and pass the wall, you would then face some of the sternest, most capable of us all. Our young are taught by the best of us, you see."

" 'Your' young," Yareth echoed resentfully.

"You must make the best of it," the Guardian said. "Believe that it is an honor to give up a daughter into Witchdom—"

"It is no honor that I recognize."

"No," Eirran said, fearful that Yareth would rouse the Guardian's anger. "Surely there is some other way—*hic!*— some agreement we can reach—"

"Nothing," the Guardian said. "The matter is ended."

A knock sounded at the door and, without waiting for an invitation to enter, a Witch came hurrying in. Her face had gone dead-white and had a pinched look, and her manner was distracted. She went directly to the Guardian and whispered in her ear. As the Witch spoke, the Guardian's features took on some of the worry and concern that the other showed. She clutched at the Jewel at her throat. "Thank you," she told the Witch. "We will deal with it directly."

The other woman bowed, then left the room. The Guardian turned to Yareth and Eirran. All at once Eirran realized that the Guardian was a young woman.

But, she thought, the Guardian is supposed to be old, and experienced— Then she remembered the Turning, and how so many of the Witches had died. This one couldn't have held her position then; she must be relatively new-come to it.

"There is great trouble," the Guardian said without preamble. "Your daughter may truly be dead. Hounds of Alizon caught the six children and the Witch escorting them, on the road between here and the Place of Wisdom. The Witch sent word by mindtouch, but it was—interrupted, before the message came clearly enough for us to know what really happened."

Yareth began to tremble with rage. "Hounds—" he said in a choked voice. "You let Hounds of Alizon touch my child—"

Hastily, Eirran drew him aside. "No!" she whispered passionately. Unaccountably, her hiccups had vanished. "You can't afford to give in to anger! Think, Yareth, think! There's still a chance. She said the message was interrupted. Right now, she needs us—or she might, if we can persuade her we are the best ones to go searching."

He stared at her out of his hawk's eyes. Gradually, the eyes became those of a man again as reason began to return to him. "Not 'we,' Eirran. This will not be work for a woman."

She was so relieved to have avoided a fatal outburst of temper on his part that she chose not to argue.

He turned back to the Guardian. "I will go and find your fledgling Witches for you if they still live," he said.

The Guardian nodded. "No one else among the Guardsmen could have so strong a desire to recover them as you," she said.

"There is one thing more," Yareth said. "When I do find them, and when I return them to you, my child is mine."

The Guardian's gaze was steady, her expression unfathomable, her voice even. "You will have our everlasting gratitude if you can return the girls to our care." She pulled a bellcord. "Now go and rest yourself for a little while. You are tired from your journey. You cannot go rushing off into Alizon alone, without knowledge, unprepared, no matter how brave you may be."

"That is true," Yareth said. He glanced at Eirran. "My lady wife is tired. Also, she has helped me begin thinking as a warrior again. A good warrior faces facts, unpleasant as they might be, for to do otherwise is to invite disaster. If the children are dead, then they are dead. If they still live, their captors have taken them alive for a purpose. In either case, too much haste accomplishes nothing."

"Tomorrow you will choose men to accompany you. By then we may know a little more to help you with your search. We will give you what you need to accomplish your mission. For this short while, our goals are identical, Falconer."

With a nod, she dismissed them. It was not until they were following the servant to the room they had been assigned for the night that Eirran realized the Guardian had not really agreed to Yareth's terms. "Everlasting gratitude" was all that she had promised.

But then, Eirran thought, the everlasting gratitude of the Guardian of the Council of Witches in Estcarp was not something to be dismissed lightly.

The room was not much larger than the Guardian's chamber. Hot water and clean towels waited on a side table and, gratefully, they washed themselves clean of road grime. The bed was fresh, newly warmed, and very inviting. Loose garments of soft blue fabric lay waiting and Eirran realized that they were expected to put them on for sleeping. She had never known such luxury. At home, she slept in an old, castoff shift and Yareth slept in a threadbare shirt long past mending. Selfconsciously, they donned the unfamiliar garments and climbed into bed. Eirran sighed. Exhausted, she settled down beside Yareth and, without expecting to, fell asleep.

III

"No," Yareth said. "Absolutely not. I will not have you going on this dangerous journey, Eirran. We are likely to be facing Hounds of Alizon! Don't you know what that means?"

Eirran didn't, not really. But these Hounds couldn't be any worse than Karsten soldiers, or the rough-mannered riverbargemen who sometimes frequented her uncle's tavern. "Jenys will be frightened. And the other girls as well. They'll need a woman to comfort them when we find them."

"They'll be lucky if they're still alive when we find them." He buckled on the sword a servant had brought him and checked the new, freshly-filled dart gun that had come from the same source. They had new garments as well—blue shirt and leather trousers and jerkin for him, a flowing blue dress with a touch of silver embroidery on the sleeves for her. Yareth looked at her, the frown on his face softening slightly. "You can help choose the men who will go with me. Will that make you feel any better?"

"No." But as it was the best that Yareth was presently prepared to allow, Eirran decided to make the best of it. The Witches had been searching all night by magic, trying to learn what had really happened on the road between Es City and the Place of Wisdom before sending out the rescue party. They would not leave until they were armed with as much foreknowledge as possible, and in that time Yareth might yet change his mind.

She followed him through corridors lighted by more globes placed high on the walls, from which a steady, if pale, glow radiated. Her footsteps were soundless; she now wore cloth slippers of the same type as some of the Witches themselves wore indoors. She had begun to think Yareth had lost his way when another man came toward them.

"Ah," the newcomer said. "You must be Yareth, the Falconer. I'm Girvan. The Guardian has assigned me to be your guide in case we have to go into Alizon itself. Been in and out of there many's the time myself."

Eirran looked at the man curiously. He had pale green eyes that caught the light oddly and blond hair so light it was almost colorless. His blue Guardsman's uniform looked somehow out of place on him, contrasting wrongly with his green eyes. He noticed her scrutiny.

"And you must be this fellow's, ah, lady. The little girl's mother." He laughed. "Aye, lady, I was born Alizonder. That's how I can go back and forth so easily without getting caught."

"I am Yareth. My wife's name is Eirran," Yareth said. "I told her she could help me pick the men who'll be going with us."

"Oh?" Girvan said without much interest. "Well, I've already lined up some good men to choose from. Come this way." He led them past a sentry and into a wider hall where a group of Guardsmen lingered at breakfast. "Have you eaten? No? Ranal, get our guests some food."

The man addressed as Ranal promptly got up from the table and dipped two bowls of porridge out of a full pot. A second pot, scraped empty and set aside, signified that a large number of men had recently breakfasted from it.

"Here, dip me another spoonful, will you?" another Guardsman said, holding out his bowl. He was a slightly built man, the kind who sometimes shows an astonishing appetite.

"You need more food, Kernon," Ranal said good-naturedly, "so you can grow big enough to match the rest of us."

Still, he did as he was asked. Kernon attacked the fresh porridge with a good appetite but Eirran pushed her bowl aside with a sudden pang of nausea. The state of her nerves must be worse than she thought. This stuff . . . her sense of smell had always been entirely too keen. Yareth also ignored the bowl in front of him, intent on his task.

"You are all volunteers?" he said. The men nodded. "I want to travel with as few as I dare and still have a party strong enough if it comes to a fight. There will be eight of us all told."

A Guard got up from his place at the table. "Then you'll need me," he said. "I'm Weldyn." He held one arm crooked, hand lightly clenched into a fist, as if by habit. Looking at the man's coloring and features, Eirran realized he had been born a Falconer despite the Guardsman's uniform he now wore. "I was with the men who brought the children to Es Castle in the first place."

Yareth nodded. "Yes," he said. He glanced at the rest of the Guards. "No Sulcarmen," he said. "You're too conspicuous." Two large, light-haired men shrugged at his words. "And none of the Old Race. We'll be going as blank shields, our story that we're sick of the eternal strife and conflict in Estcarp—"

"Not to mention being ordered about by women," Weldyn said.

Yareth glanced at him and nodded. "Whatever our reasons, we'll be pretending to seek employment in Alizon."

"Sounds like a good plan," one of the Sulcarmen said. "You want men who won't stand out in a crowd, then. Hirl's a good man. Ranal."

"Aye," a slim, dark-haired man said. "And Loric."

"Don't overlook me," Kernon said, looking up from his porridge. "I can out-ride any man twice my size and I'm a demon of a fighter."

The other Guardsmen laughed. "True enough!" one of them said, slapping Kernon on the shoulder. He was fair-featured, with light brown hair. He glanced up at Yareth good-naturedly. "Got more to prove, you see."

"That makes seven, including myself," Yareth said. "I want a company of eight. How about you?"

The guardsman got up and bowed from the waist. "Dunnis of Gorm, at your service," he said. "When do we leave?"

"As quickly as we can," Yareth said. He turned to Eirran. "Do you have any objection to my choice in men? Anybody you would prefer to any of them?"

"No, none," she said.

"Then would you go and find out from the Guardian what she has learned, for I am eager to be on my way."

"Gladly." Eirran got up from the table. A fresh whiff of the contents of the bowl assailed her nostrils. She left the mess hall at once, unwilling to stay and have to smell it. Really, she thought, the cooks in the Guardsmen's barracks must be poorly trained, to have burnt the porridge so badly.

IV

An hour later she entered the Guardian's presence. She had gotten lost again, but another of the gray-clad Witches showed her the way. "Is there any news?" Eirran said.

"Some, and not all of it good," the Guardian replied. "One of our sisterhood is dead. But we believe that the children are still alive."

Eirran went a little weak, her head spinning. She hoped she would not faint.

"Sit down," the Guardian said, indicating a footstool nearby. "You are very pale."

"I am relieved, that's all. I feared my daughter had perished. And the other children as well," she added quickly.

"And the other children. It may have been better that they had died, however. From what little we have been able to find out from this distance, the ones who attacked are taking the children northward. Toward Alizon."

"Toward Ali—" Eirran's breath caught in her throat. "But why?"

"Who knows? But if the Hounds are involved, it can be nothing good, that much is certain."

Eirran slipped from the footstool onto her knees. She clasped her hands at her breast. "Oh, Lady, please. Help me."

"What is it this time?"

"Yareth is forbidding me to go with him, searching for our daughter. But I can't go back to Blagden alone, to wait! My husband, and my child, both in danger? What if they kill her? What if they kill Yareth?"

"And what if you did go with him and they kill him and the child, and you as well?" the Guardian said with unexpected gentleness.

"Then I'd be with him at the end," Eirran said. She set her jaw stubbornly. "And my daughter. Please, Lady, I beg of you. Find a way to persuade him to take me along."

The Guardian sat back in her chair. "That might not be necessary," she said.

"Lady?"

"I got word only a few minutes ago that one of the men your Falconer picked has fallen ill. Something he ate did not agree with him."

A sudden memory of the bad-smelling porridge rushed over Eirran. That smell hadn't come from its being burnt and her imagination had not been playing tricks on her at all—the grain must have been spoiled! She was suddenly very glad that neither she nor Yareth had touched a bite. "I am sorry the man is sick," she said, "but I don't understand. What does this have to do with me?"

"Your husband is a very stubborn man. But now there is a way where there was none before—" the Guardian said.

Suddenly, Eirran realized what the Witch was saying. She blinked in surprise. "Shapechanging?"

"It will be quite easy, really. Kernon is of relatively slight stature."

"Oh, yes, yes, please!" Eirran cried. "I'll do anything—"

"Bring the children back to us. That will be enough."

"I pledge it on my life's blood."

"Come with me." The Witch led Eirran to a star-shape inlaid in the floor and picked out in brilliant blue stones. "Stand in the center," she said.

She gestured at a nearby brazier and flame suddenly spurted from its interior. A reddish mist began to fill the place where Eirran stood. A little giddily, she found herself wondering if it were confined to the area of the pentagram or if it filled the entire room. She could barely make out the shape of the Witch's form. The sound of someone singing came filtering through the haze, as if the musician stood at a great distance. A new kind of dizziness assailed her as, willing or not, she inhaled the smoke. The song entered her being, became one with her, bone of her bone and flesh of her flesh. Throbbing with a strange, unsettling warmth, she closed her eyes. She didn't want to look at what might be happening. Dizzily, she fancied that if she did look, she could see her body dissolving into the mist and draining away to re-form into a new and different shape, one wiry and muscular, not much taller than her own—

The song faded. "Open your eyes," the Guardian said.

Eirran obeyed. The mist had turned gray, and even as she blinked, it dissolved and dissipated into nothing. She looked down at herself, unable to keep back an exclamation of disappointment. "Oh! It didn't work!"

"Did it not?" the Guardian said. She took a square of polished silver from a nearby table and handed it to Eirran. "Tell me what you see in there."

She gasped again, this time in surprise. "Why—why it's Kernon's face!" She gazed at her hand, slender and fine-boned, then held it where she could catch its reflection in the metal. There it was a different image entirely—sun-darkened, heavier of bone, calloused on palm from hours of practice with the sword and dart-gun—definitely a man's hand. "And, I suppose Kernon's hand. But how—" She gazed at herself again, staring at the man's face she had last seen that morning over his second breakfast of spoiled porridge. Only her eyes were still her own.

"You can't see the magic because you're inside it," the Guardian explained. "But others will. You can only see it reflected in mirrors, like this, or in still water."

"How long will it last?" asked, half-unbelieving of her good fortune.

"As long as necessary. Beware that your husband does not learn your secret, however. He's the one who could penetrate the illusion, as he knows you best. If he does—" The Guardian shrugged. "Well, you'll just have to hope that you're so far on your journey that he won't dare send you back alone."

"Oh, thank you, Lady, thank you."

"There's no time for that. Go and dress you, and arm yourself with Kernon's gear. You leave within the hour."

"But won't Yareth wonder why I am not there to bid him farewell?"

The Guardian smiled frostily. "Not if he thinks you have gone already."

Eirran nodded slowly. "I do have a temper. And we did quarrel." She made up her mind. "Yes. It may create trouble between us later, but it will work." She bowed to the Witch as a man would, and then hurried off to do her bidding.

V

An hour later eight men dressed for the road, all cloaked and wearing chain mail and bearing fully-laden saddlebags, rode out of Es Castle. Half a league past the city gate they turned off the main road onto the lesser one leading north and west, in the direction of the Place of Wisdom.

Eirran carefully maneuvered her horse so she was near the back of the party. All of them rode sturdy, road-wise Torgians like Yareth's and Weldyn's, though Witches had changed the other horses' appearances before they left. It would have looked suspicious if all of them had been so well-mounted. Now Eirran seemed to be riding a scrubby roan. Rangin and the other Falconer's Torgian were unchanged, however; Falconers' fondness for the finest in horseflesh was well known and if they had appeared to be mounted on less, that fact would have occasioned the comment they wished to avoid. Both men carried birds on the forks of their saddles. Eirran's concern was not only that Yareth might recognize her eyes looking out of Kernon's countenance, brief though his acquaintance with the man might be, but also that Rangin or even Newbold might be able to see through her illusion disguise, so she kept a prudent distance from all of them.

She could detect Yareth's secret anger in the set of his shoulders, the tightness of his jaw. She knew he must be furious because he thought she had left without even a farewell.

But it couldn't be helped. It was enough that she was with him, enough that only a few people knew that one of the men riding out to rescue the Witch-children was really a woman.

Four

I

$\mathcal{M}$ouse thought that she had never seen anything so magnificent as the gray-green walls and towers of Es City and the great castle it sheltered. Though she had promised herself she would not act like the mouse she was named for, fresh from the country and green as grass, she couldn't help looking from side to side as the travelers rode in, singing. She felt a little better when she discovered that the others were doing the same thing. Lisper was even looking upwards as well, as if new wonders might come pouring from the sky at any moment. Lisper caught Mouse looking and the two girls had to put their hands over their mouths to hold in their laughter, lest the others start giggling too and the song be spoiled.

People stopped and stared at them as they rode straight down the main street, through the castle gatehouse and to the great stables were men came out and took the horses and ponies and led them away. Rhinfar saluted smartly and Bee dismissed him with her thanks. Then he and his men marched off, taking a different direction once they were within the castle grounds.

"Where are they going?" Flame asked.

"To the barracks. That's where they stay, when they're in the castle." Bee smiled at her charges. "Come children, let's go inside now. Don't tarry."

"So soon?" Star said. She sounded startled. "Are we going to start our lessons today?"

"You've forgotten. This is where the Guardian lives."

"But how do we get in, Bee?" Cricket said in dismay. "There are no doors!"

Bee laughed. "It's a simple trick, to fool the unwary. I'll show you. You won't be staying long here, just overnight. Another lady will take you to the Place of Wisdom—" An outburst of "No!" from six little girls, all in chorus, interrupted her and she shushed the children firmly. "My job is finished, bringing you this far. My work is here, at the Council, with the Guardian. She wants to talk with each of you, however, before you go. Come along, we've got fresh clothes so you can change and make yourselves presentable."

Bee showed the children the trick of how to see through the illusionary walls barring the entrance. Then she herded her charges through double doors and into high, echoing corridors that led to a large dormitory room plastered and painted white, decorated with a band of painted red and blue flowers, high up where the ceiling met the walls. There were six beds with a stand beside each, and each stand held a basin filled with warm water. Beside each basin lay a cake of soap. But Mouse scarcely paid any attention to any of the dormitory's fine furnishings or even the water, eager as she was to wash the road-dust off her face and hands. To her astonished delight, on the beds lay six gray robes, identical except for size to the one Bee wore. And on the floor, just under the edge of the beds, lay six pairs of gray cloth slippers, to replace their clumsy footgear, and there were new sandals as well.

The children, squealing with delight, rushed forward to examine their new garments.

"Oh, can we really, really wear these?" Flame asked. She already had her shoes off and was wriggling her feet into her new slippers.

"Of course you may," Bee answered. "But not until you are clean."

The girls immediately stripped to their undergarments and began splashing in the water so enthusiastically the floor and walls were soon splattered and dripping. Bee had to examine each child in turn, to see that she had gotten at least a little of the water on herself as well. As for the soap, it seemed to be a lost cause. Finally she gave up, sent for a fresh supply of water and supervised each little girl, one by one, as she bathed, making certain she washed everywhere—with soap—even behind the ears.

"You children," she said, shaking her head with mock disapproval at Lisper, who was last in line for the baths. The other girls giggled and squirmed, proud of their new garments and how very fine they looked in them. "You're never going to learn how to behave. I just hope you won't act like this when you're with the Guardian."

"We won't," Cricket said. "I'm hungry!"

"Me, too!" the others said.

Mouse had been sniffing the strange soap-smell—green, like herbs, and not at all like the soap Mama made, that smelled like fresh flowers—and thinking that it was very nice in its own way. Suddenly she discovered that she too was ravenous. "Can we eat just a little before we go see the Guardian?" she asked.

"Yes, of course. It will be one of our last times together for a while," Bee said. "But I'll try to come and have breakfast with you tomorrow. Now, line up. Let me look at you."

When Bee was satisfied with their appearance, she led them to another room. Windows opened onto an inner courtyard, and there was a door to the outside as well. There were six places laid at a long table—bowls, spoons, wooden cups. Mouse sighed a little.

"What's wrong, Mouse?" Bee said.

"Oh, nothing."

"Come on, now, what's wrong?"

"This is just like what we had at home."

"And you expected something finer than wood bowls. Silver. Or pewter at least."

Mouse nodded, ashamed. "I always put flowers on our table when there were any."

"Well," Bee said, "Witches don't set much store by finery. You must learn that. But we can have some flowers."

A rose vine grew just outside the door, and several buds were just breaking into bloom. Bee brought the flowers in, put them in a vial of water and set it in the middle of the table, close to where Mouse was sitting. "Is that better?" she said.

"Oh, yes, thank you, Bee," Mouse said. Contentedly she spooned barley soup into her mouth. From time to time she touched the roses. They were beautiful and smelled wonderful.

Later, because the Guardian was busy and couldn't see them just yet, they were allowed out into the courtyard. There they played happily in the sunshine. But this time, there was no uproarious game of Catch Me, as there had been on the road when they had been overexcited and had to work off excess energy or burst. Now that they were actually in Es City, and in the very middle—or so it seemed—of Es Castle, it seemed that this rare moment of peace filtered into them and made them calm. Cricket found a length of string and amused herself with teaching Lisper how to work cat's cradle; Mouse and Bird giggled together softly as Lisper made mistake after mistake, trying to follow Cricket's instructions.

"You're the worst at cat's cradle I've ever seen," Bird said contentedly. "Far worse than I ever was."

"Am not," Lisper said. Her fingers twinkled in the sunlight and suddenly the string formed a very complicated arrangement that Cricket had definitely not showed her. "Thee?"

Mouse looked at her new gray slippers, wriggling her toes with pleasure. She had never had slippers like this before. She would wear the sandals over them, she understood, when she went outside the walls of Es Castle. Later, when summer finally arrived, she would leave off the slippers and put the sandals on over bare feet, just as she had done all her life. She thought this arrangement was probably the nicest idea anybody had ever had about shoes, and slippers, and feet. Her feet always got so cold in the winter, and now they weren't cold at all.

Star wandered about the courtyard, looking at everything

but not touching anything. Flame simply sat very still in the middle of the garden, wrapped in her own thoughts, and the other children did not disturb her.

II

That afternoon, the girls lined up to go in and have their interviews with the Guardian. All at once, now that the moment had arrived, the children turned very shy. Bee had to choose which one went first, which one second, and so on, for the children seemed utterly incapable of it. Mouse was fourth in the line of suddenly subdued little girls, sitting on a bench outside the Guardian's door. Either there was another door leading out of the room or they all stayed inside once they went in, for nobody came back to tell them what the interviews were like. Mouse thought it was probably for the best that Star, the most composed of them all, was also the last. She could stand the waiting better than any of the others.

Before she knew it, it was Mouse's turn to go in. She gulped hard. She stared at the handle on the door. It was made of bronze, cast in the shape of some unimaginable creature. Mouse fancied that its eyes winked at her and it leered and writhed in her grasp. She nearly let go. Right at that moment she wanted nothing more in her life than to run away and hide, anywhere where she didn't have to look at hideous beasts on door handles, didn't have to wear gray dresses, didn't have to go to some unimaginable school a world away from Mama and Papa, didn't have to go and meet a strange old lady who was as terrible as her door handle and probably twice as ugly. Then the moment of rebellion passed. Resolutely, she grasped the metal beast again so firmly it stopped squirming in her hands. Heart pounding and her mouth so dry she could hardly swallow, she twisted the handle, pushed the door open, and went inside.

To her surprise, she discovered a very pleasant room indeed. It was small and cozy, with tapestries on the wall and a fire burning on the hearth. Another lady waited inside, dressed in gray, and she looked very much like all the other gray-clad ladies, and not at all old or ugly or beast-like, even if she did have a dreadful handle on her door. Another lady was coming through a small door at the far end of the room, carrying a tray. She set the tray down and departed the way she had come.

"Welcome, my child," the Guardian said. "I was just going to make some tea. Have you ever had tea?"

"Oh, yes, Lady, thank you," Mouse said politely. "My Mama used to make it all the time and she would let me drink a little when I was good."

The lady's mouth twitched. "Then you must know just how to do it. Will you make it for me? And since Bee tells me you've been very good indeed, you shall have a cup all for yourself."

Proudly, Mouse sat down across from the lady and began measuring out the sweet-smelling leaves from the jar. Frowning with concentration, sticking her tongue out from between her teeth, she poured just the right amount of hot water into the pot and let the brew steep. Cautiously, she checked at what seemed the proper time. The tea was perfect. As she handed the cup to the Guardian, she realized she had been very silly to be afraid. She had never had a single thing to worry about, for this lady was every bit as nice as Bee. She felt very much at home and presently she and the Guardian were chatting like old friends about anything that Mouse wanted to talk about.

"You have a pretty necklace, too," Mouse said, staring at the bluish-gray stone hanging from the silver chain around the Guardian's neck. She glanced down at her new gray dress, thinking how much she wanted a necklace just like it, and how nice it would look around her neck. "It's like the one Bee wears."

"This is more than an adornment," the Guardian said. "It is part of our mystery. Each Witch has her own Jewel, and it is hers alone. It helps us do wonderful things. Watch."

With that, she picked up the Jewel and set it in the palm of her hand. To Mouse's astonishment the gem began to glow. As she watched, the light grew brighter and brighter until it became so intense that it overpowered all the other light in the room, creating strange shadows that flickered over the Guardian's face.

Mouse sat open-mouthed. Her skin tingled, as if hundreds of crawling things danced over it. But there was nothing, nothing that she could see. Awe-struck, Mouse realized that this was part of the Power that Bee had spoken of on their journey. Power fairly crackled through the room, its flow strongest between the Jewel and the Witch who held it. The Guardian's black hair had been caught in a silver net. Under the force of the light, the net fell away. The hair, loosened from the tight net, began to stir and lift. The force intensified until the Guardian's hair streamed upward in the light the Jewel was giving off, as if she were standing on some high mountainside, facing into a cold and bracing wind. Mouse forgot to be frightened, she was so fascinated. And also the Guardian was looking at her and smiling a little, so even if she were afraid she couldn't possibly allow herself to show it.

Then the lady looked back at the gem and blew on it lightly. The level of Power immediately dropped and Mouse became aware that she had somehow been hearing as well as seeing it as the strange and noiseless sound died away. The thumping in her ears lessened until it became only the sound of her own heartbeat. She moved, discovering that she had been held frozen, unable to stir while the marvel was going on.

"Oh, thank you!" Mouse breathed. "That was wonderful. I wish I had a silver necklace with a Jewel in it. I'd do that all the time."

The lady smiled. For no reason that Mouse understood, she suddenly looked tired. "No, you wouldn't, I'm afraid," she said. "But I'm glad you want to. Would you like to touch it?"

"Ooh!" Mouse whispered. "Could I? Really?"

"Yes, of course."

Hesitantly, Mouse reached out and put a fingertip on the milky gray stone. Suddenly it flared to life with a burst of light and Mouse snatched her hand back as if it had been scalded. She stuck her finger in her mouth, but it was unharmed. The gem was perfectly cool. Perhaps the flash of light had been the last spark of what the lady had shown her, the way a fire will blaze up just before it dies for good.

The lady chuckled indulgently. "You will have a Jewel of your own one day, you know, when you are all grown up and have learned all your lessons. You must study very hard, and mind your teachers so you can grow up tall and straight—"

All of a sudden, the lady sounded just like Mama. "I'll bet you're going to tell me to eat my vegetables," Mouse said mischievously.

The lady laughed out loud. "Yes, you'll have to eat your vegetables," she said. She tweaked Mouse affectionately on the ear. "And when you do grow up, you'll have a Jewel of your very own. You will be a Witch, just like the rest of us, and you'll live for many, many years."

III

The next morning, Mouse and the other girls met Leaf, the lady who was going to take them to the Place of Wisdom. Leaf and Bee both had breakfast with the children.

"I hope you have better luck with this lot than I did," Bee said. She used the tone of voice that told the girls she was teasing, pretending to be displeased with them. "They are quite impossible, and haven't learned any manners at all, despite my best efforts to teach them."

Leaf smiled. The corners of her eyes crinkled in such a way that Mouse realized she was very kind. "Oh, I don't think we'll have much trouble. Will, we, ladies?"

"Oh, no, Leaf," the girls answered, almost in chorus.

"I'm sure we'll all be on our very best behavior with *you,* Leaf," Cricket added irrepressibly. The rest of the girls giggled.

"Do you see what I mean?" Bee said. "Full of mischief, every one of them."

"Full of life, and that's what we need just now," Leaf said. "Well, come, ladies, finish your breakfast. We must get on our way."

"Will we ride our ponies?" Flame asked.

"And will we have guards like last time?" Bird wanted to know.

"Yes, to both," Leaf said, "though we won't need as many guards here in the middle of Estcarp. Two ought to be plenty."

"Shall we wear our old clothes?" That was Star, the practical one.

"Oh, no!" Cricket said. "Please, let us wear our new ones. We'll be very very very good, and stay clean, and not get muddy or anything."

Leaf pursed her lips, thinking. "Perhaps you should," she said. "No reason why you shouldn't begin acting as much like Witches as possible."

"Then Lisper's hopeless!" Cricket said, nudging her in the ribs and giggling. "I never heard of a Witch who couldn't even talk right!"

"That'th becauth you don't know everything even if you think you do," Lisper retorted, nudging her in return. Leaf leaned forward to break up the scuffle.

"I've heard of Witches who lisped, and Witches who were hard of hearing, and even Witches who couldn't see with their physical eyes," she said. She glanced up at Bee. "I'm beginning to see what you meant."

"Well, I'll leave you to it now," Bee said. "I have other duties waiting."

"Yes. The Guardian is very pleased and wants to have another Incalling as soon as we get these girls settled. If we are lucky, you won't have long to rest."

The two women clasped hands and kissed each other on the cheek. Mouse turned a spoonful of porridge over in her bowl, watching wide-eyed, hastily putting the spoon in her mouth when Leaf turned back to her charges.

"When you are finished," she said, "we will depart."

Cheerfully, the children scraped their bowls and stacked them for servants to attend to. Then they lined up for Leaf's inspection.

"You do need cloaks," she said. "It is still cool in the mornings. Why don't you all go in and look on your beds?"

The little girls rushed squealing back into their dormitory. Mouse discovered that while she had been having breakfast, someone had placed a warm gray cloak on each bed. Her old cloak was gone, taken away somewhere. But she didn't even miss it; it had grown too short on her by now anyway. In her pleasure at the fine new garment, she forgot that it had been Mama who had sewed the old one for her. Delighted, she picked it up and held it to her face, enjoying the wonderful, unique smell of an article that had never been worn before. And it was long, like the ones grown-up ladies wore! Almost long enough to brush the ground. Only the tips of her new gray slippers would show. What could the fabric be woven of? It wasn't wool, though it was warm under her hands. Instead, the texture was what she had always imagined silk would feel like. And it was feather-light.

Quickly, she put her cloak on. The other children donned their new garments as well, sliding their feet into their new sandals. With that, they were ready to depart. Dressed all in grey from top to toe, they looked as demure as a covey of quail as they followed Leaf out of the castle and into the courtyard where their ponies waited for them. Two Guardsmen, neither of whom were among the ones who had accompanied them on their journey to Es City, stood nearby, horses saddled and ready. One of the Guards led a third horse forward for Leaf and very courteously helped her climb into the saddle.

"Fair morning, Lady," he said.

"Fair morning indeed," she replied, "when we have precious cargo like this to convey!" She gazed at the children proudly.

Mouse sat very straight and still on her pony, hands folded over the reins the way she had seen Papa sit on Rangin. She wondered if she would be allowed to keep her pony when they got to the Place of Wisdom or if Leaf and the two Guardsmen would take the ponies back for other little girls to ride when they came to Es City to be Witches. She rather hoped she would be allowed to keep the pony; she had grown fond of the fat, dappled animal on their journey. But she remembered one of Bee's lessons—Witches cared nothing for material possessions, for things of the world. All they cared about was magic, each other, and their Jewels.

IV

Mouse had come almost to believe that Estcarp was grayish-green throughout, that where one saw this color of the land, there was Estcarp. But gradually, the hues and tones of the landscape began to change as they rode north and west, becoming gray-green mixed with buff brown. Mouse realized this must be because they were coming closer to the sea, and the sandy shores that edged it.

The road bent. There was an island of isolated gray-green rocks erupting from buff brown soil, the foot of a low mountainous area, and rather than go through, those who had built the road veered from their straight path to skirt around it. This area looked like a wild place, where no one but a huntsman would ever go. Mouse wondered what Papa would think of a spot like this. He liked hunting and mountains, even if these weren't much, as mountains go.

They rode through a notch cut through the rocks at the very toe of the ridge. There were high places on either side. Just as they reached the middle of the notch, there was a scrabble of claws on rock. Mouse gasped as a pack of white dogs leaped out of hiding, swarming down onto the roadway and surrounding the riders. The air filled with their savage barking and snarling. The dogs nipped at the hooves of the ponies and horses, and jumped at their throats. The animals whinnied and shied away, trying to avoid the dogs and almost unseating their riders. A band of armed men came leaping out of hiding places in the rocks, following on the very heels of the dogs. From somewhere a hunting horn sounded and a man's voice rose, urging them on.

Leaf fought for control of her horse. The animal reared and plunged, panicked, threatening to throw her to the ground. The two Guardsmen fought their mounts under control. They spurred forward at once, scattering dogs in their wake as they drew their weapons. From someplace up in the rocks came two flat, hissing *zwwats!,* the second hard upon the first. One of the Guardsmen gave a cry and fell backward, caught in the trappings of his saddle. An ugly, stubby shaft, like an arrow only shorter and thicker, protruded from his chest. At almost the same moment something whizzed by Mouse's cheek, so close she blinked and flinched, crying out at its passing.

"Watch your aim!" one of the attackers shouted.

The girls clustered together, screaming in terror, their wild-eyed ponies shuffling aimlessly, out of control. The ponies weren't bred for combat and they didn't know what to do, or how to react. Quickly, Leaf got her mount under control.

"Get back, girls!" she cried. She snatched the sword from the body of the man who had been killed and rode forward to the other Guardsman's side. He was in danger of being pulled down by the attackers who rushed at him from both sides. Leaf scattered the men as she hurled her horse straight at them. Her sword rose and fell, and one of the attackers fell with it.

Though they dug their heels into their ponies' flanks and struck them with their reins, none of the girls could make the animals stir from that spot. A flash of movement from above caught Mouse's eye. She looked up. Another man now stood high on a point of rock where he had a commanding view of the struggle going on below. He had removed his crested helmet so he could take better aim with the crossbow he held. Mouse stared, unable to move, unable to cry out, while every detail of the man's appearance etched itself on her mind.

His blue-green jacket laced from throat to waist, and over it he wore a wide belt. There was a device on the right breast of the jacket, something white. He wore skin-tight breeches of the same color as his jacket, and his boots rose in high peaks on the outside of his legs. Sidearms and pouches hung from his belt. His white hair blew in the wind. Calmly, as if he were shooting at a target, he aimed the crossbow and squeezed the trigger. A third *zwwat!* sounded and the remaining Guardsman fell. The skinny white dogs yapped and howled and snarled, leaping at Leaf as if they wanted to pull her down into the dust as well. Some of the hounds broke away from the turmoil and rushed at the children.

Then, as abruptly as it had all begun, it was over. Before the hounds could do them harm, the white-haired men strode forward, slapping the dogs away, avoiding Leaf's futile efforts to strike with her sword, pulling the struggling Witch from her horse. Other men gathered the ponies, brooking no nonsense from the frightened beasts. They lifted the children to the ground and shoved them to one side. A couple of the men stood guard over them, ready to grab any who looked as if she might run away.

"Well done!" shouted the leader up in the rocks. He started down, jumping from foothold to foothold. Mouse hoped he would fall and break his neck. But he didn't even slip, not once.

"Kill us and you'll never live to reach the Alizon border," Leaf said fiercely. She still struggled in the grip of the men who held her, and one of them slapped her sharply across the face. Blood oozed from her lip.

The man leaped the last few feet to level ground and walked arrogantly toward Leaf. "True enough, we don't have the luxury of tarrying to enjoy, ah, Estcarp hospitality. But you needn't worry about us killing your charges. We're under other orders about them. But you— Well, we can spare a few minutes, eh, men?" He looked around, grinning, and other grimly smiling faces answered him.

Leaf's struggles seemed not to be so much to free herself from the men who held her as attempts to grasp the Jewel that hung around her neck. The leader watched for a moment. Then, without haste, he stepped forward, grasped the gem, and pulled sharply. The chain broke. Leaf cried out, and blood trickled from her neck where the thin chain had cut her skin.

"None of that, now, Witch," the leader said. "We know all about your tricks." He turned and threw the Jewel away, high into the spot where the ambushers had lain hidden. It clattered against some rocks. He nodded to the men. "We'll have to hurry, in case she managed to get a message back before we caught her. But we can make sure she won't send another. Ever again."

At once, Leaf's captors dragged her off the road toward a spot where stakes had already been hammered into the ground. They flung her down and tied her arms and legs so she couldn't move at all. She screamed and tried to bite them, using the only weapons remaining to her, her teeth, so when they ripped her gray robe from her body, they took part of it and stuffed it into her mouth.

"Leaf!" cried Cricket. It was a shout of pure despair.

"Are we going to be next?" Flame said fearfully.

"No," Star said. "They have other plans for us."

"I can't watch," Bird said. "I think I'm going to be sick."

Cricket was clinging to Mouse; she managed to put one arm around Bird as well. All the girls huddled even closer together, beginning to cry. But nothing would blot out the sounds coming from the spot by the side of the road. Men jostled with one another, making coarse jokes. Leaf moaned and screamed through the gag in her mouth.

Some of the dogs had come back to the men who commanded them and a few sat nearby on thin haunches, panting, regarding the children with curious eyes. Mouse thought she had never seen anything so ugly as those pale, skinny hounds with their narrow, snake-like heads. Bird's frail body shuddered. Then she leaned forward, retching. Mouse pushed aside her own nausea, finding the strength to help Bird.

The noises around Leaf ceased and Mouse looked up, hoping to find that the men had let her loose. Instead, one of the men stood over her, sword upraised. Leaf spat out the gag in her mouth. Her gaze and Mouse's locked. Something went tingling through the air between them and Mouse reeled back as if she had been struck.

"It's yours, Mouse! Use it to—"

The sword fell. Leaf gave a great shudder, and was still.

Mouse stared and stared, numb with shock, unable to speak, unable to move. She scarcely knew when she was bundled up and slung across the front of somebody's saddle. She lay half conscious, wanting only to find some place to hide until she could cleanse that horrible picture from her mind. But those last few moments when Leaf died repeated themselves over and over, a second image overriding what she must think of as reality. The scene sprang out like a moving tapestry embroidered on the backs of her eyelids if she slept or tried to blot out the sight of the white-haired men and their gaunt hounds by squeezing her eyes shut. That first terrible day passed, finally ended, and another. And still another.

She knew it was day only because she was on somebody's horse, riding, riding, riding to somewhere unknown. She knew it was night only when she was tossed onto the ground with the other girls to huddle together, tearful and afraid. Mouse lost count of the days and nights that had passed before she came back to herself enough to realize that the other girls were in almost as bad shape as she, though only Star had happened to be looking in that direction when the man had slain Leaf.

"It really happened, didn't it?" she asked Star tremulously.

"Yes," the other girl said. "It really did. Are you all right now? I was afraid we were going to lose you."

"She spoke my name."

"I know. I heard."

"I don't think I'll ever be the same. But I'm better."

"None of us will ever be the same." Star's voice was somber. She moved closer to Lisper, who cuddled against her, glassy-eyed, thumb in mouth.

For the first time Mouse felt strong enough to try to call out to her Mama, from inside, to make her *hear* the way she had used to. Mama had never known why she always knew to come when Mouse needed her, and Mouse had never told her. But something told her now that she could call and call but it wouldn't be any use. Mama was too far away.

"I want to go home," Bird said. Her face was dirty, streaked with lines where tears had washed some of the grime away.

"We all want to go home," Flame said.

"But we can't." Cricket wiped her nose on her sleeve.

"We can't *yet,*" Mouse said. Cricket and Bird stared at her. "Not yet," she repeated a little more strongly. She knew—she just *knew* her Mama and Papa would come and find her and her friends and take her home.

Then, with a pang that made her catch her breath she realized that she had no idea which home she wanted to go to—home home, with Mama and Papa, or the home with the Witches of Estcarp where she knew she belonged.

Five

I

*A*ll too clearly, the tragedy at the foot of the mountain revealed itself even to the eyes of someone who didn't know how to read trail-sign, like Eirran. Loric and Dunnis hurried forward to untie the Witch's body. The Hounds had simply left it there, abandoned, when they tired of the atrocities that had killed the woman. Loric took off his cloak and covered the broken corpse until such time as they could bury it. Ranal and

Hirl, grim-faced, set themselves the task of gathering their comrades' bodies and placing the dead all together in one spot. Eirran forced herself to go and help.

I am disguised as Kernon, she reminded herself, so I must be Kernon. I must not get sick, I must not cry, I must not get the hiccups.

Yareth and Weldyn sent their falcons aloft to keep watch lest the enemy still be near and return to fall upon the small band of would-be rescuers. Then the two Falconers prowled through the immediate area, noting each detail of the ambush and subsequent battle with great care.

"There must have been twenty men," Weldyn said. "And as many dogs."

Hirl exhaled sharply through his nose. "They didn't want to take any chances, then. Those are strong odds."

"They left the bodies of the Witch and the Guards," Loric said. "But we see no children's bodies."

"That is because they must have stolen the children," Girvan said. He stared northward, frowning.

"Yes. By their tracks, the horses were carrying heavier burdens away with them than they brought." Weldyn followed Girvan's gaze, and an even deeper scowl settled on his features. It was more an expression of concentrated thought, however, than of outrage and contemplated vengeance.

Hirl shook his head. "If only we could have come in time. We could have evened those odds a little, I think. Saved our comrades. Perhaps the lady would not have suffered."

"And perhaps we would have died in the effort," Dunnis said. "Twenty Hounds, with their hell-dogs, to our eight—ten if you think our dead comrades might have lived past the ambush. Even those aren't odds I'm comfortable with."

Weldyn returned from searching the heights to either side of the ambush site. Something dangled from his hand. "Now we know why the Witch didn't get a more detailed message back," he said. "They tore this off her before she could use it properly."

He stared at the pendant in his hand. "Might as well bury this with her body. They say the things are worthless after their owner dies."

"No," Eirran said before she could think or stop herself. All eyes turned in her direction. "I mean," she said nervously, "the lady was a good sort. I hate to see all trace of her disappear."

"A sourvenir?" Weldyn said. He tossed the Jewel to Eirran and she snatched it out of the air. "Take it, then. The silver is worth something. But I don't want it."

Carefully, Eirran put the Jewel away in her doublet. Perhaps it had been her imagination, or a trick of the light, but she thought she had seen a faint spark in the Jewel's depths. Perhaps, perhaps— Oh, she didn't know why she had been moved to save the artifact. But some force, possibly the effect of the male disguise that hid her true form, had bidden her act as she had, and she dared not disobey. She moved off to the side, pretending to stir a fire that was burning perfectly. Yareth had come back into camp as well and now he was looking at her in a very puzzled manner, as if wondering why she had bothered to take a lifeless Witch Jewel.

Then he turned to the three bodies waiting burial, two strong men cut down in their strength, and the third a slight form mercifully covered with Loric's cloak. "I am not one who loves the Hags of Estcarp," Yareth said. "Indeed, I have great cause to feel otherwise. But neither would I willingly see such things done to one of them."

"Nor I," Weldyn said. "It has gone hard with me, these past few years, taking orders from a woman. But the times being what they are, one must do the best one can." He looked at Yareth curiously. "You're the one who is actually married to a woman, aren't you? How does it feel, always to be with one of *them,* always to be at her beck and call? Always to be in her bed."

Yareth merely shrugged and made no answer. "We must bury these bodies decently, and start trailing the Hounds," he said. "We'll have to keep well back, out of sight, sound, and smell of those war-dogs of theirs until we see some chance that we can prevail against them. If we are not careful, they'll kill the fledglings out of hand and not wait to take them back for whatever purpose they stole them."

Weldyn turned the corners of his mouth down. "Concern about your own fledgling, I can almost understand, even if it is a girl-chick. But why should you care about the others?"

"It was my promise."

"Promise! To a woman!"

Ranal spoke up. "It's a good thing we're out of earshot of the Witches—or at least you think and hope we are," he said, and was rewarded by the flash of apprehension that flitted briefly across Weldyn's face. "You warble an entirely different kind of song back in Es Castle, Falconer."

"We are what we are," Weldyn said with a shrug. It was no apology. He glanced again at Yareth. "Except when some of us give up what we are to become something else."

"Let's get about our work," Yareth said. "The sooner we're finished here, the sooner we'll be on our way."

II

They carried the bodies away from the ambush site and buried them on a ridge of low mountains overlooking the open gray-green countryside between there and Es City. They built a cairn of rocks, both as a marker and as protection against any prowling wild thing that might be attracted by the scent and further desecrate the dead.

North they rode, and still north, following an ancient route. Once there had been a high road, well-kept and tended, symbol of happier times between the lands north and south. Now, the farther they went, the more the road degenerated until it became something little better than a track through the land. In these perilous times it was used only by those few traders who dared carry their wares from country to country, and by the brave garth-holders who clung to their estates along the edge of

the Alizon Ridge. And spies, of course, both Alizon's and Estcarp's. The Tor Fen stood between, feared and hated by Alizon
and Estcarp alike. To venture into Tor Marsh was to resign
one's self from this life. Those who entered therein did not
return and only the darkest rumors circulated as to their fate.
The greenish-gray countryside of central Estcarp changed as
well as they went, growing darker and less welcoming as the
rescue party neared the land of the Tormen, and the swamps
and fens and moors of that dismal spot.

Perhaps another people had once dwelt to the north, and had
built and used this road in bygone years. But now Alizon's
barons lorded it in the northern land, glorying in the horses they
bred from Torgian stock, and in the thin-flanked hounds they
used for hunting and for war.

All the men—even Weldyn—chafed at the necessity of keeping their distance and not closing with their enemy openly, and
as soon as possible. Unspoken among all the pursuers was the
question of why the Witch-children had been taken, and what
might be happening to them now. To Eirran this last was the
hardest of all the difficulties she found herself facing on this
most peculiar of journeys.

Their first night on the road, habit almost made her fall to
working alongside Yareth, making camp, and she had to restrain herself. The first few days of their acquaintance, when she
had virtually been his prisoner, she had flatly refused any assistance in his upkeep. But when they had made a wary peace, they
discovered they worked together very well, as if they knew each
other's thoughts without either having to speak. Then they had
been traveling, seeking a home for them both after their near-
disastrous adventure in the Barrier Mountains. She had taught
him how to find wild vegetables and edible roots, where before
he had been content to eat what game he could take or what
birds the falcon, Newbold, could hunt. And she had taught him
a finer art of camp cookery than he had known. In turn, he had
taught her how to build rabbit-snares, and which ground ro-

dents made good eating and which to avoid. Together, they lived off the land quite well; apart, each missed what the other brought to the partnership.

Following the clear trail the Alizonders left, the eight riders found the campsite chosen by the Hounds for their first night on the road northward. The Falconers searched it thoroughly for whatever information could be gleaned. But all that they could learn with any certainty was that the children were still alive at the time of this camping, and that they had slept close together, as if for comfort. But without a word passing among them, the pursuers decided to bypass this unhappy spot and seek their own night-place elsewhere.

The Falconers sent Newbold and Sharpclaw aloft on the lookout both for enemies and for game fowl. While Weldyn went out of camp and hunted for other meat, Yareth searched the area for edible plants and wild herbs for seasoning. Somewhat to Eirran's surprise, he proved quite good at this homely task; she had taught him better than she thought. Weldyn had given him a hard, sideways glance as he left, but said nothing.

With the other men, Eirran helped prepare the place for the night. They picketed the horses, fed and brushed them, and gave them water. Then they swept the area around the campfire clean so their rest would be untroubled by rocks digging into their backs. By the time they had finished these tasks, Weldyn had returned with a brace of rabbits and the falcons had brought down a bird apiece. Dunnis took them and began preparing them for cooking. The shadows lengthened, turning late afternoon into evening.

"Do I remember correctly, Girvan? You did say you are Alizonder, are you not?" Yareth said. He now sat out of the way, stroking Newbold and feeding him tidbits while Dunnis tended the pot. Weldyn sat opposite, occupied likewise with the feeding of Sharpclaw.

"I *was* Alizonder," Girvan said. His tone was, perhaps, a trifle more brusque than it might have been had the eight riders not been pursuing others of Alizon breed. He fiddled with a buckle that had come loose on his horse's harness. "I am of Estcarp now. Of Estcarp."

"Still, you were once of Alizon and know of Alizon, else the Guardian would not have recommended you as guide. While we are waiting for the meat to cook, I beg you tell us what you know of the place, since it would seem that this path takes us closer with every step."

Girvan nodded. "You are right, Yareth. From the looks of things, the Hounds—" he spat to one side "—are taking the children straight to Alizon, and us with them. Forgive my short temper. It is hard, knowing that kinsmen of mine might have been involved in—in what we found earlier. Very well. I'll tell you what I know. But you must remember that it's been four months at least since I was last there. Things may have changed in the meantime. And I may be repeating what some of us already know. Still I will tell it once again, so we may know better what we are facing."

Without a word, the other men settled themselves a little closer to listen, and Girvan began his tale.

III

That Alizon hated Estcarp and all it represented was so well and widely known that nobody even bothered to mention the fact. For many, many years, the Alizonders, under their ruling Baron Facellian, had carried on a war of attrition against Estcarp, barely contenting themselves with raids from time to time, and with capturing the occasional Estcarpian who ventured too near the border. The men were killed immediately; but the women—particularly any Witch who might have gone seeking information about Alizon's activities—were dealt with in much the same harsh and deadly fashion as had been the luckless woman escorting the Witch-children to the Place of Power.

But now there was a fresh reason for enmity, above and beyond all previous reasons Alizon had, or thought it had, for

Alizon had come to such a fever of hatred that it blamed Estcarp for its defeat in its attempted invasion of High Hallack.

The reasoning, slanted though it inevitably was, went like this: first, Alizon was barred from invading Estcarp, as it would have had the Council not closed the Alizon Gap with both magical and military means. Second, High Hallack, across the sea, and bound to Estcarp by philosophy and inclination rather than by treaty, could nevertheless be expected to come to Estcarp's aid sooner or later in its struggles against Alizon, and the Dalesmen were fierce, skillful fighters. Therefore, it only stood to reason that Alizon must keep High Hallack out of the conflict while it worked simultaneously on means to break the bottleneck that was the only thing keeping Alizon and Karsten from cracking Estcarp between them, like a nut.

The Kolder, for once in complete agreement with a people of human stock on this world, joined forces with Alizon. The Kolder would contribute support in the form of their awesome machines of war, capable of knocking down any keep's walls with an ease that must be demoralizing to the enemy, and for its part, Alizon would contribute the manpower. And so, thus armed, Alizon invaded High Hallack.

But Simon Tregarth of Estcarp and his Witch wife Jaelithe— both of cursed memory in Alizon where feuds and memories of feuds spanned entire generations—these two meddled and spoiled this most excellent of schemes. Between them, Simon and Jaelithe found the Kolder's island stronghold and destroyed the Gate the Kolder had come through while their Sulcar allies scoured clean the Kolder Nest itself. If it hadn't been for this unforeseen calamity, the Kolder would have been able to keep the supply lines open, and thus maintain the machines operating in High Hallack. But without supplies, the machines failed, and Alizon faltered as well. Unexpectedly, High Hallack's scattered clans united under a single leader and, for the first time, the Alizonder invaders began losing battles. Then the Sulcar, eager for more after that one taste of success against the Kolder, and encouraged by Estcarp, sailed to High

Hallack's aid. So successful were they in crushing the Hounds between them and High Hallack's forces that ultimately Alizon was defeated and thrown back into the sea.

The loss of the war brought about Baron Facellian's downfall. It took very little effort for Mallandor, his successor, to convince the country that all of Alizon's ills, past, present and future, could be laid squarely at Estcarp's doorstep.

During Girvan's telling all this, Dunnis had quietly brought each of the eight their food and they ate as they listened, scarcely tasting the savory mixture.

"But what about the children?" Loric asked. "What have the children to do with any of this?"

Eirran leaned forward a little from her place at the far edge of the circle, her plate of stew half-forgotten on her lap. She was the most eager of all to hear this, even more so than Yareth who, she knew, was carefully keeping himself from thinking not so much about the *why* of it than the *how* of the rescue itself.

Girvan tipped his plate to his mouth and slurped the broth. "Well," he said, wiping his mouth on his sleeve, "the last time I was in Alizon, I did pick up a rumor or two. Hadn't wanted to mention it before now, not without proof, if you take my meaning."

"I think we need to know everything you have learned, proved or otherwise, so we can make our plans accordingly," Yareth said. "Later is soon enough to find out whether it is true or false."

The other men in the circle of listeners nodded agreement. Girvan raised his hand in acquiescence. "Very well. The rumors boil down to this: I learned that Mallandor has set his scholars to work at trying to find a way to open a new Gate to the Kolder world."

Every listener uttered a sharp exclamation of protest. Weldyn recoiled and Sharpclaw flung himself, screaming, into the air. "Loose those demons on us again!" the Falconer cried. "Pray that it's only a rumor, Girvan! I've fought them. I know what they're capable of."

Shudders racked Eirran's body and she tried to control herself as a flood of comprehension washed over her in the wake of Girvan's words. Like the others, she knew of the Kolder; they were, simply, the embodiment of all that was Evil in this world or any other. If there were still Kolder living— That *had* to be the reason why the children had been kidnapped! As much trouble as she had with the concept of her Jenys being, in Yareth's words, a "fledgling Witch," she realized that the little girls represented a cumulative source of Power, raw and untrained talent though it might be. Perhaps it was this Power that the Alizon scholars needed, as a last step in fulfilling their quest to open this terrible Gate!

Fresh horror swelled her throat. If using the children in this way doesn't kill them, she thought, they will most certainly be put to death the moment the Gate is opened and their usefulness is at an end. Oh, please, don't let me start hiccupping now! We aren't so far from Es City that Yareth won't send me back, and I can't be left behind, not now, not when my Jenys is in even more terrible danger than we feared!

Something nudged at her mind and she jumped a little, swallowing hard.

Jenys!

It was as if the child were just out of sight a few feet away, calling her.

Jenys?

But there was no response, nor was the fluttering sensation at the edge of her mind repeated. Eirran forced herself to calmness, forced herself to think and remember. Often, back in the cottage at Blagden, she had had this same feeling, and always, she had discovered that Jenys had wanted or needed her. Could this have been a sign of Jenys's burgeoning Power, her talent as a Witch?

If so, then this fleeting contact must surely mean that Jenys was still alive—unless her mind was playing tricks on her. Could she answer? Could she find out whether this half-felt contact was real? Or was this just something that her imagination had supplied under the goad of her frantic worry about her child's welfare. Frowning, she tried to concentrate on returning the feathery touch she had felt, just at the edges of her thought. But she didn't know how to do it. Panic threatened to overwhelm her.

Jenys!

By sheer will power alone she stifled the hiccups that hovered just under her breastbone, threatening to erupt. Grimly, she ordered herself to stop, to quit thinking and feeling, to wrap her emotions in a veil even more impenetrable than her Witch-given disguise. I must not be discovered, she thought. I must not. Her stomach rebelled and she set her plate to one side.

"Not eating, Kernon?" It was Ranal, and he was staring at her quizzically. "What new thing is this?"

Eirran remembered the man she was impersonating and the legendary appetite that had provoked so much good-natured teasing back at the castle. She made herself shrug. "The news about the Kolder Gate has put me off my feed," she said.

"Thinking about Kolder is enough to make anybody lose appetite," Ranal said. He stared glumly into his nearly-empty dish.

"And anyway," Eirran continued, "I think I must have eaten something bad this morning at breakfast. I'm going to give my stomach a rest for a while."

IV

As a woman living as a man among men, Eirran strove to keep to herself as much as possible. Perhaps the real Kernon was a solitary kind of man; after that one inquiry about the false Kernon's lack of appetite, the others let Eirran alone as much as she desired.

She took full shares of the work, and was glad that each man by habit tended his own mount. Long ago Rangin had developed a fondness for her because of the barley-sugar she occasionally brought him as a treat. She had no idea whether the Witch-magic that changed her shape now veiled animals' eyes the way it did human vision, but she didn't want to risk Rangin giving her away by nudging at her the way he always did when asking for his sweet.

For much the same reason she avoided Newbold as well. The falcon, while never openly affectionate with her, didn't regard her with the same hostility he and Sharpclaw displayed with non-Falconers. The other men carefully kept their distance from the fierce black-and-white birds, allowing Eirran's careful avoidance to go unremarked. Strangely enough, Yareth and Weldyn could, within limits, handle each other's falcons. But an outsider ran a considerable risk if he presumed too far with them.

The only female—in fact, the only other person—Newbold ever really liked, was Jenys. From the time the child had been able to toddle, she treated Newbold with respect and care, and Newbold responded with what might have been called love, if such an emotion could be thought of as coming from a Falconer's bird. But Newbold allowed Jenys to carry him about with her; once in a while, in a rare burst of affection, he even leaned his head against her. It had become a jest between Eirran and Yareth, how Newbold had decided that Jenys was his "pet human."

Perhaps it was only her fancy, but it seemed to Eirran that Newbold had regained a little of his youthful vigor, which had been lacking of late. Perhaps he even realized that they were going to rescue his beloved Jenys. But that was silly, she told herself. For all that Newbold was an exceptional creature, he was only a bird, with only a bird's limited consciousness.

Perhaps the hardest part of this journey, in a strictly personal sense, was the way Weldyn kept at Yareth. It was plain that Yareth's "weakness" in forming a relationship with one woman and continuing to live with her rankled the other Falconer.

"Come," he was forever saying. "Show us how to lay a fire,

season the food, make up a bedroll. Your, er, wife must have taught you a far daintier way than ours. Are you lonely? I wonder that you didn't bring your, er, wife with us."

Yareth would simply stare at him out of his amber-brown eyes, never uttering a word of defense for himself, for Eirran, or for any of his actions. Eventually Weldyn would give up for a while and subside into silent disdain, only to begin his tirades all over again at the next opportunity. The other men learned to give the Falconers a wide berth when Weldyn was going on at Yareth like this.

Yareth is still angry at me or he would surely answer back, Eirran thought miserably. He is still offended that I was not there to bid him farewell. Nor can I blame him. He has a proud heart, and I shamed him. Isn't it enough that he has defied all Falconer tradition in taking a wife? Must she also be shown to the world as a weakling who runs away, who can't even bother to stand by him when he rides off to rescue their child?

Warily, she kept an eye on the moon. But her woman-time did not appear. Eirran found this more a relief than an additional worry; in fact, worry might well be the reason for its absence. She was all too familiar with the effects of strong emotion on a woman's most intimate functioning. And also, she realized, it might well be a part of the shape-changing she had undergone. A woman wearing a man's form would find such a thing difficult to explain, to say the least, and so the Guardian might have foreseen the problem and suppressed it as a kindness to her.

Their progress northward slowed even more. Once the haste to get away from the ambush site was over and they seemed reasonably satisfied that no one was in close pursuit, the Hounds dropped their pace. Now they traveled not as a band of outlaws fleeing from danger but rather as a group of travelers returning home in an unhurried though expeditious fashion. Still Yareth and Weldyn sent their falcons skyward at regular intervals and twice the rescue party had to turn aside and find places of concealment when some of the Hounds back-trailed for a league or two.

"They aren't complacent fools, we have to give 'em that," Girvan said. "We'll have to be extra careful going through Alizon Gap or I miss my guess. There's magical wards and I don't know what else set there and it's all made in such a way it turns you aside into the swamp."

Eirran found herself nodding her understanding with the others though she had no experience at all with these matters of the northern countries. But even as far away as Karsten and later in Blagden, she had heard about the fearsome Tor Marsh, and how the men who ventured there did not return.

"Yet you've been through the Gap many times," Yareth said. "So there must be a path somewhere. Don't you know the safe places to go?"

"No. The path keeps changing, and it shifts at random intervals. Maybe a week goes by, maybe a day, maybe six months, and no way to tell. Like I said, it's been four months since I've been north. The wards might have shifted once or a dozen times since then. But we can be certain the Hounds came through as close to a shift as possible, and that they'll go back the same way they came. We'll just have to follow their footsteps, that's all, and not get caught either by them or by the wards."

"Then why not take the short way straight through the Alizon Ridge?" Yareth said. He scanned the low line of mountains in the distance. To the east, the lofty peaks from which this spur had broken and sprawled across the land, forming a barrier nearly drowned in swampland, reared cold and purple. Their tops were lost here and there amid banks of thick cloud. Beside these terrible peaks that raked the very sky, the Alizon Ridge presented no barrier at all. "It looks easy enough."

"Easy indeed even for an ordinary man, let alone a Falconer," Weldyn said. There was a boastful note to his voice. "You were probably too young to remember, but the Eyrie was so high those 'mountains' ahead of us look like anthills in comparison. But I must tell you there are dangers in them nonetheless, dangers enough that even the Hounds take the longer road around. You've probably been too, ah, busy of late to have heard about it."

Yareth gazed at the other Falconer expressionlessly, then turned away without a word.

Ranal spoke up hastily, filling what could have been a dangerous silence. "Isn't there some way you can tell when you're coming close to one of these magical wards on the road?"

"Not until you've set it off and are trapped in it. Rolling smoke thick enough to choke you, phantom armies, beasts with teeth as long as your foot—oh, the Witches have some pretty tricks set up for the traveler in these parts. The worst is when it looks like there are ridges you think you have to work your way around, and the only way you can go is toward the swamp. The land leads you there, you see. Unless you know each rock like it was your cousin and can tell the false from the true, you'll go blundering off and never know the difference." Girvan shook his head. "I don't know whether any of it's real or not, even to the ground under our feet. But that doesn't matter. What counts is that it mostly keeps the Hounds penned up and not worrying away at Estcarp's flanks."

"Until lately," Ranal said. "Well, if we've got horrors in the mountains, swamps and marshes to the other side, and magic in the middle, I'd say the magic offers us the least danger in the long run."

"Don't forget the Hounds," Dunnis said. "They'll be waiting for us, if we live through this part of our journey.

"I'm not forgetting anything. But by this time they've decided they got away clean, I'll warrant. They won't be looking over their shoulders."

Eirran couldn't keep herself from speaking. "Surely—" her voice broke a little "—surely the Witch-children could sense if they were approaching something magical." She glanced around; Hirl and Ranal were looking at her. "I mean, that's why they're so important to the Hounds, isn't it? That they have magic bred in them?"

"That makes good sense," Dunnis said. Even his pleasant nature was somewhat shadowed by the dangerous prospect that now faced both the riders and the children they had traveled so far to rescue. "The Hounds, as we know, are no fools."

"Aye," Girvan said. "But the Hounds didn't catch the children just so they could smell the way back through Alizon Gap for them, and no mistake. There's darker deeds they've got in mind or I miss my guess."

Eirran needed no reminder. Jenys, she thought. If only I could contact you, mind to mind. If only you'd try reaching me again. And Yareth. If only we could find comfort in each other's arms.

She looked at Yareth. He was staring towards the north, and the muscles in his jaw were working the way they always did when he was deeply and silently angry about something. Eirran wondered if his anger was greater at the Witches—the Hags, as he called them—, at the Hounds, or at her.

Six

I

*M*ouse had long ago stopped crying. She simply had no more tears, nor did the other girls. Once, from the depths of her shock, she cried out for her Mama. But Mama was back at Blagden, still wondering where Mouse had gone, and knew nothing of what had become of her. The cry for help was not repeated.

Day after day the Witch-children rode on the front of saddles, carried by those of the white-haired men who had drawn
lots for the duty and lost. Hounds of Alizon they were, from the
enemy land to the north. Mouse could feel her daily guardian's
resentment as they traveled with her huddled on his saddlebow.
She felt no more important than a sack of grain—less, for one
could eat the grain and, little as they were fed, the children
consumed supplies that must begin to run low sooner or later—
and she wondered why the men were going to so much trouble
on the behalf of six little girls.

Even if they could have somehow found the opportunity to
escape, they could not have gone far, not on foot. The northern
horses were much too large for them to manage. Anyway, they
answered only to their masters' commands. And the little girls
were hungry, so hungry. They were beginning to grow weak.
They wouldn't have lasted a day on their own.

Now that the raiding party was beyond all reasonable pursuit, the men slowed their pace, conserving their mounts'
strength. Nevertheless, Esguir, the leader, sent back-trackers
periodically to scour the trail behind them and be certain that
no one was following. Each time these back-trackers returned
and reported seeing nothing and no one, Mouse's spirits fell a
little lower, her hopes of being rescued grew dimmer, and she
found it harder to put an optimistic face on things. In spite of
their adversities, however, the children had the resilience of
youth. They were beginning to get over the shock of Leaf's
death and of being kidnapped, even Mouse, although by unspoken mutual consent they kept very quiet about it. Who knew
if some show of resistance on their part would annoy their
captors, bring the leader's sword down on their necks as well?
They huddled together very quietly at night, speaking in the
lowest of whispers, if at all.

Sometimes, when circumstances permitted, they searched out
edible roots which they shared raw, just before bedtime. It
helped them sleep better if they were fortunate enough to find
a bite of fresh food to supplement the stale rations the Alizon-

ders gave them. But they were seldom so lucky. On the nights when they could find nothing they clung together even closer, if possible.

"Where are we going?" Lisper's eyes were wide and shiny, and she looked beseechingly at Star as though she thought if she asked the same question often enough, Star would somehow conjure up the answer.

For the first time, she had a reply. "North," she said. "We're going north."

"How can you tell?" Cricket whispered.

Like the other girls, Star had acquired a tight, wary set to her lips as she struggled to cope with her ordeal. Now her expression softened a little. "My Witchname," she said. "I know the stars. And I can tell by the direction we're traveling that we're heading north. Sometimes we veer a little to one direction or the other; that's how I could tell for sure. But then we always turn north again."

"I thought you got your name because you were so bright." Mouse clapped her hand over her mouth, fearful that she had spoken too loudly.

"Me, too," Bird whispered. "You're about the brightest person I've ever met, besides my Mama and Papa. And the Guardian," she added virtuously.

"Thank you," Star said. "But what use is it to know which direction we're going if there's nothing we can do about it?"

Flame reached out and touched Star's hand. "I'm sure we'll be able to think of something, when the time comes," she said with her characteristic firmness.

"Perhaps."

Star settled down, pulled her thin blanket over her shoulders, and closed her eyes. Suddenly, Mouse *heard* what Star was thinking. It was the first time it had ever happened with anyone besides her Mama. But this was as clear as if she had somehow slipped inside Star's head and become one with Star's thoughts. The other five children leaned too hard on her for advice and leadership, and she felt very small and alone, unequal to the task. Mouse lay down beside Star, snuggling up against her and spreading her own blanket over the both of them. The children had quickly learned that shared warmth was doubled warmth, and the nights were still quite chilly.

"I'll help, Star," Mouse said in a very small voice. "We all will. Don't worry. You don't have to do it all yourself, alone."

Star just sighed. Perhaps she was already asleep. Nearby, the other girls settled themselves likewise for sleep in pairs as Mouse and Star had done, seeking the maximum warmth out of the inadequate blankets they were given. Bird and Flame were already asleep but Lisper and Cricket jostled each other and complained about a stone that dug into first one's side, and then the other's. At last Cricket sat up, rummaged around until she found the offending pebble, and tossed it away, careful not to throw it in the direction of one of the white-haired guards.

"There," she said disgustedly. "Baby. Good thing we're all here to look after you."

Lisper said nothing, but Mouse thought she heard her snuffling to herself. Of them all, Lisper was the one she worried about most, and, she felt, so did the other four.

Oh, why did they have to be in the power of these dreadful white-haired men, and not safe in the Place of Wisdom, as they should have been, being instructed in their craft? Why hadn't Mouse paid more attention to Bee when she was lecturing to them about magic, on the road to Es City?

North, Star had said. Mouse knew, with a sinking feeling, that what lay to the north was even more of the white-haired men, that they were heading in the direction of their homeland, Alizon. She hoped with all her might that it was still a long way off, that it would take many days to get there. Anything to prolong the time before she would discover why it was that the strangers had taken her and her sisters, and what they intended to do with them once they got there.

II

The travelers began to slow their pace as they neared the toe of the low mountains barring their way. The buff-brown land had given way to the red-brown of dried blood. It was as if centuries of decaying vegetation—or something worse—had been harrowed into the soil, though no farming implement had ever broken the crust of the land. The vegetation had gone gray-green again, though somehow it looked unhealthy and not at all like it had around Es City.

Unclean, Mouse thought. This land has a kind of sickness. I do not like it here.

Something wailed in the distance, and the lank white hounds lifted up their muzzles and howled a challenge in reply. The men hurriedly snapped leashes onto their collars and the dogs leaped and strained, trying to escape and chase after whatever had called to them.

There was a far-off hint of moisture in the air, though Mouse knew instinctively that this was no smell of the sea but rather of something far darker. In some strange way it smelled the way the land looked—diseased. For several mornings they had ridden through fog that lifted only reluctantly, as if it had a sentience all its own and didn't welcome intruders. Now, as they traveled, the mist came spilling over the rims of hills and washed over the level ground like soundless gray waves. It swirled around the horses' feet, and the travelers slowed still further. The horses might have been wading through sluggish water, groping their way across the dismal landscape. The fog gradually rose to the horses' knees, to their flanks, until it enveloped all in a steadily thickening blanket of dirty gray.

Though the road in this area looked considerably more passable than other stretches they had covered, now leagues behind them, the Alizonders brought their horses to a walk. A few of Esguir's elite Hounds dismounted and began to lead the way, eyes to the ground as if searching for something. At midday, the travelers stopped to rest, and to eat a quick and cheerless meal.

"Where are we now, Star?" Bird said. She shivered; the day had grown cold and the stale bread with a lump of flavorless cheese gave them no warmth.

Star gnawed an edge off her hunk of bread and then wrapped it in a fold of her cloak and put it away. They had all learned to do this; their body heat sometimes softened the hard crusts enough so they could be chewed rather than splintered. "I think we're near Tor Marsh," she said through a mouthful of crumbs. She wiped away a patch of mold and bit into her cheese.

"Oh," Lisper said in a soft, decayed voice. "That'th a bad plath, ithn't it."

"Dangerous, rather than bad," Star said. "We always avoided it when my parents and I were out during the trading season, traveling in the wagons. Preferred to deal with garth-holders in the foothills, when we came this far north."

Mouse swallowed a bite of bread and cheese together; it tasted like ashes. With a pang, she remembered the cheese Mama used to make, and what a good flavor it had. She might never see Mama again, might never even eat a bite of decent food again— No. She mustn't allow herself to think like this. Unappetizing as this food was, this was all she had to ease her hunger, so she'd better set to eating it. She had to stay strong, so she would live. Her slab of bread was slightly less stale than the others', and she ate determinedly, refusing to taste it, until it was all gone. In her preoccupation she didn't notice Esguir striding towards them until he and a few of his men were virtually in their midst.

"I need the services of a Haglet," he said brusquely. "That one. Take her."

Cricket cringed away from Esguir's pointing finger and the men who stepped forward to do Esguir's bidding. Her half-eaten crust of bread and bit of cheese fell to the ground as they grabbed her by the arms and hustled her off, following Esguir who had gone back the way he had come.

"What are they going to do to her?" Lisper said fearfully. Her eyes were unnaturally big in her pinched little face, and they shone with unshed tears.

"Nothing," Flame said. She picked up the bread and cheese from the ground where Cricket had dropped it and brushed the dirt off. "Nothing that we can do anything about," she amended.

Lisper began to snuffle again.

"Oh, stop that," Bird said irritably. "If they were going to kill her, they would've done it long ago. The rest of us as well."

Star nodded. "She's right. In any case, we have to stay calm."

Some of the Alizonders came then and forced them to their feet. "We're going now," one of them said.

The children hastily stuffed whatever remained of their food into cloak pockets, having long since learned to do as they were bid and do it promptly. Flame put Cricket's food away for safekeeping, carefully placing her remnants in a different pocket in the inside of her cloak. As usual, one man was assigned to watch each of them while they were moving, and they forced the children to walk along just in front of them.

Mouse couldn't get the bit of food in the pocket of Flame's cloak out of her mind. I didn't save back anything to eat, she thought. Her cloak is beginning to get shabby. So is mine. Whenever will this torment end?

Ahead, a child's cry pierced the fog. The Witch-children stopped as one, hearts in throats. But their captors nudged them onward. They stumbled through the deep mist, barely able to see the backs of the men they followed.

"Turn a little to the left," Bird's guardian said. They led the Witch-children, in turn following the men who walked just behind Esguir and Cricket. "Keep a sharp watch and go in the footsteps of the one that's gone before you if you know what's good for you." He looked back at the others and grinned through the mist. "Better hope the Haglet does a good job finding where the wards have shifted. I heard Baron Esguir say if he is pleased, he'll give you hot soup tonight. If she fails—" he drew a finger across his throat in a graphic way that made Mouse shudder "—it's finish for all of us."

Shaking so hard she could scarcely walk, Mouse tried hard to place her feet exactly in the footsteps of the man in front of her. Futilely, she attempted to brush the mists aside. It was like pushing feathers out of the air. Palpable as the mists were, they rushed in again as quickly as she cleared a space where she could see. She dared not look to either side, fearful of what might be waiting for her out there. She sensed dark shadows, wavering and dancing just beyond her vision. Or was it because she herself was moving that they seemed to mimic her progress?

Another wailing shriek like that of a doomed spirit pierced the fog, and was answered immediately by the wild yammering of the dogs. They leaped and strained at their leashes. The little girl at the head of the column cried out again.

What terrors Cricket must be enduring out there all alone, acting as their living shield! As frightened as Mouse was, she knew that what she was feeling was nothing compared to what Cricket must be going through. Grimly, not knowing how to do it, Mouse strove to send Cricket as much of her own strength as she could. She hoped the other girls were doing the same.

Because she was concentrating on where they were going and watching only the direction of the footsteps in which she had to walk, Mouse began to be aware they were veering off a straight path. And each time they turned aside, the angle of their departure was sharper than that of the correction. She thought they must be getting near a bog; a cold, wet wind made her shiver and pull her cloak tighter. The wind did nothing to lessen the thickness of the fog.

A sudden outcry from ahead made her look up, though there was nothing to be seen.

"This way!" a man shouted angrily. Esguir, from the sound.

Cricket cried out again, but this time more in annoyance than in fear or pain. "No!" Her high-pitched voice was firm and cut clearly through the muffling fog. "Let go of me! We must turn right."

"There's nothing but ridges over there. This way's the road."

"This way leads to the swamp. Turn, I tell you, or walk on and let the Tormen or something worse get you."

There was a silence and Mouse could imagine the Alizonder leader pondering Cricket's words. She sounded strong enough and Mouse wondered if her efforts to help, even at a distance, had been of any use. Mouse hoped the man wouldn't hurt Cricket. He had sounded very angry.

"Very well," Esguir said at last. "We'll turn right. Everyone! Look sharp! This Haglet is leading us off the road, so mind where you put your feet!"

With infinite caution, the line of men, horses and children started moving again. Mouse smiled to herself as she heard muffled exclamations from walkers ahead of her. The "ridges" dissolved as they approached, and presently she heard the sound of boot heels ringing on the true road. She realized they had all wandered from it unknowing, lost in the heavy fog. As they regained the road the mist gradually began to grow thinner, and soon she could make out the outlines of the men ahead and then of Esguir and Cricket at the forefront of the column.

"Well, curse me if you weren't right," Esguir said. "It was another of your damnable traps. Good thing for all of us even the young ones can smell out your own work. Very well, get back with the rest now. We can find our way from here." He raised his voice. "Mount up! I want to get a league between us and this cursed place before nightfall!"

The men hastened to obey. One of them snatched Cricket up and placed her on his saddlebow before she could reach the others. Flame stifled an exclamation.

"Please," she said to the Alizonder whose saddle she shared, "may I give her the rest of her food? She didn't have time to eat and she must be very hungry."

"Very well," the man said. "I suppose she's earned it."

He nudged his horse until he was even with his companion's. Flame handed over the packet of bread and cheese. Cricket looked too exhausted to eat, but nevertheless she unwrapped the unappetizing bundle and began to suck at a crust. As it softened enough for her to swallow, a little of the pinched grayness left her face.

Mouse discovered she was riding near Lisper. The little girl had that raw, shiny-eyed look Mouse had come to know and dread.

"What is it, Lisper?" she said.

"I—I'm tho athamed," Lisper said. She scrubbed the backs of her hands over her eyes. "When they took Cricket, I hoped Flame would thare out the bread and cheethe, and we could eat it."

Mouse thought about this in silence, remembering her own thoughts at the time. "You mustn't be ashamed," she said finally. "You're just hungry. We all are."

Though he had made no mention of it and Mouse was certain that he had forgotten, Baron Esguir sent the children a hot meal that night. And though when it arrived from the Baron's camp-fire the broth was mostly water, one of the men guarding them that night added a little meat and a generous handful of barley, cooking it until it thickened. Mouse thought she had never tasted anything so wonderful and satisfying before in her life. She smiled at the man who had been so kind to them. Somehow, on him, the white-blond hair and green eyes didn't look so hideous as it did on the others.

"I wanted you to know that I don't hold with starving children," he said a little gruffly. "I can't do much, but I'll look after you when I can. My name is Talgar."

"I am Mouse."

Solemnly, he took her hand and kissed it. "I am honored, Lady Mouse."

She giggled; she couldn't help it. It was the first time anybody had ever kissed her hand or called her Lady anything.

"Eat up," he told the other Witch-children. "You'll sleep well tonight anyway, with your bellies full for once. You'll need your strength. Tomorrow we'll give the horses their heads. We're nearly home."

"Home," Mouse repeated faintly. Her moment of mirth dwindled and vanished. She had never felt farther from home in her small life.

"Be of courage, child. I said I'd look after you, as much as possible."

For the first time since the ambush Mouse felt a trace of hope. Surely there must be more like him, even in Alizon.

III

Leaving the darkness of Tor Swamp behind, they rode the next day through wind-scoured rolling plains. As Talgar said, their pace increased dramatically. Once free of the perils of Alizon Gap, the horses could scarcely be held back. They sensed their home and seemed happy to be returning. The dogs, loosed from their leashes, coursed madly back and forth, yapping and barking, quarreling among themselves.

Though the countryside was mostly barren, an occasional stand of gray-trunked trees grew in the shelters formed between one rise and another. Their lacy foliage at the tops, where the wind could reach it, was blown to tatters, leaving nothing but bare twigs with shreds of leaves still clinging to them. There were few houses within sight. Rows of thorny bush lined either side of the road, marking individual fields and meadows. Someone—or perhaps many someones—laid claim to this country, and had put their indelible mark on it. Every field was full of dirty gray sheep or, in the big meadows, herds of horses.

Talgar had found it easy to trade duty with one of the men whose lot it was to look after the children, and now he rode with Mouse on his saddlebow. "This all belongs to our mighty land-barons," he told her. "They own everything, and rent out farms to ordinary folk. My father has a farm much like one of these, only on the far side of Alizon City."

"I've never seen anything like those," Mouse said, pointing to the bushes. Now that they were closer, she could see that many more types of plants made up the thorny barriers. Ivy and berry vines, just coming into bud, were nearly lost among the thorns. Here and there she recognized wild flowers and lesser weeds. And the wild tangle didn't grow directly from the ground, but seemed to spring from rows of buff-toned rocks half-hidden under the savage growth.

"The hedgerows?" Talgar said. "These are ancient. They were here when the first Alizonders came to this land." He smiled. "The barons tried to root them out, but the hedgerows defeated them. Most of the barons hate them, say they're made up of the vermin of the plant world. But I don't mind." His face hardened. "It keeps the barons from riding through a man's grainfields if that pleases them. . . ."

Mouse kept quiet, letting Talgar talk. He told her of the nobles on horseback with their dreadful white snake-headed dogs, hunting, careless of the ruin of a poor man's crops. Thus they had dealt with Talgar's father, laughing while they destroyed the only way he had of paying his rent to one of them. And in order to keep his father from the punishment a tenant faced when he could not pay, the eldest son took service with Baron Esguir, the powerful man who was the Master of the Hounds of Alizon.

"The pay is enough so I can send enough to my father to ensure his rents," Talgar said. "Until now, I've always had guard duty at the castle, and the life wasn't so bad. At least, most of the time. But this, what we've had to do—" He made a sound of disgust and gestured in a way that Mouse understood to mean the ambush and kidnapping. "This was not good."

She twisted a little to look more closely at the man who held her as they rode. Like the others, he wore the blue-green uniform with the symbol of a dog's snarling head on his breast, the boots with high peaks on the outside of the leg. Mouse wished she had discovered this almost-friend among the Alizonders much earlier in their journey. Perhaps, with his help, they could have escaped, could have found their way back to Es City. Surely the Guardian would have welcomed the man who had rescued the Witch-children, would even have found him a place among her guards. . . .

Mouse hated the thought of their journey's end more than ever. But Talgar had been correct when he said they would soon be home—his home. Within a few days they were entering the gates of Alizon City.

The castle and the towered walls that surrounded it had been constructed from the hard buff-brown stone that everywhere pushed through the thin layer of fertile soil that was the best this part of the world afforded. Centuries ago, during some unthinkable cataclysm, an enormous knob of rock had thrust its way out of the ground. The outcrop was huge enough to cause the Alizon River to change its course and flow around the foot of the cliff. Now the river formed the sea-wall for the arrogant and mighty castle that rode the crest of the rock as if saying, "Here I am and thou shalt not pass."

The town itself sprawled out over the plain, having overgrown its walled boundaries long ago. Still the walls formed an outer defense that was not all for show. Armed sentries paced the walkways and guarded the towers, and the enormous gates, five layers of wood thick with each layer cross-grained to the one beneath, looked fresh and strong.

It was just as well that the children had wept away all their tears; Mouse knew it would have been undignified if they had been carried wailing into an enemy city. Her throat was as dry as her cheeks as the Alizonders rode with them through the great main gatehouse. Looking up, she glimpsed the sharp teeth of a portcullis waiting to slam down between would-be invaders and the inner door, trapping them so the defenders could destroy them at their leisure. She shuddered.

They rode through the twisting streets of the town, until they reached the foot of a steeply sloping ramp. They crossed a wooden drawbridge, passed through a central tower, then across another drawbridge that led through another, even stronger, barbican and gatehouse and thence into the outer ward of the castle. Mouse's heart sank at the very thought of soldiers trying to assault such a daunting place.

Inside the gatehouse, Baron Esguir and his personal pack of Hounds dismounted. The men carrying the Witch-children swung them off the saddlebows and set them on the chill stone pavement.

"You are dismissed," Esguir said harshly. "Go back to your regular duties."

The Master of Hounds strode rapidly through the outer ward, arrogantly certain that his men were dragging the Witch-children in his wake. Mouse looked back over her shoulder, trying to get a last glimpse of Talgar, but he had vanished from her sight. Flushed and self-assured with his success, Esguir made straight for a large, multistoried building and ran up the outer stairs with the ease of a man thoroughly familiar with his surroundings. At the top of the stairs a door opened onto a third-floor hallway. Mouse got a jumbled impression of more doors, more rooms, more white-blond men and a few pale, lank-haired women in long, trailing dresses. Then, a last door opened and they were inside a private room, much like the one the Guardian had occupied, only more richly decorated with much bright paint on walls and ceilings. A white-haired man wearing a gold circlet with a green stone sat on a velvet-cushioned chair. He leaned on one elbow, unsurprised at the Baron's entrance.

"Sir," Esguir said. He inclined his body from the waist and the men with him bowed even more deeply. Mouse and the other children just stared, wide-eyed, too frightened to move.

The man in the chair acknowledged the Hound-Master's greeting with a languid wave of his hand. "You are very timely, Esguir," he said. "We are pleased."

When she dared look at her surroundings, Mouse discovered there were several more men in the room. Most were the silver-blond Alizonders she had grown accustomed to seeing, but one was not. This one was a very strange-looking individual indeed. Mouse had thought she would never see anything she hated more than the green eyes and silver-white hair of their captors until she caught sight of this man. With the same kind of instinct that makes one draw back in horror from a snake or scorpion even if one has never seen one before, she loathed him on sight. Around her, the other girls drew in their breath audibly and moved closer together.

The stranger wore a gray robe belted at his middle, and a gray cap on his head. Then Mouse understood her error. Though she had thought him a man at first, she realized it was because he happened to have a man-like shape. In reality, he didn't look like any kind of man Mouse had ever seen before. He had a wide, flat face and a narrow chin that was almost no chin at all. All the Alizonders had proud, hooked noses; this one had a little sliver in the middle of his face with pinched slits in place of nostrils. He glided toward the velvet chair, bent forward a little and began to make a series of peculiar noises Mouse thought might have been an attempt at speech.

"Oh, talk so everyone can understand," the man in the chair said irritably. "That gets on my nerves, if you must know."

The man inclined his head. "As you wish, Baron Mallandor." His words were heavily accented, and the clicking and whistling of his native language made its way through the common tongue. "I was saying, they will do. They will do."

He moved closer to the Witch-children, staring at them out of yellowish eyes until Mouse wished she were her namesake so she could run away and hide. Shakily, she reached out and caught Bird's hand, discovering that Bird was trembling as well.

"Yes. They will do." Abruptly he pointed an inhumanly long finger at Flame. "We will start right away. With that one."

"No!" Shock jolted the word out of the Witch-children's throats, Flame's denial most vehement of all. But it was to no avail. The man who had escorted her to this dreadful place now held her firmly while the other girls' guardians began dragging them away.

"Take them to the upper tower room," Mallandor said.

"It will be done, Sir," Esguir said. "I will set the guards myself."

To Mouse's shame and dismay she discovered she had not cried away all her tears after all. Though she hated showing any weakness before this Mallandor and his horrible minions, she couldn't help it. She wailed aloud and the other four likewise had wet cheeks.

Flame did not weep. Mouse struggled to free herself of the guard's grip, wanting to run back to Flame, to comfort her, to save her—

But they were just children, small girls in the grip of large and strong men. Effortlessly, the Hounds picked up their charges and carried them off. More corridors, some narrow circular stairs, another door, another even narrower winding stairway. One by one, the men flung the children down into the straw on the floor. Then they hurried out, and shut and locked the door behind them.

Slowly, the children stirred, stretching cramped limbs, rubbing chafed wrists, trying to get their bearings again in this latest of their new surroundings. Lisper lay in a corner, racked with hard, shuddering sobs. Star and Cricket went to tend her as best they could. Mouse was trembling as well, though not as convulsively as Lisper.

"Are you all right?" Bird said.

Wordlessly, Mouse nodded. But she couldn't get the picture of Flame's stricken, tearless face out of her mind. She had looked so little and so lost, in the Alizonder guard's grasp. And the strange man-creature in the gray robe was stretching out his oddly shaped hand to touch her on the cheek.

Seven

I

*G*irvan, Weldyn and Yareth paused frequently to confer over the trail they were following. Though they lost the horses' prints on those stretches of road that were still intact and had not been scoured of a layer of soil by the wind, somehow they always managed to find them again. Girvan never wavered, confident of the route the kidnappers had taken. Now, they had entered the area of magical protection; they stopped to rest a moment before going on. They all dismounted, to give the horses a breather as well.

"The Hounds are fairly certain nobody's following," Girvan said. "See? The leader's not sending back-trackers nearly as often as he did at first. Now he's doing it just enough to satisfy a cautious man. And we can be sure this fellow's careful. We could tell that back in Estcarp, by the way the ambush had been laid out."

Weldyn looked up, scanning the countryside that lay ahead. "That must be the edge of Tor Marsh to the left, where the heavy mists are. Alizon Gap must lie beyond the bend in the road, where the Alizon Ridge ends. Hills. Just hills."

Yareth also gazed at the Ridge, lying purple-smudged and hazy on the horizon. His eyebrows quirked speculatively. "That's the direction we are headed. It's the kind of country where I feel comfortable. We could go unseen. Everything considered, it is probably the safest route."

Girvan stared at him in disbelief. "No! Absolutely not! The Gap is at its safest right now, on the heels of those who've gone through and set off the wards. They'll need time to gather energy and reset themselves."

Yareth didn't seem to hear. "Now that we are close enough to see with our own eyes what lies ahead I think we should leave the road. Find a way through the hills. We can do it easily enough." His voice sounded curiously flat.

"For once I fully agree with you, my brother Falconer," Weldyn said. His voice had the same intonation as Yareth's. "We'll avoid the Marsh. Go through the hills."

It did seem reasonable, Eirran thought, now that they were here, and could see what they were facing. Why risk the dangers of the swamp? Around her, the other began murmuring in agreement as well.

Girvan scowled at them. "The magic in this place must be scrambling your brains," he said in disgust. "Weldyn, you're the one who first mentioned dangers in the heights."

"I've changed my mind."

"Listen. I come from the southern part of Alizon. There has to be a reason the people who live there call Alizon Ridge the Forbidden Hills. Nobody but those with something to hide dares go there. So if you want us to look like a band of thieves, robbers and cutthroats, I commend you to find your way into the country from that direction."

"Aye, but we may have less to fear there than on the road. They're bound to have somebody, someplace, watching the Gap. In the hills, we can send the birds up to spy out anything dangerous in our path. If the kidnappers have perchance left a man to watch the road at the Gap, we can avoid him altogether."

"If it were so easy, the Hounds would have used that way and as you can see, they didn't," Girvan said. "They've got a lot of reasons to hurry, but they chose the Gap with all its danger and magics. Don't you think there's a reason for that?"

"Of course." Yareth smiled coldly. "No Hound ever whelped could match a Falconer in anything he set out to do."

"And also," Weldyn said, "the stink of magic is not one that

I have come to love. Some of us are shape-shifted. What if the disguises the Hags gave them and their horses are affected some way by the wards?"

Eirran listened intently; this was a question that troubled her even more than it did the others who were, as yet, unaware that her own magical disguise made her appear a man like they were. It made the choice of going through the hills that much more attractive to her.

Girvan snorted with derision. "Don't you think the Witches are smart enough or skillful enough to think about such things? Their shape-changings aren't so easily done away with."

"My nature urges me to the hills," Weldyn said stubbornly. "And so does my brother Falconer's."

Yareth nodded. In this one matter, at least, the two Falconers were as one, however much they might disagree entirely about other matters, such as women, and wives.

"Well, there's one thing you haven't considered."

Weldyn looked at Girvan, displeasure written on his face. "And what would that be?"

"The pretense we're traveling under, that we're blank shields looking for employment with other than the Hags of Estcarp. Honest men wouldn't come slinking into Alizon through the Forbidden Hills."

"That must be taken into account," Yareth said reluctantly.

"And another matter." Girvan smiled a little, like a man who is about to play his top card. "If you go through the hills, you'll never know if the Hounds or their captives made it through themselves. You might be walking straight into the enemy land and have nothing to go for once you were there."

There was a long silence. All at once, Eirran took a deep breath, as if she had been deprived of air for too long. The Witch's Jewel, hidden in her doublet, seemed to tingle against her skin.

That's my imagination, she thought. That's impossible. The Jewel died with the Witch. I don't know why I'm still carrying it.

But she made no move to throw it away. Instead, she flexed her shoulders, working an unexpected stiffness out of them.

She glanced around; the others had begun blinking and moving uneasily as well, as if coming out of a trance. With its vanishing, Eirran recognized the persuasive magic that had been working on them, trying to lead them away from their goal. But Girvan had told them that the wards were designed to take an intruder toward Tor Marsh. This magic, or whatever the strange impulse to enter Alizon Ridge was, had sought to send them in the opposite direction.

Yareth, pale of face, stared down at the toes of his boots. A damp breeze had sprung up and the horses, sensing water nearby, had become restless. They stamped and snorted, dragging at their reins. "Your arguments are unwelcome, but convincing," he said at last. "I like it not, but you speak harsh truth. So I will take your advice, Girvan. We will keep to the road even though it leads us into illusion and deception and I long with all my being to turn aside."

Girvan relaxed perceptibly. "As I said, sometimes the illusions are quiet, after someone has passed through recently," he said. "Let us hope that this is the case with us, Yareth."

"Let us hope also that you are right that the magic in this place is working on Weldyn and me in a different and more subtle fashion than on another, and that you are keeping us to the right path." The Falconer stretched and loosened his muscles much as the others had done.

"Aye," Hirl said. "While you were making your argument for the Alizon Ridge, it sounded very reasonable. The only way to take, actually. I was ready to follow you there. But Girvan's words have made me see the situation in a different light."

"I agree," Ranal said, and the others echoed him.

Girvan allowed himself a bitter smile. "For once I'm glad I am Alizon stock," he said, "if it helps me keep a clear head when the rest of you are ready to rush off to your doom."

"We are grateful for it," Yareth said.

They turned to take one last look at land that was undeniably

Estcarp. Then, with renewed purpose, they mounted their horses, nudged them forward, and once more took up the pursuit. As they rode, however, both Falconers ever cast longing glances toward the low mountains lying so close and so tempting.

II

Try as he might, Girvan could find no explanation for the strange urge that had come upon the Falconers to enter the Forbidden Hills and which had in turn communicated itself to the other men. As for the Gap itself, the rest of the company made no secret about hoping it would be as the guide had predicted. And to their intense relief, they were allowed to proceed without incident.

"As you said, the magical wards and defenses set by the Witches must indeed lie quiet for a time after being triggered," Dunnis said.

"Or perhaps the spells are growing thin after so much time and use," Loric commented.

"Or weren't much to begin with," Weldyn said sourly.

Ranal spoke for all. "Whatever the reason, the situation as it is suits me more than I can tell you."

Though dense fog arose as the band of Guardsmen pretending to be blank shields rode onward, the mists felt like those born naturally of the earth and the nearness of the marshlands where they traveled rather than fashioned out of some malevolent magic. Nor did the land appear to change its shape, to try to drive them toward the swampland lying behind the sullen wall of cloud. To everyone's relief, both Falconers began to behave in a fashion more nearly normal, as they began concentrating once more on the trail and the task at hand.

"Ah," Weldyn said. He leaned from his saddle, examining the ground beneath his horse's hooves. "They left the road here. The tracks are plain."

Equally obvious a distance beyond was the spot where the

Hounds had stopped for a while, probably to eat a hasty meal, and had then begun walking on foot, leading their mounts. Here and there the trackers pointed out where the ground had been torn by dog-claws, as if the animals had had to be forcibly restrained from running—not away, as reason dictated, but rather toward Tor Marsh. Eirran shuddered, not wanting to think about the kind of magic that could have prompted such a reaction.

The Falconers dismounted and, leading their horses by the reins, followed the footprints slowly, gleaning every scrap of information they could gather from the appearance of the trampled ground.

"What can you expect to find?" Loric said. "There are too many footprints, all on top of each other."

"Notice that they tried to be very careful to walk where the first in line had trod," Yareth said. "But they did not always succeed. See here."

He pointed at a single clear print of a tiny foot, to the right of the main body of tracks. It was as if the diminutive owner of that foot had started to go in that direction and had been pulled back by force. But a few steps farther on, the entire company had turned right, to the east and away from the marshlands.

The muscles worked in Yareth's jaw. "They put one of the fledglings in the van, to smell out the magic, just as Kernon suggested they might."

Eirran closed her eyes, trying to keep her voice steady. "Can—can you tell which one it was?"

"No," he said. "But their tactic was successful. The fledgling led them back toward the main road, though it looks like someone didn't agree with the direction she wanted to go." He straightened up and gazed westward. An enormous bank of thick fog obscured anything that lay beyond, as solid in appearance as a wall. Its very presence forbade a traveler to venture in that direction. "The Tor Marsh is cut off from the rest of the world, thoroughly and without recourse even when the other magic is quiet. I wonder why."

"I can answer that," Ranal said. "The Tormen blundered badly, back during the war. They gave aid to the Kolder, capturing some high-ranking prisoners and turning them over to the Kolder for a price—"

"High-ranking indeed," Hirl said. "It was Lord Simon himself, and Lady Loyse of Verlaine. Never understood how the two of them got caught, or why the Tormen would deal with the Kolder for that matter."

Ranal shrugged. "Whatever their reasons, they did it. And the Witches sealed off the Tor Marsh from that time forward. The Tor people aren't quite what you'd call human, so the stories go, and they never cared much for the outside world in any case. Now, so the stories go, the Witches have fixed it so you can blunder in easily enough if you're not careful but you'll never find your way out."

"Convenient way to put a stopper in the Alizon Gap," Weldyn said. "Well, we've learned what we could from this place. Let's be gone before the magic regains its power and snares us."

III

The entire company felt uneasy, exposed, once they cleared the toe of the Alizon Ridge, the range of low mountains that divided Estcarp from Alizon, and entered the enemy land. But no one—neither the occasional traveler on the road nor the even rarer toiler in the wide fields and meadows—cast more than an incurious glance in their direction. Eirran, however, stared openly, as did the others who had never been this far north before. Even the Falconers riding proudly in the van, birds alternately perched on the saddle horn or soaring overhead, did not scorn to examine the countryside through which they passed.

These thorn fences, Eirran thought. They keep a traveler to the road, willy-nilly. They'll give us trouble if we have to flee cross country if we rescue the children. When.

Newbold came stooping back to Yareth's fist and "spoke"

with him in falconsong. Yareth transferred the bird to his perch on the saddle and turned to Girvan. "Is there some secret to getting through these hedgerows?" he said. "Newbold tells me it's like a jumble of boxes when seen from the air."

"Not through them," Girvan said. "But there are openings, little gaps between one holding and another. Paths you can take if you know where they are."

"We will have to teach our falcons to recognize these openings and paths," Weldyn said. He spoke to Sharpclaw in the same avian language as Yareth and Newbold had used, and sent him winging skyward. A few moments later Newbold joined him aloft.

But though the birds quickly learned what was expected of them, the openings in the hedgerows proved to be both infrequent and ill-placed for the convenience of someone who was in a hurry to cross the country without using the road.

"It's simple," the light-hearted Dunnis said. "We shall simply have to find a way to get out of Alizon as easily as we got in. Perhaps the Falconers' birds can teach us how to fly."

The other men laughed, even Weldyn, but Yareth merely smiled a little. Eirran shared his concern. The farther they rode, the stronger her feeling that they had escaped one trap only to ride headlong into another.

That is nonsense, she told herself sternly. We can't fail, now that we've come so far. We just can't.

She had begun to think the entire country of Alizon was tightly sewn into squares with the hedgerows representing the seams, when the thorny boundaries ended abruptly and the land opened out. A scattering of houses, wattle-and-daub over stone foundations, made up the outermost of the villages that inevitably cluster around a stronghold.

"Just beyond that rise is Alizon City," Girvan said. "You can almost see the tallest turrets from here."

Gooseflesh rose on Eirran's limbs and she shivered.

"Are we still agreed? We go in, pretend to join their Guardsmen—I mean Hounds—and then begin searching for the children? They could be anywhere by now, and we'll get farther in looking for them if we can work from the inside, so to speak. As one of them."

Weldyn brushed fastidiously at his sleeve. "I wish we could clean up first. I hate to be seen covered with road-dust."

Yareth stood in his stirrups, shading his eyes as if this slight additional height would allow him to catch sight of his goal despite distance and intervening countryside. "Plenty of time later. Let us not pause to rest, now that we're so close."

He set spur to Rangin and the Torgian leaped ahead. Weldyn, unwilling for the younger Falconer to go ahead of him, dug his heels into his own horse, and the others were not far behind. After this fresh burst of speed, however, the party of Estcarpians settled back to a more moderate pace. They fell into their accustomed riding order—the Falconers in front, followed by Hirl and Girvan, then Loric and Ranal. "Kernon" brought up the rear with Dunnis. Eirran liked Dunnis because of his pleasant nature and had been pleased when it worked out that Dunnis was her usual trail companion.

Even though she thought she knew what to expect, she couldn't stifle an exclamation of surprise mixed with dismay when the town and castle came into view. It was far more daunting than she had expected. Compared to this, Estcarp's main castle was no more than a fortified dwelling-place and its city walls frail and ill-defended. But then, their purposes could not have been more dissimilar. Es Castle housed wisdom, and the kind of Power that did not come through feats of arms. What Alizon Castle housed, Eirran did not wish to think. The others were similarly affected by the sight and only the Falconers and Girvan did not cry out involuntarily.

"Castle Alizon has never fallen, except through infiltration or treachery from within," Girvan said. There was a note of pride in his voice. He stared at the heavy, unyielding town walls, an unreadable expression on his face.

This could not be pleasant for him. Eirran wondered if he could be thinking that he was, by some lights and in some views, a traitor to his native land.

But she didn't have long to ponder what Girvan's thoughts might be. The eight men pretending to be blank shields looking for employment were already crossing the threshold of the mighty gate of Alizon City.

IV

The eight dismounted once they got into the town proper and at Girvan's suggestion put their horses in a public stable where they could be fed, watered, and properly groomed for the first time since they had left Es City. The Torgians acted as if they still had leagues of travel left in them, but they all accepted nosebags of oats with more eagerness than they had shown for trail rations.

"I'll ask around at this tavern," Girvan said. "I'm better at this than the rest of you would be. After all, I'm an Alizonder by birth. People will be more likely to talk openly with me."

"We will wait here in the town square," Yareth said.

While Girvan went about his errand in the tavern, the others strolled around the square, getting their first good look at an Alizonder city. Though Ranal, Loric, Hirl, Dunnis and "Kernon" didn't rate many second glances, the same was not true of the Falconers. Birds on fists, they attracted open stares from every side. But, proudly, they pretended to be oblivious to the attention they garnered.

"Don't see one Falconer every day, let alone two," Dunnis whispered in amusement to Eirran.

She shrugged and said nothing.

By chance they had arrived on market day in Alizon City, and small farmers had come from everywhere, setting up their wagons and displaying their goods. Despite the poorness of the soil, there were many stalls offering late winter vegetables for sale. Eirran knew what was involved in growing foodstuffs. Remembering her own garden at home, she could imagine how the farmers had painstakingly added soil to their small plots of ground, nourished and cared for it, digging in all their table scraps and animal droppings so as to enrich it enough that seeds could take root and grow. So had she done at home, though the soil around Blagden was a hundred times better than Alizon's.

She paused by a booth where a farmer's wife was selling finely-made shirts. The woman had done exquisite decorative stitching at neck and cuffs, geometric patterns in dark thread on the creamy linen. Eirran, only a tolerable seamstress, fingered one of the garments to admire the work, thinking that Yareth needed some new clothes. If this had been market day in an Estcarpian town, and if she had had any money. . . . The woman, sensing a prospective sale, hurried over.

"That shirt'll last you years, young sir," she said. "Only five copper bits."

"A fair price," Eirran said. "Another day, perhaps, when I get paid—"

The woman looked her over with a knowing eye. "Come to join the Hounds, have you," she said. "And the other blank shields with you."

"Yes."

"Well, they're usually hiring, some times more than others."

"And now?"

The woman shrugged. "Don't know. But you'll have better luck, I'll warrant, if you stay close to those fellows with the hawks. Don't know when it was I last seen one of them."

Eirran's blood went cold at the thought of a Falconer—any Falconer—having joined the Hounds of Alizon. "Oh?" she said carefully. "Then there've been Falconers here before?"

"Oh, now and then, as prisoners. But never looking for work. Esguir would be tickled no end having one of them on his payroll, let alone two."

"Esguir?"

"Aye. Baron Esguir, Master of Hounds." The woman looked Eirran up and down again. "High Captain of the Estcarp Guards, where you come from."

"Is it that plain?"

The woman shrugged. "No matter. A blank shield is a blank shield, wherever he hails from. Shall I save back the shirt for you, young sir?"

"No. If you get a chance to sell it before I return for it, do," Eirran said.

"Next market's a sennight from today, right after the Hounds get paid." The woman grinned. "I'll be looking for you then."

Another customer paused by the booth and the woman turned away. Eirran rejoined her companions just as Girvan came out of the tavern. He was surreptitiously wiping his mouth with the back of his hand and the smell of ale was strong on his breath.

"We've got throats full of road dust, too," Hirl said reproachfully.

"Agreed," Girvan said, "but you also need to keep a clearer head than I do. Time for celebrating when we've gotten what we came for, if you take my meaning."

"We do," Yareth said. "What did you learn? Are they hiring?"

"Yes. We have to go to the castle, and see the Master of Hounds, Baron Esguir. He's the one to talk to about finding work. Or anything else."

Eirran started to speak, then thought better of it. Girvan hadn't learned a thing inside the tavern that she hadn't discovered in a few minutes' talking with a farmer's wife. So the man wanted a drink. No harm done, really. They were in the very heart of the enemy land. Eirran felt they were so close to finding Jenys she fairly tingled with the child's nearness. Why start an argument and run the risk of calling unnecessary and unwelcome attention to themselves? She fell into place beside Dunnis as they marched toward the huge, buff-brown castle gleaming in the afternoon sun.

V

As befitted the highest-ranking commander of the Hounds of Alizon, the Master had his headquarters in the spot where the fiercest fighting would be expected to occur in case of attack—the gatehouse of Alizon Castle. The barracks—the Kennels—stood in the outer ward, against the south wall.

All eight applicants entered the gatehouse tower and climbed the winding stone stairs. They were kept cooling their heels for the better part of an hour in an outer chamber, while the Hound Master attended to some business within. Through an open door, they could see into the room directly above the gate passageway below. Piles of stones cluttered the floor, ready to drop on an invader through the murder-holes that were now covered with wooden hatches. A stack of iron pots stood nearby, waiting to be filled with sand or water and heated before the contents were cast down along with the stones. But the pots were dusty and covered with cobwebs; Alizon Castle had not undergone siege in many, many years.

Only to treachery, Eirran thought. The castle has fallen only from within. And what are we then, if not spies and infiltrators? Her nerves grew tighter with every passing second and she had to force herself to stay calm with every ounce of self-control she could muster.

What if the Master of Hounds turned them away? What if the Hounds discovered the real reason these new "recruits" wished to join the ranks of Alizon soldiers, and killed their captives out of hand? What if the children—if Jenys—were dead already? A hiccup hovered somewhere in the middle of her stomach, threatening to escape, and she resolutely swallowed it down again.

At last a man wearing the uniform of the Hounds appeared in the doorway. "You," he said. "Baron Esguir will see you now."

"Right behind you," Girvan said.

The men and Eirran got to their feet and followed the soldier up another flight of stairs. They entered the large room that spanned the entire width of the gatehouse building. There were windows on either side, so none could leave or enter the castle unremarked. The room was crowded with people, soldiers coming and going. A white-blond man wearing a Hound's uniform with a gold band circling the badge on his breast sat at a table, looking over some papers. He glanced up as they entered.

"Well?" the man said brusquely. "My man said you wanted to speak to me personally." His manner conveyed the feeling that these new "recruits" thought over-highly of themselves to have asked for the privilege.

"Indeed we did, my lord," Girvan said. He moved beside the desk, turning to face the others. "Or, rather, I did. I thought you'd like to see these Estcarpian spies personally before you put them in prison, to examine at your leisure."

He snapped his fingers and before any of the company could move, they found themselves seized by their arms and pinned.

"Traitor!" Weldyn shouted. "Filthy Alizon spawn! I'll have your life for this!"

The Estcarpians were not the sort to submit meekly, once they had been found out. All of them—even Eirran—fought fiercely with the Hounds. Loric came close to breaking free, and almost got his hands on Girvan before being caught again and flung to the floor, his arms forced painfully behind his back. Newbold and Sharpclaw screamed and beat their wings against the Falconers' captors as the men struggled. Other soldiers tried, without success, to capture the birds. Yareth screeched something in falconsong and Newbold immediately streaked for the door, evading the shouting men who clutched at him. Weldyn's order echoed Yareth's. Sharpclaw was right behind the older falcon; both birds shot through the nearest window and streaked out of arrow-range before any guard at arrow-slit or on the walls could react. Eirran's heart dropped and she sagged in the grip of the soldiers who held her.

Oh, to have wings! she thought. To escape, go free, and attack again another time! But the birds, without their masters, could do nothing. Still, she knew, it was better they were gone. A Falconer would never yield to questioning or even to torture, but who knew what kind of torments the Hounds would devise for a bird? Far easier to unlock a Falconer's lips that way than to question him directly. And for that reason she was savagely glad the Hounds had not caught them.

"Take them to the prison tower," the Master of Hounds said. His voice cut clearly through the din in his chamber. "Let them cool their heels for a while. We will examine them at our leisure, tomorrow perhaps." He turned to Girvan. "My thanks. I wondered why you had come back to Alizon with a company of seven Estcarpians. I would have kept your secret, however, and let you play out your charade."

Girvan shrugged. "The game was up. My usefulness is at an end, as far as Estcarp is concerned. I could never go back now, not after this adventure, so better I am thought dead with the others. I was ready to come home anyway, before I got caught. They've come after the children."

Esguir's colorless eyebrows rose. "Have they now."

"Aye. It was all I could do to keep them from running up against your Hounds on the road. But I figured you'd want to talk to them, wring whatever information they might have before you, er, dispose of them. And that was better done here."

"Indeed. You've done well, Girvan. Well, you were promised a place on my personal staff when you ceased spying. I'm happy to say you've earned it."

"Thank you. Oh, by the way. That one—" he indicated Yareth "—he doesn't know anything of Estcarp or its doings. But he is the father of one of the Haglets."

"Better and better. Oh, you have done well. I must see to it that you get a more tangible reward in addition to what you have coming to you already."

Girvan bowed. "Sir."

Baron Esguir glanced at the Hounds who were still struggling with the men from Estcarp. "Well, what are you waiting for? Knock some sense into their skulls with your sword-pommels if you have to, but get them into the prison at once."

The Hounds renewed their efforts, and, with considerable difficulty in spite of their superior numbers, managed to carry out their commander's orders. Eirran had a jumbled impression of the stairs they had come up, then being dragged a short distance across the outer ward, into a large room and through a door opening, oddly, from a window embrasure and hidden from casual view behind a curtain. Thence the prisoners were shoved down more stairs into the dankness of the lowest cell. Part of the dungeon had been blocked off by a thick wooden wall, pierced by a narrow, heavily barred door. One by one the prisoners were flung through the door onto a floor covered with a thin layer of sour-smelling straw. Just before it was Eirran's turn to undergo this humiliating treatment she caught an incongruous whiff of bread baking nearby. Then she went hurtling through after the others. The door clanged shut behind them with reverberating finality. Darkness settled down almost tangibly, relieved only by what light got through a single small hole high in the outer wall, the only source of ventilation for their prison. The men slowly picked themselves up, straightening their garments and rubbing bruises.

Eirran swayed dizzily. *"Hic!"* A sensation as if she had walked through a veil of cobwebs made her shiver. Something shifted on her skin, but whether the sensation came from within or without she didn't know. She tried, unsuccessfully, to stifle another hiccup.

A man's hands lay on her shoulders. She looked up to see Yareth staring into her face. She tried to twist away, and hiccuped again.

"Eirran?" Yareth said hesitantly. "Eirran! By the Great Falcon, it is you!" He clasped her to him and then held her at arm's length again. Now he was scowling, uncertain. "But how— Why— What are you doing here? You stayed behind—you left Es City and didn't even say farewell to me."

"Only—*hic!*—because I rode with you."

"But how? Tell me that."

"The Guardian. She—*hic!*—shape-changed me. She told me to be careful and not get too close to you, that if you recognized me, my disguise would fail. I—I suppose it has. You see, Kernon had gotten ill—"

"I thought there was something wrong," Ranal said. Despite the puffiness of his lips where a Hound had struck him, he smiled one-sidedly. "Kernon never had such a dainty appetite as you." He wiped his lip with the back of his hand. "Well met, lady."

"Oh, Yareth—*hic!*—I had to come. I couldn't stay tamely behind when Jenys was in danger. Please, please forgive me."

Yareth still held her, stiffly, at a distance. They stared at each other. There was silence in the prison cell except for Eirran's hiccups. She was acutely aware of Weldyn glowering disapprovingly to one side. Then Yareth pulled her into the circle of his embrace again, holding her tightly, stroking her hair and burying his face in it. Her arms went around his neck and they stood thus for a long while.

"What does it matter," Yareth said at last. "You are here, and I am here. Whatever happens now, we will be together."

Eight

I

*W*here are we?" Cricket said. "Besides locked up."

"I'll look." Star got up, shifting Lisper's head from her lap to Cricket's, and went to the window opening, set high in the wall.

Lisper lay watching with huge, shiny eyes. Her thumb was in her mouth again. Cricket stroked Lisper's hair.

"Do you need any help?" Mouse said. She hurried over to the window. Star dangled, half-in and half-out of the embrasure. She clutched at a shutter, struggling to get up onto the ledge. Mouse lent a helping hand from below, and Star managed to scramble into the deep recess.

"Thanks. Oops!" Star disappeared from sight. "Don't worry, I'm all right. The window ledge slopes down from the edge, and I wasn't expecting it. I can see now. It's just a narrow opening in the wall, and not a real window at all." She sat back on the edge of the embrasure, studying the sliver of window, and the peculiar, slanted opening in the thickness of the wall. "I think this must be where soldiers are supposed to stand and shoot arrows down on other men." She scooted back into the recess for another look. "You can see a lot of the wall platforms from here. We're up high. But we knew that. All those stairs. Made me dizzy. I can't tell what's below— Wait. I can just see some rocks. And water. There's land on the other side, so it must be the river."

"Is there any way out?" Bird said.

"Only if you can fly, like your namesake." The children

smiled at Star's feeble joke. "The window opening is too narrow, even if we could climb down the walls. And there's a wind blowing even if we could take out some of the rocks. We'd never make it."

"Then we're stuck here."

"I'm afraid so."

The children lapsed into silence. Lisper sucked at her thumb a little harder.

Star jumped down again. "Well," she said decisively, "we can't just sit here. What would Bee think of us? She'd call us lazy, and good-for-nothing, and she'd be right, too."

"What do you want us to do?" Cricket asked.

"We can brush ourselves, and tidy our clothing. We can set this room to rights."

Mouse looked around. There was very little in the room to get disarranged. A bed, without even a mattress, the rope lashings sagging with age and use. A chair with a broken leg. A bowl and a pitcher on the floor near the door, half-full of stale, tepid water. Some clothes pegs hammered into the stone wall. Marks in the straw where a clothes press had once stood. "We could sweep some of the straw together to make a bed and put a couple of our cloaks over it and use the rest for cover," she said.

Star smiled. "That's a start."

Before long, the children had pushed the useless bed to one side of the room out of the way, had scraped the cleanest of the straw into a pile, and had set the bowl and pitcher on the chair, making it serve as a bedside table as it could not be sat on without collapsing. Mouse and Bird put their cloaks over the straw and Cricket urged Lisper to lie down on it. The little girl snuggled into the makeshift bed, and Cricket spread Lisper's cloak over her.

"I think she'll go to sleep now," Cricket said. "She was almost nodding off before."

"It'll be good for her," Star said. "She worries me," she added in a low voice.

The other girls glanced at Lisper, but as Cricket had predicted, the child appeared asleep already. Her thumb had fallen
out of her mouth and her breathing had become deep and even.
And yet her slumber was not peaceful. There were dark circles
beneath her eyes and she trembled and whimpered a little as she
slept.

"She worries me, too," Mouse said. "Do you think the Alizonders would send us a doctor for her?"

"She's not sick," Cricket said, "even if they would, which
they won't. I couldn't feel any fever. I think she's scared. More
than any of us."

Mouse digested this in silence. There was certainly enough
for the children to be frightened of. But, vaguely, she felt it
wouldn't do for them to show it as openly as Lisper did. They
would just wind up scaring each other until they were all as
badly off as she was. "How can we help her?"

Star shook her head. "I don't know. We don't know very
much at all."

A sound at the door made them all turn their heads. The lock
creaked as the key turned in it. Then a white-blond man in a
Hound uniform entered, carrying Flame. Two more Hounds
followed close behind. One carried a sack, which he let fall near
the door.

"Aha, I see you've been busy." The Hound strode over and
dropped Flame onto the straw bed. All three turned to leave the
room again. "We'll be back later," the Hound said, just as the
door closed behind him.

Lisper sat up groggily, rubbing her eyes. She stared at
Flame's limp, white-faced body, and began to scream. "Oh, no!
The'th dead the'th dead the'th dead the'th—"

Star slapped her sharply across the face. "Shut up!" she said
fiercely.

Lisper put her hand to her cheek. Then the hurt and fear
welled out of her eyes and she began to weep—not the frightened snuffling of the past few days, but open sobs, heartfelt and
healing. Mouse knew instinctively that Lisper needed to be left

alone for a little while to cry it out, so she joined the others clustering around Flame.

"She's breathing," Bird said. "Just barely."

"Oh, look," Mouse said. Gently, she brushed Flame's hair back from her face. There were marks on her temples, looking something like a burn and something like a bruise, but which were neither. "What did they *do* to her?"

"Nothing good," Star said grimly. "She's got marks like that on her arms and legs, too." She tore a strip off the bottom of her dress, dipped it in water, and began to bathe Flame's hurts. Flame stirred and moaned faintly.

"She's coming to," Cricket said.

Flame opened her eyes. "I'm here," she said. She seemed dazed.

"Yes, you're here. With us. Drink some water," Star said. "But not too much. It's all we've got."

Star held the jug for Flame and she lapped at it, like a cat. Her lips were so dry and cracked they were close to bleeding.

Bird had been investigating the sack the Hound had dropped on the floor. "They brought us some bread," she said. "And a bottle of something." She opened the stopper, sniffed, and made a face. "Whew! That's awful!"

Mouse sniffed it in turn. "That smells like Mama's medicine bottle, the one she kept hidden in the cabinet and I wasn't allowed to touch."

Star took the bottle and put it to her own nose. "Ha!" she exclaimed. "You babies don't know anything! This is just spirits, and not the best, either, not half so good as my father used to make. But strong as anything, I'll bet. Here, Flame, take a mouthful of this. It'll make you feel better."

Mouse wanted to ask if Star's father had made his medicine—spirits—back in an out-of-the-way patch of woods the way Rofan did, back home. But she held her tongue, knowing that the other girl was her superior in knowledge of the world outside her little village of Blagden. Star was holding Flame's head up so she could sip the powerful brew. Flame coughed and spluttered, but managed to swallow the dose. A touch of color came back into her face and she seemed strengthened by the medicine.

"Can you tell us what happened?" Cricket asked.

"I'll try." Flame took a deep breath. The other girls settled down to listen. Even Lisper stopped sobbing and moved a little closer. "There was a machine, a dreadful machine, and the gray-robed man—there are three of them and I heard somebody call them the Kolder—the Kolder put me in it. . . ."

II

The machine occupied an entire room of its own. Like the man's robes, the machine was gray, dull and lifeless, a series of huge connecting boxes lining the room, and the room itself was covered—floors, walls, ceilings—with still more gray. The material gave a little underfoot and was so smooth it looked like it had been poured onto the original surfaces, allowed to pool, and then had dried in place. It gave voices an odd, muffled sound, and made footsteps completely silent. An enormous map occupied one wall. Flame thought it looked as if someone had gone high, high in the air, to see the plains and mountains and ocean, and had then modeled what he'd seen on the map. She recognized the jagged coastline, the Great Mountains, the shape of Estcarp, the Alizon Ridge and Tor Marsh with the Gap between, recognized the unfamiliar shapes of Alizon to the north and Karsten to the south. The Barrier Mountains still showed on the map, so Flame knew it couldn't have been a very recent one. But she guessed there had been an effort to bring it up to date. The map was hooked up to the machine some way, for it was set with tiny light-globes—yellow in Estcarp, red in Alizon. A few spots of green still glittered in Karsten, but most of the light-globes there were dark, as were the ones along the Sulcar peninsula and the island of Gorm.

A table stood directly in front of this map. One of the three

Kolder sat at it. Somehow, to Flame's horrified realization, he had been made a part of the machine. He had a metal cap on his head and wires came out of it, connecting him to everything in the whole room. He didn't ever move, except for his long fingers touching a panel of buttons and levers and other things Flame didn't have a name for. The Kolder never once even opened his eyes but Flame knew he was aware of her presence.

The third Kolder had been standing by the one that was wired to the machine. He came and helped the first one fasten the struggling child onto a table in the center of the room. She kicked and tried to bite them, but they were too strong for her. They put straps all over her so she couldn't move and attached a lot of wires to her, sticking them on her arms and legs with cold stuff that burned where it touched. Last, they put a cap on her head similar to the one the Kolder at the table wore except that this one had a clamp that fit over her temples. When they had finished she felt they had made her almost as much a part of the machine as the Kolder was.

Then the other two went over to separate parts of the room and stood waiting beside panels of more dials and buttons. The machine-Kolder ran his fingertips over his control panel. Lights began to flash about the room. Dials lighted up. One Kolder twisted a dial. The other pushed a series of buttons in an intricate pattern.

Flame had no words for what happened next, except that she knew at one point she was screaming. The entire room closed in on her until she could scarcely breathe. And it made her terribly, dreadfully sick.

She turned her head to one side. "My head hurts," she said plaintively.

Bird got the bowl in place just in time before Flame threw up. Mouse swallowed hard, willing her own rebellious stomach to remain quiet. When Flame was finished, she lay down again. Oddly, she looked a little better. Star gave her another restorative sip of the spirits.

Lisper cuddled up to Flame, putting her arms around the other girl. "I'll hold you, and keep you thafe," Lisper said. "Go to thleep now."

III

Later, after Flame woke up, the children shared out the bread and ate it, though Flame could hardly touch her portion. There was hardly any water left, and they gave it all to Flame. Her mouth was still dry and cracked. She gulped the flat-tasting stuff gratefully. Daylight faded, and a sour-faced woman-servant in a grimy smock brought them more water and a dented pewter cup. She glared at them as she thumped the jug down on the chair seat that served as makeshift table, hard enough to make the chair teeter and fall. Bird grabbed the jug before it hit the floor. The cup clattered away into a corner.

"Ordered to bring you this," she said. "Better make it last. Won't be more till tomorrow. If it was up to me, you'd go thirsty. What you deserve." She spat on the floor. "Haglets." Then she slammed her way out of the chamber.

For a moment the children stared at the closed door, shocked. They had never experienced such open hatred, not even during their journey north when the Hounds had them prisoner. But then, the Hounds were bound to their own form of military discipline and castle servants were not.

"I never saw such a disagreeable woman," Cricket said clearly. Her face looked more pinched than it usually did. "It would be a real pleasure to turn her into a bug and squash her. Only I don't know how." Then she splashed a little water onto the glob of spittle, took a handful of straw, and wiped the floor clean.

The children took turns with the cup. Then, their thirst slaked, they lay down to sleep, all six huddled together for mutual comfort, arms around each other.

The next morning, another servant brought them more bread and another jug of water, taking the empty one away with him.

He said nothing at all to them, and didn't even glance their way.

"Please," Cricket said, "do you know anything about why we are here? And what they plan to do with us?"

The man turned. By his coloring and the cast of his features, he was no Alizonder; what his origins were, however, no one but he would ever know. He shook his head and pointed at his mouth. "Uuunh, gahh, hhaah," he said.

"They've cut out his tongue," Flame said.

Fresh shock reverberated around the room, almost tangible in its intensity.

The man shuffled out and locked the door behind him. The children stared at one another.

Bird shuddered. "I'd rather they killed me and had done with it."

"Don't thay that!" Lisper's cheeks were pale, but she set her chin resolutely. "I don't want to be killed. And my tongue doethn't work very good, but I don't want it cut out, either. I want to go home."

"So do we all," Flame said. "But there doesn't seem to be much chance of that just now. Well, let's have breakfast. I think I could eat a little this morning."

Mouse shook her head. "I couldn't."

"You'd better." Star was already busy tearing the loaf into six more or less equal pieces. "If you get sick now you're done for." She looked at the bread and the corners of her mouth turned down. "I wish we had some of that awful cheese we hated so on the road. Well, at least the bread's good. And fresh, for a change."

Mouse nibbled at a crust, and discovered she could eat after all. The children limited themselves to half a cup of water each, remembering the warning the maid servant had given them the night before. Maybe she had just been mean, trying to frighten them, but they couldn't afford to take the chance that she wasn't telling the truth. If the water had to last until the next day, they could not afford to be greedy.

"We'll just have to make a game out of it," Bird said. "Pretend we're on rations, and make it last as long as we can."

Lisper smiled wanly. "I like gameth. But not thith one, very much."

There was another noise at the door. It opened and two of the Hounds from yesterday entered. The one who had taken Flame strode into the room, while the other stood by the door.

"Well, which one is it to be today?" the Hound said. He stood looking at them, a disdainful expression on his face, his fists on his hips. "What, no volunteers?" He laughed. It was not a pleasant sound. "All right, then, I'll pick one myself. And, I pick *you!*" He turned and lunged at Mouse so abruptly she jumped and shrieked in spite of herself.

"No! No—"

"Oh, yes, yes. My masters would be very angry if I came back without a Haglet for them. And we don't want that to happen, now do we?"

Mouse's temper flared. "I wouldn't care if they got so mad at you they cut your neck in two!"

"Oh-ho, spirited this morning, aren't we. Well, never mind. Come along. Mustn't keep them waiting." With that, he grasped Mouse's arm in a grip hard enough to bruise, and dragged her kicking and struggling from the room and out onto the tiny landing just outside. The other Hound closed, locked, and barred the door behind them. "Vicious little beast," Mouse's captor muttered, sucking a bitten finger. "You take her, Willig."

The other man shrugged and grinned at his companion's discomfiture. "You don't know how to manage 'em," he said. "Keep company with a widow who's got a houseful of brats and any one of 'em is ten times worse than all these Haglets put together, and you learn." Nonchalantly, he picked Mouse up around her middle and tucked her under his arm where all her kicks and flailings had no effect whatsoever. "Nothing to it. If you know how."

"Good. Then you've got the duty of carrying them to and fro from now on," the other Hound said. "Let's get moving."

Mouse could hardly breathe, the way Willig held her. She quit struggling, lest she knock her head against the wall of the narrow stairwell. She hoped he would put her down so she could catch her breath when they reached the floor below, but he didn't. She caught a glimpse of someone, another man, she thought, out of the corner of her eye. He was coming toward them, and he looked familiar, somehow.

The two men stopped abruptly, and both bowed. "My lord Baron," they said.

"Is this the Haglet you have chosen for today?" When he moved within Mouse's range of vision she saw that it was the man who had been sitting in the velvet chair when the children had been brought into the brightly painted room. The man who had sent the Hounds after them. Baron Mallandor. "Scrawny, ugly things, all of them. I've decided to watch this session. Come along, Rhyden, Willig. Don't dawdle."

He led the way down the second, slightly more commodious stairway, and through a maze of corridors and rooms. All too soon they arrived at a door different from the others. Mouse recognized it at once, from Flame's description. It was of metal—or something like metal—and was the dull gray of the strange race called Kolder. It returned no reflection. Mouse loathed the looks of it on sight, the instinctive way she had reacted to the Kolder. Her heart began to thud heavily and her stomach lurched with apprehension.

"You knock," said the Hound called Rhyden.

"I can't," the other man said, more than a little satisfaction in his voice. "I have the Haglet. You have the pleasure."

Rhyden cursed under his breath. Then, taking a deep breath, he stepped forward, braced himself, and pounded on the door. It seemed to Mouse that he hated touching it. The peculiar material seemed to absorb sound much as it did light. Rhyden had to pound twice more before it finally opened.

"Baron." The Kolder inclined his head slightly. "You do us honor."

Mallandor strode through the door, Rhyden and Willig close behind. "I want to see what is happening in here. My man told me what you're doing nearly killed the first Haglet, with nothing to show for it. You must be more careful with them. It won't be easy, getting any more. They're bound to have tightened their guard in the south."

"Like every inquiry into unknown matters, we learn as we go," the Kolder said. His voice was as flat and as gray as the room he stood in. There was no echo; the material coating the room really did absorb all extra sound. "The young one lives?"

"Yes," Willig said. "Here's the next one you asked for."

"Put her here."

Though Mouse knew it would do no good, she couldn't help fighting as Flame had. Willig placed her, none too gently, on the table in the center of the room. The two Kolder already had the straps ready. She barely got a glimpse of the map, the table, the seated Kolder Flame had described before they were settling the cap on her head and tightening the clamps against her temples. Then they fastened gray-coated wires to her arms and legs with the sticky, cold-hot paste.

But what happened next she did not expect at all. The Kolder opened her dress and one of the Kolder touched her abdomen. He held another wire. She screamed and tried to twist away.

"Placing this here may help the transmission," the Kolder said. He smeared some more of the sticky paste over the wire to hold it in place. "If this doesn't work, we'll put it over the heart on the next one. Then, we'll start putting the wires under the skin."

"Is that really necessary?" Willig asked. He seemed repelled by what was happening, in spite of himself.

The Kolder turned an expressionless face on the Hound. "Your master commands."

"And I'm beginning to think it is just a waste of time," the Baron said. "An excuse to torment Hags so young they can't retaliate. You said you knew what to do with the first one, that it would work with her and you wouldn't even need the others."

"Leave us alone," the other gray-clad Kolder said. Their voices were identical, full of the clicks and whistles of their own tongue. "It is a new thing that we are doing. If we are to subdue the ones that break but do not bend, we must experiment."

"I'm the one they'll blame. It was my picked men who brought them here. I'm the one they'll come after."

Willig frowned and shook his head. "But why use children?"

"Because they are children," the first Kolder replied. "They have not yet been taught the ways that keep them from accepting our power. When we learn how to make these little ones our own, then we will know how to put their elders under our domination." He nodded to his companion, and the two of them moved to their respective control panels.

Despite the deadening of all noise in the room, Mouse heard the skittering of fingertips over buttons and the faint click of a relay closing somewhere behind her. Then another sound filled her ears, first so high she could barely hear it and then so low she felt it in her teeth. Her mouth went dry and her tongue stuck to the roof. She clamped her jaws tightly together and the pain in her teeth subsided a little. The room spun and she had to close her eyes before she spun away with it and was lost forever. Once she managed to open her mouth to scream and discovered she could make no noise at all. The machine had stolen all the sound in the world and left her none. And it had put it all into this room and was beating at her with the waves of sound, beating and pounding over her, drowning her in it, pummelling her until she was certain her head was going to burst. Her teeth began aching with renewed savagery and she clenched her jaw again. Her belly swelled with the relentless pressure filling her body. It was going to split, the skin was going to peel back like a grape and everything inside her was going to burst out and be whirled away and lost like the rest of the world. . . .

Gradually, she became aware of something else. Somewhere, woven through the waves of painful sound battering her to near insensibility, a voice came echoing into her, reverberating and vibrating throughout her body. She heard not only with her ears, but with her teeth, her bones, her blood.

Bend, bend, the voice crooned. Give over. It's easy. Give over and all this unpleasantness will stop and you will be at peace, all pain forgotten. Peace.

No, no! Mouse cried inwardly.

Yes, yes. You don't want to hurt, do you? Then let go. Surrender. It's so easy. So peaceful.

The voice was smooth, tempting, and despite her best efforts, Mouse felt her hold on herself begin to loosen.

The pounding in her head and body subsided for a few moments, and she could hear, faintly, in the background, the voices of the men. They seemed to be discussing her reactions with no more emotion in their voices than if she had been a slab of meat on a butcher's block. All but the one who had carried her—she no longer remembered his name, or her own for that matter—the one who had objected and who now seemed kindness personified. Like the one who had been so good to them on the road. The voices made her realize that the machine hadn't really stolen all the sound in the world to use as a weapon and hurl it at her. It only seemed that way. No wonder the room itself had sounded so dead, so flat. It was all here. She was in a bubble of sound and the men outside weren't even aware of what was happening inside, where she was.

The Kolder began manipulating their control panels again, and Mouse closed her eyes. The incredible pounding welled up to swallow her, and the seductive voice started its litany again.

Give in, bend. You will have peace. There will be no more pain. . . .

The wires burned, the clamps against her temples burned, her brain felt on the verge of boiling inside her skull. She kept her eyes shut tightly, for fear they would burst. The sound diminished again. She couldn't even sob, she was so empty.

Another voice, from another direction.

She simply couldn't stand a third level of attack, so she

fought to block it out. But then she realized that this one wasn't coming battering from the outside. Rather, it seemed to come from somewhere deep inside her. She hadn't heard it at all while the first barrage was going on, might not have heard it if the people tormenting her hadn't relented for a moment so she could gather her few remnants of strength. How long had it been speaking to her?

Hold on, the tiny voice said. Hold on. It sounded a little like Bee, a little like Leaf, a little like the Guardian. And a lot like Mama, though that was impossible. Mouse listened closer.

You can do it, the voice said. You can keep them from destroying the essence of you, from burning it away so all that's left is an empty hull the Kolder can turn to their own dreadful purposes.

But how can I? Mouse asked. I don't understand.

Yes, you do, down deep.

I don't, Mouse said plaintively. I'm just a little girl. I'm only six years old. I hurt, and I feel sick. I want to go home.

Hold on. Just hold on.

But Mouse knew she couldn't hold on. The next time, she thought, the next time I'll do what they want. Maybe Star could have beaten them, she's so strong and smart, but I can't. I'll bend to their will and that will be the end of me. I will be truly lost. All my strength is gone. I can't last another minute when they start again.

She gritted her teeth tightly, trying to be brave. Her jaw was tired. All she could do was keep her eyes closed and brace herself for the next onslaught of battering by the gigantic waves of sound. She was vaguely glad that the others—Cricket, Bird, Star, and particularly Lisper—would be spared this agony, that the Kolder had gotten what they wanted without hurting them, too. The thought of the dreadful wires being stuck under Lisper's skin. . . . She would have died, even before the sound began to rise. Let it come, Mouse thought. Let it come now. I hope it won't hurt too much, once I am all gone.

But the expected crescendo did not occur. The gray-clad men

were at the table, bending over her. Cold fingers unsnapped the bindings on her limbs. Sharp pain shot through her as the Kolder began ripping away the wires pasted to her body. Hardly daring to believe what was happening, she kept her eyes closed except for just a bit to see through as someone—yes, it was the kindly one—fastened her dress again and picked her up.

"Take her back," one of the Kolder said. There was no disappointment in his tone, nor any other expression at all. "We will use another tomorrow. By the time we have worked through all of them, the first will be recovered enough to use again."

"Well, you'll do it without me." That was the—the Baron. Mallandor. Mouse's head hurt abominably and she was sick and dizzy, but she was beginning to think again, after a fashion. Strange. The Baron sounded sick, too. "I have no stomach for tormenting children, even if they are just Estcarpian Haglets."

"Our experiments do not need your presence."

"Good." The Baron turned away. Then he looked at the man who held Mouse. "Well, what are you waiting for, Willig? You heard. Take the girl back. And Rhyden, have some scraps from the table sent up to them this evening."

"Aye, my lord," Rhyden said. His face swam into view and Mouse could see that even he looked shaken by what he had witnessed.

Willig. That was the name of the man carrying her back through the corridors, retracing his steps until he came to the door of the room where her sisters waited anxiously. He was kind. This time he carried her properly, in his arms, instead of slinging her under his arm like a sack of hay. The way Papa would have carried her.

The second set of winding steps was too much for her whirling, aching head. Sickness welled up, overwhelmed her. To her mortification and despite her best efforts to wait until she was decently inside where her sisters could tend her, she threw up all over the man's uniform.

Nine

I

The prisoners collected their wits as quickly as possible, assaying their situation, quickly going over any and all assets they might have available to them. There was no time to be wasted languishing in the dungeon cell, though Eirran could see no possibility of escape. The dungeon cell was too deep, too strong.

"They took our weapons, but at least we still have our mail," Loric said.

"The better to weigh us down when they hang us," Ranal commented sourly. "What's to say Girvan wasn't lying to us all along, and the children aren't even here in Alizon City, let alone in the castle? He seemed to know a lot about what the Hounds' plans were. He could have led us completely off the trail."

"They've got to be here in the castle somewhere," Yareth said stubbornly. "It's the strongest spot, the most secure place to keep them. It's where the adepts would choose to open their gate to the Kolder world. Using the children. My daughter."

The men sat on the straw, backs against the stone wall, knees drawn up and arms clasped. Eirran sat close to Yareth, basking in his warmth and nearness, her hiccups subsided. She rubbed her cheek against his sleeve. "Jenys," she said softly.

"Aye," Hirl said. "You're right. They're here, I'd lay odds on it. But what good does that knowledge do us here?"

"Enough good that we can start making some real plans for escape," Weldyn said.

The men all looked up. Until now, none of them had even

mentioned escape. They had seemed as resigned to the futility of their imprisonment as Eirran did.

"What plans?" Hirl said. "I'd like to hear them. They hustled us here so quickly I'm not even sure of where I am, let alone where the children might be."

"Well, I know where we are at least." Weldyn scowled. "Only too well. Years ago, I knew another Falconer named Ysher. He was my trusted companion. My friend."

Yareth turned to look at Weldyn; the other men nodded their understanding. The close bond one Falconer frequently formed with another was well known in Eastcarp. Many a time, one of such a pair of close friends had gone on a quest to hunt down and destroy whoever—or whatever—had slain his companion. That Weldyn spoke of Ysher in the past bespoke of this kind of quest. Falconers were typically reluctant to relate such stories, so every man listened closely, now that one of this tight-lipped breed seemed willing to talk. Eirran listened with interest as well, suddenly curious to know more about this strange and bristly man.

It was—Weldyn said—shortly before the Turning, when Falconers had begun joining forces with the Guard and leaving the Eyrie to go and fight side by side with them against their common enemies.

Ysher and he had been serving in the northern part of Estcarp, very near the Alizon border. It was their duty to keep the Alizonders from infiltrating into Estcarp, and also to rescue the occasional fugitive spy fleeing from Alizon with priceless information for the Council.

During one such skirmish with a pack of Hounds, Ysher had been captured, his falcon killed, and Weldyn wounded. Though he could not prevent Ysher's being carried north, to Alizon City, the fact that Weldyn had been left for dead let him escape his friend's fate.

Ysher had been incarcerated in the very dungeon those from Estcarp now occupied. Occasionally he had been taken from this cell to one and then another of the buildings in the inner ward, where he had been questioned severely by various officials and minions of the late Lord Baron Facellian. During these times of relative freedom he noted carefully every detail of building, defense, maintenance and garrison, in hopes he could live to relay the information to Koris of Gorm, who was then serving as Captain of the Guard.

Eventually, when his captors despaired of obtaining any information from him, Ysher had been taken from Alizon Castle and sent with a group of other prisoners down the river road toward Canisport. There they were to be turned over to the Kolder. Ysher was then to be taken by boat to Gorm, and processed as one of their mindless slaves, forced to fight those who had once been his friends and allies. However, the prisoners managed to overpower their guards two days out of Alizon City. During the resulting confusion Ysher escaped and, despite being severely wounded as he fled, he made it back over the border and to the garth that was serving the Guardsmen as base camp. There, before dying, he told Weldyn what he knew of the Alizonder fortifications.

"I've waited all these years for a chance at revenge," Weldyn said grimly. He clenched his fists unconsciously, until the knuckles cracked. "The Hags took Ysher's information about Alizon Castle, but during those dark days, there was neither the time nor the manpower to spare to send an army against it. Far better that our company of Guards was recalled to Es City and the Hags used magic to put a stopper in Alizon Gap while we dealt with enemies closer to hand. And then, later, we had even fewer men to spare, and no Koris to lead them. Aye, I know this place, through Ysher's eyes, as thoroughly as if it had been I and not he penned up here." He looked up, scowling.

"Little good that does us. They're going to kill us," Dunnis said. His sunny nature, for once, seemed thoroughly dimmed. "I only hope they're quick about it and don't decide to turn it into some kind of show."

"If only we had the least weapon," Loric said. He smacked one fist into the other palm. "But they took everything, even my boot-knife."

The light from the hole in the wall dimmed and everyone looked up. A small black form marked with a "V" on its breast emerged. With a burst of falconsong, Newbold plummeted down to Yareth's upraised fist. In a moment, Sharpclaw followed, settling on Weldyn's glove. The Falconers stroked and petted the birds.

"O wise and venerable feathered brother!" Yareth said. "I knew you would find me, best and cleverest of falcons!" The falcon screeched and bated, and Yareth switched to falconsong until the bird settled down and began smoothing its feathers. Weldyn did likewise with Sharpclaw, gentling and stroking the bird; being younger, his falcon took more time to calm himself than did the veteran Newbold. The Falconers glanced at one another, then got to their feet.

"We have weapons now," Weldyn said grimly. "We can begin."

Eirran stared at them. Weapons? Those frail creatures of flesh and blood? But her husband and Weldyn were acting as if the birds were quite enough for any blank shield worthy of his hire. Yareth and Weldyn differed so much they could scarcely be cordial, let alone become friends the way Weldyn and Ysher had been—even if she had not stood between them—but Falconer would always understand Falconer in a way other men could not. Now they stationed themselves on either side of the prison door, holding the falcons lightly on their fists, as if waiting.

"Call the guard, Eirran," Yareth said.

Suddenly, in a flash of insight so clear they might have been speaking mind to mind, she realized what Yareth was planning—and the other Falconer as well. And she was the only one of them who could provide the kind of bait they needed to make the trap work. A random thought about how Weldyn must rely on a "useless" female almost made her smile. She leaped to her feet, dragging Dunnis with her.

"You foul barbarians!" she cried, pitching her voice toward the door. "Don't you Alizonders know enough to put men and women into separate cells? Don't you have the least shred of decency? Leave me alone, damn you!"

Dunnis just gaped at her as if she had taken leave of her senses. "What are you doing—"

"Struggle with me," she whispered fiercely.

"Struggle! B-but Kernon—I mean, Eirran—"

"Do it! Struggle with me! *Hic!*" Oh, no, not now! She hiccuped again.

Dunnis touched her shoulder halfheartedly, pretending to shake her a little.

"No," she said. "Do it right!" She slapped him soundly across the face. Dunnis started back in surprise and put his hand to his cheek. "Do it!" She kicked him, began scratching, gouging, trying to bite.

At last he began to retaliate. He had to, before she inflicted some real damage. He pushed her away and she waded in again. "Now see here—" he began.

"See here nothing! Fight me!"

"I will, Eirran," Ranal said. He started toward them where they stood facing each other in the center of the cell.

"Good! Two of you, that's even better!"

At last Dunnis began to comprehend what Eirran wanted of him. He grasped her shoulders, and Ranal caught her around the neck. The three of them were struggling in earnest by the time the uniformed guard opened the door and stepped inside.

"Here now, stop this, stop it at once! Lady, we'll put you someplace else—"

Two black falcons flew into his face. Instinctively, he dodged, hands shielding his eyes against the falcons' attack, and blundered into the cell. Weldyn and Yareth struck in unison and the man crumpled to the floor. With quick efficiency they finished him off.

"Keys," Yareth said in satisfaction. He took the ring from the guard's belt.

"Dagger," Weldyn said. "And dart gun." He handed the dagger to Yareth and examined the gun. "Not much ammunition and this fellow doesn't have any spare clips. And it's dirty, to boot. But this ought to do until we can get more weapons."

Eirran didn't have to be told that they would be taking weapons from other dead Hounds. She glanced at Dunnis; the mark of her fingers was plain on his cheek. "I'm sorry," she said.

"The apology is mine," he said gallantly. "I was slow to understand."

The others crowded around, eager for action. "What next?" Loric said.

"We leave this place." Yareth started toward the door.

Birds on fists, the Falconers led the way out into the small portion of the prison level of the tower. As secure as the dungeon was, Weldyn told them, the Alizonders were always a little lax in guarding it. The man they had eliminated seemed to be the only one on duty. Silently, the men and Eirran climbed the wooden steps and made their way through a narrow corridor. The falcons shifted and bated, eager to fly into battle. Whispers of falconsong filled the air.

"I hope this is the way we came," someone—Hirl—whispered.

"It is," Weldyn replied. "There isn't but the one way in or out, through this little wall tunnel that opens in the window embrasure in the Great Hall. Ysher was very sure of that. Nobody is supposed to know the deepest part of the tower even exists. The Baron would give his judgment, and off the prisoner would go, vanished forever— Hello."

They had come to the door. Cautiously, Yareth opened it and pushed the curtain aside just enough to allow him to peer out into the Hall. There was a lone person in sight, a servant sweeping up stale rushes, preparatory to scattering the fresh ones lying stacked on the long table. Weldyn took quick aim over Yareth's shoulder with the dart gun. The weapon spat, and the man dropped in his tracks. Cautiously, one by one, the Estcarpians emerged from the narrow corridor, avoiding the body. The man, obviously not an Alizonder by his looks or coloring, lay face upward, a look of astonishment congealed on his face. His mouth was open.

"He was unarmed!" Eirran said. She knelt beside the body, examining it for a sign of life.

Weldyn turned a cold face to her. "He could have given the alarm."

"He wasn't an enemy. The man had no tongue."

The Falconer nudged the man with the toe of his boot. "Hmm. Probably someone they captured somewhere. Too bad, but it can't be helped now." He examined the dart gun, made a sound of disgust, and dropped it beside the man he had killed. "Don't these Alizonders ever maintain their weapons? This thing is jammed useless. Yareth? You go over there."

The Falconers quickly crossed the room toward the two entrances in the Great Hall to have a look into the outer ward, hoping to get their bearings. Weldyn took the far doorway, the one the greater distance from potential aid in case a fight broke out.

At least, Eirran thought, no one can fault him on bravery. But I wish he hadn't had to kill the poor servant.

"The inner ward is this way," Weldyn said, "behind yonder wall." Everyone hurried to where he stood and jostled one another for a look through the door he had opened a bare crack. "We'll have to cross that open spot before we get to the gate. But that will be where they're keeping the children, or I miss my guess. It's the strongest part of the castle. Where the Baron's living quarters are located."

The wall separating the inner and outer wards looked as

strong as any wall in the castle, with its own gatehouse. The gateway was guarded by what looked like a tower. Beyond the tower, a double door stood open.

"By the way my stomach feels, it's noontime. The guards are probably inside, eating," Hirl said.

"Aye." Loric rubbed his chin. "And more of them will be in the tower besides. This won't be easy."

Here and there, Hounds crossed the ward, going about their business, or on private errands. A number of them were making for the barracks across the ward, talking to each other in the manner of men on their way to a midday meal. The Estcarpians waited in scant patience until, as far as they could see, the outer ward was empty.

"Find Jenys," Yareth whispered to Newbold, and released him.

The falcon winged upward. For a moment, he seemed confused and sailed back and forth just under the enormous stone arches supporting the roof of the Great Hall, as if feeling his way. Then he picked up a direction. He screamed and stooped for the door and Weldyn opened it just in time to keep the bird from smashing into it—or knocking it open. Bursting out of the building, the Estcarpians made a headlong dash after him.

As they pelted through the ward, Eirran realized that what they had thought a tower was, in fact, a covered well-house. They were fortunate in their timing. By some miracle, the six men and one woman reached the middle gate undetected in their impetuous dash.

Jenys! Eirran called in her mind. *Jenys, I'm coming! Hold on. Mama's coming.*

Four Alizonders looked up from the table in the guard room just off the passageway through the gatehouse. One of them was just uncovering the contents of a basket. Sharpclaw hurled himself at one of the men and the Hound went down with Hirl on top of him. Dunnis and Ranal overpowered another. Weldyn, as if seeking personal satisfaction for the defective dart gun, grappled with the third.

Yareth engaged the fourth, steel to steel, while Eirran watched with her heart in her throat. He hadn't handled a weapon in so long— The Hound pressed to the attack and Yareth was forced to give ground. The Hound lunged, certain of victory. Eirran cried out. But Yareth turned aside at the last moment. The Hound's sword blade slid past harmlessly, and the man impaled himself on Yareth's dagger. Yareth and Eirran exchanged glances and she began to breathe again.

Hirl rose grinning, the Hound's sword and dagger in his possession, and met Weldyn emerging triumphant from his own battle.

"Well done," the Falconer said, and Hirl's grin widened at the unaccustomed praise.

"They've got a basket of bread and meat here, untouched," Dunnis said. "I can eat and fight at the same time, and I'm not at all proud about accepting Hound leavings."

"We haven't touched a bite since last night," Weldyn said. "Go ahead. But hurry."

They all began hastily digging into the basket, taking as much as their hands would hold.

"No!" Eirran cried. They all turned to stare at her. "The children," she said. "They might be hungry."

"You're right," Dunnis said. He put his share back into the basket. "We'll take this to them." He gave Eirran a shadow of his old merry smile. "Like a picnic."

Quickly, Yareth distributed the captured weapons. Now, among them, they had four swords and five daggers. Eirran clutched the dagger he handed her. Then, with all due caution, they hurried out of the gatehouse. Newbold had disappeared.

Weldyn said something in falconsong to Sharpclaw, and the bird rose in the air, following Newbold.

"Wait!" Eirran said. "Call him back!" All heads turned in her direction. "I—I can hear Jenys."

"That's impossible," Weldyn said. Nevertheless, he whistled Sharpclaw back to his fist.

"Nevertheless, I hear her," Eirran said stubbornly. "I know the way to go."

"I believe you," Yareth said. "Which way?"

"The building in the far corner. And high. Very high."

They entered the first doorway they came to, only to run up against another group of Hounds. They seemed to run in packs of four within the castle walls, Eirran thought. She ducked under a Hound's guard and buried her dagger in his chest before he could react. Quickly and silently, the grim-faced band of Estcarpians dispatched the rest and added their weapons to the ones they had already captured. Eirran cleaned her dagger and tucked both it and her late opponent's into her belt. Then she picked up his sword. Even if the rest of the men had not been armed by now, nobody—not even Weldyn—would have disputed her right to the weapon. It felt good, solid and reassuring, in her hand.

"Let's go before more of them find us," she said.

"Sssh," Yareth said. "Listen."

From somewhere far away, the fugitives could hear the faint sounds of screeches and thuds.

"Your Newbold is determined, isn't he?" Weldyn asked.

Eirran stared at him for a moment. It was the closest thing to a joke the man had ever made. "He loves Jenys," she said. "He'd fight his way through a solid door to get to her."

"Sounds like that's what he's doing." Weldyn hefted his captured sword. "Come on."

They met two more Hounds on the first flight of circular stairs.

"Escaped prisoners! Get help!" the closest one shouted. "I'll hold 'em here!"

The other turned and ran. Weldyn, narrowly shoving past the rest to be first up the stairs, found himself hampered by the central post. The stairs had been designed so it would be in his way, while the defender had free play for his sword.

"Boost!" Yareth shouted.

Weldyn immediately flung himself down on the stairs against

the outer wall. Yareth leaped onto Weldyn's shoulders just as the other Falconer rose again, hurling Yareth straight into the startled defender's face. The Hound went down, and Yareth scrambled over him to go after the other man. In a moment, both Hounds lay dead with Falconer steel in their hearts.

Grinning, Weldyn looked at Yareth. "Haven't forgotten everything, I see," he said, panting a little. "In spite of—you know."

Eirran brushed past him. She didn't see Newbold anywhere. Then she heard an angry falcon hissing and screeching, and talons scraping against wood. She ran toward the sounds. The corridor ended in two doorways—one, she surmised, leading to the outer wall and the sentry walk. The other opened on another short flight of circular stairs, even tighter and narrower than the first, leading to a barred door at the very top of the tower. Newbold was flying at the door, striking at it repeatedly. A pile of slivers on the floor of the small landing attested to the fury of his attacks.

"Newbold!" The falcon reluctantly returned to Yareth's fist. "Take the keys," he said, handing Eirran the ring he had removed from the prison guard's belt. Awkwardly, he tried to push the bar up with his free hand and Eirran rushed to help him remove it from the door.

"Do you think any of the keys will work?" she said.

Dunnis was right behind Yareth. The landing was so tiny he couldn't wedge himself onto the landing but had to remain standing on the stairs. He grinned. "Why not?" he said. "There're just so many keys and locks anybody would want to keep track of. Try them."

Eirran was already fumbling the first key into the lock. It didn't work. She tried the second, and the third.

The fourth key on the ring turned, with a little jiggling, and the lock mechanism reluctantly gave way. Eirran opened the door. A group of little gray ghost-children huddled on a makeshift pile of straw in the corner, terrified. Newbold darted into the room, screeching triumphantly. The ragged little gray creatures ducked and squealed, scattering like chickens. Newbold swooped overhead before landing on the back of a rickety chair and beginning to preen his feathers.

"What did I tell you?" one of the little ghosts said. "You're all so silly! You didn't believe me!"

Another grasped the one nearest her by the hands and began to dance around. "She told us, she told us," she sang. Her song shifted. "We're sa-aved, we're sa-aved!"

Eirran's range of vision narrowed abruptly. Only one of the children registered clearly in her sight, the one who had first spoken. "Jenys!" she cried. She rushed across the room in a few strides, flung herself down on her knees, and snatched the child to her. "Oh, Jenys, what have they done to you? What have they done to you all? You are so dirty! And so thin!"

She hugged and kissed Jenys as if she could never stop. The other children, even the ones who had been dancing in joy, clustered around her then, each seeking to clasp an arm, her waist, anything. Their little hands were so urgent, Eirran felt as if they sought to draw life and sustenance from her. She sought to include as many as possible in her embrace. One of the girls clung to her leg with one arm while the other thumb remained firmly in her mouth.

"Oh, Mama," Jenys said weakly. "I was afraid you'd never get here."

"Well, I'm here now. And we're going to take you out of this terrible place." She got up, took Jenys by the hand, pulled her to her feet, and started for the door. Jenys sagged and fell. "What's wrong?" she cried.

"She can't walk just yet," one of the other children said. "Flame can't walk, either, not very fast."

Eirran paused, looking at her daughter more closely. Only now did she see the terrible marks on her temples. "What did they do to you?"

Jenys's face crumpled and she seemed very near tears for the first time. "They hurt me, Mama," she whispered.

"Who hurt you?"

"Men. Gray men."

"They are Kolder," said the child who had begun singing and dancing with her friend. "My name is Star. I can tell you what you want to know."

By now the other Estcarpians had hurried up the stairs and into the relative shelter afforded by the room. Hirl stood guard by the door, in case someone came to investigate.

"Are you hungry?" Eirran asked.

The chorus of "oohs" that greeted her words and the way all the children fell upon the food made her even more glad that she had saved back the guards' meal.

"Meat," Lisper said. The deep satisfaction in her voice told Eirran exactly how long it had been since the children had been decently fed.

Quickly, between bites, and with a presence of mind far beyond her years, Star told them all that had happened, from the time they had been kidnapped, their adventures going through Alizon Gap, what had befallen Flame and Mouse—

Mouse? Eirran thought in confusion. Oh. She must mean Jenys.

—what had befallen Flame and Mouse since they had been brought to Alizon Castle.

"They want to find a way to bend all of the Old Race and make us into their slaves. They thought if they used us children, they could find a way to beat us. The Kolder, I mean, not the Alizonders." Star made a face.

"We thought the Alizonders were going to try to use you children to attempt to open a new Gate to the Kolder world," Loric said. "That's what Girvan told us."

"Girvan," Ranal said in disgust. "An Alizonder through and through. A spy for the Hounds. I don't know how he could ever have been allowed to join the guards."

"His story was excellent," Weldyn said. "He came to Estcarp wounded, telling us someone had tried to have him killed for a traitor and pointing to his hurt as proof."

"And so he was a traitor, but not in the way we thought."

Loric scowled. "This is very bad news. Kolder still alive in our world. I thought they were all destroyed when Lord Simon laid waste to their Nest."

"These must have been stationed here, coordinating the Alizonder invasion across the sea."

"Where is this room you spoke of?" Yareth said.

Jenys and the child called Flame began describing the route they had taken. Between them, they provided sufficient detail that any of the rescue party could have been confident of finding the way.

"What do you have in mind?" Loric asked.

"I'm thinking," Yareth replied.

"Well, first we have to get the children out of here," Eirran said. She started to pick Jenys up.

"No, Eirran," Dunnis said. "Let me."

"She's my child!"

"Yes, but you said yourself we had to get them out of here and I can go faster carrying her than you can."

Eirran bit her lip. "Very well," she said. She surrendered Jenys to Dunnis. The little girl looked very frail and weak indeed, in the Guardsman's arms.

"I'll take the other one who's hurt," Loric said. "We'll get them out of the castle, never fear."

"Oh, we can help, too," the little girl called Star said confidently. "We know some tricks to do."

"Good," Eirran said, not really listening.

Yareth and Weldyn exchanged glances, and nodded. "Hirl, you and Ranal go with them," Yareth said.

"What? Aren't you coming?"

"In a while."

"But—"

"Never mind about us. We'll catch up with you outside the city. Get the horses out also, if you can."

Ranal turned a little pale; nevertheless, he saluted. "Count on me." He started for the door.

The children set up a protest, pulling back and balking at

leaving part of the company behind. "Oh, we must all go together!" Star cried. "If we don't, we can't—"

"We have to root out the evil here in Alizon Castle," Yareth said. "Or it will rise again, somewhere else. It must be done, and we are the ones who must do it."

Eirran just stared at the Falconers, appalled. What could Yareth and Weldyn be thinking of? They had what they had come for. Now they should all leave, borne on the impetus of their very rashness, while they had even the slightest chance of escape. Hirl and Ranal had a child clinging to each hand, as they had clung to Eirran. Newbold launched himself from the chair back and floated through the door, as if he would go with Jenys. Eirran turned to go after them as well, but Yareth put his hand on her arm.

"These may be the last Kolder left in our world," he said. "We have to destroy them and their machine."

Eirran hesitated, torn. She wanted to stay with her husband, and she also longed to escape with her child. How could she choose? The Witch Jewel, nearly forgotten until this moment, burned against Eirran's skin. Of its own volition, her hand reached inside her clothing and took the Jewel out of its hiding place. She stared at it for what seemed to her to be a long time, seeking an answer in its cloudy gray surface. But though it spoke not to her, looking at it made her realize what had to be done.

Her decision made, she ran after Dunnis, and pressed the Jewel into Jenys's hands. "This may help you," Eirran said. "We found it where—near the spot where you were taken."

Jenys looked at it wonderingly. "It was Leaf's," she said.

Star glanced at the child who kept her thumb in her mouth. "Lisper?" she said. "Can you work with so many?"

"Yeth," Lisper said. "I think I can do it. I'll try, anyway. You'll all have to help me, though."

As if in answer, Mouse held up Leaf's Witch Jewel. "We have this to help us," she said. "And when we aren't using it, it's yours to try to see with, Bird."

"Thanks."

Bewildered and not understanding what they could be talking about, Eirran touched each of the other girls in turn, stroking one's cheek, ruffling another's unkempt hair. She kissed Jenys, her heart nearly breaking. "Run, those of you who can," she said. "Stay with these men, and run as fast as you are able!"

"Don't worry about us," Star said. "And don't worry about yourselves. We'll help a lot, we promise."

With that, the children followed Loric and Dunnis out of the tower room, gone except for the sound of their footsteps pattering down the stairs.

Eirran faced her husband. "I let you leave me behind once before, and we both suffered for it. Now *we* have to destroy the and I won't have you tell me no," she said fiercely. "We'll do it. You and me."

"And me," Weldyn said. He frowned at Eirran. "Two Falconers can fight an army of Hounds, let alone three Kolder with one of them locked into their controlling machine. But this woman—"

"This woman," she said clearly, "is the mother of one of the children these unspeakable monsters have hurt. They hurt another woman's child, and would have hurt more before they were through with their foul work. Nothing is more important than that I punish them with my own hands for what they have done."

Weldyn raised his brows sharply. "Well," he said to Yareth, "I have Sharpclaw. And you have Newbold. But if she insists on going along with us in this venture, this, this woman must not expect me to come to her aid."

"You don't need to worry about Eirran," Yareth said. "She can take care of herself when she needs to." He whistled. Newbold flew back through the door and settled on his fist.

Then the three of them, swords drawn and ready, descended the narrow stairway and began making their way through the maze of corridors, seeking the gray door behind which the Kolder would be found.

Ten

I

M ouse opened her eyes. "Mama is here!" she said, surprised.

"You're dreaming, silly," Star said. "We all want our Mamas. But we haven't got them. What happened? You look terrible. Here, drink this." She held a bottle of something to Mouse's lips.

Mouse swallowed automatically, expecting to taste water. Fire suffused her entire body. She coughed and sputtered, and her eyes filled with tears, but when the burning died down a little she realized the raw, evil-tasting liquid had made her feel a little better.

"Was that the spirits?" she asked.

"Yes. Good thing the Alizonders gave it to us. It's the only thing that's pulled you and Flame through the first hour or so. I wish I had something to give you to eat, but they haven't brought us anything yet."

"I couldn't eat anyway. I heard the Baron give orders that we were to get table scraps tonight."

"Ooh," Lisper said. "That would tathte so good. It'th been tho long thinth we had any real food."

"And I'll bet the Baron eats well," Cricket said. She made a face. "I never thought I'd look forward to getting table scraps, but I am. And I'll eat them, every one."

"Could I have some water now?" Mouse said.

"Yes. All you want. We've saved it back for you. Can you tell us what happened?" Star said.

"I think so." Mouse shifted on the bed of straw, trying to sit up. But her head throbbed so and she was so sick she had to lie down again. She licked her dry lips. Star held the cup so she could drink a few drops. Mouse had never tasted anything so good in her life. She could feel the water soaking into her parched body. She took another sip, and Star patiently held the cup until she had drunk all she wanted. "They nearly beat me down, Star. They nearly made me give up. I was ready to do what they wanted me to do. The sound, and the voices—"

"What sound?" Flame said. "I didn't hear any sound. Or any voices."

"What did you feel?" Cricket said.

"There was something all around me, something I couldn't see. It was a kind of pressure, I guess you'd call it. Like something squeezing me, really hard, and never letting go. It hurt me dreadfully. I thought it was going to squeeze my insides out."

Lisper took her thumb out of her mouth. "And you didn't know why?"

"No."

"Well, I did," Mouse said. "It was all around me, too, hurting just like you said. And I couldn't see what it was. But I heard it, all right. Maybe we were feeling the same thing, only we're talking about it in different ways. Did you feel it in your ears?"

"I thought they were going to pop."

"Me, too. That's what made me think it was sound. But I really did hear a voice. Two voices. I think it might have been because of the other wire."

"What other wire?"

Mouse lifted her dress and showed the others the blackened place on her abdomen. "Here. They fastened the wire here. I heard them say they were going to put it over the heart on the next one." She swallowed hard, thinking, considering whether to tell them the rest or not. Well, there was no use in keeping secrets; better to let her sisters know what lay in store for them, so they could prepare as best they could. It would be no favor to hide from them exactly what they could expect. "They said, if the one over the heart didn't work they were going to stick the wires right in us next time."

Shocked exclamations arose from every side. "What do you mean?" Bird cried.

"I mean in us, stick them under our skins," Mouse said.

"Ooh, that would hurt!" Flame looked profoundly shocked. "A lot more than what happened to you or me."

Lisper had gone dead white and she sucked even harder on her thumb. Mouse's eyes filled with tears. "They're not going to stick wires in you, Lisper," she said. "If they come back and choose you, I'll go again in your place."

"Not you, not again. Me," Cricket said.

"No, me," Bird said.

"No," Star said. "I will."

Mouse took Star's hand. "I kept thinking that you could have beaten them, even if I couldn't. Well, that was just for that time. We might not even have to worry about it. I think it was worse with me than it was with Flame." Her head hurt and she knew she was choosing her words poorly. Nevertheless, she persisted. No matter how badly she was stating things, she had to make them understand. "Maybe they twisted the dials differently or something. I think it will be even harder with the next one. And if it is, they'll have what they want, even if they pick you. But if they get what they want, then they'll leave us alone."

"Or kill us," Cricket said.

"We have to find a way to help each other," Mouse said. "I've been thinking about it. You see, when I was just about to bend, to give in, there was another voice—"

"Yes, you mentioned that," Star said. "What voice?"

"Somebody—you're going to laugh, but it sounded like my Mama—somebody kept telling me to hold on. So I did. But if they had done that sound thing with the wires again, I couldn't have held on, not another minute."

"Your Mama!" Bird said. "That's silly. Your Mama is 'way back on the other side of Estcarp."

Mouse shook her head and immediately regretted the action. She closed her eyes until her head stopped thumping. "No, she isn't," she said. "She's close by. Near enough that I can *hear* her."

"Then she's got to have a really loud voice." Cricket sounded nearly as scornful as Bird.

"She did say something about her Mama being here when she first woke up," Star told them. "How do you know?"

"I told you. I can *hear* her."

"How?"

"In my head. Like this." Mouse concentrated. Star jumped, startled.

"'How did you do that?"

"It's easy," Mouse said. "I'll show you."

II

The girls all wanted to learn how to *hear,* how to do this thing that Star called touching with the mind. Mouse showed them, one by one, and they giggled as they tried it out on each other. Mouse felt a little better as long as she had something to keep her mind off how sick and dizzy she felt. And it was something for them to do, as well. Part of the awfulness of being captive was the waiting, with nothing to do, nothing to keep them occupied.

Soon, with a little practice, the children could all *hear* one another by mindtouch with varying degrees of proficiency, though it tired them considerably to do so, as if they had been running and playing hard for hours. It was strange. As Bird put it, it was as if they were not so much learning something new as remembering something they had forgotten long ago.

They sat resting for a while, silent. From far below, the sounds of boats on the river drifted up to them. Mouse wished she were on a boat, going far, far away from this place.

"When I was little, my Mama never let me have a kitty to play with," Flame said shyly. Her eyes were closed and she lay back on the bed. "So I used to make one out of clay. I'd *think* about it very hard, and then it would be a real kitty for a while. We'd have ever so much fun. And then it would become clay again."

"Can you do it now?" Bird wanted to know.

"I can try, but I don't have any clay. I'd have to use some of this straw."

"Oh, please, do try!" Cricket said.

Enthralled, all the girls watched while Flame sat up and began gathering bits of straw and smoothing them into a bundle, which she tied with gray threads from her dress.

"This is going to be the kitty's body," she said. The other girls nodded their understanding.

Encouraged by their interest, she then made four smaller bundles—the legs—and tied them onto the body. Forming a roundish clump on one end to represent the head and sticking another piece of straw on the other end for the tail, she added the finishing touch of a strip of fabric which she tied around the "neck" in a bow.

"Well," she said, eyeing her creation judiciously, "this is as good as I can do. We'll see what happens now."

She closed her eyes and began to *think* so hard Mouse could see it happening. She breathed loudly through her nose. Mouse watched, fascinated. Flame paled, faltering visibly.

"I—I can't," she said. "I'm still too sick—"

"I'll help," Star said. She reached out her hand toward Flame and Mouse saw—or thought she saw—a spark, a flash of something pass from Star to Flame. Flame took a deep breath, and suddenly a kitten stood, wobble-legged, before them. It was not a very pretty kitten, and its coat was a bewildering mixture of gray and straw-colored fur. But it looked as real as real could be.

A sudden longing for Pounce, who used to sleep on her bed sometimes back home, came over Mouse. "Ooh," she breathed, "may I touch it? May I pet it?"

"Of course," Flame said. "You may all play with it, if you don't hurt it. I don't know how long it will stay."

She handed the kitten to Mouse who cuddled it in her arms. It purred, gazing at her out of yellowish eyes, and batted at her fingers. Then it licked her hand. Its tiny pink tongue was as rough as its fur.

"Let me have it for a while," Lisper said, and Mouse reluctantly gave the kitten to her. "Hello, kitty. What'th your name?"

The children petted the kitten, and dangled bits of straw enticingly for it to play with. It danced and purred, happily romping from one child to the next, sharing their attentions equally. But the spell couldn't last long; when it was Flame's turn for the kitten, she touched it and it fell apart, a bundle of straw once more. She untied the threads and let the straw drift to the floor.

"I thought you weren't going to be able to do it at all," Cricket said. "How did you manage, there at the end, just before it turned into a kitty?"

"I don't know," Flame said. "It was as if somebody helped me, only I don't know how—"

"That was me," Star said. She looked a little abashed. "I gave you some of my strength."

III

Star had used to do that, lend her strength to people who needed it, when she and her family were out on the road, and everyone was getting tired before they could make camp.

They all lived together, these traveling merchants, with no wedded wives and husbands but all living in one group with an ever-shifting pattern of relationships. None of the children could be certain who their fathers were, even if their mothers knew, which they often did not. Furthermore, their mothers' identity sometimes grew hazy in their minds. Women mothered children indiscriminately, and just as casually ignored them if they chose to do so. But there were usually enough women in the mood at any given time that no child went without maternal attention for long. Star had no more idea of who her real father was than any other child in the caravan, but she chose to believe he was the leader among them, and he was the only one she called "Papa." She was very proud when he came to stay with her mother, which he did more often than with any of the other women.

On the road, Papa would be trudging along, thinking, Star knew, about having to set up the wagons, having to tend the horses, having to mend whatever had broken that day. And about having to watch through the night lest thieves come and try to steal their poor stock of goods or the small chest of money that was kept under Mama's bedroll. From the seat where Star rode, she found it easy to *push* somehow, to send a surge of strength out like a puff of fog, enveloping Papa. She could almost see it when it left her body, could always tell when he inhaled it, or it sank into his skin, or whatever happened. He would straighten up, as if he had been unaware of the kink in his back.

"Come on now, just a little farther and we're there," he'd call to the people in the wagons following theirs. And the others would take heart from the renewed vigor in his voice.

Sometimes, if Star hadn't sent more strength to Papa than usual and she wasn't too tired, she would *push* a wave of it out to someone else in the caravan—whoever seemed to need it most. Nobody had taught her how to do this. It was something she just naturally seemed to know. And so it had not been at all surprising to her when Bee and the guardsmen had found her family and had taken her away to be trained and become a real Witch some day.

"And that's what I did with Flame," she said.

"That's a very nice thing to know how to do, give someone a little extra strength," Mouse said thoughtfully. The other girls began to talk, one by one, telling of what they could do, and though Mouse listened, part of her mind was busy, turning something over and over. There was a drawback, somewhere. But if Star could show them how to *push,* the way she had taught them how to *hear* when others spoke, and if some of the other girls had useful talents, even untrained. . . .

IV

"I can change the way I look," Cricket said.

"No!"

"Really."

Cricket was the child of a couple who lived in a small village in southern Estcarp. Her father had a small farm that barely fed his family and, for a little extra on the table, her mother did sewing for the village women. She had one brother, a little older than she, and her mother was expecting another child any time.

"Though how we'll ever feed another mouth is more than I'll ever know," Cricket's mother would say, sighing.

It was especially hard on Cricket's brother, Gwannyn. He was hungry all the time. And so was Cricket, until she stumbled onto the knack of making other people believe she was her brother. She would just *want* it so, and it was.

It was very convenient, this ability of hers. She could go into the pantry any time she wanted, could take a bite or two, and he would get the punishment. It was lovely. She did have to be careful, though, when Mama had extra money and made spice tarts, not to eat too many of them and get sick. That would have been very difficult to explain.

Whether it was a trick of the light, or something else, Cricket didn't know. Only sometimes, when Gwannyn was nearby, she would have to *want* herself into looking like someone else. And usually, she could. She hadn't thought anything at all when Bee and the guards had come and gotten her. She had simply thought it was a very nice thing for Bee to think of doing. She hadn't any idea that everyone couldn't change their shape—in another person's eyes, at least—the way she could.

"Oh, that'th nothing," Lisper said. "I uthed to keep people

from theeing me altogether. I could walk right under their notheth, and they wouldn't notith."

Lisper had been a very quiet, withdrawn child, easy to over-look in the large establishment of Gweddawl Garth. Everyone who lived there seemed far too busy to have time for the small, thin girl-child who couldn't speak clearly, even if she was the daughter of the garth-holder and, as such, could have been considered minor nobility. Lisper felt invisible most of the time. And one day, to her surprise and wonder, she discovered that when she *wished* it hard enough, she really was invisible. In fact, all that she could see of herself was a thin shadow, as if she were made of fog. She could look right through her hand, the way you did sometimes when you held your hand to the light and it shone all red and you could see the outlines of your bones. But even her bones went transparent when she *wished* it so.

Now she could go anywhere, see and overhear anything—especially the secrets over which the grownups were always hustling her away so they could discuss them in private. They called it business and sent her out to play. But Lisper knew it was because they just didn't want to be bothered with having her around. And none of the other children would play with her anyway. When she was invisible, though, everything was dif-ferent. It was all very exciting, being where she had always been forbidden to go, though she really didn't understand a tenth of what was going on once she got there. The only serious draw-back was that she had never learned to *wish* her clothing trans-parent as well, and unless she wanted it to appear that her dress had suddenly gotten up and gone for a walk, she had to take it off. And her other clothing as well. This made her secret activi-ties a thing best confined to warm weather. Invisible she might be, but she could still be heard. The sound of her chattering teeth would surely have given her away, and she didn't have any idea what would have happened to her if she had been caught spying, and without her clothes, and invisible to boot. Further-more, she didn't want to find out.

After Bee had come for her, she had been so happy with her

sisters that she hadn't even thought about *wishing* herself unseen, not even once.

"That ith, until the Houndth caught uth. And Leaf." Lisper's thumb went back into her mouth.

Cricket sniffed. "I'll bet that if I had *thought* myself into looking like a Hound—or," she amended practically, "one of their rotten old dogs anyway, they're closer to my size—if I'd *thought* that, or if you'd *wished* yourself invisible, they would never have caught us."

"Maybe not. But it all happened too fatht."

"I'll bet I could do that right now—walk out without being noticed, or make the Hounds think I was somebody I wasn't."

"I'll bet I could do it better. Tho there."

Mouse privately thought the two of them were bragging more than just a little, but she didn't say so out loud. She was still working on her idea, but something was bothering her. She almost had it, if only her head didn't hurt so much—

"What can you do, Bird?" Lisper asked.

"Nothing much. Sometimes, if things are just right, I can *see.*"

"What do you mean, you can see?" Star asked.

"Oh, you know," Bird said, blushing. *"See.* I always called it going deep."

V

Bird's Papa was the blacksmith in the village where she used to live, and probably the richest man anywhere for leagues around. He was a big man, bluff and handsome.

Bird's Mama had been the village beauty when she was young, and she still liked to go as handsomely decked out as possible. Her husband indulged her, as much as he could. Her dresses were of the finest material and sewn by the best seamstress in the village. She had carved combs of shell for her hair and red leather shoes for her feet. Bird knew she was something of an embarrassment to these handsome people—a thin, scrawny wraith of a child, plain of face and not likely to grow into any sort of beauty. Bird held no resentment over this; it was just a fact, like any other, and something she couldn't help. Still, it was hard sometimes when strangers looked at her Papa and her Mama and then at her, with a look on their faces that clearly asked, "Why?"

Mama had many pretty things, ornaments and ribbons, clothing and trinkets, and Bird loved it when Mama let her take one of these things for a day and keep it near her. Bird did this with any lovely object that caught her fancy—a perfect flower, a glittering rock—and she would look at it until, as her Mama put it, she had "all but looked all the prettiness out of it." One of her favorite things was a piece of crystal on a silver chain that Mama wore sometimes. The crystal was perfectly clear—a smooth, round stone polished with no distracting facets or engraving on it, and despite its plainness it caught every stray beam of light, glowing like a living thing on Mama's breast.

Then one day, Mama lost her beautiful crystal necklace. She looked for it, but it was nowhere to be found.

"Even though it was such a plain thing, I liked it because you gave it to me," she told Bird's Papa.

"Oh, well, don't fret," Papa said. "At the next fairing, we'll buy you another, even finer."

Mama smiled and quit looking for her necklace then, for if there was anything she liked better than pretty things, it was new things. "Next time let's look for one that sparkles and makes rainbows when the sun shines on it," she said.

When Bird found it much later, out under the bay-tree where Mama had been walking, it never even crossed her mind to take it back to her. The silver chain had broken, and that was why it had fallen off Mama's neck. Since it was by far Bird's favorite thing, she thought Mama might even let her keep it for herself now, and maybe Papa would even get a new chain for her to wear it on. After Mama got her new necklace, of course.

She started to put it in her pocket. But then, moved by some impulse she didn't understand, she looked into it, in a different manner from the way she had done before. This time, she really looked until she could began to *see*. The more she *saw,* the more she felt as if she were swimming into the crystal, the way fish swam in water. To her surprise, she discovered pictures in its depths, pictures that moved, of things that were happening a long way away. There was Mama, back at the cottage, combing her hair and humming to herself. Fascinated, Bird tried "going deep," so she could *see* more. The picture in the crystal faded, shimmered, and resolved into her Papa, who had gone over to the next village that day, to buy a new riding horse. Bird could see him ever so clearly, and the horse, too. It was red, to match Mama's hair.

After that, Bird began wearing the crystal on a string around her neck, carefully keeping it hidden from sight. She would go into it and *see* every chance she had. It was fascinating. She discovered she could *see* people she knew, almost every time. Once in a while, though, all she could *see* was something like a closed door, and gradually she began to understand that the person was occupied in something private, and if she had looked, she would have been intruding. That seemed fair to her. And, she also discovered, she could not *see* people or things she did not know, or had only heard of, such as the great ones in Es City, no matter how "deep" she went. It was no great surprise to her when Bee came. Though she had not *seen* Bee, exactly, she had "gone deep" and had watched herself riding away from her village, in the company of five small shadows and one larger one. She had been very pleased that Bee had had on the kind of necklace she wore. She thought Bee must use it the same way Bird used the piece of crystal. It seemed so right and natural that Bird had not even thought to take her necklace with her when she left to go to Es City.

The other girls ooh'd and aah'd when Bird finished her story.

"That'th wonderful, Bird. Could you *thee* what'th happening with my Mama and Papa? If I helped you, I mean? I'd let you *hear* inthide my head, tho you could do it."

"Maybe. But I don't have anything to look into."

"Would this do?" Flame poured a little water into the cup and handed it to Bird.

"I don't know," Bird said doubtfully, "but I could try."

She looked into the cup, tilting it so the water could catch the light. Mouse watched intently, wishing it were her Mama that Bird was trying to see. Somehow Bird's appearance changed, and she knew the very moment when Bird "went deep."

"I *see* something!" Bird exclaimed. "Does your Mama wear trousers like a man, and carry a sword?"

"No, of courth not."

"That's my Mama!" Mouse exclaimed. Heedless of her aching head, she scrambled over the straw to where Bird knelt, and peered into the cup. "I know it! I just know it! Show me how to do it, Bird. Please!"

"Oh, it's gone!" Bird said. She glared at Mouse. "You ruined it."

"But I just know it was my Mama. I heard her, and now you saw her! She's here, she's in Alizon, I just know she is."

"You're crazy."

"I'm not."

"Yes, you are."

"Stop it, both of you," Star said. "Mouse, you've been talking about your Mama ever since you started telling us about that other voice you thought you heard. She can't be here. It's impossible."

"I did hear another voice. It sounded like Mama, even though it sounded like the Guardian, too, a little. I just know that Mama is near, and that she's come to get me. And even if I'm wrong, even if I'm crazy like Bird said, none of us would have known what each other could do and we wouldn't have learned anything if I hadn't told you about *hearing* her. Maybe the things each of us can do will help us. How far away did you have to be to *push*, Star?" Mouse asked.

Star looked at her, frowning a little. Then her expression changed and Mouse knew without *hearing* or using mindtouch that she understood what Mouse was driving at. "Not very close at all. Do you mean I should *push,* and help the next one of us who goes into the Kolder room?"

"I think it's the only way we can keep from giving in."

"Well, it's worth trying," Star said. "I don't know if I can do it all by myself, though. And what if I'm the one who's next?" Then she answered her own question. "Of course. I'll teach everyone how, just like you did with that *hearing* of yours. We all ought to teach each other how we do things."

Mouse closed her eyes, relieved. The idea was out, finally, even if she hadn't been the one to voice it. There was still something wrong, though. She couldn't think about it. Her head still hurt too much.

Bird laughed. "What good does making a kitten out of straw do us? Except to pass the time, I mean."

"I don't know," Mouse said stubbornly. "But Cricket can make people believe she looks like somebody else, and Lisper can make people think nobody was there at all."

Bird glanced at Lisper, and as clearly as if she had spoken the words aloud, Mouse *heard* her say, A lot of good that will do us.

"It will do some good," Star said, and Mouse realized she had *heard* as well. "Lisper can teach us how, just like Mouse taught us how to *hear* the way she does."

"Well, suppose we could turn ourselves into shadows and walk right out the door the next time the Hounds come for us," Cricket said. "What about Mouse and Flame? How can we manage? They can't walk."

"I can so," Flame said stoutly.

Star ignored her. "We'll wait until they're better."

"By that time," Cricket pointed out, "somebody else will be sick. Even sicker, if the Kolder do what Mouse said they were going to do."

"Oh."

Suddenly, the thing that had been bothering Mouse became clear enough in her head that she could tell the others. "I heard voices when the Kolder were working on me, and I was the one who could *hear* with my mind. I think that means something."

"Maybe. But what about Flame?" Cricket said.

Star's eyes narrowed. "Maybe it's the Kolder machine, turning our, our talents against us. In that case, Flame's ability wasn't something it could fasten on, that's all."

"Then we've hurt ourselves and not helped, by sharing what we can do!" Bird cried, horrified.

Every eye turned toward Bird; what horrors would she see when she was entangled in the Kolder machine?

"No, I don't think so," Star said slowly. "I think we might be stronger together than we are separately."

"My Mama will come for us," Mouse said. "She'll save us."

"Oh, hush," Star said. She sounded more tired than irritated. "Don't hold out hope for us when there isn't any. The best we can do right now is learn and practice each other's abilities, and try to work together so we can hold out when we're under the Kolder machine." She shivered, and Mouse caught a glimpse of what Star was thinking: herself, lying helpless on the table in the Kolder laboratory, screaming while the Kolder pushed sharpened wires into her.

Mouse knew that Star was right. Even if they could manage to escape, they couldn't leave anyone behind, and despite her brave words, Flame was only in slightly better condition than Mouse was.

"Yes, Star," she said. "The *hearing* and the *push* you do when you share your strength—that's what we ought to concentrate on. That's what we'll need most, until the Kolder are through with us."

The other girls shuddered, knowing as well as Mouse did herself, that the only way the Kolder would be through with them would be when they had bent to the Kolder will, or were dead.

Eleven

I

*Y*areth and Weldyn stalked through the corridors, falcons on fists, at the ready. Eirran had never seen Yareth like this before, not even when they had been battling with the beast in the Barrier Mountains. There they had been overmatched. Here he was in his element, doing what he had been born for—a confident, surefooted warrior, unafraid, eager for battle, going side by side with another Falconer fully his equal. It was a sight to daunt an entire company of Hounds, a sight to inspire confidence in one who fought beside them. Eirran followed close on their heels, glancing frequently over her shoulder, expecting any moment to see a hundred Hounds erupt in pursuit. Even the bold Falconers couldn't prevail when outnumbered like that. But, so far, their luck seemed to be holding.

Down this hallway, through that door, up a short flight of stairs, following the directions Flame and Jenys had given them. They were in another part of the complex now, on the top floor of a large stone building set against the castle wall. Eirran remembered passing by the place during their headlong dash across the inner ward toward the northeast tower, toward the spot where she thought she had heard her child calling to her. That had been so strange. Eirran had been very sure she had actually heard Jenys, and yet that was impossible. She must think about that, later, when she had time.

The Falconers came around a corner and halted. Eirran nearly blundered into Weldyn; he glanced over his shoulder at her, disdain for her clumsiness written clearly on his face.

"This is it," Yareth said quietly. "That gray door yonder."

"The woman stays out here. She'll just get in our way."

"No, I won't."

"You hold that sword as if it were a stick."

"Then I'll use it to club the Kolder who hurt my daughter."

"Quiet," Yareth said. "She stays with us. Our luck won't last forever. We're bound to run into more Hounds and she wouldn't stand a chance if we left her outside and she had to deal with them alone."

Weldyn scowled, and then nodded reluctantly. "Very well. But she'd better keep out of my way or I won't be responsible for what happens to her."

"Fair enough," Eirran said grimly. "Now, how do we get in?"

For answer, Yareth crept forward, careful not to betray his presence by click of bootheel or jingle of chain mail. She and Weldyn followed, just as cautiously. As they drew closer, Eirran became aware of a curious deadness to the air, a kind of absence of sound that swallowed up all noise and gave back none of the normal echo and resonance that was so much a part of her normal surroundings she didn't even notice it until it was gone.

The Falconers must have been experiencing the same thing; they exchanged glances with eyebrows raised.

"It must be the Kolder metal, or whatever it is, on this door," Weldyn said.

Yareth stared at the gray surface. "Or the effects of the machine in there. Perhaps both."

Gingerly, Eirran laid one fingertip against the door; the material—not wood, not metal as she knew it—yielded slightly under her touch. But it was as cold and lifeless as the aura it exuded, and somehow *hungry,* as if it would drain all the life force out of her if she touched it long enough. She drew her hand back, as if she had been scalded.

"I'd bet you could shout the castle down and nobody would hear it inside," Weldyn said. "They might not even notice an ordinary knock. You'd think they would hang a bell inside, or some such. Anything to keep from having to touch that stuff."

"They don't care about that. If there's no bell and they would have trouble hearing us even if we wanted to knock politely, let's take a more direct way to open the door and hope that somebody is inside to receive visitors."

The men stepped back a pace. The falcons clutched the men's gloves, striving to keep their balance, as the warriors aimed kicks squarely in the center of the door. The lock burst. The door flew open—not with a crash, but with something like a muffled thud—and the three people and two falcons leaped inside. The birds were at the highest point in the room, ready to go arrowing down at the enemy, even before the two men and the woman with them had cleared the door.

As they rushed in, Eirran got a confused jumble of gray and green-blue shapes—three gray-clad horrors masquerading in the form of men, and the green-blue uniforms of four white-blond men. One of the Alizonders shouted an alarm and pulled a dart-gun from the holster at his side.

From above, Newbold screamed a challenge. He stooped toward the head of the Kolder seated at the table. Swift as thought, the falcon ripped out tubes and wires and carried them off in his talons. Somewhere in the room a high-pitched whine droned to a stop. Lights on the map died, dials dimmed and went out, and the Kolder slumped like a doll that had lost its stuffing. The metal cap came off the Kolder's head and dangled, useless, from the few wires still attached to the machine. The cap had replaced most of the creature's skull. To Eirran's horror, the sickening contents began spilling out. Newbold banked, stooping for a second attack.

Zzzzzt! The dart-gun in the hands of the Alizonder spoke, and Eirran ducked instinctively. But none of the human attackers had been the target. Newbold screeched in a note Eirran had never heard before—a cry that should have been impossible for a bird's throat to produce. He flapped feebly, still trying to fly. Time slowed and Eirran watched, in excruciating detail, as the black-feathered bird slipped sideways out of the air and fell to the cold gray floor. He seemed to fall forever, drifting down as helplessly as a feather. A blotch of red stained the white "V" on the falcon's breast.

Her own voice jarred her back to reality. "No!" she screamed.

Weldyn shoved her out of the way and hurled himself onto one of the Kolder. She scrambled past Yareth who had leapt to the attack, engaging sword to sword with two of the Alizonders. The man with the dart-gun turned the weapon in her direction.

Zzzzzt! The dart whizzed past, and the scalp over her ear stung furiously. She flung herself at the man but she did not move more swiftly than Sharpclaw. The second falcon flew straight into the man's face. Instinctively, he covered his eyes before Sharpclaw could blind him. Eirran lunged at him with the sword. His hands dropped, grasping at the blade, and he stared at her in utter disbelief before he collapsed. She pulled the sword free and turned, looking for another enemy to destroy.

The Kolder Weldyn was struggling with presented a tempting target, but she dared not interfere, lest she blunder and wound—even kill—the wrong one. The third Kolder fumbled with the apparatus Newbold had ripped from the controller. He seemed to be trying to fit the cap onto his own skull. Eirran ran forward, raised her sword and brought it whistling down on the spot where the neck joins the shoulders. The Kolder fell. Something hit her, hard, from behind and she went down in turn, struggling with the Alizonder who had attacked her. She had lost her sword. The Alizonder raised a dagger. Desperately, she caught his wrist with both hands before he could bury the blade in her body. She couldn't even defend herself. The two daggers in her belt might as well have been back in Blagden, for all the good they did her. The Alizonder was too strong. Inexorably, the dagger point came closer, until it was scraping against her chainmail.

Weldyn appeared over the Alizonder's shoulder. With quick, brutal efficiency, he hauled the man up by his hair, stabbed him, and hurried on to Yareth's assistance. By the time Eirran scrambled out from under the dead man, the last two enemies lay dead.

Weldyn hastily checked the insignia on the Alizonders. "Underlings," he muttered in disgust. "Minor barons at best, having a cozy chat with their Kolder masters. Well, I suppose it was too much to ask that we'd catch Mallandor in here with them."

"You're hurt!" Yareth hurried over to Eirran and touched the spot on the side of her head.

"It's nothing," she said. "We've all got a cut or two. Newbold—"

Yareth had not seen what had happened. With a cry he flung himself down next to the falcon and picked him up as tenderly as he had handled Jenys when she was an infant. "He lives yet," he said brokenly. "He's still breathing."

"He killed one of the Kolder unaided," Weldyn said. "He acquitted himself well."

Eirran touched the bird cautiously, trying to examine him. The dart, ugly and bloodstained, protruded from the falcon's chest. "He's gravely wounded. I'll take him."

Weldyn put his hand on her arm. "No," he said.

She gazed at him a moment, then nodded. It was only fitting that Yareth bear his feathered brother in honor from the field of battle. It didn't matter one way or another that Yareth could scarcely carry Newbold and fight at the same time. The odds on their living to reach a place where she could tend his hurt were shortening steadily. Chances were they would be captured, or trapped and shot down with darts or arrows within the hour.

"Come on, then," she said. "The last place I want to be caught is in here." Yes, she added to herself, let's get it over with. Let us go running headlong to our doom.

Weldyn whistled Sharpclaw back to his fist. Yareth, cradling Newbold tenderly in the crook of one elbow, hefted his sword. Eirran retrieved her own sword from where it had lodged in the Kolder's body, and the three hurried out of the gray chamber.

"Which way now?" she asked.

"This way." Weldyn pointed toward the end of the corridor. "There should be a stair down, and a wall passage where we can go without being seen from either ward. Then we'll have to get out the main gate and find the other men and the children."

"Is that all?" Eirran gave a short laugh in spite of herself. She could see the crossbowmen now, waiting atop the wall to catch them in a murderous crossfire. "Well, let's get on with it."

Once again, the information Ysher had given his friend Weldyn proved correct. The three of them ducked into the narrow walkway hidden inside the great wall of the castle. The darkness was alleviated by the light from an occasional arrow-slit and by small oil lamps set at intervals in holders on the walls. A smell of dampness came through the arrow-silts from the river below. As they hurried past, one lamp guttered and went out.

"The Alizonders must not have the power machines Estcarp has, to light and heat their strongholds," Weldyn commented. "Either that, or their machines have fallen into disrepair. Perhaps that's one reason they keep trying to overrun us."

Yareth made no reply, but moved ahead in that long-legged stride Eirran knew so well. She hurried after him, and Weldyn, for once, was forced to bring up the rear.

"Yareth!" Eirran caught him by the sleeve. Intent on Newbold, he had failed to look ahead, to anticipate what they might encounter in the passageway.

Five Hounds accompanied by their snake-headed white dogs of war were coming toward them at a dead run.

II

Without a word, Yareth passed Newbold back to Eirran and rushed forward to the attack. His dagger appeared as if by magic in his other hand.

One of the hounds leapt out in front. "Wait!" it cried in an unaccountably childish, high-pitched voice. "It's us!"

Yareth halted in his tracks. "W-what—" he said. He gripped his sword a little tighter.

"It's us! It's me! Cricket! We're disguised!"

Two of the Hounds carried white dogs in their arms. Eirran tugged on Yareth's sleeve again. He shrugged her off. One of the unencumbered Hounds laid his sword down very carefully and took a step forward, displaying empty hands.

"Please," he said. "Listen. Or kill me if you wish. I am Alizonder. The others are disguised, as this little one said."

"Alizonder? What are you doing with the others, if you are one of the enemy?"

"My name is Talgar. I befriended one of the Haglets—I mean, the Witch-children, on the way to Alizon City."

Yareth tightened his grip on his sword. "You stole my child—"

"I was under the orders of Baron Esguir, Alizon's Master of Hounds. It is death to disobey. I risked much, even doing what little I was able to do. Could you have done as much, dared to defy your commanding officer?"

The thin white dog in the arms of another of the Alizonders spoke up. "It's true, Papa. He was very good to us on the way. He's trying to help us now!"

The bizarre prospect of an animal using his daughter's voice was too much for Yareth. He brushed at his eyes with the back of the hand that held the dagger. He had begun to tremble slightly. Eirran found the situation far easier to accept, perhaps because of her own recent experience with shape-changing.

"It's a trick to fool us into giving up! The Hounds are using magic!" With a muffled exclamation of disgust, Weldyn started to shove past them.

"No, wait!" Eirran cried. "Look, Weldyn, Yareth! That Hound—I mean, child—is it really Jenys? It is! She has the Witch Jewel around her neck!"

Weldyn stopped abruptly. "By the Great Falcon! The woman is right! But it could still be a trick. They could have taken it from her. How came you by that bauble, dog?"

"Becauth we gave it to her," another of the hounds said. "We all tried to make it work, but it wouldn't do anything for anybody but Mouth." Then it giggled.

In spite of herself, Eirran began to laugh as well. Relief and the absurdity of their situation made her giddy. "Nobody—not even the most careful magic-worker in all of Alizon—would think to make one of the hounds, the children, whatever they are, nobody would make one of them lisp. Oh, how wonderful—*hic!*—how perfect! We went to rescue them, and they wind up rescuing us!"

"Stop it, Eirran," Yareth said. "Don't get hysterical on us."

Both Falconers stared at the impossible assortment ranged before them—Alizonder, Estcarpian Guardsmen in the guise of Alizonder, Witch-children wearing the forms of thin white dogs. "Well, what is it to be?" Weldyn said finally. "Are we to be turned into Hounds as well?"

"If this little one has the strength to do it." Talgar laid his hand on hound-Cricket's head. The dog form danced a little, tongue out, claws clicking on the stone floor. The Jewel on hound-Jenys's neck gave off faint sparks of blue light in the gloom. "If the Witch-children can't manage to include you in their illusion, we'll just march you out of the castle, pretending that you're our prisoners. Off to let the dogs chase you. It's one of the things we do to captives."

Yareth found his voice. "You—you seem to have thought of everything."

"We couldn't have done it if the children hadn't turned us invisible and gotten us as far as the outer ward," said the "Alizonder" who held hound-Jenys. Eirran recognized Dunnis's voice.

"That wath me."

"Oh, quit bragging, Lisper," hound-Cricket said.

"Well, it wath."

"You did it through Mouse and the Jewel and you know it!"

"Argue it out later," Talgar said. "Come, lady. Sirs. Whether you go as a Hound or in your own guise, you must leave quickly. The Ha— The Witch-children can't keep up their illusion forever."

The Falconers and Eirran moved forward to join the others. Hound-Janys struggled to sit up in Dunnis's arms. "Newbold!" she cried. "He's been hurt!"

"We can't do anything about it until we get out of the city," Weldyn said harshly. "Sharpclaw can fly, but how do you propose to disguise the other falcon?"

"Don't let Sharpclaw fly away," hound-Star said. The dog— no, the *child*—spoke with such ridiculously calm self-possession that Eirran had to stifle an urge to laugh again. She hiccupped instead. "Someone is bound to see. They might figure out that we've escaped."

"What then?" Yareth's face was haggard. He took Newbold back from Eirran and stroked him so gently Eirran's heart broke for him.

"We're giving all our strength and powers to Mouse, and she's channeling it through the Jewel," hound-Star went on. "What do you think, Mouse? Can you change them? We could disguise the birds as puppies."

"I think so. Everybody, let's try."

Even in the disjointed strangeness that had surrounded the Estcarpians since the moment they had found the children, the sight was weird enough to make Eirran stop hiccupping. All six of the "dogs" came to attention and turned their gaze toward the Falconers and Eirran. As they stared, concentrating, Eirran saw thin lines of faint blue light begin to form between them, like a web of power linking one to another. She shook her head, positive that she had begun to hallucinate. The strands of light grew brighter, though their glow did nothing to alleviate the gloom of the passageway. Then, with a rush that made the Witch Jewel flare into brief brilliance, the power-web concentrated and focused. It shot out and enveloped the three humans and two birds. Eirran and Yareth staggered and nearly fell, and Weldyn took a step backward. A faint, scorched smell drifted through the corridor.

"Is that it?" Weldyn examined his hand. "I'm not any different."

"You won't seem so, to your own eyes," Eirran said.

Yareth turned to look at them. "You are both changed," he said.

"And you appear to hold a puppy in your arms." Eirran touched Newbold's head gently.

Weldyn looked at the "puppy" that, incongruously, perched on his gloved fist. "Now I believe," he said, and spoke to Sharpclaw in falconsong. With much coaxing, Sharpclaw allowed himself to be held much as Yareth was holding the wounded Newbold. To Eirran's relief, Newbold, in his disguised form, did not appear injured, nor did he resist being carried. There was no blood; the "puppy" looked as if it were merely asleep.

"Well, let's go," the older Falconer said gruffly. "Sharpclaw won't put up with this for very long."

"He won't have to," Hirl said. "Just until we get outside the city walls, and beyond Alizonder sentries' sight."

"The sooner we're out of Alizonder form and back into our own, the better, I say. And you, woman, keep your mouth shut. Your voice isn't changed this time, and if you begin to babble like women do, you'll betray us all."

III

Trying to hide the tension they all were feeling, the Estcarpians and the one real Alizonder strolled as casually as possible through the outer ward and toward the castle gatehouse. Everyone's nerves jangled almost audibly, and Eirran dug her nails into her palms to keep herself from screaming. Once they reached the open, hound-Jenys and hound-Flame walked, though hound-Jenys shivered and limped, leaning against Dunnis as often as she could.

"Talgar!"

The Estcarpians stiffened and more than one hand went to

sword-hilt, but the one who hailed their companion had no challenge in his voice.

"Off duty?" the Hound said. He walked up to the band of disguised escapees, glancing at them incuriously.

"Yes, and on my way out to run the dogs a little," Talgar said.

"A couple of them don't look very well."

"They've been off their feed."

The newcomer grinned. "You always were too soft on your dogs. You should let 'em fight for their food, the way the rest of us do. Makes 'em tough, weeds out the weaklings."

"We thought a little exercise might do them some good."

"Yes. It might. I see you've got pups as well. Didn't know there were any pups in any of the kennels this time of year. It's early yet."

"Oh, you know how it is. You get a female that's determined enough—" Talgar shrugged expressively, and the other man laughed.

"Well, can't start training 'em too young, I suppose. Luck to you." The Hound nodded courteously to Talgar's companions and walked on.

Eirran began to breathe again.

Talgar turned to the others. "Shall we ride?" he asked, loudly enough to be overheard if anyone was listening.

It was Yareth's turn to shrug. "I'd rather not run along with the hounds," he said, "though I'll carry this little one for a while."

"And I." Weldyn's mouth twitched and for a moment, Eirran thought he might smile.

"Might as well carry these sickly ones while we're at it," Dunnis said. "At least until they get a whiff of fresh air." He picked up hound-Jenys, and Ranal picked up hound-Flame.

"But let's not coddle them too much," Ranal said. Surreptitiously, he stroked hound-Flame's snakelike head.

"Lead your horses at first, until we get well away from the town," Talgar said. "The hounds will get too excited and they might overrun someone's garden, and then there'll be trouble from Baron Esguir."

"Oh, we know all about Baron Esguir," Loric said. "Never fear, we'll be very careful."

They made it out through the castle gate without further incident, and only a few curious glances followed them as they strode quickly through the town. Ranal and Dunnis set their charges down as they neared the place where their horses were being stabled, and the "dogs" all moved close together.

At first, the stablekeeper was reluctant to let the men have the horses. "They belong to someone else," he said. "New recruits for the Hounds. Girvan told me so when he paid me."

"Those men turned out to be spies from Estcarp, and Girvan turned them in." Talgar spat into the straw on the dirt floor of the stable. "All their goods forfeit. Baron Esguir has given the horses to these men. Reward for past service."

"Oh." The stablekeeper peered at the disguised escapees, looking them up and down. Eirran swallowed hard, trying to stifle a threatening hiccup. "And I suppose you want to try 'em out, eh? Take 'em for a run. Very well." He shot them a suspicious look. "But don't try gettin' any refund for the stable fees."

"Keep it, keep it," Yareth said. "Your part of the reward."

The stablekeeper relaxed perceptibly. "Well, that's all right then. Come again, gentlemen, any time."

The Estcarpians quickly claimed their mounts before the man could change his mind. Talgar accompanied them as they went on foot half a league beyond the city gate, leading the horses. They paused on the road, well away from any house or sentry, yet still in sight of the city walls.

"Here I must leave you," the Alizonder said. "It is up to you now, to get out of the country in one piece. If you can. It won't be easy, that I know."

Yareth nodded. "You have already done more than— than—"

"Than you would have expected of a Hound?" Talgar's smile twisted bitterly. "Not all of us are monsters. I don't make war on children. And when I heard what the Kolder were doing to them in that private room where nobody goes without having business there— Well, I was on my way to see what I could do to help them when I met your companions coming out."

The canine shape that was hound-Lisper giggled again. "He meanth, we thcared him thilly," she said. "We dithcovered a way I could make uth all invithible without taking our clotheth off, tho I did it and then when we thaw Talgar, Mouth thaid we thould let him thee uth. He jumped like anything."

"We were trying to figure out what we were going to do about you three," Loric said. "Keeping six children and four men invisible was wearing on this little one, even with the others helping her." He tugged hound-Lisper's ear affectionately. "Then, when we met Talgar, everything just fell into place. Cricket said a disguise was a lot easier for them to maintain. You know the rest."

On impulse, Eirran grasped the Alizonder's hand. "Come with us, Talgar," she said. The other Estcarpians turned to stare at her as if she had taken leave of her senses.

Talgar shook his head, and gave a short laugh. "No, lady. I may disagree with Mallandor and his barons on some of the things they do. But make no mistake. I'm an Alizonder and no friend to Estcarp."

"I believe I know what Eirran may have meant with her rash invitation," Yareth said. "It's only a matter of time before all the prisoners are discovered to be missing. When they find that our horses are gone as well, there will be inquiries and the trail will lead directly to you. She would spare you, because of your kindness to our child."

Talgar's face twisted. "You overstep your bounds, Hagman. We are enemies, you and I. Unfriends, I think you'd call it. If you and your company hadn't been necessary to get the children out of the clutches of the Kolder, I would have let the Master turn the Hounds loose on you and never lifted a finger to help you. I'll take my chances back in the barracks."

"The Kolder will never harm anyone, ever again," Yareth said. "Go your way, and return to your kennel if you will."

Talgar turned abruptly and stalked back toward the city. Something cold nudged into Eirran's hand, and she jumped. It was hound-Jenys, close by her side, putting her dog's nose into Eirran's palm as if seeking warmth or comfort.

"Why did he go away like that? I thought he liked me."

"He did," Eirran said. "It's, it's complicated. I'll try to explain later."

"Get on your horses," Yareth said, "and each of you take a child with you. We have to put more distance between us and this place. It's just a question of time before the Hounds discover what's happened and come after us. I want our trail to get as cold as we can make it in what time we have."

He looked at the "puppy" he still held cradled in the crook of his elbow and Eirran knew what he was thinking as clearly as if he had spoken aloud. "We'll stop at the first sheltered spot, and I'll tend him," she said. "Come, Jenys—"

"Mouse," the white dog said.

"Mouse, then. You ride with me." She took the dog in her arms and climbed on her horse. Without thinking what she was doing, she stroked the animal's thin sides. She could count every bone. The Alizonders must have starved the children. . . .

Yareth lifted hound-Lisper to the front of his saddle, somehow managing to hold her and Newbold and still control Rangin. Each of the other men did the same, except for Weldyn. Only he rode alone.

IV

As soon as the escapees dared, they let the horses have their heads and went galloping pell-mell through the Alizon countryside. For the first time, Eirran was glad for the shelter of the ugly, brutal hedgerows. They might be difficult to go through, but they did keep the fugitives out of easy sight.

They didn't stop until they came to a small copse growing beside a bend in a stream. Weldyn hastily made certain the spot offered the shelter it promised. "We can hide here, and defend ourselves if necessary," he said. "You do what you need to do, woman, and I'll stand guard."

"I'll gather what medicinal plants I can find. You and Yareth both have a cut or two that need attention."

"Nothing worthy of a song," the Falconer replied. "Save your poultices and remedies for when they're needed." He walked off stiff-legged, back straight and proud.

Sometime during their wild ride, Jenys—Mouse—had let go the strands of power that kept the disguises in place. Eirran became a woman again, holding a child and not an ugly white dog. As soon as Weldyn let him, Sharpclaw took to the air with an angry rustle of wings and flew straight up until he was a dot almost lost in the vastness of the sky.

Jenys and Yareth were kneeling beside Newbold when Eirran returned with a handful of moss and some nettles. These were almost useless for a healing, but nettle leaves, boiled, would stop hemorrhaging. Hoping against hope to find even the smallest bit of illbane, instead she had found elderflower and mullein, false sage and primrose. If she had been looking for ingredients to make a beauty cream, she could have done no better. But of true healing herbs, there were none. The best she could do now was to extract the ugly dart from Newbold's breast, apply the boiled nettles, bandage the wound with moss, and hope.

The Witch-children stood nearby, watching with big, curious eyes. She told them to start a fire, and instructed Jenys—

Mouse—to put some water on to heat. Then she turned her attention to Newbold. By some miracle, the falcon still lived, though he was very limp and heavy, and his breath rasped in his throat.

"I don't know if I can help him at all," she told Yareth.

"Do what you can."

As gently as she could, Eirran grasped the end of the dart and began to pull. Newbold was so far gone he didn't even stir. That might be for the good; if he fought, she might wind up doing even more harm to the bird. Gradually and steadily, she eased the dart out of the falcon's body, wiping away the darkened blood that came with it and applying a wad of dampened moss to the wound.

"Live," she muttered. She began massaging the bird's wings and legs, testing for resistance in his talons. "Live. Jenys, get those nettles ready."

Newbold stiffened and Eirran's heart leapt. For a moment she thought he might be coming around, relieved that the terrible dart was removed at last. She looked up at Yareth, the beginnings of a smile breaking over her face. But he just stared at Newbold in growing disbelief.

Newbold shuddered in her hands. She looked back at him, and the breath caught in her throat. His head lolled, and a thread of scarlet showed on his beak. He took a deep breath, shuddered again, and went limp.

"Oh, no," she said softly. "No."

Her words were drowned out by Yareth's cry of agony echoing through the little clearing where they knelt, and, following close upon it, Mouse's equally stricken wail.

Twelve

I

The Jewel burned where it lay on Mouse's chest. She touched it, and for the first time in her life, she found herself able to *hear* Papa as clearly as she had always *heard* Mama. But to her surprise she found this went even further than *hearing*—perhaps even farther and deeper than what Star had called it—mindtouch. Startled, Mouse discovered she had become one with him. She was no longer Mouse, and he was no longer Papa. *They* were Yareth. Yareth the Falconer. Bits and pictures of his life flashed across her mind, each moment as vivid, as clear and pure as it would have been if she had lived it all herself.

With him, she remembered his boyhood with a strong, dour Falconer mother who never touched him except when necessary and never with affection, for that was the proper way. The Falconer way. With him she remembered his yearning for the Eyrie he had never seen and never known, where he might take his place and at last be accepted as one of them. With him, she served a term as a marine on a Sulcar ship, and with him, she retched, seasick, in the lightest swell. She knew the thrill that shook him when he first caught sight of Mama—Eirran—on his journey back to find what there was left of the Eyrie. With him, she knew that what he had thought was his dream of rebuilding the place taking fire was, in fact, the beginnings of the love he felt for her. With him, she quarreled with Eirran and came, grudgingly, to a kind of respect for her unwillingness to back down from what she considered right, even in very trying circumstances. With him, she fought the beast in the mountains, retreated from the shattered mountains, traveled with Eirran seeking a permanent home for them both, hesitantly felt the kicking lump in Eirran's belly that would one day be Mouse. She looked upon her own infant face through his eyes when he held her for the first time and put her into the cradle he had made with his own hands. With him, she guided the girlchild to her first steps, to her first spoonful of food eaten on her own. With him, she put the child that was herself on his saddlebow, listening to her squealing and holding her while she squirmed with delight, and galloped off to ride into his beloved mountains.

His falcon, and his horse, and the mountains—those were the things a Falconer was allowed to cherish openly and without shame. To his confusion and occasional shame, Yareth had allowed more into his life. She knew his anger when he discovered that his child had been taken by the Hags of Estcarp, his dismay and gratitude that Eirran had found a way to accompany him though he had forbidden it, and felt his joy when he found his daughter again.

Eirran was everything to him. She was what he had lost, what he had never had, what he would always seek. And because Mouse had come from the two of them, out of their love, his feelings for her were no less intense. Without her and Eirran, he would be even more lonely than he had been all his life.

And as she knew what he knew, felt what he felt, she also basked in the warmth of the love he felt for her, for Eirran, for Newbold. At last she understood why he seldom spoke about the way he felt, knew about the way Falconers avoided talking about their emotions, how they denied and disciplined themselves against all things of beauty and of love, lest they mistakenly be thought weak. But Mouse knew he wasn't weak, even if Yareth the Falconer didn't quite believe it in the depths of his heart. The love he was so ashamed of allowing himself to feel made him a complete man, far more so than his brother in flesh, Weldyn—

The falcon breathed its last and at that instant a sharp blade of grief stabbed through the man whose mind she inhabited. So enmeshed was she in this new sensation, this being one with Yareth the Falconer, that the pain threatened to carry her away entirely. It was as if someone had taken the Alizonder sword that now hung at his side and cut clear through him. And because she was so close—not only touching his mind but winding through every part of it—the sword cut right through her, too. She couldn't help crying out aloud as she spun down toward the welcoming blackness. Something—a shadow with rustling wings—swirled down with her. Newbold! He soared closer to her. She knew she was going with him, and was glad for his company on the journey. Journey—could this be death? If so, it was not at all the way she had always thought it might be. The darkness was nothing to be scared of at all, not with Newbold to keep her company. It was quiet. And comfortable. . . .

"Come back, Mouse!" the other Witch-children called. The words echoed in her mind, filtering down through the dark mists through which she fell. "Come back!" Star added to her, mind to mind. "It isn't death, not yet. You aren't going to die if you come back now. We need you! We all need you! Remember, you are the only one who can make the Jewel work!"

They were right. Farewell, Newbold, she said. The falcon's spirit hesitated a moment, then flew on.

Now panic set in. Wildly clutching the Jewel, grasping at the help offered by her sisters, she scrambled out of Papa's mind. She caught her breath, aware that she had had a very close call. There was danger in wearing the Jewel, unwittingly letting it take her deeper into another person's mind than she knew how to manage or control. Papa bent nearly to the ground, his hands over his eyes.

"Oh, no," Mama said. "No." She laid Newbold's body down, turned, and put her arms around him.

Mouse blinked, gradually beginning to come back to herself. It was difficult, almost like being born again, this reclaiming of herself as a separate person after having been a part of him. She had always known that Papa had loved Newbold, though she had never quite understood it until now. And the falcon had loved Papa, too. Sometimes, when they were talking to each other in falconsong, the sounds that came pouring out of their throats simply filled the air around them. When she tried, she could *hear* the notes sparkling and glittering with love. It was like what Papa and Mama felt for each other, only different. Something very simple and direct, that a bird could understand. With Mama and Papa, it was much more complicated. What she *heard* when they were together was a soft chiming that melted and floated over their heads, enclosing them in a singing bubble that Mouse thought must be as safe and as private as a private sky. She had sometimes wondered whether Mama ever *heard* it, and then decided that Mama didn't have to. It was enough that she moved through her days in a bubble of comforting love-song.

Now, for the first time, Mouse *saw* what she had only *heard* before. Blue sparks like the notes of a clear silver bell were flowing out of Mama as she held Papa tight, and it looked just the way she had always thought it might, in her mind.

"Oh, I'm so sorry, Yareth," Mama said. "There was nothing I could do—"

"I know." Papa's shoulders slumped just a little. A muscle twitched in his jaw, the way it did when he was trying to hide the way he felt. He just held her hand, hard, for a moment. "You did the best you could. He should never have been wounded. He could have avoided that dart."

"He was getting old, my love. He wasn't as quick as he used to be. And he did kill the Kolder, all by himself, and the machine he was a part of. We should do so well as he did, to take a mighty enemy with us into the Void."

"Yes. It was an ending worthy of a song. But he is gone, Eirran. And a Falconer without his falcon is only half a man."

"You will always be the most wonderful man in the world to me." In full view of everyone, she kissed him.

It was as if they had forgotten the entire world outside of the spot where they knelt, mourning over Newbold's body. The globe of sparkling blue surrounded them, almost blinding in its intensity, shielding them from everything but each other. But Mouse could tell, despite the love, that Papa had a big empty place inside, where Newbold had lived, and Mama was close to emptying herself as well, trying to help Papa ease his pain. The other children stood nearby, holding hands and watching, their faces showing the sorrow and sympathy they felt for the stricken Falconer and his wife. Star looked at Mouse and nodded. Together, the children all helped her *push* strength to him. Privately, Mouse *pushed* a little extra strength to Mama as well. Papa's shoulders straightened once more.

"We must bury Newbold," Papa said firmly.

"Yes."

"He has gone, and what is left is only a shell, but I will not abandon it to be eaten by scavengers."

Weldyn came back into the clearing. He took in the situation at a glance. "The Hounds are abroad already," he said brusquely. "They will pick up our trail before long. We can't tarry."

Papa looked at him out of what Mama called his "falcon's eyes," the same look he used to get when he and Mama talked about Rofan and the way he was so cruel to Belda back in Blagden. He had looked like that the day he had punished Rofan.

"And if it had been Sharpclaw who had fallen, would you drop his body by the roadside as you ran to save your own skin?"

Weldyn's face got red and he frowned. "Bury him then, by all means, but be quick about it." He strode away. A few red sparks glittered in the air after him and Mouse knew he was very angry.

"We'll help you, Papa," she said.

"Shall we go and search for a suitable place?" Mama said. "Someplace hidden?"

"Here," Papa said. He pointed to where Newbold's body lay. "Right here."

"But if the Hounds are out and searching, and if they happen to find this copse—"

"Here," Papa repeated stubbornly. "The spot where he died."

II

They set a guard, and dug a small hole in the center of the clearing at the place where Eirran had worked over the stricken falcon. The Guardsmen, even those who were standing watch, found a moment to come to Yareth and express their regret and sympathy over his loss. Weldyn, having said what he had to say, left the copse with Sharpclaw, to try to discover where, exactly, the Hounds were ranging.

Moved by some obscure sense of ceremony, the little girls wanted to sing a song over Newbold's grave. Mouse knew that the ordeal they had all been through had left its mark on them. If they had still been as young as they were when they left home, they might not have thought of doing it.

They gathered in a circle around the grave, and all held hands. Then they began to sing. The only song they all knew was the one they had sung when they had ridden into Es City that day so long ago—when they had still been children. It wasn't quite the right sort of song for the occasion because it was all about being very happy to be going somewhere. But when they sang it, their clear, sweet voices made it sound very fine, and nobody minded about the words at all. Papa and Mama held hands very tightly and Mouse thought that they both looked a little better by the time the children were through.

"Aren't you finished yet?" Weldyn's voice cut through the little clearing, severing the mood. "The Hounds are close on our trail. We'll have to run for it."

Papa glared at him, then swallowed hard. Mouse knew he was putting Newbold's memory into a safe place, where he could take it out and examine it later, when the hurt had died down a little. But he had his falcon's eyes again.

"Very well," he said. "It's a good thing we are all riding Torgians, and that the disguises on all but Weldyn's and mine still hold. Let's hope the Alizonders didn't choose their best horses to chase us. Everyone, mount up as before. We're going home."

Home! What a wonderful word! And then Mouse realized, with a pang that clutched at her heart, she didn't really know which home she wanted to return to—the one with the Witches in Estcarp, or back in Blagden with Mama and Papa—any more than she did when she had first been kidnapped by the Hounds. Then all the children had yearned for a haven to flee to, a place of safety that, for lack of a better word, they all called "home." Now, Mouse seemed to be the only one not to know where it was.

"Don't worry so much," Star said, and Mouse realized she had been thinking so hard Star couldn't help *hearing.* "You'll make the right decision when the time comes."

"I hope so," Mouse said. She felt really bad. First the Witches had come for her and she had gone off without a second thought. Then she and the others had been kidnapped. Then Mama and Papa had come after her—and had gone through some very dangerous times, she knew, from listening to them talk—and poor Newbold had gotten killed in the fight with the Kolder, and now she couldn't even make up her mind where she wanted to live, once they got back to Estcarp. How could she ever explain it to them? Either Papa and Mama, or the Guardian? She huddled into a miserable lump on Mama's saddlebow, aware as she did so that Papa's wonderful Torgian, Rangin, was getting old, too, and one day he would die, too.

And as if things weren't bad enough, Weldyn—who still refused to carry one of the Witch-children—had begun to pick at Papa. It was as if he didn't realize—or didn't care about—the danger involved.

"If you were back at the Eyrie, you'd have no trouble replacing your falcon with a new fledgling." He lifted Sharpclaw on his fist and sent him winging into the sky again. "This is my third."

"I understand you reared your birds from the egg, before the Turning," Dunnis said. He had been the one who had carried Mouse out of the castle. He was very nice, and sometimes very funny, too. Now he held Lisper in front of him. Lisper's thumb was in her mouth as her gaze went from Papa to Weldyn, and back. Mouse knew he was trying now to avoid possible trouble, to get Weldyn and Papa off a sore subject, and she watched with as much attention as Lisper did.

"We did," Weldyn said. "But the Mews were destroyed just as the Eyrie was."

"Few men know that as well as I," Papa said. There was a dangerous edge in his voice that Mouse knew very well, but Weldyn didn't seem to hear it any more than he recognized the look in Papa's eyes. Or if he did, he didn't seem to care.

"Really." Weldyn's voice was flat, and disbelief laced through it.

"Yes, really. I tried to find the Eyrie. I was going to rebuild it, and the Women's Village. . . ."

Weldyn looked at Papa, and then at Mama. A mockery of comprehension broke over his face. "Ah!" he said. "And that was when you first met this, this woman, why you took her with you on your journey. Too bad you were too weak of will to carry through your quest."

Mama spoke up and Mouse thought she had never heard her use such a sharp tone with anybody. "Weak-willed? I would rather you had fought the beast my husband battled! You would be singing a different tune now, Falconer!"

"That has nothing to do with it, Eirran," Papa said. Still, he and Mama reached again for each other's hands and clung to each other, hard.

Weldyn made the strangest sound, a kind of strangled snort through his nose. He dug his heels in his horse's sides and galloped a distance ahead of the others.

It didn't take long for Mama and Papa and the other men to catch up. Everyone went fast, because the Hounds were very close on their trail by now.

"Shouldn't we try to cut across country?" Loric asked. He shifted Bird on the saddle in front of him.

"Not yet," Weldyn said. "For the present, we'll make better time on the roads. As long as Sharpclaw can keep us informed of where they are, we don't have much to worry about. My concern is that they'll try to go around us, catch us between two packs of them."

"We'll need to stop eventually," Ranal said. Flame leaned against him, white-faced, her eyes closed. "These little ones can't go on much longer."

Mouse knew exactly how Flame felt, for she leaned against Mama the same way, except she forced herself to watch everything that was happening.

"They'll have to go on as long as we do," Weldyn said. "They don't have any choice in the matter."

"They've been starved and mistreated and tormented by the Kolder, and if they don't get some rest and some decent food, they're going to die." Mama nudged her horse right up next to Weldyn's. "You're always telling everyone how wonderful you are, how great all Falconers are against the Hounds. I know my husband's abilities. Now show us how good you are."

He looked at her, his own hawk's eyes almost colorless. "I would have thought you wouldn't need to ask, after the fighting in the Kolder chamber," he said. "Nevertheless, I will yield to what your, your *husband* wishes. It is his errand, not mine. And so it was he and not I the Guardian set to lead us."

His tone of voice stated clearly that he thought the wrong Falconer had been chosen for that duty. But Papa just nodded and held Lisper closer to him. He glanced at the sky; the sun was nearly down behind the hedgerows.

"Send Sharpclaw up to find us a place where we can rest. Then, when we make camp, I will go and find something for us to eat."

"We can't afford the luxury of a fire."

"We still have journeycake hidden in our saddlebags," Eirran said. "And we can find roots and tubers, if we're lucky. It's too early for berries."

Weldyn turned on her, the look of disgust plain on his face. "Oh, yes, you're the *woman* who taught a Falconer how to forage like an animal."

"And I suppose you think—"

Papa put a finger in his mouth and whistled sharply, making all the horses start and Sharpclaw screech and bate. Weldyn brought both mount and bird into line with some difficulty. "Do as you're told," Papa said. "This is no time for quarreling."

III

They found shelter for the night in an abandoned stone building. Perhaps it had once been a barn or even a farmhouse; most likely, it was a peasant's practical combination of the two. The thatched roof was missing in places, but there was room enough inside for all, including the horses. Outside the house, Eirran discovered the remnants of a garden. It had long since gone to weeds, but there were a few edible plants still struggling to grow through the rank growth that threatened to strangle the life out of them. Pleased with their luck, Papa even decided it was safe to risk a small fire, after it grew too dark for enemy eyes to pick out the rising smoke and use it to track them by. Loric went out hunting with Weldyn, but game was scarce in this part of Alizon. They had to settle for taking a lamb from one of the flocks that grazed unwatched in a nearby field. Papa fared a little better. He snared a brace of rabbits while Mama gathered what there was to be had from the ruined garden.

Soon, the lamb turned on a spit over the fire. Mama looked very contented as she worked with Papa, preparing the rabbit stew and stirring up a batch of trail biscuit. And six little girls sat in a row, watching and waiting. Their stomachs growled

with hunger, and Mama gave each of them spoons to put in
their mouths until supper was done.

Weldyn stroked Sharpclaw, talking to him and feeding him
tidbits while he waited for his own meal to cook. Mouse hoped
he would let Papa alone for a while, but he wouldn't. He acted
as if he were just talking to the bird or the other men, but Mouse
knew he wasn't. And so did everyone else.

"Good Sharpclaw," he said. "Fine, brave bird. There'll never
be another like you, for all that we found each other in the wild.
The Mews may be gone, but the black falcons live on." He
glanced sideways at Dunnis. "That's how I got this fellow, you
know. Some of the birds got away, when the mountains began
to fall, and now they breed in the wild. When Fangfoot died,
this beautiful fellow sought me out. And we've been together
ever since, eh, Sharpclaw? You knew a *proper* Falconer when
you saw one. Not one who's let himself get corrupted and go
soft, and turn to consorting with a wo—"

"That'll do right there, Weldyn." Papa stood up straight and
tall. His face had gone pale and he frowned so fiercely Mouse
would have been terribly afraid if he had looked at her like that.

"You're no true Falconer," Weldyn said flatly. "Not any
more. If I were you—and I thank the Great Falcon that I'm
not—I wouldn't hold any hope a wild bird will find you."

Papa took a step toward Weldyn. The firelight flickered
across his features. His falcon's eyes glittered dangerously. "I
have had enough of you and your remarks. I have tried to hold
my temper, tried to remember my mission meant nothing to
you, because it was merely a search for my daughter and this
was something you could not understand. I let you insult me,
I let you insult my wife. I could rise above your words and, I
thought, Eirran would never know. But now you have gone too
far and I can swallow nothing more. Come outside, and we will
settle this matter here and now, Falconer fashion."

"No!" Mama jumped up and stepped between them, bran-
dishing the spoon with which she had been stirring the stew.
"All during the journey to Alizon I listened to you making your

nasty insinuations to Yareth, and I wondered that he defended neither himself nor me. Now I understand. Yes, you have a quarrel. But—" she moved closer to Weldyn and shook the spoon under his nose "—you will wait until we are back in Alizon to settle it or you will both answer to me!"

Papa smiled and actually laughed out loud. He turned to the men who had watched this exchange, not daring to interfere. "Well, gentlemen, my wife has spoken and that is how it shall be," he said. "It is a matter I'm sure you all understand—even if Weldyn never will!"

A wave of relief mixed with nervous laughter went through the men in the room. They could relax a little; the danger seemed, for the moment, to be allayed. Mouse and her sisters exchanged glances.

Mama turned. "Who's ready to eat?"

Six spoons came out of six mouths and the little girls squirmed excitedly. "We all are—" Lisper said. "Pleath, what thould we call you?"

"Oh, Eirran will do."

"Thank you, Eirran." Cricket held up her plate. "The quarrel isn't over between them, and they won't forget about it, you know," she added so softly even Mouse barely heard her.

"Yes," Mama said. She looked at Papa, worry in her eyes. "I do know."

IV

That night the children slept on another bed of straw—this one even staler and worse-smelling than the one in the castle. And yet, for all the animal smells and the rustle of small creatures whose nests had been disturbed by the Estcarpians, Mouse and her sisters snuggled into it with even greater content than they had known their last night at Es City. But tired as they were, and drowsy from the good meal, they didn't go to sleep at once, but lay whispering quietly to each other for a while.

"Do you think we'll get home safely?" Bird shifted in the straw, raising a cloud of dust.

"We have to," Flame said. "Oh, I feel so much better, now that I've finally had something to eat. How about you, Mouse?"

"Better than I thought I ever would." Mouse hugged herself, happy to be feeling the warm lump in her middle where her supper was digesting. "Another day and I'll be back to normal."

"Another day and we'll be back in Escarp, if we can keep up this pace," Cricket said.

"Not quite." Star stifled a sneeze. "But two more days, maybe."

Mouse squirmed her way over close to Bird, and the children began whispering to each other. "Did you see the blue sparks around Mama and Papa today?"

"Of course. And the red ones, too. I see things like that all the time."

"I never saw anything like that before. I only heard it."

"I never knew other people didn't. I think I heard it this time, too."

"Maybe we'll be able to do it any time we want to, now."

Mama's voice cut through their conversation. "Ssh. Quit that whispering. Go to sleep."

"Yes, Mama."

"Yes, Eirran," the others said, all but Cricket, who echoed Mouse and said "Yes, Mama," which sent everybody into the first real fit of giggles they'd had since leaving Es City. But, obediently, they settled down and fell into a sound slumber.

Before dawn had clearly outlined the land next morning, the fugitives were in the saddle and riding. Papa and Weldyn kept their peace; they moved very carefully around each other, speaking only when necessary, and then only about matters at hand.

"You continue on this road, and make as good time as you can," Weldyn said. "Sharpclaw and I will backtrack and spy out the strength of our pursuit from a distance."

"Use caution," Papa said. "It will not go well with you if you are caught."

Weldyn smiled, but Mouse couldn't see any humor in it. "You don't need to give me lessons in Falconer-craft," he said. "I'll catch up with you soon."

This day Mouse rode on Papa's saddlebow and Star shared Mama's mount. Mouse tangled her hands in Rangin's mane. He turned his head, looked at her as if to say, Oh, it's you. Then, with a toss of his head, he danced a little just like he used to when she did this back in Blagden. So long ago.

Now that the first rush of their escape was past, they settled into a steady pace calculated to eat up the leagues and bring them quickly to the Estcarp border, where the Hounds would, expectably, be loath to go. She didn't even want to think about how they were going to get back through the Alizon Gap. It had been so frightening before, with all the mists and the way the very land had risen against them, trying to push them into the Tor Marsh. Then, when they were in safe country once more, Mouse knew Papa and Weldyn would settle their differences, once and for all. She didn't want to think about that, either.

"Papa?"

"Yes?" He sounded distracted.

It could wait until later. "Nothing. I love you."

"I love you, too."

Presently Weldyn caught up with the main body of escapees. "We have trouble," he said to Papa.

"We knew that."

"More than you thought." Sharpclaw screeched and settled onto the Y-shaped saddle fork. "They've got good horseflesh under them. But there's more urgent news than that. The Hounds pursuing us have someone tied to his saddle they're forcing to ride ahead of them. It looks like our 'friend' Talgar. It was hard to tell, he was such bad shape. Every now and then, someone would ride up and lash him again. I think they were very annoyed when they discovered it was he who betrayed them."

Papa's jaw twitched a little. "It's unpleasant news you bring, but not unexpected. We tried to warn him. Is that all you have to report?"

"Would that it were." Weldyn wiped his forehead. "I've learned the reason they haven't ridden us down before now, even if they hadn't been amusing themselves along the way. They've sent a pack of Hounds ahead, by a way through the hedgerows we didn't know existed, to wait for us at the Gap."

"They hope to take us between them, then." Papa gazed southward, toward the smudgy line of the Alizon Ridge. "And leave our bones there, where our friends may find them, as a warning. Girvan seemed sincere enough about the dangers we would face, when he was warning us against going through the mountains. Now it's beginning to look as if that's our best way to avoid meeting the Hounds and the fate they have planned for us."

"I wouldn't mind it," Hirl said. "It's agreeable work, fighting Hounds."

"And you would risk the lives of those we set out to rescue." Papa shook his head. "I would far rather cross steel with the Hounds myself, rather than avoid them as we must. The fighting in the castle was only enough to whet my appetite for more Alizonder blood. They who would treat with Kolder—" He broke off with an exclamation of disgust.

"I must agree with my brother Falconer," Weldyn said. "But not for the same reasons. In other circumstances, we could take either pack of Hounds, even if the infant Witches had to run for cover while we six fight."

"Seven," Mama muttered, but Weldyn paid no attention to her.

"Together," he went on, "they outnumber us at least four to one. And they are armed with dart-guns as well as steel. Even if those weapons aren't as well cared-for as the one I took from the guard, they're bound to be able to pick off a few of us before they're useless. Those are odds even I don't care to face. So I agree. It's the mountains."

"Then we shall take Loric's suggestion, leave the road and start across country," Papa said. "Now."

Weldyn nodded. With a word of falconsong, he sent Sharp-claw into the air, to begin searching out the way they must go.

Thirteen

I

*T*hey discovered a side lane connecting to the main highway, and turned off at once in hopes that the Hounds would expect them to flee the country by the most direct route, and would follow the main road without question. This much smaller road angled off the main thoroughfare in an eastward direction, and then turned directly east. Neither Yareth nor Weldyn showed the least concern. Their goal, ultimately, was the Alizon Ridge; what did it matter at which point they entered it, as long as their present path had even a hope of shaking off the Hounds pursuing them?

As they rode, Eirran couldn't help sending puzzled glances at Mouse—Jenys—who traveled this day with her father. The Witch Jewel around her neck took on a milky glow in the morning light. She could scarcely believe the change that had come over her daughter. It wasn't just the clothing—for, tattered and dirty as it was, her garments and those of her friends were clearly recognizable as Witch garb in miniature—nor was it the wan and wounded condition in which she had found Mouse—

No, not "Mouse." Jenys. It was the name she and Yareth had chosen together.

Still, it was incredibly easy for Eirran to call her Mouse, as the others did. Surely it would do no harm, at least until they got back home. . . .

She had thought Yareth and Weldyn were going to come to blows last night. And she feared for Yareth, if that happened. When. Yareth had issued the challenge. And, even if Weldyn was inclined to back off, she knew her husband never would. The older Falconer was both heavier and a little taller, and he had a hard edge that frightened Eirran when she thought about him and Yareth in mortal conflict, for such it was bound to be when Falconer pride was involved.

"You are worried, Eirran," said Star, the child who rode on her saddlebow. "I can feel it in the way you move, the way you sit your horse."

"Yes," she said. "I am. I am afraid that I won't be able to keep them from fighting. He will kill Weldyn. Or worse, Weldyn will kill him. And then what will become of me?"

Star didn't have to ask who "he" was. "I can't tell you not to worry," she said, "for you have a right to be troubled. But I can tell you that it does no good to worry beforehand. Much may happen to change things long before the Falconers come to blows with each other."

Eirran turned the little girl so she could look into her face. "Another one who is six years old going on forty! Are you all like that?"

"Yes, Eirran. Except for Lisper sometimes," Star added honestly. "In some ways she is still very immature."

In spite of herself, Eirran laughed at hearing these words coming from such childish lips. "She is long past the age when she should have given up sucking her thumb, but surely—"

"There are other ways. Thumb-sucking isn't all of it. She was very weak on our journey to Alizon, when we were kidnapped. We feared for her if she went under the Kolder machine. Still, she is one of us. Our sister."

An unexplained chill went over Eirran, making gooseflesh

rise on her arms. To change the subject, she said, "Tell me about the Jewel."

"Well, when we left you behind in the castle, we began to test it as fast as we could, to see if we could make it work."

Though all of them had tried, Star explained, Mouse seemed to be the only one among them who could use it to channel her thoughts and untrained powers. They quickly discovered that they could use it to channel also, but only through her.

After a false start or two, and with the other five helping her, Lisper managed to turn the entire company invisible, though it was a shaky undertaking and the men in particular kept discovering they had an arm or a foot showing. It was a relief when they had met Talgar just as they were emerging from the tower building into the inner ward. On Star's order, Lisper relaxed her control, and everyone swam back into view. All at once, then, Lisper had to sit down.

It had been very funny, watching Talgar's reaction. When he had gotten over his shock at seeing four men and six little girls appear out of nowhere, he agreed to help them get clear of the castle and the town.

"After that, though, you are on your own," he said.

"Oh, please." Mouse was near tears. "My Mama and Papa and another man are still in here someplace. They've gone to fight the Kolder."

"Kolder, eh?" Talgar looked thoughtful. "It was the Kolder who have been behind all of Alizon's ills these many years past, or at least so I think." He smiled suddenly. "And what I think is what matters now, since I am the one the fickle Lady of Chance has chosen to help you. I have no love for the Kolder. Very well. If your Mama and Papa live through the fighting in the Kolder hole, we will take them out of the castle with us."

Quickly, with greater efficiency than Lisper had shown, Cricket had transformed everyone into Hounds and white dogs, and, with Talgar to lead them, they had gone searching for the three who stayed behind. For speed's sake, and to stay out of sight as long as possible, Talgar had led them through the wall passage.

"And the rest you know," Star said matter-of-factly.

"That still doesn't explain how you children could use the Jewel. I thought each Jewel belonged to but one Witch."

"We believe Leaf willed the Jewel to Mouse before she died," Star said. "She called her by name and tried to say something. Baron Esguir threw the Jewel away. We think Leaf wanted her to go find it and use it to get us all back to Estcarp. We weren't allowed to go and look for it. So, we had forgotten about it until you gave it to Mouse."

"I see." They rode in silence for a while. Eirran thought about the impulse that had made her tuck the artifact into her shirt, where it had stayed, forgotten by her as well, until it made its presence known and found its way into the hands of the one who could use it, even without clear knowledge of how to do so.

A muffled cry came floating back from the rider in front of the little band of escapees. "Here! A way through the hedgerows!"

Eirran nudged her horse into a brisker pace. Ahead, just around a turn in the narrow lane, Ranal had discovered a place where two hedgerows offset each other, leaving a space where one person could go—or one horse, provided it carried no weight, either of rider or extra flesh. It was very cleverly constructed. One part of the fence divided into arms that wrapped around and enclosed the other section, forming a U-shaped passageway. At the base of the U, a hinged gate, now rotting from lack of use, closed the path. A cow or sheep—or even a horse—might blunder partway in, decide it had gone the wrong way, and retreat without ever knowing it was just a few paces short of freedom. A tangle of weeds and thistles—integral parts of the hedgerows themselves—grew around the stone foundations; overhead, the "vermin" vegetation snarled into a solid canopy above the stones, and the entrance was all but obliterated. Ranal and Yareth were already hard at work, hack-ing away the worst of the overgrowth. Mouse and Bird, who had been riding with Ranal, were trying their best to help but were succeeding only in getting in the way.

"The brush growing atop the wall covers the entrance and makes it look all of a piece, from above," Ranal told Weldyn. "That's why your falcon couldn't see anything but a spot where the hedgerow looked a little thicker than usual."

The Falconer nodded and spoke to Sharpclaw in falconsong. "Now he knows what to look for," he said. The bird went soaring into the sky, searching for the next break ahead in the impenetrable barriers between the Estcarpians and the mountains that were, now, their sole refuge from the pursuing Hounds of Alizon.

Even though the Torgians they rode were as fined-down as their long journey had made the men, woman and children, each of the riders had to dismount and lead their horses, coaxing them to scrape their way through the opening. The height of the passage, even if it had been wider, was such that everyone would have had to crouch as low as possible and still stay mounted. "This is going to slow us down," Loric muttered to himself. He loosened his blade in its scabbard. "I agree with Hirl. I'd rather turn and meet the Hounds head-on."

"It may come to that," Hirl said, grinning. "They may yet catch sight of us crossing the open ground."

"Providing they ever find out we didn't take the main road after all and finally come looking for us down this one."

Eirran looked out over the field they would have to cross. It was bigger than the usual area fenced off by these impassable hedgerows, and the land sloped upward without any dips she could see, so that they would, indeed, be exposed to full view of anyone pursuing them. Once across, they were that much closer to the Alizon Ridge that lowered, greenish-purple, on the horizon. But was there another passageway through the inevitable hedgerow on the other side?

When everyone was through the wall, Yareth and Weldyn

went back to brush away the marks of their passage and pull some of the weeds back in place over the opening before rejoining the others.

Sharpclaw came stooping down out of the sky to soar over Weldyn's head, falconsong bubbling from his throat. Weldyn smiled in satisfaction. "These rows are riddled with passageways!" he said. "If we had but known what to look for, we could have saved much time, both going and returning. We can expect that most have lain unused for years, as this one has. The Alizonders, at least around here, prefer to build stiles over the hedgerows. We can't cross them, except on foot. But if we hack our way through each passageway, we will leave as clear a trail as any pursuer would want to follow."

"That can't be helped. We have to reach the mountains, and we can't wait until we get to the Gap," Yareth said. "All right, everyone. Ride as fast as you can. Let us hope we can find shelter from searching eyes, or the Hounds are too busy tormenting that poor fellow who helped us and don't notice we aren't on the main road until we are far past pursuit."

II

Past the wide meadow and through another similar labyrinthine passageway, Eirran began to nurture a faint hope that their ruse had worked and they had shaken off their pursuers. Then the thin notes of a hunting horn came floating to them, borne by the breeze.

"Well, that does it," Weldyn said grimly. "We make it to the Ridge and hope Girvan was right about the Hounds not daring to go there, or we get caught out in the open and have to make a stand then and there."

In this portion of Alizon, buildings of any sort were scarce. Here and there, a ruined tumble abutted a hedgerow, seeming almost a part of it. Usually there was a stile nearby. Whether these buildings had once been dwellings, or had been intended as rude shelters for shepherds or animals, it was impossible to tell. They would offer poor protection if the fugitives had to seek recourse in the rubble when the Hounds began to bombard them with darts.

The riders spurred the Torgians into a gallop. They wasted precious time searching the next hedgerow for an opening, but what Sharpclaw had spotted and guided them toward was only an unusually abundant growth of thorn bushes. Openings to the south had now become few, and far between. There weren't even very many stiles. The fugitives didn't dare turn west, as that would bring them closer to the Hounds; so again, they were forced to turn east, where they finally located the hidden access to the meadow they had crossed. When they had cleared the weeds and thorns away and had gone through, Weldyn struck flint to steel and set fire to the tangle. Within moments the top of the hedgerow was ablaze. It made a smoke column big enough to be seen at the Alizon Gap, but it would halt pursuit for a while until the embers cooled. Eirran only hoped that there was not another opening, unknown to them, that the Hounds could use and avoid the delay.

Again, the north wall gave them no access, but at the east hedgerow they finally had a stroke of luck. There, they discovered a proper gate in the fence where the ground had been trodden into mud with the passage of many animals back and forth. The fugitives dashed through the gate and past the incurious herd grazing on the lea—but not, however, before Yareth closed the gate behind them and lashed it tightly with a cord which he tied into intricate knots. "There," he said. "The fire seems to have bought a few extra minutes. Maybe this will, too."

The next gate led to an open ground that held a cottage and barn—no doubt the dwelling place of the peasant who looked after this estate for the Alizonder baron who dwelt in the city and gave never a care to his land except for the revenues it brought in. The farmer, attracted by the noise the horses made on the hard ground, had come out of his house to investigate. He held a hay-fork as if it were a weapon, but clumsily; patently, he was no fighter.

"Who are you and what d'you want on my land?" he demanded. The look in his eye made Eirran think he was not at all amused by the prospect of anyone—Hounds with their snake-headed dogs, or fugitives fleeing from them—riding across his fields, ruining his crops and upsetting his livestock.

"We apologize for the intrusion," Yareth told him. "And if you will, you can help us be gone that much sooner."

"Hmm," the farmer said thoughtfully. "You the ones who set the fire?"

"We are. We hope it will be confined to the hedgerow only. It was to delay pursuit."

"I saw the smoke." The man looked at Eirran, and at the children who clung to the riders' saddlebows. "Well, I have no love for the Hounds. If you're running from them, you must have a good reason, not that they need much cause to go after a man. Though I hadn't thought they had begun persecuting women and children as yet."

"They put me in prison," Eirran said, "and they were torturing these little girls." She stroked Star's hair. Perched on Dunnis's saddlebow, Lisper sucked her thumb and stared at the farmer out of enormous, shiny eyes.

The farmer spat on the ground at his feet. He gazed off into the distance. "I have a wife and two daughters myself. And a son who is thinking about joining the Hounds rather than staying on and helping me. But you've picked a poor place to run to. There's no place to hide hereabouts and it would be my death if you were found in my cottage or barn."

"We've no intention of putting you or your family in danger, sir," Yareth said. He pointed toward the mountains that loomed very close by now. "Yonder is our destination."

The farmer looked startled. "No! Surely nothing you've done is so bad you'd risk that place rather than the Hounds! They've been known to show mercy, if the mood was on 'em. The Forbidden Mountains don't."

Weldyn stepped forward. "We're Falconers, he and I. No mountains in this world hold terrors for us."

"Be that as may be, there's dark things roam those mountains. And folks with any sense stays away. There's those as says we tempt the wickedness enough, living here as close as we do."

"Yet that is where we would go." Yareth set his jaw stubbornly. "Better the risk of dangers we don't know than the certain knowledge of the kind of death we'll face at the hands of those who pursue us." He gazed at Eirran across Mouse's head.

"Well then, if you're set on it—" the farmer glanced at each in turn, and all nodded agreement, even the children "—there's a crofter's cottage two fields over and one field south. Used to use it when I ran flocks in those meadows. Gave it up when— Never mind that. The cottage lies athwart the hedgerow. Used to be part of it. It's all in rubble now, no roof, walls mostly down. If you was careful you could pick your way through and get to the other side. But as I told you, I wouldn't want to do it."

"Thank you, good sir," Yareth said. "We'll trouble you no further—"

"Aye, but I'd trouble you for one favor."

"Name it."

"The Hounds are close on your heels. If they're as eager to catch you as you say, it'll go hard with me that you've even ridden through my spot of land. If you could just kindly cosh me a little on the head, say, not enough to do damage, but enough to show the Hounds, convince 'em I didn't help—"

Yareth frowned. But then he swung himself out of the saddle and strode toward the farmer, leaving Mouse clutching Rangin's mane.

"Close your eyes," he said. Then, drawing his dagger, he hit the man neatly just over the temple with the hilt. It opened the skin enough to make an impressive show of blood, and a lump was already forming by the time he eased the farmer gently to the ground.

Eirran caught sight of a woman's white face at the window, and a child's eyes peeping out over the sill. The woman looked at Eirran and nodded slowly. "I'm sorry," Eirran said, knowing the woman couldn't hear her. Then she nudged her horse into a gallop, following the men in their headlong flight from the pursuing Hounds. Behind them, the horn sounded again, much nearer.

III

They wasted precious time searching for the ruined cottage because the farmer had been off in his directions. It lay three fields to the east, rather than two, and in the far corner beyond a sharp rise. Between their traversing the fields and the lane they had traveled down, Eirran judged they must have come several leagues farther east than most of them would have chosen. But otherwise, it was as the man had said. This was the boundary; it was also the last hedgerow, and the tallest. Here the stone foundations were built high as the walls of any house, as if early inhabitants had wanted to put a barricade across southern Alizon, trying to keep at bay whatever they feared in the mountains. The cottage had been constructed as an integral part of that barricade. When the cottage had been abandoned—for whatever reason, Eirran didn't wish to know—the resulting ruin had created a chink in the defenses. The thorn bushes and the weeds and ivy hadn't as yet filled in the gap completely. A few more stones pulled down from the back side of the wall— the men rigged ropes to saddles and immediately set the horses to the task—and they could go through.

The children clustered around Eirran while all this was going on, and she put her arms around as many as she could manage. "Will they be in time, Eirran?" Lisper asked fearfully.

"I hope so," she replied. "If it's at all possible, yes, my

husband will get us out before the Hounds catch up with us."

Bird stiffened. "'They're coming!" she cried, pointing behind them. The horn sounded again.

Eirran turned. There they were, outlined against the sky. There must have been two score of them. Their helmets gave them a weird, unworldly look. Even as she watched, the Hounds came galloping over the rise and spreading their ranks out across the meadow. Now the sound of yapping and baying dogs mingled with the horn and the eager war-cries of the men as they drew closer. They sounded like wild animals who had scented blood—the men as well as the dogs. Even the horses neighed and shrilled their challenges. Their eyes rolled in their heads, and there was foam around their jaws. In a moment the Hounds, their dogs of war, and their horses would be upon them.

"Yareth!"

He didn't hesitate. "Go! Now!" he shouted. The men abandoned the ropes and went pounding back to where the horses waited. They scrambled into their saddles and snatched the children up with them. Eirran was already mounted, Mouse in her arms.

"Get a good running start!" he cried. "You'll have to jump for it!" He slapped Eirran's Torgian across the flanks and the startled animal leaped forward.

There were stones littering the ground, ready to catch and trip a horse, even one picking its way with care. Eirran leaned forward, holding Mouse tightly, and closed her eyes. It must, it must, it must, she found herself chanting over and over. Then she felt the Torgian tense under her thighs, lift. A sensation of flight seemed to last a long time. The horse landed heavily, nearly stumbled. Miraculously, it regained its footing and kept going. Behind her, she heard more sounds of galloping hooves, the pause and thud, as the men followed her over the wall.

"Keep going!" It was Dunnis. He urged his mount onward, keeping close to her side, lashing both horses to their utmost speed. A dart whistled past but it was almost spent and spiraled off harmlessly into the ground. Lisper clung to Dunnis's neck, holding on for all she was worth. "Just a little farther, and we'll be out of range!"

"Where's Yareth?"

"Following— No!" He turned his horse against hers, preventing her from pulling up.

"I've got to go to him—"

"He's all right! He and Weldyn stayed long enough to see that all the Witch-children got over safely, and then they followed. He sent me to look after you."

They entered a patch of woods. No more darts zinged through the air, so he allowed the horses to slack their pace. They slowed to a halt and stood, heads down, needing a breather after their hard exertions. Dunnis turned and stood in his stirrups, craning to see through the tree branches. "There they come. Loric has Flame and Cricket both with him. And— yes, yes! There they are! The Falconers are safe."

Eirran sagged with relief. She loosened her grip on Mouse. "Let's get down," she said to her, "and let the poor horse rest. He's earned it."

Dunnis dismounted, bringing Lisper with him. The little girl had to be pried loose from his neck. "I hope this little monkey isn't scared senseless—"

But rather than being terrified, as Eirran expected, Lisper was exhilarated and bubbling with excitement and pleasure. "Oh, Dunnith, that wath fun!" she said. "Pleath, let'th do it again!"

"I hope not—ouch! Let go my hair!"

Lisper and Mouse both dissolved into a fit of giggles. Now that the danger was past, Eirran began to laugh as well.

Presently everyone but the Falconers had regrouped in the edge of the wooded patch, and those who waited could see them coming. They appeared unhurt. Hirl had a dart lodged in the sleeve of his chainmail, just piercing the skin, but he shrugged off any attempt Eirran made to tend the wound.

"If it festers, then I'll come looking for you," he said. "But the last I heard, the Hounds had not begun to put poison on their darts."

"Just in case, I'll start gathering what medicinal herbs I can, while we rest and get our bearings."

"Our bearings!" Ranal laughed. "The moment I'm in country with ridges higher than my head I'm as good as lost. No sense of direction even with the sun to guide me."

"I never knew that. You must fare badly on campaign then," Dunnis said good-naturedly. He was checking various parts of his tired horse's saddle and bridle. "Next time, I'll remember to let you ride along in my dust."

"Oh, I do well enough, as long as someone else is there to point which way I should go. But by myself I'm hopeless."

Yareth and Weldyn came riding up just then. Eirran rushed to her husband's side. "What happened? Are they following?"

"No, they aren't." Yareth and Weldyn swung themselves from their saddles, and sent their horses off with the others to rest and crop what grass they could find under the trees. "They stopped short at the wall, though they did pepper us from the top of the wall with their dart guns. Good thing we were almost out of range before they got there."

"I don't understand why they didn't follow us."

"I don't either," Weldyn said. He didn't seem to notice that he was talking to the woman he had treated with scorn ever since her true identity had been discovered. "That fellow Talgar was no longer with them. Perhaps they finished him as soon as they caught our scent."

Eirran shuddered. "Oh, I want to put as much distance between us and Alizon as I can!" she cried.

"We will," Yareth said. "And quickly, too. Girvan and the farmer were right. The Hounds do not go beyond their boundary walls, into the Alizon Ridge."

"I hope he is all right—the farmer, I mean."

"I didn't hit him hard. Only enough to stun him and, I hope, save his life."

"I still want to be gone from here as soon as we can. The

sooner begun, the sooner we're there, and the sooner all this is behind us and we can go on with our lives as before!"

He laughed. "That's my practical Eirran! Very well, we seem to have all caught our breath by now. Off we go through the mountains, where a proper Falconer belongs."

He turned and walked away with Weldyn. Something had changed subtly with both Falconers. Their quarrel now seemed entirely forgotten and both men appeared tense, excited—even a little feverish, as if on the verge of some long-delayed and greatly anticipated adventure. Eirran decided to ask what had happened back at the last hedgerow, tonight when she and Yareth were alone. For now she was content to follow the brisk pace they set. The more distance between her and Alizon before nightfall the better.

The going was remarkably easy, even for Eirran who had no love of mountains or heights. They wound their way through valleys between peaks, climbing ever higher. To their left, they could see the cold and inhumanly tall crests of the Great Eastern Mountains, of which the ridge they traversed was but a spur. Eirran knew that the Barrier Mountains, between Karsten and Estcarp, likewise joined the Great Eastern range. But they did so as one giant meeting a greater giant, merging into one as they wound away into unknown lands. Here, however, it was as if leftover peaks—so small in comparison they could easily be thought of as insignificant—had simply spilled off the shoulders of the Great Eastern behemoths, leftovers from when they had been formed, in the beginning of the world. And what else had spilled into the Alizon Ridge, from the heartless, forbidden ranges to the east?

Don't be ridiculous, Eirran admonished herself sternly. It is only your own silliness that makes the air feel heavy and hard to breathe, only your own imagination that populates the shadows among the trees with other, darker shadows with red and unblinking eyes. I will not give in to fear, I will not, now that we have come so far—up through Estcarp and through the Alizon Gap with its magical wards and dangerous proximity to

Tor Marsh, to Alizon City and prison. And the near-miraculous escape from the castle, aided by more magic that seemed to be channeled through Mouse—her Jenys!—thence through the hedgerow country and into the mountains where the Falconers who rode at the head of their little column felt most at home. *What have I to worry about?*

They were working their way along a little stream that meandered through a deep defile where cliffs rose steeply on either hand. Tall trees with slender, almost leafless trunks clawed skyward, seeking the lifegiving sunlight. Here by the streambed, they could see the sky and could also catch an occasional glimpse of the sharp cliff edge overhead. The sun was beginning to descend on their right. A few gold beams filtered through the trees, just enough to intensify the gloom within the forest and outline the many large rocks in the streambed that had fallen from the cliff overhead. An occasional dead tree leaned against its neighbors until it finally decayed enough to fall to the forest floor. As they went deeper into the defile, bird sounds, sparse in this area at best, died away entirely and even the rustle that spoke of small arboreal creatures going about their business ceased among the leaves. There was no sound save that of the stream chuckling its way over clean-scoured river pebbles, and the sounds they themselves made as they rode.

Eirran was not the only one to notice the unnatural stillness. All the Estcarpians began looking keenly from side to side, and even the Falconers, intent as they were on whatever was driving them, came to full alert. Without a word, Yareth passed Cricket to Loric again and he put her behind him while Flame rode, as usual, on the saddlebow.

"Hang on," Loric said quietly. Greatly magnified, the words echoed from the rocky cliffs overhead, as if they were a signal.

And something answered.

A shrieking roar came bellowing down from the heights. The horses shied, startled, and everyone looked up.

There, sharply outlined against the sky, crouched a misshappen thing. It looked to be part giant cat, part bear, and part something Eirran didn't want to think about. It stretched one taloned paw down toward the column of riders. Tossing its head, it roared again. A shower of pebbles, shaken loose by the dreadful cry, came rattling down on their heads.

Then the creature leaped at the men at the head of the column.

Fourteen

I

*O*nly the Torgians' instinctive reaction saved both Falconers from being killed immediately. The horses' sole impulse was to get away from the thing hurtling down on them. The beast landed heavily in the spot where the Torgians and the Falconers had been just a moment earlier.

For a moment, Eirran saw the thing clearly. Its little red eyes glittered like malevolent crimson gems. The lips were drawn back from teeth too long and sharp to be contained in its ursine muzzle. It crouched on misshapen, catlike haunches but its taloned forelegs were almost like the arms of a man. But there was nothing human in the length, the angulation, or the number of joints. Saliva dripped from its fangs. It recovered more quickly from its missed attack than its intended prey and drew back a ropy forelimb, ready to slash at whatever was within reach. Its appearance called back an old memory, one Eirran had tried for more than seven years to forget. . . .

"Eirran, get back!" Hirl shouted. He plucked Star off the saddle and set her down. The child was running before she fairly touched the forest floor. "Look after the children!"

Loric let Cricket and Flame slide down also and spurred his horse forward. His sword was already out. Eirran dismounted hastily, leaving Mouse in the saddle, and hurried her mount toward the edge of the forest and what she hoped might be shelter, away from the battle. She called the children toward her. Bird was already down from Ranal's horse, but Lisper was giving Dunnis some trouble.

"No!" she shouted. "I want to thtay with you!"

As gently as he could, he pulled her grasping arms from around his neck. "Not this time! Do as you're told!"

"Lisper!"

The immense sound filled the clearing, booming back from the cliff face, making even the ravaging beast pause for a moment in mid-attack. It was Star's voice, but echoes of four other childish trebles augmented the command. Eirran looked at Star, startled, then at Mouse. Mouse held the Jewel, and Eirran could almost swear she caught a glimpse of a fading burst of light that had emanated from the stone. Reluctantly, Lisper loosed her grip on Dunnis and allowed him to set her on her feet. The beast snarled and slashed with a taloned paw at Rangin, who danced out of reach.

"You stay here, with me!" Eirran said, gathering the child into the group that huddled, frightened, behind her. She kept a tight grip on her horse's bridle. If worst came to worst, she would put all the children on the animal's back, lash its flank with the reins to make it run, and she would flee into the forest on foot, taking another direction to try and confuse the hideous thing.

The very air in the little defile trembled with the shattering noise—bestial snarls, hooves clattering on loose stones, men's shouts, Torgian stallions screaming their war challenge. Riders vied with each other, jostling to get a good vantage point from which to strike. Sharpclaw swooped and soared, harrying and distracting, dodging the beast's claws by a feather's breadth.

Eirran's lips drew back from her teeth in instinctive hatred of the form and nature of the thing which had attacked them.

Yareth slashed at the beast. Rangin reared, striking with his hooves. The beast flinched and drew back. Weldyn's horse landed a heavy blow from the other side. The beast reeled, and Yareth scored it with his sword. Hirl's blade rose and fell, and the beast staggered. One of the horses screamed, this time in pain. Ranal pulled back, out of the conflict. Blood stained his Torgian's shoulder and the animal's eyes rolled in its head. The others renewed their attack.

With a roar that shook the trees, the beast fought free of its attackers and fled, trailing something that might have been blood save for its unnatural color. The sheer speed of the thing as it bounded along the stream made Eirran tremble all over again. And she had thought she or the Torgian, burdened with the Witch-children, might outrun it. . . .

Weldyn and Loric started to spur after in pursuit, but Yareth called them back. "Let it go! Let it go. You'll never be able to catch it anyway."

A scattering of loose rocks pelting down told of the beast's efforts in scrambling up the cliff again, thereby putting itself well out of reach of pursuit. A dismal wail echoed through the defile. Then there was nothing but shocked silence.

"What made it give up?" Dunnis said. He breathed hard and his horse danced in nervousness, heavily lathered on shoulders and muzzle. He regarded his stained swordblade with distaste.

"It didn't think we'd fight back," Yareth said.

"You sound like one who speaks from experience," Weldyn said. He whistled, and Sharpclaw returned to his perch on the Falconer's saddle. "I suppose you're going to tell us that was one of the things that lives in the mountains these days, like what you met near the Eyrie."

"Yes," Yareth said, "only this one was smaller and far less fierce. At the Eyrie there was only Rangin and Newbold and me to fight it."

Weldyn looked at Yareth, a grudging respect in his gaze. "Yet you managed to live. Even with a woman to burden you and make your sword-arm weak. There may be more to you than I first thought, Falconer."

Yareth shrugged. "Ranal, let's see how badly your animal is injured."

Eirran was already busy with moss, stanching the three parallel slashes that scored the Torgian's shoulder. The wounds had bled freely enough, she thought, to have washed it clean. If the beast's claws had been poisoned, it must be nearly bled out by now. "The cuts aren't serious or deep," she said. "Just through the skin. No muscle damage. But we shouldn't push the horse just now. We should make camp as soon as possible. Let me brew a poultice."

"We must keep going." Yareth frowned and once again Eirran sensed the feverish hurry and anticipation in him. "Let us get away from this spot with all speed, at least."

Eirran stood up. Now that the danger was past, she began to tremble. "That—that vile beast. . . ."

"It's gone now."

"Unspeakable—"

"Put it behind you. We must move on. Now."

Eirran stared at him. Another time, he would have put his arms around her. But now, all she could see in him was this peculiar impatience to be gone, to go deeper and deeper into what the Alizonders called the Forbidden Mountains. She began to hiccup.

II

"What was that thing?" Mouse asked. "Papa said you had seen one once before."

Saw it, Eirran thought, and cringed when its arm came snaking into the cave where we hid, trying to catch us and pull us out. No. Mustn't upset the children any more than they are already. Turn it aside, try to talk of something else. "I was hoping you and the other children might tell me what it was," she replied half-jokingly.

"I don't think it was a creature of the Shadow, Mama. It wasn't natural, but I don't think it was really evil. I think it was just hungry."

"Well, I saw that Jewel you wear flashing in a place where there was no sunlight."

Hirl and Star rode near her, close enough for them to hear. "We all did that," Star said. "We had to make Lisper hear us, and obey. She was in danger."

"I see." But Eirran didn't see, not really. She rode on without speaking, deep in her own thoughts. An hour later, she insisted on halting for the night, despite the protests of both Falconers. Ranal's horse had begun to limp badly.

"If we don't stop and let me poultice the poor beast's wounds, he'll go crippled entirely. And—" she looked pointedly at Weldyn "—most of us are riding double as it is."

Weldyn made an impatient noise and stamped off. Yareth stood staring at her out of his falcon's eyes. "We'll make it a cold camp. No fire, lest it bring unwelcome visitors. And whether Ranal's animal is fit or not, tomorrow we ride on."

"Agreed."

Her mood was as grim as his. All her moods, she had noticed lately, were more pronounced than usual—the good as well as the bad. Nerves. She wanted to be gone from this cursed place as much as Yareth did, but at least she was willing to stop long enough to tend an injured horse. She defied him to the point of building a small, sheltered fire, needing a way to heat the water enough to boil the poultice of leaves and moss. She was going to have to rely on the heat of the compress and the Torgian's natural stamina, given the scarcity of beneficial plants in this part of the mountains. He came stalking by as she worked, looking at her sharply. She pretended not to notice, but stirred the mess in the little pot, murmuring to herself as she sometimes did when putting together a herbal recipe, and making certain he knew what she was doing. He said nothing, but merely walked on.

She had no idea why he was on edge, or why it was only the Falconers who were so affected. Everyone wanted to be gone from Alizon, but the other men gave in to weariness after the battle. They seemed content to lie still, munching on journeycake or trying to catch a few winks of sleep. Not the Falconers. Together and separately, they paced the camp, fingers drumming nervously on sword hilts. They had paused only long enough to clean the beast's malignant ichor from their weapons. Long after Eirran had done the best she could for Ranal's Torgian, fed the children a cold and cheerless supper, and settled down with them for the night, she could hear the restless treading of the Falconers' boots as they continued to walk back and forth, back and forth. It was as if their impatience to be gone had translated itself into this kind of nervous wakefulness; she felt nothing short of death could have made either of them sleep that night.

Before dawn had fully broken, they were moving through the camp, urging everyone to their feet. By this time, even the other men had begun to notice the Falconers' strange behavior, and to complain about it.

"What's our hurry?" Ranal said. "I want to see to my horse. And surely we can pause long enough to have breakfast. We can afford a fire now that it's morning."

"You can eat while you ride," Weldyn said irritably. "It's just trail rations, after all."

"We could cook something. And I still have to see to my horse."

"We can't delay," Yareth said. He had dark circles under his eyes; Eirran realized he hadn't rested at all during the night. "We must keep moving."

She put her hand on his arm. "Yareth."

He looked at her and through her, as if she didn't quite exist.

"Don't try to stop us." Then he strode on, urging the men to move faster.

Eirran woke the children, who were sleeping deeply like the essentially healthy young animals they were. "Get up, now," she said. "The men want to go. We need to get through these mountains as quickly as we can."

Star rubbed her eyes. "Then why are the Falconers leading us the longest way?"

"What do you mean?"

The little girl yawned. "The shortest way is due south. But we're going at an angle through the mountains. Why?"

"I don't know." Eirran swallowed an uneasy sensation. "They are both more at home in mountains than they ever were on the plains. And you know how well they guided us there. They must know what they're doing."

"My Papa knows everything," Mouse said. But Eirran knew her daughter. A certain confidence was lacking in her words; Eirran knew that for the first time Mouse doubted her father's wisdom.

Unwilling to examine closely what she could not do anything about, Eirran went to where the horses were picketed, to see how Ranal's animal had fared through the night. To her satisfaction, the wounds the terrible beast had inflicted looked much better this morning. She didn't think it was her own efforts that had made the difference—unless, as she had hoped when stirring the poor mixture of leaves she had been able to find, the heat of the poultice had done its work and drawn out much of the soreness. The horse looked fit to travel, if it wasn't pushed too hard.

"Weldyn, can you take Bird with you today?" Eirran said.

Weldyn simply stared through her, even more so than Yareth had, and she dropped the subject. Bird didn't weigh much—not enough to make any difference, really.

In a very short time they were on the move again. This day the sky was overcast and gloomy, threatening rain. Ground fog made the footing treacherous, even near the stream bed. The horses picked their way carefully, refusing to go faster even under Yareth's and Weldyn's urging.

Good old Rangin, Eirran thought. He has more sense than Yareth has today. Wonder what's gotten into him? And now the falcon has begun acting strangely as well.

Sharpclaw couldn't be content to ride on the fork of Weldyn's saddle, and whenever he tried to fly he kept racing ahead so far Weldyn would lose sight of him. Back he would come in response to Weldyn's whistled signal, only to shift uneasily, bating continually, until he took wing again.

"All this is getting on my nerves." Dunnis guided his horse toward Eirran's. "What is eating those two? Three."

"I wish I knew." To her irritation, she started hiccupping again.

Around them, the shade of the trees appeared to grow a little lighter. No sun broke through the clouds, but the ground fog began to lift. Yareth's head came up a notch, and Weldyn looked as if he, too, were sniffing the air, as if they had caught a familiar and welcome scent. "This way!" Weldyn cried.

The Falconer reined sharply to the right, dug his spurs into his horse's flanks, and was off into the forest at a light gallop, with Yareth close on his heels.

"Wait!" Eirran cried, but too late. The rest of them could only follow, the best way they could. Already the Falconers had left them behind, and the ferny undergrowth closed in their wake with no sign of their passing. There was nothing to do but plunge ahead, hoping that they had not taken another abrupt turn and lost the others entirely.

"Stay with me!" Dunnis cried. He had one arm around Lisper, who rode with him, lest a low-hanging branch sweep her off his saddle. Lisper looked back at Mouse, wide-eyed.

"Mouth!"

"Yes, I know. We're going the right way. I can *hear* him."

Eirran was too busy trying to keep branches from knocking the both of them out of the saddle to ask what Mouse meant. Gratefully, she fell in behind Dunnis, with Ranal, Hirl, and

Loric following her. Ranal's mount was favoring its wounded shoulder. Single-file, they emerged suddenly into a large clearing. Eirran stifled an outcry at the bizarre sight they stumbled upon.

There was a circle of dark stones, like pillars. Half were topped with a life-sized carving of a bird. Half had a carving of a larger-than-life-sized egg surmounting the pillar. They alternated, bird, egg, bird, egg, except for the opening in the circle which was flanked by two larger pillars, carved in the shape of man-sized birds with outspread wings and open beaks. A road emerged from the forest floor, leading straight through this gate. The road, like the pillars, the gate, and the paving of the area inside the circle, was made of dark stone. Eirran had the dizzying feeling that the road had been under their horses' feet all the time, hidden by the soil and detritus of the forest, and this road was what had been drawing the Falconers unerringly to this spot. For, in the center of the paved area of the circle, stood a gigantic stone bird—a falcon, subtly different from any falcon breed known in the present world, yet clearly recognizable in spite of its oddities. It stood as Eirran had seen Newbold standing a thousand times—poised as if for flight, wings close by its sides, ready to launch itself skyward in the blink of an eye. Its beak was open and Eirran almost put her hands to her ears lest she be deafened by the kind of scream that might issue from that great stone throat.

Without realizing it, she had dismounted and discovered that everyone else had also. They were now standing in a group. Everyone, even the children, stared awestruck and stunned at the sight of this temple—for such it must be—hidden away in the mountains of the Alizon Ridge. "The Great Falcon!" Hirl breathed from behind her. "It is so beautiful. . . ."

She heard the longing in his voice. And in spite of herself, she also yearned for the privilege of being admitted to the inner circle of the temple, there where all mysteries would be made known, where all questions would be answered.

Yes, she thought numbly. Hiccups forgotten, she stood gazing upward in terror and dismay. This is the Great Falcon that drew Yareth and Weldyn hither, beckoning to them even as we rode through the Alizon Gap. There was no magic left there to muffle its allure. And if even I feel its call, what must be happening to Yareth?

The scrape of a boot on stone made Eirran reluctantly tear her gaze away from the enormous bird-form.

Both Yareth and Weldyn stared up at the statue, their faces utterly rapt, unreachable. Weldyn had started walking along the stone road toward the gate. Sharpclaw, quiet at last, rode proudly on his fist. Yareth stood at the edge of the road where it emerged from the ground, as if waiting his turn.

Another scraping sound. This time it was the slow, inexorable grind of stone against stone that made her look back toward the statue. A set of stairs was emerging from the paving; it rose until it touched the carved feathers of the bird's breast. Above the stairs, individual feathers began moving outward and turning flat, forming an extension of the steps. And as she watched, the sharp beak opened wider and still wider until the hook at the bottom formed the last step of all. As Weldyn put his foot on the bottom step the eyes sprang to life, glittering a dull red shot through with black. And from the depths of the statue, an answering red glow began to flicker on the back of the cruel stone gullet.

III

"No!" Eirran screamed—and discovered she could only whisper. Panting from the effort it took, she turned and looked at the others. The men all gazed at the statue. They seemed almost as affected as the Falconers. One by one, they moved stiffly, as if under the direction of a will not their own, toward the spot where Yareth waited his turn to start along the road toward the monstrous stone form.

Dimly, she understood that she must not—*must not*—look back again, must not, in spite of all her longing, gaze at the hypnotic sight that had ensorcelled her husband and the men who rode with him, and the children—

The children!

She scarcely dared move, lest the power of the Great Falcon twist her head around, force her gaze to meet that of the terrible stone eyes. Sooner or later, she knew, she would be able to resist no further. Then she, too, would take the first step along the road that led she knew not where.

The children were standing together, grouped behind Mouse who was holding the Jewel and staring into it.

"Mouse—"

The little girl's concentration wavered. She glanced up at her mother. And in that moment, somewhere inside her the thing snapped that had been keeping Eirran from looking at the Great Falcon. She turned, irrevocably its captive now, and, stumbling, took her place in line behind Loric.

A sound filled her ears, one she had not been aware of as long as she had avoided looking directly at it. A kind of drumming echoed the pulsating red glow coming from the maw of the enormous statue. Weldyn had reached the steps and had already climbed halfway up. In perfect harmony with the music, he took another unhurried step, and then another. Those waiting their turn swayed in time to the rhythm.

Brroom-DOOOM, sang the drums, an immense throbbing heartbeat. *Brroom-DOOOM.*

Another sound, a jarring antiphony to the drum. She tried to shake it off, blot it out, but it persisted, as shrill and irritating as insect-drone.

Brroom-DOOOM. Weldyn set foot on the feather-steps. He reached the beak. He paused a moment, outlined against the red glow. Then, proudly, he stepped forward, and disappeared. The glow blazed high. A wisp of oily black smoke and the faint scent of scorched feathers drifted out onto the air.

Brroom-DOOOM. Yareth started on the road to the Great Falcon's temple. His face was as exalted as Weldyn's had been. He bore his left hand before him, fist clenched, as if an invisible falcon, Newbold's ghost, rode there. He took one step.Then another. *Brroom-DOOOM*.

Suddenly, Eirran realized what the irritating noise was. It was coming from the children, from Mouse and her companions.

No. It was coming from the Jewel.

Don't they realize what a distraction they are causing, she thought. If I had the time to spare, I would turn and see what they were doing. And make them stop.

Brroom-DOOOM. Yareth had reached the foot of the stairs. The Great Falcon had grown eager now, greedy to share its secrets with those who longed to receive them. Hirl was next behind Yareth, passing through the gate, and Dunnis had just taken his first step upon the dark stone road outside the circle. Behind him Ranal and Loric crowded close, as if each was impatient and fearful that the other would be allowed to go before him. If she had had the strength, Eirran would have pushed ahead of both men. But threaded through the insistence of the drumbeat was the mysterious sense of the orderliness of their passage. This one now, that one later, you last of all, and so she must force herself to wait her turn.

Brroom-DOOOM. Step by step, gracefully, Yareth ascended the steps. Hirl was nearly at the foot of the stairs. Ranal went through the gate. Loric set his feet upon the road.

A tremulous thrill went through Eirran. In a moment, just a moment, she, too would be following the path, in the slow and solemn dance toward the place where every mystery life has to offer would be unraveled. The music of the drum swelled up in her, emptying her of everything she had once known, filling her with the rapture of what now dangled enticingly, just barely out of her grasp. . . .

The whining insect-drone rose, almost drowning out the deep, soul-stirring throb of the drums. With all her will, Eirran tried to close it off, tried to ignore it, wished it away. But the sound lifted higher, becoming a clear, pure note as if from the throat of a singing crystal. Higher and higher it soared, and louder and louder throbbed the *Brroom-DOOOM* of the Great

Falcon's heartbeat. The warring sounds fought in Eirran's head. She wanted to put her hands over her ears, but she was not allowed to move. Yareth was so close. In another moment, with another step he would be standing upon the great beak where Weldyn had stood before being admitted to the inmost mysteries of the temple.

The booming of the drum and the song of the crystal rose unbearably high, unbearably loud, unbearably strong—

—and the world shattered into oblivion.

IV

Eirran came to herself slowly. She discovered she was lying on the ground at the edge of the clearing. With a great effort, she turned her head. It threatened to splinter and fall into a dozen pieces. Yareth was lying nearby, limbs composed, face white. And still, so still.

"Yareth—"

Dunnis lifted her and set a water skin to her lips. "He lives yet. He was closest to the—I guess you'd call it an explosion, when the temple was destroyed."

"But what— How—"

"Drink first. Questions later."

Obediently, she drank a little water. Then, with help, she sat up. Dunnis's arms trembled; he appeared shaky and none too well himself. The other three likewise bore stunned expressions.

They look, she thought, like I feel.

"The children—"

"They are well." Dunnis managed a ghastly parody of a smile. "I don't know why. But they are almost untouched by what happened to the rest of us. They are tired, that's all. It is a mystery."

"Yareth. I must go to him." She groped her way on hands and knees across the space that separated them. His chest rose and fell with his breathing, but so lightly it would have been easy to have overlooked the movement. She put her hand on his forehead. It was cold. "My love." She kissed his cheeks, his eyelids, his mouth. It may have been her imagination, but it seemed that a little color began to come back into his face and his breathing became stronger.

"Mama?"

Still intent on Yareth, she answered absently. "Yes, Mouse?"

"I broke it."

She looked up then. Her daughter knelt on the ground beside her—her daughter. Not Mouse, not a fledgling Witch, but Jenys. Her face was puckered, her eyes had deep smudges under them, and she looked on the verge of tears. She held the silver chain the Jewel had hung from. But the Jewel itself had vanished. Nothing was left but the setting, and that was cracked and blasted as if it had been blackened by an immense fire.

"You broke it? Oh, Jenys." She took her child into her arms, rocking her softly and whispering into her hair. "My poor baby."

Star was at Jenys's side, and behind her the other children stood watching. They looked as weary and wrung-out as Jenys. For once, in spite of what they had all just gone through, Lisper didn't have her thumb in her mouth. The children moved closer, and Jenys pulled herself from her mother's arms and joined them. They all took each other's hands.

Jenys vanished, and Mouse stood in her place. "We stopped it, Mama. All of us. Even though the Jewel got broken when we did it." She looked at the other little girls. "I'm sorry I cried. I shouldn't have."

Eirran regarded the six Witch-children, deeply puzzled by Mouse's words. They had no meaning for her. Finding nothing to say, she merely nodded her head. Then she left them to each other and returned to tending her stricken husband.

V

"I don't think she understood," Mouse said.

"How can she?" Cricket said. "I barely understand it myself, and I helped do it."

The children wandered along the edges of the dark temple. All the columns were half-melted, their carved finials mere blobs of cooling stone, and the large birds that marked the entrance to the inner circle had been so mutilated by the force of the destruction that they were scarcely recognizable for what they had once been. But it was in the center of the circle that the full force of what they had done was most visible.

The great statue had virtually been obliterated. Nothing remained above the level of a standing man's head. What little was left—the carved legs and the stairway that had emerged from some subterranean hiding place—bore great rifts and scorch marks. It looked as if the next breeze would tumble it to join the scattered rubble that littered the paved area. A faint wisp of smoke still issued from the depths of the ruin, where it had fallen in on itself. Were it not for that, the place would have looked like it had been abandoned for centuries. All it needed was a kind veiling of ivy or other creeping vine, to soften the outlines of the devastation that had been visited upon it.

"I *saw* it right away," Bird said. "Oh, those sick, nasty colors all over everywhere, from everything inside and out. The eyes were the worst."

"Yes, I know. And when that beak opened and they lit up—"

Bird turned to Flame. "But all the eyes were glowing from the first, all red and black, even the ones on the little birds on top of the pillars. And the eggs—oh, they pulsed in time with the drum. There were red and black flashes of light everywhere, and a dreadful sick green, too. The colors made me want to throw up."

"Do you still *see* them?" Flame frowned, as if trying to *see* as well.

"No, they're gone. There's nothing left."

"This place was evil," Star said soberly. "It was completely of the Shadow. It had your Mama and your Papa, Mouse. And the other men, too. I could feel it *push* when it took Weldyn. I think it would have gotten stronger with each one it swallowed, and it would have been strong enough to get us, too, by the time it had finished."

"I never knew anybody could do the thing we did," Mouse said. She looked at the piece of scorched silver that had once held a Witch Jewel. "And I still don't know how we did it."

"It wath the Power. We uthed it. Or maybe it uthed uth."

"That's more likely," Star said.

Mouse bit her lip. "I hope we don't get in trouble for ruining the Jewel."

"We'll just have to tell the Guardian what happened, and hope she forgives us."

"And I hope my Papa is going to be all right."

Bird looked at Eirran working over Yareth. "Yes, he will be fine. I can *see* him getting stronger by the minute."

"That's good," Mouse said, relieved. "Now we can go home."

"I suppose you've finally made up your mind, then, about what you're going to do once we get there."

Mouse stared at Star. "How did you know?"

Star smiled. "You taught us all how to *hear,* remember? This has been on your mind ever since your Mama and Papa found us in Alizon Castle."

"I'm going to miss them terribly. Even Rangin. He can't have many years left in him, you know. Papa's had him, oh, since before I was born. And Newbold."

Her sisters moved close, holding her hands, patting her. "Yes, it is very sad," Cricket said. "Even more for your parents than it was for my Mama and Papa. They had my brother, and the new baby, but you're the only child Eirran and Yareth had."

"When we can travel again," Mouse said, "I'm going to ride

with Mama one day and Papa the next. And I'm going to put off telling them I won't be going back with them, as long as I can."

Fifteen

I

*D*espite the children's assurance that the evil was dead forever, no one could bear the thought of lingering at this spot. Overcoming their weariness and the lingering shock of their brush with the evil falcon-temple, Eirran and the four men managed to carry Yareth away from the area. With the help of the children, they set up a hasty, makeshift camp. Then, hoping no beast such as they had met the previous day would find their scent and devour them while they slept, Eirran lay down beside Yareth and closed her eyes.

When she opened them again, Yareth was awake and moving about the camp. He looked thinner, somehow—as if the light would show his bones if he stood between her and the sun. She sat up abruptly, wanting to go to him and hold him in her arms. But something in his demeanor stopped her.

Things between us stand on a sword's point, she thought. He might blame me for everything. The thought made her stomach turn over. She swallowed hard. If I hadn't been away from home, tending to the hurts that worthless Rofan caused, I might have turned the Witch away from the door and none of this would have happened.

But perhaps not. Mouse has become a Witch in miniature since I last saw her in Blagden. That's very plain to me at last, now that my head is clear enough to understand what has happened. But Yareth didn't see her as I did, didn't hear her telling me how she and the other Witch-children had stopped the evil that threatened to engulf us all. And still being child enough to mourn because the Jewel had gotten destroyed in the doing.

She is gone. I have lost her. And have I lost my husband as well?

A shadow fell over her. She looked up; he was standing there, gazing at her with an unreadable expression on his face. "Can you ride?" he said.

"Yes."

"We must get out of these mountains, before we come upon another place like the last."

And be unable to fight, because our sole weapon is now blunted, Eirran thought. "Yes," she said aloud. "I agree. The sooner out of this terrible place, the better."

A muscle worked in the side of his jaw. "We have a spare horse now. Ranal, you ride that one and lead yours."

Ranal nodded. "In another day, we can load what spare goods we have on my animal, and ride easier ourselves."

"I want to ride with you, Papa," Mouse said.

"Up you go, then."

"I'll ride with you, Eirran," Star said.

All that day they pressed as hard as human and horse flesh would allow. There was none of the usual banter among them. The others seemed to have caught Yareth's mood—or, perhaps, they were all still recovering from the aftereffects of their near brush with the Shadow.

Eirran's mood was no lighter, and her stomach no easier until well past midday. It seemed to her that the mountains gradually grew less wild as they traveled, and that the forest became somehow friendlier as they descended into the foothills. The tall, stark trees gave way to more familiar oaks and a smaller variety of evergreens. Their shed needles made a carpet that gave off a refreshing fragrance as the horses trod it underfoot.

Here and there a drift of grayish-green mistletoe clung to an oak branch. Eirran's nerves calmed, her stomach settled a little, and she breathed easier here. So, it seemed to her, did the others. If only Yareth would talk to her. But he had wrapped himself in his Falconer's pride, and when he was like that she knew better than to try to reach him. He would have to come out of it on his own. She didn't want to think about what his thoughts and feelings would be when he finally did.

Late in the afternoon they stumbled on what looked to be an old path, now disused and overgrown. But a path meant people and people meant habitation. Suddenly, Eirran longed for a roof over her head, and a hot meal cooked properly, in a fireplace. And hot water. She ran her hand through her hair. She must look dreadful. No wonder Yareth was avoiding her.

Eventually the path led to a house—but such a ramshackle structure, the very sight of it made Eirran smile in spite of herself. There was such an air of absentmindedness, almost of frivolity, about it that she was charmed. The dwelling had evidently started out as a single, all-purpose room, the way most houses were built. But at various times, judging by the differences in workmanship between one section and another, the original structure seemed to have been built onto at random, apparently as the owner needed more space, and with little regard as to what had been built on before. Oddly shaped rooms branched off in several directions; often, a new addition was of a different height than its predecessor, and the various roofs weren't even of the same materials twice in succession. Here was a slate shingle roof; next to it, thatch. Next to that, wood shakes. But the place seemed in remarkably good repair, considering how long it must have been since it was lived in, if one judged by the weeds choking the garden. One of the shutters had come loose, but the others were still sensibly shut, blocking out the elements until the owner—who, Eirran thought, must surely be as eccentric as his dwelling-place— came back to reclaim his home.

Dunnis looked at the house, and traces of his good humor

began to reappear. His mouth twitched with amusement. "Well, surely nobody will mind if we borrow this, er, *unusual* building for a while. I'm sure all of us would be glad for a bit of rest."

"Do you suppose there is still furniture inside?" Loric seemed as taken by the structure as Eirran was.

"Perhaps a cupboard bed. Or several," Dunnis amended. "But I wouldn't count on finding any mattresses."

"It will do for tonight," Yareth said brusquely. "Hirl, you see to the horses while the rest of us search the house and surrounding area. I am weary of surprises."

Once they had untied the stiff leather thongs securing the front door latch to a peg hammered into the outside wall and had gone inside, Eirran found the dwelling's interior no less bewildering than its exterior. Many of the fireplaces were stopped up and unusable, but eventually she found a clear one in a room at the end of a twisted passageway. She tied a bundle of twigs to a stick and made a makeshift broom to sweep the rough stone hearth. Then, while Ranal gathered wood and built a fire, she industriously proceeded to sweep the rest of the house. The broken shutter had let an incredible mess of leaves, dirt, and other debris sift through the rooms. While she worked, the children, released from the tedium of travel with adults too distracted to entertain them, ran squealing through the house, involved in a boisterous game full of rules recognizable to no one but themselves.

By the time she finished sweeping, Ranal had a pot of water heated for her, and had begun preparing a meal from their own supplies and a couple of birds someone had snared. "No sense in letting you do all the work," he said, grinning. "You go and wash up. Ladies always like to do things like that."

She accepted the water with a grateful smile. "The one who gets you will be a lucky woman," she said. "Now if only the owner of this house had left some soap."

Nevertheless, when she had washed the top layer of grime off her skin, she felt much better. She went back to the little room, now cozy and cheerful with the fire and the smell of cooking food, heated more water, and used it to repair the children's appearance as best she could.

"Stop! We'll just get dirty again," Mouse said.

"If I listened to arguments like that," Eirran said, as she scrubbed the back of Mouse's neck, "you'd have been caked with filth from head to foot ever since you could walk."

"We just about are," Cricket said impishly.

Eirran smiled contentedly as she dealt with one set of grubby hands and face after another. "I think your giggle-box has turned over!" she said. She gave Star's face a final wipe, and was rewarded by seeing even that solemn little person dissolve into gales of laughter. That set off the others. She was happy the children seemed to have recovered so well. And the others were also regaining their normal composure—all except for Yareth. He alone seemed subdued, burdened by thoughts and feelings he would not—or could not—express.

The house was empty of all furniture, and the single cup-board bed still standing was unusable. Even the ropes that had once supported the straw mattress had vanished—probably stolen—long ago. That night Eirran slept on the floor, rolled up in her blanket, close to the banked embers of the fire. Mouse snuggled up against the crook of her body, with one of the other girls—she couldn't turn over to see who—wedged against her back. But much as she relished having her child so close, knowing as she did that these moments would end all too soon, she longed to be lying in Yareth's arms instead.

II

At dawn the next day, the travelers cleared away all traces of their occupancy. Loric had repaired the broken shutter, and when they left they closed everything neatly again, tying the front door as securely as they had found it. By mid-morning they had descended from the foothills and discovered a small village. It was so small, it boasted of only a single all-purpose shop to serve the needs of nearby hill farmers. But Eirran welcomed the sight as another woman might exclaim over a gigantic port-town bazaar.

Her recent encounter with near-cleanliness had set up a longing in her that now came close to becoming an obsession. She longed to be free of road-grime, to be back in women's clothing again and out of men's garments that pinched so abominably in the waist. But most of all, she wanted a bath all over, and clean hair. "Soap!" she exclaimed.

"Food," Dunnis said. He grinned. "We're about out of everything. Wouldn't want to starve between here and Es City."

"And these children eat like pigs," Hirl said. He hugged Flame affectionately. "Who has coins?"

"I have a few." Ranal rummaged in his saddlebag and brought out a small pouch. "Good thing I hid this and the stablekeeper back in Alizon didn't have the wit to search our belongings before he learned we were spies."

Loric nodded. "That ought to buy us everything we need. Chances are the storekeeper here bargains in kind most of the time. I'd bet he doesn't see two coins from one year's end to the next."

"Well, he can have the whole bag if he has something sweet for sale. I haven't had anything sweet since we left Es City."

"We will conclude our business quickly and be gone," said. His severe tone and manner put a damper on the men's banter.

"Yareth," Eirran said in protest.

He turned his falcon's eyes on her. "Es City is just the midpoint of my journey," he said. He looked at Mouse, who rode with Eirran. "I am eager to be in my own home again, with my child."

Our, Eirran thought. She gritted her teeth to keep from making a sharp remark that would not help matters a bit. Our journey, our home. Our child. Only she isn't ours, not any more. Oh, damn that Falconer upbringing of yours that turns you cold and selfish at the most inopportune times. If you weren't in such a mood, I could help you ease the disappointment that you are bound to know when we get to Es Castle and you learn that only your wife will be accompanying you back to *your* home."

Resentfully, hiccupping again, she hovered in the background while Yareth conducted his business with the storekeeper. There wasn't much to look at—tack for horses, both riding and plowing; sacks of unground grain; a few bags of dried fruits and vegetables; some crockery bowls, slightly cracked and gathering dust and fly-specks on a top shelf. A barrel of salted meat gave off a sharp smell that made Eirran's stomach lurch queasily.

Nevertheless, the travelers were in no position to be overly choosy or fastidious. Their supplies were far too depleted for that luxury. With crisp efficiency, Yareth made his selections from the storekeeper's wares, even to some of the salt meat that hadn't yet gone off altogether. Dazzled by the quantity of coins he was offered, the man threw in a bundle of honey-straws for much less—he claimed—than the usual cost. Eirran stepped forward.

"Yes, lady?" the store-keeper said. "Is there something special I can do for you?"

"Soap," she said. "Please. *Hic!*"

The man frowned, thinking. "What's it used for?"

The notion that somewhere in the world there were people who did not know about soap astonished Eirran. Even in Blagden, every woman guarded her soap recipe jealously. And in Es Castle it was an amenity as commonplace and as unremarked upon as the water that flowed at a touch, and the light globes in every hallway. "Why, you use it for washing!"

"Oh. Like clothes, or cooking pots. We mostly use fine scouring sand hereabouts." The man's face cleared suddenly. "But my wife has a mixture she makes out of froth-plant. Regular as can be, every new moon, she rubs it on herself and then rinses it off. Would that do?"

"Oh, yes!" Eirran exclaimed in relief. If froth-plant grew locally, she could manage, but she didn't want to have to stop and search for it—not given Yareth's present mood. "How much—*hic!*—is it?"

He scratched his head. "Well, I don't know. It doesn't seem right, somehow, to charge for something you can gather yourself. Tell you what. I'll go and get it, and you take it as thanks given for your good patronage."

"Thank you."

"Are you finished?" Yareth said. "Is that all you want?"

Even if the storekeeper had had a case of trinkets to catch her fancy, Kernon's borrowed money-pouch had never had any coins in it. And in any event, she had lost it long since—pilfered, she expected, when the Hounds had been hustling their prisoners down to the dungeon. "Yes. I'm ready to go now."

"Good. We'll be outside." He turned and left. The other men and the little girls trooped out after him.

The storekeeper returned from his errand in time to overhear their conversation. "That stern-faced fellow your husband, is he?"

"Yes, he is."

"Well, all I can say is, good luck to you." He put a leather bag full of thick liquid in her hands.

"I've a question."

"If I can answer, lady, I will."

"We stayed last night in the most, er, peculiar dwelling—"

The man's face lit up in comprehension. "Ah, yes. That could be none other than old Ostbor the Scholar's house. Long dead, you know. Had a helper living with him for a while. Stayed on after, then she went away. Can't remember her name. Nobody ever goes near there anymore. House is said to be haunted."

"But it isn't. It's a wonderful house. It needs to be lived in, that's all, by someone who will love it and care for it."

"Perhaps," the storekeeper said skeptically, "but it would have to be someone moving in from outside. Nobody local would dare."

"That's a pity. It's a wonderful house, full of surprises."

The storekeeper rummaged a curtained niche, coming out at

last with a small sack that seemed to be filled with pebbles. "For the little girls," he said. "Sugared nuts. Don't let them eat them all at once. You're a good woman with a kind heart."

"Thank you," Eirran said. "Thank you for your generosity."

She put the delicacies away, hurried out and put the cherished bag of froth-plant essence into her saddlebag. Then she climbed into her saddle. She could hardly wait to see the children's faces when she began sharing out the nutmeats, as a reward for allowing themselves to be scrubbed clean the night before they all went riding back in triumph into Es City.

III

The Guardian might not have moved at all, for all the difference between this audience and the last time Eirran and Yareth had been in her presence. They were in the small room again, with what might have been the same fire burning on the hearth, and the same light streaming through the single window. Only this time the room was considerably more crowded. Their daughter was with them, as well as the other five children. Their four companions had left them at the gatehouse, to return to their barracks; Eirran found that she missed having them with her, to act as a kind of buffer against Yareth's uncertain moods. And her own, she had to admit.

Now Yareth stood straight, tall and Falconer-proud. "I promised I would return your fledgling Witches to you, if they were alive. And here they are."

"And, as I promised, you have my everlasting gratitude." She glanced from Yareth to Eirran, and Eirran thought she saw a hint of a smile touching the Witch's stern lips.

"Then our business is concluded." He turned to Eirran and Mouse. "Come. We are going home."

Mouse took a step forward. Her young face wore an expression of resolve, and Eirran's heart thudded at how much, at that moment, she resembled her father.

"No, Papa," she said. "My home is here now."

Eirran almost reached out for Yareth, hoping to stave off the angry explosion, or—if she couldn't—at least to direct it at her and not at her child. But to her astonishment, Yareth bowed his head, and his shoulders slumped as if he were impossibly weary. "I had feared as much," he said. For the first time in her life, Eirran heard a note of defeat in his voice. Then he looked up at the Guardian. He made a visible effort and his shoulders straightened once more. "You have won. I don't know how, but you have won. You have taken my daughter from me. May you have joy in your victory." Then he turned and strode out of the chamber.

"Forgive him, lady," Eirran said. "He is distraught. He lost his falcon, Newbold, in the fighting. And now this. . . ."

"I know," the Guardian said kindly. "Be gentle with him. He will need you in the days to come."

"Would that it were true."

"It is, Eirran. Believe me." The Guardian's mood shifted. "It was a most unpleasant surprise to learn that there were still Kolder alive in our world. You and your husband may have put an end to them at last. For that mighty accomplishment alone, we are deeply in your debt. The animal that bore you to Es City waits for you now in the outer ward. It is laden with a few gifts, tokens of our gratitude. Please keep, as our gift also, the weapons and armor you used, and the horse you have ridden on this adventure. It is so little payment for the great deeds you have done."

A second Torgian! Unheard-of wealth, and so casually bestowed! And even more gifts. Eirran stammered her thanks.

"It is nothing," the Guardian said with a shrug. She smiled mysteriously. "There are gifts, and there are gifts."

Eirran didn't know how to respond to that.

The Guardian fingered the blackened silver setting that had once held a milky gray-blue stone, and twined the chain around her slender fingers. "Most extraordinary, the way they used the Jewel against that Place of Power in Alizon Ridge. Most extraordinary. And most extraordinary also the form the Shadow took in that Place of Power. The Great Falcon. Could that be something from Falconer history that they will not speak of?"

"I don't know, Lady," Eirran said. "I did hear Weldyn call on the Great Falcon the way some men swear oaths. But Yareth never mentioned the name until after he had been in Weldyn's company for a time."

Yareth. She couldn't tarry much longer. She turned to Mouse. "I will not burden you with any tears of farewell," she said. "I said my goodbyes, I think, on our way back here. Just be good, and obedient, and learn all there is to learn."

"I think all of these girls are going to be outstanding pupils," the Guardian said.

"Goodbye, Mama," Mouse said. Then, a little girl again for perhaps the last time in her life, she flung herself into her mother's arms for a last kiss and a tremendous hug. The other children clustered around her as well, as if she substituted for their parents in this final farewell.

"Goodbye, goodbye," they said.

"Pleath, Eirran." Lisper tugged at her sleeve and she bent down until she was on a level with the child. "I'll mith you and Yareth, too. I could thay both your nameth without any trouble at all!"

"And I'll miss—I'll miss—" Abruptly, Eirran got to her feet and rushed out of the room. She had promised Mouse no tearful farewells, and unless she left then and there, she would be unable to keep her word.

She had expected him to be far down the road toward home by now. To her surprise, she found Yareth waiting for her, holding Dorney's reins. The gentle old gelding was laden under an enormous bundle of goods—the "few gifts" the Guardian had spoken of. Without a word, he handed her the reins, and she fastened them to her own saddle. Then they rode slowly out of the castle, through Es City, and onto the road to the east.

She was unwilling to disturb his silence, being disinclined herself to aimless chatter. After a time, she scarcely noticed it. Too much had happened since she had followed him along this same road, seeking the child the Witches had taken. A child no more. Whether it had been the kidnapping, the harrowing experience under the Kolder machine, the incredible manner in which Mouse and her sisters, untaught and unknowing, had drawn Power through the borrowed Jewel and saved them all from the Shadow—or whether it was the fact that Mouse was, indeed, a born Witch—she was no longer a child, for all that she was just six years old.

Eirran glanced at Yareth, wondering what he was thinking. Newbold's death and Mouse's loss had been hard enough on him. Had the death—or worse—of his brother Falconer affected him more than he had shown? There had been bad blood between them at the last, and she would not have mourned overmuch if the two of them had fought it out and Weldyn had fallen at Yareth's hands. But suppose Yareth had been the one who had fallen—

A sudden surge of nausea at the thought brought bitter fluid flooding into the back of Eirran's throat and she had to swallow hard to keep from being sick. Strange, she thought. It has all been so very strange. I wonder if I will ever understand it all.

IV

They kept to the main road on this journey back home, though it was a longer route. It seemed just too much effort to go cross-country. In a few days, they came to the Great Fork where the road split, one branch leading to Lormt and the other turning south, toward Blagden. Eirran could see the outlines of the towers of Lormt gleaming cool and remote in the distance. Perhaps now, she thought with a sigh, there would be time for her to go there for a few months and study, as she had always wanted to do. Yareth wouldn't miss her. He had scarcely spoken a dozen words to her since they had left Es City.

A wild cry echoed from the sky. Eirran looked up, alarmed. A small black speck, hardly bigger at that distance than a sparrow, came hurtling down toward them. As it dropped closer, the white "V" on its breast became visible and belatedly she realized what she was really seeing.

Startled, Yareth just managed to get his fist up in time for the bird to land on it. Ecstatic falconsong came pouring out of his throat. But the bird just cocked its head, as if puzzled by the sounds. Yareth switched to the *eek-ik-eek* speech he used to speak in casual "conversation" with Newbold. And the bird answered.

Yareth turned to Eirran. "This is a wild falcon!" he exclaimed delightedly. For the first time in far too long, he laughed. "It's a fledgling, born from one of the ones who escaped the destruction of the Eyrie during the Turning!"

"Oh, Yareth!" Eirran reached out to lay her hand on his arm and the young bird bated, as if annoyed or upset at her proximity.

Yareth stroked the falcon's head gently and the bird grew calmer. "Sssh," he said. "Get used to her. She's a friend. And what is your name, my fine fellow?"

"I can't believe what I am seeing—you, with that bird on your fist!"

He glanced up at her. "It's been bred in them for centuries to find one of us and bond with him. All of this young one's nestmates are gone, fallen to beasts and other birds when they were still in the eggs, or chicks unable to fly. He has been terribly lonely." The little falcon screeched something and Yareth made *eek-ik-eek* noises in return.

"What did he say?"

"His name. He wants to be called Boldwing." Yareth smiled reminiscently. "After the falcon before him. I wonder how he knew." He stroked Boldwing again. "He's completely untrained, of course. I'll have to work with him quite a lot."

Eirran closed her eyes thankfully. Oh, Guardian, she thought. Could this be your gift? If so, you could never have found anything more suitable, or more desperately needed. Now, perhaps, all will be well with my Yareth once more.

Without either of them saying anything, they picked up their pace. Finding the fledgling had broken through Yareth's dam of silence. He spoke mainly of inconsequentials and what they had found, however, still not ready to talk about what they had lost. The wounds were too recently scarred over for that.

Eirran's spirits improved also, to the point that she could think about something other than her despair over Yareth. She investigated the contents of some of the parcels Dorney carried, full of feminine curiosity. And the Guardian had given with a lavish hand. Fine clothing for both, made of the blue silky stuff they had worn in the Castle. A pair of dart-guns, with an enormous bundle of ammunition. A hunting bow and arrows tipped with a strange blue metal. A silver scale, for measuring herbs. A mortar and pestle, of blue stone that felt very good in her hands. A set of a dozen silver spoons. And more, still untouched. She decided to save the rest for when they arrived back in Blagden.

That night, she put on one of her new gowns.

"You should save it for a special occasion," Yareth told her.

"This is special." She touched his cheek tenderly. "Very special."

He looked at her, momentarily puzzled. She could almost see the change occurring behind his eyes. Deliberately, she shifted from being the good trail companion they both knew she had to be when they were surrounded by other men and by young and impressionable children, and once more became Eirran. His wife. His beloved.

He took her in his arms and that night, for the first time in far too long, they made love under the stars.

With this enormous barrier overcome at last, it was almost the same as it had always been between them. Eirran rejoiced at their progress and began to hope that their lives would, somehow, resume their normal course once they were back home. He had his fledgling falcon to fill the void of Newbold's death, and they were returning with unthought-of riches bestowed by the Guardian. Only she still had an empty place in her heart. Her daughter—

Resolutely, she put the thought away. How could she be so ungrateful in the face of their wonderful good fortune? Mouse was safe, she was alive, she had found her place in life. All was settled, and all for the good. The ache would recede in time, though she knew it would never be entirely forgotten.

V

Blagden was much the same as it had been when they had left it—so long ago, it seemed. But summer was barely beginning; the vegetables in the gardens were not even close to ripe.

Conscious of how strange they must look to their friends and neighbors, both clad in chainmail, riding Torgians and leading a third horse laden with gifts from the Council of Estcarp, Eirran followed Yareth through the village and turned down the lane where the Falconer's cottage waited for them.

Aidine came running out of her cottage, crying her greetings. A huge tiger cat bounded along at her heels, stopping short and fluffing its fur when it caught sight of the strange falcon riding on Yareth's saddle fork.

Eirran tossed the reins to Yareth and slid out of her saddle. "I'll be there in a minute."

"Don't be long." He nodded and trotted on toward their barn with the animals while she ran and embraced her friend.

"Aidine! Oh, it's so good to see you! And is this Pounce? What have you been feeding him?"

"Oh, snails and tadpoles," Aidine replied, laughing. "My, you do look different. I wouldn't have recognized you in that armor. Well, never mind. Your home is all clean and waiting for you, and there's supper on the hearth, too—"

"But how did you know?"

"I've done it every day for the past two weeks. Hefin says he's never eaten so well since we were first married."

Eirran laughed. "You must tell me all the news."

"Rofan beat Belda again—" Aidine made a face "—I know, I know. But he's left town now, we hope for good. Two of his good-for-nothing friends went with him. The baker's oven caught fire and nobody had any bread for a week—"

"Oh, it all sounds wonderful. I've missed all this so much."

"—and your garden is flourishing," Aidine finished. "I don't know what magic you must use— Oh, speaking of magic, what about Jenys? Isn't she with you? Didn't you find her?"

"Yes, we found her." Eirran smiled wistfully. She picked up Pounce and cuddled him. The cat began purring and kneading her shoulder. Observing his mighty claws, she was glad for the protective chainmail. "Then we lost her again. They were right to come and get her. She's a Witch, too, Aidine. And now she's going to live as one."

"Oh. I don't know whether to offer congratulations or condolences." Aidine considered her friend critically. "Congratulations are more in order, I think."

Eirran made a noncommittal sound and made as if to turn for home. Her friend took her by the arm.

"Wait. Don't you know?"

"Know what?"

"Come inside with me. Just for a minute." When they had entered Aidine's spotless cottage, she handed Eirran a polished plate. "Here. Look for yourself."

Puzzled, Eirran let Pounce drop to the floor while she looked at her reflection. It was the first time she had stopped to examine her image in weeks. Even in Es City, she had looked hurriedly only to check that she was, finally, clean. Then, all at once, she saw what Aidine had recognized instantly. There was no mistaking that special glow, even in such an unreliable mirror. She set the plate down on the table and crossed her arms across her belly. Tears began seeping from her closed eyes and running down her cheeks. Now, at last, she understood what the Guardian had only hinted at when she spoke of gifts. And all the signs! The woman-time that never came, the shifting moods, the nausea! So clear, and yet, under the circumstances, so easy to put to other causes. She must have been with child, all unknowing, before she even started to Es City with Yareth.

"Some Wise Woman you are," Aidine chided affectionately. "Some Wise Woman, indeed."

"Well, aren't you pleased? Don't you think Yareth is going to be happy about it?"

"Happy?" A familiar sensation gathered in the pit of Eirran's stomach. She hiccupped. "You have no idea. Just wait till I tell him!" she said. She began to laugh through her tears. "Oh, won't he be surprised! *Hic!*"

Afterword

WE had Eirran's and Yareth's tale from their own lips some time after their return. For in search of the herb lore in Lormt Eirran insisted upon making us a visit even as Yareth had thought she might. She was big with child when she came and Nolar and I both sensed there was something amiss.

It was not that they grieved for their daughter, for both of them realized that a child of Talent moved, by nature, beyond the bonds of kin. There was some other shadow upon them. Or rather, as I sensed, upon Eirran, and Yareth's uneasiness was rooted in concern for his wife.

She was busied with Nolar one morning, copying out some healing spells and the lists of herbs to go with such, when she asked suddenly:

"Why should I have such ill dreams, lady? It was not so when I was carrying before. Then all was happiness." She put down her pen and pressed her hands to her belly as if to shield against what she did not know.

"What manner of dreams?" Nolar asked.

"I cannot remember when I wake, but just that they are ill sendings. I know for when I do wake I am all asweat with fear, my throat aches as if I have screamed for long, and sometimes I have an urge to vomit as if I have eaten some foulness. Yet I must not let Yareth know and so— It is very hard to hide it from him as he grows more and more concerned and does not wish to leave me alone. This is not a proper bearing and I fear, oh, how I fear! That is the truth which really brought me here."

At the same time Eirran spoke to Nolar, Yareth who had been watching his falcon's careful approach to Galerider, said abruptly, speaking with his back towards me:

"Is it true that you have something of the Talent even though you be no maid Witch?" His question was sharp and, I knew, one of import to him. I answered with the truth:

"Some small power, yes, I have gained." My hand went to the pouch of crystals which rode ever at my belt.

He swung around to face me and came closer. "Then tell me," he said, his hands clasping so tightly on his belt that the knuckles stood out sharply, "is there a hold of the Dark upon me?" He faced me as a man unflinchingly faces the charge of an enemy.

Seldom had I used that mindknowing of which I am still more than a little afeared for more than surface reading, and once or twice with Nolar when we unite. Yet at this demand from him I probed deeply. However, I met with nothing but that which is human and akin to all our species. Save there was a shadow of fear, partly for himself but mainly for Eirran.

"I can find nothing."

I do not know whether he accepted that for the truth. I believe what I said brought him no relief.

"What is it that you fear?" I added.

He shook his head as one who shakes away an irritating fly. "That is it, I know not. Save there is something—like a dream."

"And do you dream?"

"I do not know—for at waking the memory goes. But it is evil and—and that evil—it is turned towards Eirran. Nothing shall come near Eirran, nothing! By me or any other thing. That I swear, by the Great Falcon!" But as those words left his lips he suddenly looked at me, his eyes wide as he repeated in a whisper which was broken by a shudder—"the Great Falcon!"

"Did you not see that evil laid?" I asked. "It may well be that the memory of that comes to you as a dream. If so, such shadows fade."

"Grant that is so." However, a shadow remained upon him as he left me.

I made a decision of my own and for the first time I took my way up stair and down a hall where long ago I had been made unwelcome. There I rapped firmly on a door. The woman who opened it stood, pen in hand, showing me as closed a face as the door had been.

"There is a need," I stated bluntly.

"What need?" she countered, but Arona, whom I had seen but a finger count of years since her coming here, could not evade me now.

"Tell me, what do you know of the Great Falcon?"

I might have drawn that sword which necessity had set me wearing again, for her hand went to her mouth and she gave back a step or two. I followed eagerly for I believed that while so shaken she might indeed forget her long-held aloofness and share something of importance.

She continued to retreat until she sat down abruptly in a chair, her eyes no longer focusing on me but past my shoulder as if there hung a roll from which she must read.

"Jonkara—the great trap of the Dark—but it was flawed, flawed because men willed it so!"

"Have you read the Chronicle of Eirran and Yareth?"

Her tongue passed across her lips as if her mouth was suddenly dry. "Yes." Her voice was hardly above a whisper.

"Then what might those two have to fear?" I pressed her.

Again she wet her lips and then asked, in a brittle voice. "Do they fear?"

"Yareth does."

"And Eirran," Nolar had come upon us both. "Would your Jonkara have any quarrel with an innocent woman bearing new life within her body? Surely what you have told me would give lie to that."

Nolar passed me to Arona's side and put hand on her shoulder. Now when she spoke her voice was softer and somehow put a wall about them, leaving me outside.

"You have the key, unlock the door."

Arona looked up into Nolar's eyes.

"But it is a legend, a story—it tells nothing of what—" Suddenly she paused almost in midword.

"There is something you remember, Arona? Let me warn you, Eirran is nearer to her time than we thought. She cannot make the trip back to her home, and she is also convinced that there is something wrong with the child. From what she has told me there may have been a sending—"

Now my hand did grip sword hilt, though I knew that no blade could defend against such a thing. Only Power itself. So I tried to believe that of all of us there might be enough of that.

Within Lormt there was knowledge certainly but it required the proper talent to wield it. I had a fraction, Nolar far more. The Stone of Konnard, was that not meant for healing? Still, for years that had served, or had been bent to serve, the Dark. Was it wholly free, even with this long space under Elgaret's guardianship?

"Arona?" Nolar prompted again.

The pen in the Falconer woman's hands snapped. Her face was white with more than just the leaching given by life ever indoors. Swiftly she arose and went to the table where lay piles of scrolls, sheets of time-tattered parchment.

"Jonkara." The name might have been breathed as an invocation. Then her head raised so she looked at me. "This is for women," she said with winter frost.

I shook my head. "Power knows neither male nor female—it answers to whomever calls it forth. When there is need what I have waits to be used. There is only Light and Dark and that depends upon the caller."

Arona did not dispute me though I expected her to. Rather she turned her attention once more to what lay on the table, and Nolar said:

"Look you to Yareth. I think we all may meet an enemy who may be one he knows—let him be prepared."

The time of our battle was not long delayed. Eirran awoke

from a broken sleep that night and her screams quickly brought Nolar and me from a nearby chamber. As Yareth held his wife in his arms he fought her, her eyes wild and unseeing. It was only after Nolar had signaled me to help break his hold on the girl and had herself grasped Eirran that she quieted. There was movement at the door and Arona brushed past me.

She held a small, wand-like stick in her hand and with that she touched Eirran's swollen belly and spoke words I did not know. The girl convulsed and Yareth aimed a blow at Arona which I parried, taking the force of it myself. I do not know she even realized what he would have done, for she said to Nolar:

"That within her is possessed."

Yareth cried out and I was shaken. For possession by the Dark can be worse than any true death. Eirran had fallen back on the bed and now her heavy breathing made her whole body shudder. Yareth looked to me, his face stricken:

"What is to be done?"

Nolar had made a quick examination of the girl.

"Birth is not yet. We must get her to the Stone!"

Though over the years we had made a fair trail on our visits to Elgaret, that was no real road. We had kept it so that others might not be moved to follow. To transport Eirran there was a task I would not have considered had I not believed that it would be fatal if we did not.

We devised a litter between the two most surefooted ponies— one such as the Borderers use for the seriously wounded—and with Derren, who also knew the road, together with Anylse his wife, a young woman who had midwife training, we headed towards the hidden shrine.

Eirran did not seem aware of our travels and Nolar considered that a blessing, ready at each halt we made with herb drinks and consultations with Anylse. Yareth spoke little, and I did not press him. Arona also appeared to ride as one whose body was present but her mind elsewhere. From time to time I saw her lips move as if she spoke to herself or something we could not see. She carried that wand with care. Oddly enough both Galerider and Yareth's falcon Boldwing seemed disturbed, now and then voicing screams which might almost be challenges. At such times Rawit would answer with sharp barking.

So we came to the shrine and Elgaret met us. Eirran cried out and twisted on the litter so that Nolar and Anylse, who had chosen to walk beside her that morning, were quick to restrain her. Though I knew little of birthing I guessed that her time was not far off.

We unfastened the litter and would have borne it within, but Elgaret stood between us and the door, her hands upon her jewel.

"Do not bring her to the Stone." Her voice was harsh as I had never heard it before. "This is of the Dark."

Yareth was carrying the forepoles of the litter. Had his hands been free I think he would have struck the Witch to the earth. His face was thunderous and his falcon flew low, screeching, yet not seeming to dare to attack.

Arona moved to stand shoulder to shoulder with Nolar before the Witch. Anylse cried out:

"Her time is upon her! In the name of Gunnora, dame, have pity!"

"Evil cannot be so easily turned away, Lady," Arona said to Elgaret. "It must be fought and in Jonkara's name I will fight. By whom or what will you do battle? Are you not sworn, as I have heard tell, by mighty oaths to use your Power when and where the needs arise? Or do you only turn mountains and blast lives in grand gestures of battle?"

So they fronted each other, one, hand on jewel, the other, fingers gripping rod, and, to my great astonishment, it was Elgaret who gave way and let us carry Eirran into the rock chamber which was the outer room of the shrine.

Then Derren went to see to our mounts. But Yareth fell to his knees and caught Eirran's hands as she writhed and moaned. Now Nolar and Anylse watched her with wise eyes and I made to leave. However, Nolar shook her head at me—pointing to a place by the door. I could feel about us something gathering as a threat.

I tried to probe it. From a formless dark it became a brooding bird, a falcon. Galerider thrust claws painfully into my shoulder. I did not know that a bird could whimper, but the sounds which came from her were close to that. When Yareth had knelt, his bird had flown to the back of a chair and I saw its eyes shine as bright as flames as it watched. While Rawit crouched at my feet, her fear harsh upon her, but she would not leave me.

At Eirran's head stood Elgaret and from the jewel she wore light glowed down about Eirran's head and face. At her feet was Arona, the wand she held pointing to that passage through which the newborn must emerge. Still I sought, to the utmost straining of my talent, to learn what harm was about to come on us.

Eirran gave a great gasping cry and the babe came into the birthing cloth Anylse held ready. There was a sound but was no normal child's wail—rather a wild, triumphant laugh such as a man might give.

Arona's wand swung down but did not quite touch the child at heart level. There was an odor, strong and foul, of burnt flesh and singed feathers.

"Name yourself, by the Great Falcon which the Dark took, by the Power of the Lady denied, aye, by Jonkara's full might— name yourself!" Her voice stilled that laughter.

There was a great silence and then, even birds and hound were still.

"Weldyn."

A single word, a name. I saw Yareth start as if a lash had been laid across his shoulders. His head jerked around, his eyes searching.

"Weldyn." It was Arona who repeated that. "There is a challenge to be given."

Almost I could hear heavy breathing, as if there were some animal—or man—crouched and waiting.

"By the Great Falcon, Weldyn," she spoke again, "do you accept challenge? Come forth and try your strength if you are what you think yourself to be."

"Against a female!" The contempt in that was as great as if it were the foulest of obscenities.

"Against me!" Yareth had leaped to his feet, his eyes still searching. "If I did not see you die, if it were all illusion—Yes, my challenge, Weldyn!"

That laugh again. "Not so, Falconer. Much as you have betrayed your kind, the kin-oath still binds you. Draw steel if you can!"

Yareth's hand did move towards sword hilt. Then I saw it stayed as if some great weight pinned it fast. There was a curdling of the air and from that formed one in Falcon helm and armor while the charnel odor grew stronger.

If Yareth could not move there were no such bonds on me. What stood there now was solid and real. Dark talent can be as great as any power if wielded strongly.

"You have done me well, half-breed." The bird-surmounted helm turned and whatever lurked behind the eyeholes of that regarded the limp body of the child. "I live and will be about my battle."

"There was a challenge," I said. "And I am not bound by any oath, nor am I a woman—"

The head swung towards me with the speed of a striking snake. Eyes which were spots of unholy fire regarded me.

Once more that thing laughed. But it made no move to draw weapon. Instead, with an empty hand, it made a contemptuous gesture—followed by a bolt of fire. Only, that which I had earlier aroused and set on guard found me alert and ready.

It was a battle strange beyond all telling which we fought there. Twice was I very hard pressed and new energy flowed into me which I knew came from Nolar. The Witch took no part in our struggle; her light held steady over Eirran though it did not touch the motionless child whom I believed dead.

My weakened legs shook, I was drained. For the third time

Nolar reached me. I saw the lips of that half-masked face form a snarl. Then the whole body of that apparition swung around, away from me, toward Anylse and the child. I knew what this thing which called itself by a dead man's name would do—enter again into that waiting body.

Only there was Arona, her wand held like the sword he would have denied her.

"By your strength, Lady, by your will!" She struck at that snarling face.

There was a jagged burst of darkness. I heard Arona gasp as her wand became flame and she had to hurl it from her. Only at the same time Galerider and Boldwing screamed and took to the air, circling the column of blackness which fell in upon itself and was gone.

Nolar caught at Anylse and clutched at the child, gathering the small form to her breast and running onward through doorway which gave upon the place of the Stone.

The last of the blackness was gone. Whatever had attempted to enter our world through the newborn had vanished from sight. I followed Nolar in time to see her kneel beside the Stone and hold out the unmoving body. The light was clear and bright upon the birthing cloth and its burden. But—if the child had been only a husk to hold that other—its true spirit dead before birth—

There was a cry, a wail. A small fist beat the air. Nolar gave a small cry also and caught that babe close to her. This was all human child. My thought had reached out and touched only that which was normal and right. The Stone of Konnard had completed our struggle and we of the Light had once more won.

Thus ends our Chronicles—each in a manner linked, close or far. And the rolls shall rest until there come those who may be of another kind, yet desirous to know of us who learned to change. It is fair and right that what was once be again known—and credit given to other days.

Duratan of Lormt

About the Authors

ANDRE NORTON

For over forty years "one of the most distinguished living SF and fantasy writers" *(Booklist)*, Andre Norton has been penning bestselling novels that have earned her a unique place in the hearts and minds of readers. Honored as a Grand Master by both the Science Fiction Writers of America and the World Fantasy Convention, she has garnered millions of readers for her most famous series, the Witch World novels. These works and others, such as *Imperial Lady* (with Susan Shwartz), *Redline the Stars* (with P. M. Griffin), and *The Jekyll Legacy* (with Robert Bloch), have made her "one of the most popular writers of our time" *(Publishers Weekly)*. In addition to her novels, which number over forty works of SF and fantasy, she has recently created the *Tales of the Witch World*. Andre Norton resides in Winter Park, Florida.

PATRICIA MATHEWS

Patricia Mathews has had stories published in various anthologies, including *Tales of the Witch World*. *We, the Women* is her first published novel. Ms. Mathews lives in Albuquerque, New Mexico.

SASHA MILLER

Sasha Miller has had stories published in various anthologies, including *Tales of the Witch World*. She has also published several novels in other genres; *Falcon Magic* is her first published fantasy novel. She lives in Sunnyvale, California.